DANIELLE STEEL
SAFE HARBOUR

RANDOM HOUSE
LARGE PRINT

Copyright © 2003 by Danielle Steel

All rights reserved under International and Pan-American Copyright Conventions.
Published in the United States of America by Random House Large Print in associated with Delacorte Press, New york and simultaneously in Canada by Random House of Canada Limited, Toronto.
Distributed by Random House, Inc., New York.

The Library of Congress has established a Cataloging-in-Publication record for this title.

ISBN 0-375-43225-6

www.randomlargeprint.com

FIRST LARGE PRINT EDITION

10 9 8 7 6 5 4 3 2 1

This Large Print edition published in accord with the standards of the N.A.V.H.

To my incredible, wonderful children,
Beatrix, Trevor, Todd, Sam, Victoria,
Vanessa, Maxx, Zara, and Nick,
who keep me safe, happy, and loved,
and whom I love so much,
May you ever be a safe harbour for each other.

And to the angels of "Yo! Angel!":
Randy, Bob, Jill, Cody, Paul, Tony, Younes,
Jane and John.

with all my love,
d.s.

The Hand of God

Always with a feeling
of trepidation,
excitement,
fear,
the day comes
when we go out
to God's lost souls,
forgotten, cold,
broken, filthy,
and occasionally
though rarely clean,
brand new on the streets,
with still clean hair,
french braided,
or faces cleanly shaven,
when only a month later,
we see the ravages of days,
the same faces no longer
quite the same,
the clothes
beyond repair,
the souls beginning
to tatter
like their shirts
and shoes
and eyes. . .
i go to mass
and pray for them

before we leave,
like matadors
        entering the ring,
never sure what the night
        will bring,
whether warmth
        or despair,
danger or death to them
        or us,
my prayers silent
        and heartfelt,
and then at last
        we take off,
laughter ringing
        like bells around us,
as we watch for the faces,
        the bodies,
        the eyes looking for us,
they know us now,
        they come running,
        as we jump out
        time and time
        and time again,
hauling heavy bags
        behind us,
to buy them one more
        day,
one more night in the rain,
one more hour . . . in the cold.
i prayed for you. . .
        where were you?
        i knew you'd come!
with shirts plastered

to their bodies
in the rain,
their pain and their joy
mingling with ours.
we are the wagons
filled with hope
in a scope we cannot
measure,
their hands touch ours,
their eyes digging deep
into ours,
god bless you,
the voices sing softly
as they walk away,
one leg, one arm,
one eye,
one time,
one life they share
with us for a moment
on the streets,
as we move on
and they remain
etched in our memories
forever,
the girl with the scabs
all over her face,
the boy with one leg
in the pouring rain,
whose mother would have
cried to see him,
the man who put down
his head and sobbed,
too frail to take the bag

from our hands,
and then the others
who frighten us,
who come prowling,
watching,
trying to decide whether
to pounce or participate,
not sure whether
to attack or thank,
their eyes meet ours,
their hands touch mine,
their lives intertwined
with ours,
like the others,
irrevocably,
immeasurably,
and in the end, finally,
trust is our only bond,
their only hope,
our only shield
as we face them
again and again.
the night wears on,
the faces endless,
the seeming hopelessness of it
interrupted by the briefest
of moments
when hope is born,
and a bag full of warm clothes
and groceries,
a flashlight, a sleeping bag
a deck of cards,
and some band-aids,

a sign of dignity returned,
their humanity
            no different than ours,
and then finally
        a face with eyes
so devastated and devastating
    it stops your heart,
        it breaks time
            into tiny fragments
            until we are either
                as broken as they
        or as whole,
            no difference between us
                anymore,
    we are one
            as the eyes search mine,
        will he let me claim him
            as one of ours,
        or will he step forward
                and kill me
because hope is too far gone
    for him to seize it.
why are you doing this for us?
because i love you, i want to say,
but rarely do i find the words,
        as i hand him the bag
            along with my heart,
    my own hope and faith
        spread thin among so many,
and always the worst face of all
            at the very end,
        after a few joyful ones,
        and some who are so close

to dead
they cannot speak at all,
but this last one,
always mine,
the one i take home
with me in my heart,
his crown of thorns
resting on his head,
his face ravaged,
he is the filthiest
and most frightening of all,
he stands and stares at me,
holding his ground,
eyes boring into mine,
wasted sometimes,
at the same time ominous
and filled with depair.
i see him coming,
he comes straight toward me,
as i want to run,
but can't and won't
and don't dare.
i taste fear,
we meet and stand
eye to eye,
tasting each other's
terror
like tears
mingling on one face,
and then i know,
i remember,
if this were my one
last chance

to touch God,
to reach out and be
touched by Him
in return,
if this were my only chance
to prove my worth
and my love for Him,
would i run?
i stand my ground,
remembering
that He comes
in many forms,
with many faces,
with bad smells,
and perhaps even
angry eyes.
i hold out the bag,
no longer brave,
but merely breathing,
remembering why
i have come into this
dark night
and for whom. . .
we stand equal and alone,
death hovering
between us,
as he takes the bag at last
whispers God bless
and moves on,
and i know once again
as we drive home,
silent and victorious,
that once again

we have been
touched
by the hand of God.

refuge

once broken,
    now renewed,
        the thought
        of you
    a place
        where i take
        refuge,
    your seams,
        my scars,
    the legacy
        of those
    who loved us,
        our victories
        and defeats
            slowly
                converging,
    our stories
        merging
            into one,
        basking
            in the winter
            sun,
    the pieces
        of me
            no longer
            broken,

and all of me
at long last
whole,
a crackle jar
of ancient
beauty,
the mysteries
of life
no longer
seeming
to need answers,
and you,
beloved friend,
my hand in yours,
as we both
mend,
and life begins
again,
a song
of love
and joy
that never
end.

SAFE
HARBOUR

1

IT WAS ONE OF THOSE CHILLY, FOGGY DAYS THAT masquerade as summer in northern California, as the wind whipped across the long crescent of beach, and whisk-broomed a cloud of fine sand into the air. A little girl in red shorts and a white sweatshirt walked slowly down the beach, with her head turned against the wind, as her dog sniffed at seaweed at the water's edge.

The little girl had short curly red hair, amber-flecked honey-colored eyes, and a dusting of freckles across her face, and those who knew children would have guessed her to be somewhere between ten and twelve. She was graceful and small, with skinny little legs. And the dog was a chocolate Lab. They walked slowly down from the gated community toward the public beach at the far end. There was almost no one on the beach that day, it was too cold.

But she didn't mind, and the dog barked from time to time at the little swirls of sand raised by the wind, and then bounded back to the water's edge. He leaped backward, barking furiously, when he saw a crab, and the little girl laughed. It was obvious that the child and the dog were good friends. Something about the way they walked along together suggested a solitary life, as though one could sense that they had walked along this way often before. They walked side by side for a long time.

Some days it was hot and sunny on the beach, as one would expect in July, but not always. When the fog came in, it always seemed wintry and cold. You could see the fog roll in across the waves, and straight through the spires of the Golden Gate. At times you could see the bridge from the beach. Safe Harbour was thirty-five minutes north of San Francisco, and more than half of it was a gated community, with houses sitting just behind the dune, all along the beach. A security booth with a guard kept out the un-welcome. There was no access to the beach it-self save from the houses that bordered it. At the other end, there was a public beach, and a row of simpler, almost shacklike houses, which had access to the beach as well. On hot sunny days, the public beach was crowded and populated inch by inch. But most of the time, even the public beach was sparsely visited, and at the private end, it was rare to see anyone on the beach at all.

The child had just reached the stretch of beach where the simpler houses were, when she saw a man sitting on a folding stool, painting a watercolor propped against an easel. She stopped and watched him from a considerable distance, as the Lab loped up the dune to pursue an intriguing scent he seemed to have discovered on the wind. The little girl sat down on the sand far from the artist, watching him work. She was far enough away that he was not aware of her at all. She just liked watching him, there was something solid and familiar about him as the wind brushed through his short dark hair. She liked observing people, and did the same thing with fishermen sometimes, staying well away from them, but taking in all they did. She sat there for a long time, as the artist worked. And she noticed that there were boats in his painting that didn't exist. It was quite a while before the dog came back and sat down next to her on the sand. She stroked him, without looking at him, she was looking out to sea, and then from time to time at the artist.

After a while, she stood up and approached a

little bit, standing behind him and to the side, so he remained unaware of her presence, but she had a clear view of his work in progress. She liked the colors he was working with, and there was a sunset in the painting that she liked as well. The dog was tired by then, and stood by, seeming to wait for a command. And it was yet another little while before she approached again, and stood near enough for the artist to notice her at last. He looked up, startled, as the dog bounded past him, sending up a spray of sand. It was only then that the man glanced up and saw the child. He said nothing, and went on working, and was surprised to notice that she hadn't moved, and was still watching him, when he turned his head again, and mixed some water in his paints, half an hour later.

They said nothing to each other, but she continued to watch, and finally sat down on the sand. It was warmer, keeping low in the wind. Like her, the artist was wearing a sweatshirt, and in his case jeans, and an old pair of deck shoes that were well worn. He had a gently weathered face and a deep tan, and she noticed as he worked that he had nice hands. He was roughly the same age as her father, somewhere in his forties. And as he turned to see if she was still there, their eyes met, but neither smiled. He hadn't talked to a child in a long time.

"Do you like to draw?" He couldn't imagine any other reason why she'd still be there, except if she were an aspiring artist. She would have been bored otherwise. In truth, she just liked the silent companionship of being close to someone, even a stranger. It seemed friendly somehow.

"Sometimes." She was cautious with him. He was, after all, a stranger, and she knew the rules about that. Her mother always reminded her not to talk to strangers.

"What do you like to draw?" he asked, cleaning a brush, and looking down at it as he talked. He had a handsome, chiseled face, and a cleft chin. There was something quiet and powerful about him, with broad shoulders and long legs. And in spite of sitting on the artist's stool, you could see he was a tall man.

"I like to draw my dog. How do you draw the boats if they aren't there?"

He smiled this time as he turned toward her, and their eyes met again. "I imagine them. Would you like to try?" He held out a small sketch pad and a pencil, it was obvious that she wasn't going anywhere. She hesitated, and then stood up, walked toward him, and took the pad and pencil.

"Can I draw my dog?" Her delicate face was serious as she inquired. She felt honored that he had offered her the pad.

"Sure. You can draw anything you like." They didn't exchange names, but just sat near each other for a time, as each worked. She looked intent as she labored on the drawing. "What's his name?" the artist inquired as the Lab sailed past them, chasing seagulls.

"Mousse," she said, without raising her eyes from her drawing.

"He doesn't look much like a moose. But it's a good name," he said, correcting something on his own work, and momentarily scowling at his painting.

"It's a dessert. It's French, and it's chocolate."

"I guess that'll work," he said, looking satisfied again. He was almost through for the day. It was after four o'clock and he'd been there since lunchtime. "Do you speak French?" he said, more for something to say than out of any real interest, and was surprised when she nodded. It had been years since he'd spoken to a child her age, and he wasn't sure what he should say to her. But she had been so tenacious in her silent presence. And he noticed, as he glanced at her, that aside from the red hair, she looked a little like his daughter. Vanessa had had long straight blond hair at that age, but there was something similar about the demeanor and the posture. If he squinted, he could almost see her.

"My mom's French," she added, as she sat, observing her own work. She had encountered the same difficulty she always did when she drew Mousse—the back legs didn't come out right.

"Let's take a look," he said, holding a hand out for the sketch pad, aware of her consternation.

"I can never do the back part," she said, handing it to him. They were like master and student, the drawing creating an instant bond between them. And she seemed strangely comfortable with him.

"I'll show you. . . . May I?" he asked her permission before adding to her efforts, and she nodded. And with careful strokes of the pencil, he corrected the problem. It was actually a very creditable portrait of the dog, even before he improved it. "You did a good job," he observed, as he handed the page back to her and put away his sketch pad and pencil.

"Thank you for fixing it. I never know how to do that part."

"You'll know next time," he said, and started putting his paints away. It was getting colder, but neither of them seemed to notice.

"Are you going home now?" She looked disappointed, and it struck him as he looked into the cognac-colored eyes that she was lonely, and it touched him. Something about her haunted him.

"It's getting late." And the fog on the waves was getting thicker. "Do you live here, or are you just visiting?" Neither knew the other's name, but it didn't seem to matter.

"I'm here for the summer." There was no excitement in her voice, and she smiled seldom. He couldn't help wondering about her. She had crept into his afternoon, and now there was an odd, undefinable link between them.

"At the gated end?" He assumed she had come from the north end of the beach, and she nodded.

"Do you live here?" she asked, and he gestured with his head in the direction of one of the bungalows just behind them in answer. "Are you an artist?"

"I guess so. So are you," he smiled, glancing at the portrait of Mousse she was holding tightly. Neither of them seemed to want to leave, but they knew they had to. She had to get home before her mother did, or she'd get in trouble. She had escaped the baby-sitter who'd been talking for hours on the phone with her boyfriend. The child knew that the teenage baby-sitter never cared if she went wandering off. Most of the time she didn't even notice, un–

til the child's mother came home and asked about her.

"My father used to draw too." He noticed the "used to," but wasn't sure if it meant that her father no longer drew, or had left them. He suspected the latter. She was probably a child from a broken home, hungry for male attention. None of that was unfamiliar to him.

"Is he an artist?"

"No, an engineer. And he invented some things." And then, with a sigh, she looked at him sadly. "I guess I'd better go home now." And as though on cue, Mousse reappeared and stood beside her.

"Maybe I'll see you again sometime." It was early July, and there was still a lot of life left in the summer. But he had never seen her before, and suspected she didn't come down this way very often. It was a good distance for her.

"Thank you for letting me draw with you," she said politely, a smile dancing in her eyes this time, and the wistfulness he saw there touched him profoundly.

"I liked it," he said honestly, and then stuck a hand out to her, feeling somewhat awkward. "My name is Matthew Bowles, by the way."

She shook his hand solemnly, and he was impressed by her poise and good manners. She was a remarkable little soul, and he was glad to have met her. "I'm Pip Mackenzie."

"That's an interesting name. Pip? Is that short for something?"

"Yes. I hate it," she giggled, seeming more her own age again. "Phillippa. I was named after my grandfather. Isn't it awful?" She screwed up her face in disdain for her own name, and it elicited a smile from him. She was irresistible, particularly with the curly red hair and the freckles, all of which delighted him. He wasn't even sure anymore if he liked children. He generally avoided them. But this one was different. There was something magical about her.

"Actually, I like it. Phillippa. Maybe one day you'll like it."

"I don't think so. It's a stupid name. I like Pip better."

"I'll remember that when I see you next time," he said, smiling at her.

They seemed to be lingering, reluctant to leave each other.

"I'll come back again, when my mom goes to the city. Maybe Thursday." He had the distinct impression, given what she said, that she had either sneaked out or slipped away unnoticed, but at least she had the dog with her. Suddenly, for no reason he could think of, he felt responsible for her.

He folded his stool then, and picked up the worn, battered box he kept his paints in. He put the folded easel under one arm, and they stood looking at each other for a long moment.

"Thank you again, Mr. Bowles."

"Matt. Thank you for the visit. Good-bye, Pip," he said almost sadly.

"Bye," she said with a wave, and then danced away like a leaf on the wind, as she waved again, and ran up the beach with Mousse behind her.

He stood watching her for a long time, wondering if he'd ever see her again, or if it mattered. She was only a child after all. He put his head down then against the wind, and walked up the dune to his small weather-beaten cottage. He never locked the door, and when he walked inside and set his things down in the kitchen, he felt an ache he hadn't felt in years and didn't welcome. That was the trouble with children, he told himself, as he poured himself a glass of wine. They crept right into your soul, like a splinter under a fingernail, and then it hurt like hell when you removed them. But maybe it was worth it. There was something exceptional about her, and as he thought of the little girl on the beach, his eyes drifted to the portrait he had painted years before of a girl who looked remarkably like her. It was his daughter Vanessa when she was roughly the same age. And with that, he walked into his living room, and sank heavily into an old battered leather chair, and looked out at the fog rolling in over the ocean. As he stared at it, all he could see in his mind's eye was the little girl with bright red curly hair and freckles, and the haunting cognac-colored eyes.

2

OPHÉLIE MACKENZIE TOOK THE LAST WINDING turn in the road, and drove the station wagon slowly through the tiny town of Safe Harbour. The town consisted of two restaurants, a bookstore, a surf shop, a grocery store, and an art gallery. It had been an arduous afternoon in the city for her. She hated going to the group twice a week, but she had to admit that it helped her. She had been going to it since May, and had another two months ahead of her. She had even agreed to attend meetings over the summer, which was why she had left Pip with their neighbor's daughter. Amy was sixteen, liked to baby-sit, or so she claimed, and needed the money to supplement her allowance. Ophélie needed the help, and Pip seemed to like her. It was a comfortable arrangement for all concerned, although Ophélie hated driving into town twice a week, even though it only took her half an hour, forty minutes at most. As commutes went, aside from the ten-mile stretch of hairpin turns between the freeway and the beach, it was easy. And driving along the cliffs, on the winding road, looking out over the ocean relaxed her. But this afternoon she was tired. It was exhausting sometimes listening to the others, and her own problems hadn't improved much since October. If anything, it seemed to be getting harder. But at least she had the support of the group, it was someone to talk to. And when she needed to, she could let her hair down with them, and admit how rotten she was feeling. She didn't like burdening Pip with her troubles. It didn't seem fair to do that to a child of eleven.

Ophélie drove through town, and shortly afterward took a left turn onto the dead-end road that led to the gated portion of Safe Harbour. Most people missed it. She did it by reflex now, on automatic pilot. It had been a good decision, and the right place to spend the summer. She needed the peace and quiet it offered. The solitude. The silence. The long, seemingly endless stretch of beach and white sand, which was sometimes almost wintry, and at other times hot and sunny.

She didn't mind the fog and chilly days.

Sometimes they suited her mood better than the bright sun and blue skies that the other residents of the beach longed for. Some days she didn't leave the house at all. She stayed in bed, or tucked herself into a corner of the living room, pretending to read a book, and in fact just thinking, drifting back to another time and place when things were different. Before October. It had been nine months, and seemed like a lifetime.

Ophélie drove slowly through the gate, as the man in the security booth waved, and she nodded. She let out a small sigh as she drove toward the house carefully, over the speed bumps. There were children on bicycles on the road, several dogs, and a few people walking. It was one of those communities where people knew each other, but stayed unto themselves nonetheless. They had been there for a month, and she hadn't met anyone—and didn't want to. And as she drove into the driveway and turned off the car, she sat quietly for a moment. She was too tired to move, see Pip, or cook dinner, but she knew she had to. That was all part of it, the endless lethargy that seemed to make it impossible to do anything more than comb her hair or make a few phone calls.

For the moment at least, she felt as though her life was over. She felt a hundred years old, although she was forty-two, and looked thirty. Her hair was long and blond and soft and curly, and her eyes were the same rusty brandy color as her daughter's. And she was as small and delicate as Pip was. When she was in school, she'd been a dancer. She'd tried to get Pip interested in ballet at an early age, but Pip had hated it. She had found it difficult and boring, hated the exercises, the barre, the other girls who were so intent on perfection. She didn't care about her turnouts, her leaps and jumps or pliés. Ophélie had finally given up trying to convince her, and let Pip do what she wanted. She took horseback-riding lessons for a year instead, took a ceramic class in school, and the rest of the time she preferred drawing. Pip was solitary in her pursuits, and was happy left to her own devices, to read, or draw, or dream, or play with Mousse. In some ways, she was not unlike her mother, who had been solitary as a child too. Ophélie was never sure if it was healthy to let Pip keep to herself as much as she did. But Pip seemed happy that way, and she was always able to entertain herself, even now, when her mother paid so little attention to her. To the casual observer at least, Pip didn't seem to mind it, although her mother often felt guilty about how little they seemed to interact anymore. She had mentioned it to the group often. But

Ophélie felt unable to break the spell of her own lethargy. Nothing would ever be the same now.

Ophélie put her car keys in her bag, got out of the car, and slammed the car door without locking it. There was no need to. And when she walked into the house, all she saw was Amy industriously loading the dishwasher and looking busy. She was always busy when Ophélie got home, which meant she had done nothing all afternoon before that and had to frantically catch up in the last few minutes. There was little to do anyway, it was a bright, cheerful, well-kept house, with clean-looking modern furniture, bare light wood floors, and a picture window that went the length of the house and afforded a splendid view of the ocean. There was a long narrow deck outside, with outdoor furniture on it. The house was just exactly what they needed. Peaceful, easy to maintain, and pleasant.

"Hello, Amy. Where's Pip?" Ophélie asked, with tired eyes. You almost could not hear her French origins at all, her English was not only fluent, her accent was nearly perfect. It was only when she was extremely tired, or vastly upset, that a word or two sneaked through that betrayed her.

"I don't know." Amy looked suddenly blank,

as Ophélie observed her. They'd had this conversation before. Amy never seemed to know where Pip was. And Ophélie instantly suspected that, as usual, she'd been talking to her boyfriend on her cell phone. It was the one thing Ophélie complained about nearly each time Amy sat for her. She expected her to know where Pip was, particularly as the house was so close to the ocean. It always panicked Ophélie to think that something could happen to her. "I think she's in her room, reading. That's where she was the last time I saw her," Amy offered. In truth, Pip hadn't been in her room since she'd left it that morning. Her mother went to take a look, and of course saw no one. At that exact moment, Pip was in fact running down the beach toward home, with Mousse gamboling along beside her.

"Did she go down to the beach?" Ophélie asked, looking nervous as she came back to the kitchen. Her nerves had been raw since October, which previously would have been unlike her. But now everything was different. Amy had just turned on the dishwasher and was preparing to leave, with little or no concern where her charge was. She had the confidence and trust of youth. Ophélie knew better, and had learned the agonizing lesson that life could not be trusted.

"I don't think so. If she did, she didn't tell
me." The sixteen-year-old looked relaxed and
unworried. And Ophélie looked anxious, despite the fact that the community was supposed
to be safe, and appeared to be, but it still infuri-
ated and terrified her that Amy allowed Pip to
wander off with no supervision whatsoever. If
she got hurt, or had a problem, or was hit by a
car on the road, no one would know it. She had
told Pip to report to Amy before she went anywhere, but neither the child nor the teenager
heeded her instructions. "See you on Thursday!" Amy called as she breezed out the door, as
Ophélie kicked off her sandals, walked out onto
the deck, looked down the beach with a worried frown, and saw her. Pip was coming home
at a dead run, and holding something in her
hand that was flapping in the wind. It looked
like a piece of paper, as Ophélie walked out to
the dune, feeling relief sweep over her, and then
down onto the beach to meet her. The worst
possible scenarios always jumped into her mind
now, instead of the simpler explanations. It was
nearly five by then, and getting colder.

Ophélie waved at her daughter, who came to
a breathless stop beside her, with a grin, and
Mousse ran around them in circles, barking. Pip
could see that her mother looked worried.

"Where've you been?" Ophélie asked quickly

with a frown, she was still annoyed at Amy. The girl was hopeless. But Ophélie hadn't found anyone else to sit for her. And she needed someone with Pip whenever she went into the city.

"I went for a walk with Moussy. We went all the way down there," she pointed in the direction of the public beach, "and it took longer to get back than I thought. He was chasing seagulls." Ophélie smiled at her and relaxed finally, she was such a sweet child. Just seeing her sometimes reminded Ophélie of her own youth in Paris, and summers in Brittany. The climate had not been so different from this one. She had loved her summers there, and she had taken Pip there when she was little, just so she could see it.

"What's that?" She glanced at the piece of paper and could see it was a drawing of something.

"I did a picture of Mousse. I know how to do the back legs now." But she did not say how she had learned it. She knew her mother would have disapproved of her wandering off alone on the beach, and talking to a strange man, even if he had improved her drawing, and it was harmless. Her mother was very strict about Pip not talking to strangers. She was well aware of how pretty the child was, even if Pip was entirely unaware of it herself for the moment.

"I can't imagine he sat still for his portrait," Ophélie said with a smile and a look of amusement. And when she smiled, one could see easily how pretty she was when she was happy. She was beautiful, with exquisitely sculpted fine features, perfect teeth, a lovely smile, and eyes that danced when she was laughing. But since October, she laughed seldom, nearly never. And at night, lost in their separate private worlds, they hardly talked to each other. Despite how much she loved her child, Ophélie could no longer think of topics of conversation. It was too much effort, more than she could cope with. Everything was too much now, sometimes even breathing, and especially talking. She just retreated to her bedroom night after night, and lay on the bed in the dark. Pip went to her own room and closed the door, and if she wanted company, she took the dog with her. He was her constant companion.

"I found some shells for you," Pip said, pulling two pretty ones out of the pocket of her sweatshirt and handing them to her mother. "I found a sand dollar too, but it was broken."

"They nearly always are," Ophélie said as she held the shells in her hand, and they walked back to the house together. She hadn't kissed Pip hello, she had forgotten. But Pip was used to it now. It was as though any form of human touch or contact was too painful for her mother. She had retreated behind her walls, and the mother Pip had known for the past eleven years had vanished. The woman who had taken her place, though outwardly the same, was in fact frail and broken. Someone had taken Ophélie away in the dark of night and replaced her with a robot. She sounded, felt, smelled, and looked the same, nothing about her was visibly different, but everything about her had altered. All the inner workings and mechanisms were irreparably different, and they both knew it. Pip had no choice but to accept it. And she had been gracious about it.

For a child her age, Pip had grown wise in the past nine months, wiser than most girls her age. And she had developed an intuitive sense about people, particularly her mother.

"Are you hungry?" Ophélie asked, looking worried. Cooking dinner had become an agony she hated, a ritual she detested. And eating it was even more distressing. She was never hungry, hadn't been in months. They had both grown thinner from nine months of dinners they couldn't swallow.

"Not yet. Do you want me to make pizza tonight?" Pip offered. It was one of the meals they both enjoyed not eating, although Ophélie seemed not to notice how Pip picked at her food now.

"Maybe," Ophélie said vaguely. "I can make something if you want." They had had pizza four nights in a row. There were stacks of them in the freezer. But everything else seemed like too much effort for too little return. If they weren't going to eat anyway, at least the pizzas were easy.

"I'm not really hungry," Pip said vaguely. They had the same conversation every night. And sometimes in spite of it, Ophélie roasted a chicken and made a salad, but they didn't eat that either, it was too much trouble. Pip was existing on peanut butter and pizza. And Ophélie ate almost nothing, and looked it.

Ophélie went to her room then and lay down, and Pip went to her room and stood the portrait of Mousse against the lamp on her nightstand. The paper from the sketch pad was stiff enough to hold it, and as Pip looked at it, she thought of Matthew. She was anxious to see him again on Thursday. She liked him. And the drawing looked a lot better with the changes he'd made to the back legs. Mousse looked like a real dog in the drawing, and not half-dog half-rabbit, like the earlier portraits she'd done of him. Matthew was clearly a skilled artist.

It was dark outside when Pip finally wandered into her mother's bedroom. She was going to offer to cook dinner, but Ophélie was asleep. She lay there so still that for a moment Pip was worried, but when she moved closer to her, she could see her breathing. She covered her with a blanket that lay at the foot of the bed. Her mother was always cold, probably from the weight she had lost, or just from sadness. She slept a lot now.

Pip walked back out to the kitchen, and opened the refrigerator. She wasn't in the mood for pizza that night, she normally only ate one piece anyway. Instead she made herself a peanut butter sandwich, and ate it as she put the TV on. She watched quietly for a while, as Mousse slept at her feet. He was exhausted from the run on the beach, he was snoring softly, and woke only when Pip turned off the TV and the lights in the living room, and then she walked softly to her bedroom. She brushed her teeth and put her pajamas on, and a few minutes later got into bed and turned the light off. She lay in bed silently for a while, thinking about Matthew Bowles again, and trying not to think how life had changed since October. A few minutes later she fell asleep. Ophélie never woke until the next morning.

3

WEDNESDAY DAWNED ONE OF THOSE BRIL-
liantly sunny hot days that only happen rarely at
Safe Harbour, and cause everyone to scramble
for the sun and bask in it gratefully for hours. It
was already hot and still when Pip got up, and
wandered into the kitchen in her pajamas.
Ophélie was sitting at the kitchen table, with a
steaming cup of tea, looking exhausted. Even
when she slept, she never woke feeling rested. It
took only an instant after she woke up, for the
wrecking ball of reality to hit her chest again.
There was always that one blissful moment
when memory failed her, but there was just as
surely the hideous moment following it, when
she remembered. And between the two instants, the ominous corridor where she had an
instinctive sense that something terrible had
happened. By the time she got up, the whiplash

effect of waking had left her drained and exhausted. Mornings were never easy.

"Did you sleep well?" Pip asked politely as
she poured herself a glass of orange juice and
put a slice of bread in the toaster. She didn't
make one for her mother because she knew she
wouldn't eat it. Pip seldom saw her eat now, and
never breakfast.

Ophélie didn't bother to answer the question.
They both knew it was pointless. "I'm sorry I
fell asleep last night. I meant to get up. Did you
eat dinner?" She looked worried. She knew
how little she was doing for the child, but
seemed to be unable to do anything about it.
She felt too paralyzed to do anything for her
daughter, except feel guilty about it. Pip nodded. She didn't mind cooking for herself. It
happened often, in fact almost always. Eating
alone in front of the TV was better than sitting
at the table together in silence. They had run
out of things to say months before. It had been
easier the previous winter when she had homework, and an excuse to leave the table quickly.

The slice of toast popped up loudly out of the
toaster, Pip grabbed it, buttered it, and ate it
without bothering to get a plate. She didn't
need one, and she knew that whatever crumbs
she dropped, Mousse would take care of. The
canine vacuum. Pip walked out to the deck and

sat on a lounge chair in the sunshine, and a moment later, Ophélie followed.

"Andrea said she'd come out today with the baby." Pip looked pleased at the prospect. She loved the baby. William, Andrea's son, was three months old and a symbol of his mother's independence and courage. At forty-four, she had decided that she was unlikely to finally meet Prince Charming and get married. She had conceived the baby by artificial insemination from a sperm donor and had him in April, a bouncing beautiful dark-haired chubby baby boy with laughing blue eyes and a delicious giggle. Ophélie was his godmother, as Andrea was Pip's.

The two women had been friends since Ophélie came to California eighteen years before with her husband. They had lived in Cambridge, Massachusetts, for two years before that, while Ted taught physics at Harvard. There had never been any question in anyone's mind that he was a genius. Brilliant, quiet, awkward, almost taciturn at times, yet gentle, tender, and once upon a time loving. Time and life's challenges had hardened him eventually, even embittered him. There had been hard years when nothing went as he wanted, and there was almost literally no money. And in the last five years, he had been lucky. Two of his inventions had made a fortune, and everything had gotten easy. But he was no longer open in heart or spirit.

He loved Ophélie and his family, they knew that, or said they did, but he no longer showed it. He had become lost in his constant struggles to come up with new designs, inventions, and solutions to problems. And he had finally made millions selling licenses to his patents in the field of energy technology. He had become not only world renowned but universally revered and respected. He had found the pot of gold at the end of the rainbow ultimately, but no longer remembered that there was a rainbow. His entire world centered on his work, and his wife and children were all but forgotten. He had all the hallmarks of a genius. But there was never any doubt in Ophélie's mind that she loved him. For all his difficulties and quirks, there was no one like him, and there had always been a powerful attachment between them. And as Ophélie had said patiently to Andrea one day, "I don't suppose Mrs. Beethoven had it easy either." His prickly character was the nature of the beast and went with the territory. She had never reproached him his quirks or solitary personality, but she often missed the early years when things were still warm and cozier between them. And in some ways, they

both knew Chad had changed that. The difficulties of their son had irreversibly altered the
father. And as he withdrew from the boy, he
also withdrew from his mother, as though
somehow it was her fault. Their only son had
been difficult as a small boy, and after endless
agonies and a tortuous road, was diagnosed at
fourteen as bipolar. But by then, for his own
salvation and peace of mind, Ted had disen-
gaged from him completely, and the boy had
become entirely his mother's problem. Ted had
sought and found refuge in denial.

"What time is Andrea coming out?" Pip
asked as she finished her toast.

"Whenever she can get the baby organized.
She said sometime this morning." Ophélie was
happy she was coming. The baby was a pleasant
distraction, particularly for Pip, who adored
him. And in spite of her age and inexperience,
Andrea was a fairly easygoing mother. She
never minded Pip wandering around with him
everywhere, holding him, kissing him, or tick-
ling his toes while his mother nursed him. And
the baby loved her. His sunny disposition
brought a ray of sunshine into their lives, which
even warmed Ophélie whenever she saw him.

Much to everyone's amazement, Andrea had
taken a year's sabbatical from her successful law
practice to stay home with the baby. She loved

being with him. She said that having William was the best thing she'd ever done, and she didn't regret it for an instant. Everyone had told her that having him would preclude ever finding a man, and she didn't seem to give a damn. She was happy with her son, and had been ecstatic over him right from the first. Ophélie had been with her at the birth, and it had moved them both to tears. The delivery had been fast and easy, and the first one, other than her own, that Ophélie had ever seen. The doctor had actually handed the baby to her to give to Andrea, minutes after he was born, and the two women had felt bonded forever after sharing William's birth. It had been an extraordinary event, deeply moving, and a memory they both cherished. It was a defining moment in their friendship.

Mother and daughter sat in the sun for a while without feeling obliged to say anything, and after a while, Ophélie went back into the house to answer the phone. It was Andrea, she had just finished nursing the baby, and said she was heading for the beach. Ophélie went to take a shower, and Pip changed into a bathing suit, and then told her mother she was going down on the beach with Mousse. She was still there, wading in the water, when Andrea arrived forty-five minutes later. And as always, she blew into the house like a gale-force wind. Within minutes of her arrival, there were diaper bags, and blankets, and toys, and a swing all over the living room. Ophélie went to the top of the dune and waved at Pip to come in, when they arrived, and shortly after she was playing with the baby, and Mousse was barking at them excitedly. It was standard fare for one of Andrea's visits. And it was another two hours before she was nursing the baby again, and things finally settled down. Pip had had a sandwich by then, and had gone back to the beach. And Andrea was sipping a glass of orange juice, as she sat peacefully on the couch, and Ophélie smiled at her.

"He's so beautiful . . . you're so lucky to have him," Ophélie said enviously. There was something so peaceful and joyous about having a baby in their midst. It was all about beginnings and not endings, about hope instead of disappointment, loss, and grief. Overnight, Andrea's life had become the antithesis of hers. Most of the time now, Ophélie felt as though her own life was over.

"So how are you? How does it feel to be out here?" Andrea was constantly worried about her, and had been for nine months. She stretched out her long legs comfortably as she settled back against the couch with the baby at her breast, and made no effort to cover herself. She was proud of her new role in life. She was a handsome woman, with piercing dark eyes, and long, dark hair that she wore in a braid. Gone suddenly were her businesslike demeanor and courtroom suits. She was wearing a pink halter top, white shorts, and bare feet, and she was a full head taller than Ophélie. In heels, she stood well over six feet and was a striking woman. And despite her height, there was an obvious sensuality about her.

"It's better," Ophélie answered her, not entirely honestly, although in some ways it was. At least she was in a house where she had no tangible memories, except those she had brought with her in her head. "Sometimes I think the group depresses me, and sometimes I think it helps. Most of the time, I'm not sure which."

"Probably both. Like most things in life, it's a mixed bag. At least you're with other people going through the same thing. The rest of us probably don't understand all that you feel." It was comforting to have Andrea admit that. Ophélie hated hearing people say that they understood what she was feeling, when they didn't. How could they? At least Andrea knew it.

"Maybe not. I hope you never do." Ophélie smiled sadly, as Andrea switched the baby from one breast to the other. He was still drinking avidly, but in a few minutes, she knew, he'd be sated and asleep. "I feel so badly about Pip. I can't seem to connect with her. I feel like I'm floating somewhere in outer space." And no matter how hard she tried to come back to earth, or wanted to, she couldn't.

"She seems to be doing okay in spite of it. You must be managing to get through to her once in a while. She's a pretty solid kid, she's been through a lot, you both have." Chad had brought his share of stress to the family in the past several years. And Ted very definitely had his quirks. Pip was remarkably well balanced in spite of all of it, and until October, so was Ophélie. She had been the glue that had kept the family together, despite countless traumas and near tragedies. It was only since October that she had finally been brought to her knees. And Andrea was convinced she'd get back on her feet eventually. She wanted to do all she could to help her in the meantime.

The two women had been friends for nearly two decades. They had met through mutual friends, and liked each other instantly, although they couldn't have been more different, but some of that was what had drawn them to each other. Where Ophélie was quiet and gentle, Andrea was outspoken and assertive, and sometimes nearly masculine in her points of view.

She was decidedly heterosexual, bordering on promiscuous at times, and she had never let any man tell her what to do. Ophélie was infinitely feminine, still very European in her values and opinions, and had been submissive to her husband for their entire marriage, and never felt diminished by it. Andrea had always encouraged her to be more independent, and more American in her behaviors. They shared a passion for art, music, great theater, and once or twice had flown to New York together to see the opening of a play. Andrea had even gone to France with her one year. And she and Ted had been enormously compatible. It was one of those rare threesomes where each person liked the other equally. She had been a physics major at MIT before going to law school at Stanford, which was what had brought her to California and ultimately kept her there. She couldn't stand the idea of going back to the snows of winter in Boston, where she was from and had gone to school. She had come out to California only three years before Ophélie and Ted, and was just as determined to stay and make a life there. Ted had loved her physics background and talked to her for hours about his latest projects. She understood far more about what he was doing than Ophélie ever had, and it pleased her that her friend was so knowledgeable. Even Ted, as

difficult as he was, had to admit he was impressed by Andrea's extensive comprehension
of his field.

She represented large corporations in lawsuits
against the federal government, and did only
plaintiff's work, which suited her somewhat
confrontational personality. It was also that side
of her that allowed her to take Ted on toe to toe
sometimes, and he admired her for that too. In
some ways, she handled him far better than his
own wife did. But Andrea could afford to, she
had nothing to lose. Ophélie would never have
dared say half the things to him Andrea did. But
then again, Andrea didn't have to live with him.
Ted behaved like the resident genius, and com-
manded a great deal of respect from all of them,
except of course Chad, who had said he hated
his father from the time he was ten. He hated
his overbearing manner, and the sense of entitlement and superiority he had because of how
smart he was. Chad had been just as smart, his
circuitry had just gone awry somehow, so none
of the connections matched up, or at least some
very important ones didn't.

Ted had never been able to accept that his son
was less than perfect, and in spite of all of
Ophélie's efforts to mitigate the situation, Ted
was ashamed of him. And Chad was well aware
of it. It had caused some very ugly scenes be-

tween them. And Andrea knew that too. Only Pip had managed to somehow stay away from it, and remain untouched by the strife that nearly destroyed their family eventually. Even as a small child, Pip had become the little fairy who flew above it all, touching each of them gently, and trying to make peace between them. Andrea loved that about her. She was a magical child, and seemed to bless all she touched, just as she did now with Ophélie. It was why Pip was so tolerant and understanding of the fact that her mother was now so incapable of giving anything to her, not even meals. She forgave her for all of it, far more than Ted or Chad would have. Neither of them would have been able to tolerate Ophélie's infirmities, even if caused by them. They still would have blamed her. Or at least Ted would. Not that Ophélie would have seen it that way, she never had. She had always worshiped him, no matter what he did, and made excuses for him. Whether he recognized it or not, she was the perfect wife for him. Devoted, passionate, patient, understanding, long-suffering. She had stood behind him unfailingly, even in the lean, angst-filled years of no money.

"So what are you doing to distract yourself out here?" Andrea asked her pointedly, as the baby fell asleep.

"Not much. Reading. Sleeping. Walking on the beach."

"Escaping, in other words," Andrea said, cutting to the heart of things as she always did. It was impossible to fool her.

"Is that so terrible? Maybe that's what I need right now."

"Maybe. But pretty soon it will be a year. You've got to get back in the world at some point, Ophélie. You can't hide forever." Even the name of the community where she had rented a house for the summer was a symbol of what she wanted. Safe Harbour. From the storms that had battered her since the previous October, and long before that.

"Why not?" Ophélie looked hopeless as she said it, and her friend's heart went out to her, as it had for nearly a year. Ophélie had gotten a very tough deal.

"It's not good for you, or Pip, to hide. She needs you front and center, sooner or later. You can't check out indefinitely. It just isn't right. You have to start your life again. You need to get out, and see people, maybe even date at some point. You can't be alone forever." Andrea thought she should get a job, but she hadn't dared say that to her yet. And Ophélie was still in no condition to start working. Or living.

"I can't even imagine it." Ophélie looked

horrified. She couldn't see herself with anyone but Ted. In her mind, she was still married to him, and always would be. She couldn't conceive of anyone else she'd want to share her life with. No one else would ever measure up to Ted in her eyes, no matter how difficult he had been to live with.

"There are some other things you could do first to get on your feet again. Combing your hair would be nice, once in a while at least." Most of the time when Andrea saw her now, she looked disheveled, and sometimes she hadn't gotten dressed in days. She showered, but then put on jeans and an old sweater, and just ran a hand through her hair instead of combing it, except when she went somewhere, like to group. But she rarely went anywhere anymore. She had no reason to. Except when she drove Pip to school. And she didn't comb her hair for that either. Andrea thought it had been long enough, it was time to pull herself together. It had been her idea that they come to Safe Harbour, and she had even found the house for them through a realtor she knew. She was glad she had, she could see just from looking at Pip, and even her mother, that it had been a good decision. Ophélie looked healthier than she had in nearly a year. And for once, her hair was combed, or close enough anyway. In spite of herself, she looked suntanned and pretty.

"What are you going to do when you come back to town? You can't lock yourself in the house again all winter."

"Yes, I can," Ophélie laughed without embarrassment. "I can do anything I damn well want to now." And they both knew that was true. Ted had left her an enormous fortune, not that she was showy about it. It was an ironic contrast to the dire straits they had been in, in their early years. At one point, they had lived in a two-room apartment in a dismal neighborhood. The kids had shared the bedroom, and Ted and Ophélie had slept on a pull-out couch in the living room. Ted had turned the garage into his laboratory. And oddly enough, despite the hardships and money worries they had, those had been their happiest years. Things got far more complicated once Ted had made it to the top of his field. Success had been far more stressful for him.

"I'm going to bug the hell out of you if you pull that recluse shit again when you come home," Andrea threatened. "I'll make you come to the park with William and me. Maybe we should go to New York for the opening of the Met." They both loved opera and had gone there before several times. "I'm going to drag you out by the hair if I have to," she said menacingly, as the baby stirred and then settled again, making the soft fluttering sounds that babies do. Both women smiled as they looked at him, and his mother let him sleep at her breast, where he was happiest, and so was she.

"I'm sure you will," Ophélie said in answer to her threat, and a few minutes later, Pip walked in with Mousse. She had a collection of rocks and seashells in her hands that she carefully deposited on the coffee table, with what looked like a gallon of sand. But Ophélie didn't say anything, as Pip pointed proudly at them.

"They're for you, Andrea. You can take them home with you."

"I'd love to. Can I take the sand too?" she teased. "What have you been up to? Have you met kids out here?" Andrea was concerned about Pip too.

Pip shrugged noncommittally. She hadn't really met anyone. She seldom saw other people on the beach, and her mother was so reclusive, she hadn't met any families either.

"I'm going to have to come out here more often and shake things up. There must be some kids staying around here somewhere. We'll have to find them for you."

"I'm fine," Pip said, as she always did. She

never complained. There was no point. She knew it wouldn't have changed anything. Her mother wasn't capable of more than she was doing at the moment. It was just the way things were for now. Maybe it would get better again one day, but obviously not yet. And Pip accepted that. She was wise way beyond her years. And the past nine months had forced her into adult shoes.

Andrea stayed until late in the afternoon, and left just before dinnertime. She wanted to get home before the fog rolled in. But by the time she left, they had laughed and talked, and Pip had played with the baby, and tickled him. They sat on the deck, soaking up the sun, and all in all, it had been a lovely, friendly afternoon. But the minute Andrea and the baby left, the house seemed instantly sad and empty again. She was such a powerful presence that the absence of her actually made things seem worse than they had been before she came. Pip loved the life-force of her. It was always exciting to be around her. And for Ophélie too. She couldn't get her own momentum going anymore, but Andrea had enough for all of them.

"Do you want me to rent a movie?" Ophélie suggested helpfully. She hadn't even thought about things like that in months, but Andrea's visit had energized her too.

"That's okay, Mom. I'll just watch TV," Pip said quietly.

"Are you sure?" She nodded, and they went through the usual dilemma about what to eat, but tonight Ophélie offered to make hamburgers and a salad. The hamburgers were more cooked than Pip liked them, but she didn't say anything. She didn't want to discourage her, and it was better than the frozen pizza neither of them ate. Pip ate her whole hamburger, while her mother picked at hers, but she ate all the salad and at least half of the hamburger for once. Things had definitely improved with Andrea's good influence on them.

As Pip went to bed that night, she wished her mother would tuck her in. It was too much to ask in her current state, but nice to think about anyway. She remembered that her father used to do that when she was small, although he hadn't in a long time. No one had. He was seldom home and her mother was busy with Chad most of the time. There was always some drama happening. And now that there was none, Ophélie seemed to be gone too. Pip just went to bed herself. No one came to say goodnight, or prayers, or sing songs, or tuck her in. She was used to it. But it would have been nice anyway, in another life, a different world than the one she was in. Her mother had gone to bed straight after dinner that night, while she was still watching TV. Mousse licked her face as she lay in bed, and then with a yawn himself, lay down on the floor next to her, as she reached a hand out of bed and stroked his ear.

Pip smiled to herself as she drifted off to sleep. She knew her mother was going back to the city the next day, which meant she could walk down the beach and visit with Matthew Bowles again. She smiled, thinking of it, as she fell almost instantly to sleep, and dreamt of Andrea and the baby.

4

THURSDAY DAWNED FOGGY AGAIN, AND PIP WAS still half asleep when her mother left for the city. Ophélie had an attorney's meeting before her group that day, and had to go into the city before nine. Amy made breakfast for Pip, and then got on the phone as usual, while Pip watched cartoons on TV. It was nearly lunchtime when she decided to walk down the beach. She had wanted to go all morning, but was afraid to go too early, or she might miss him. She thought Matthew was more likely to be there in the afternoon.

"Where are you going?" Amy asked responsibly for once, as she saw Pip walk off the deck onto the sand, and Pip turned to look at her innocently.

"Just on the beach with Mousse."

"Do you want me to come?"

"No, I'll be fine. Thanks," Pip said, and Amy went back to her call, feeling that she'd done her duty to Ophélie. And a moment later, both child and dog were bounding down the beach.

She had run for a long time when she saw him finally. He was in the same place, sitting on the folding stool, working at his easel. He heard Mousse barking in the distance, and turned to look at her. He had missed her the day before, surprisingly, and was relieved to see her small brown face smiling up at him.

"Hello," she said, as though greeting an old friend.

"Hi there. How are you and Mousse?"

"We're fine. I would have come sooner, but I was afraid you wouldn't be here if I came too early."

"I've been here since ten o'clock." Like Pip, he had been afraid they'd miss each other. He had been looking forward to the meeting just as much as she, although neither of them had in fact promised to be there. They just wanted to be, which was the best way.

"You added another boat," Pip commented, examining the painting carefully. "I like it. It's pretty." It was a little red fishing boat in the distance, near the sunset, and it added punch to the painting. She liked it instinctively and he was pleased. "How do you imagine them so

well?" she asked admiringly as Mousse disappeared in the sandgrass on the dune.

"I've seen a lot of boats." He smiled warmly at
her. She liked him. Very much, in fact, and there
was no question in her mind that he was her
friend. "I have a little sailboat I keep in the lagoon. I'll have to show it to you sometime." It
was small and old, but he cherished it. It was an
old wooden boat he went out in alone whenever he could. He had loved sailing since he was
Pip's age. "What did you do yesterday?" He
liked hearing about her, and looking at her.
More than ever, he wanted to do a sketch of
her, but he loved talking to her too, which was
rare for him.

"My godmother came to visit, with her baby.
He's three months old. His name is William and
he's really cute. She lets me carry him, and he
giggles a lot. He doesn't have a father," she said,
looking matter-of-fact.

"That's too bad," Matthew said carefully, taking a break from his work and enjoying her.
"How did that happen?"

"She's not married. She got him from a bank
or something. I don't know. It sounds complicated. My mom says it's not important. He just
doesn't have one, that's all."

He got the drift of it better than she had and
was intrigued. It sounded very modern to him.

He still believed in traditional marriages, and mothers and fathers, although he was well aware that life didn't always work out that way. But it was generally a good place to start. He wondered again what had happened to Pip's father, if anything, but he didn't get the feeling she was living with him, and he was afraid to ask. He didn't want to upset her unnecessarily, or pry. Their budding friendship seemed to rely on a certain amount of discretion and delicacy, which was both her nature and his.

"Do you want to draw today?" he asked, watching her. She was like a little elf hopping around the beach. She seemed so light and lithe, sometimes her feet barely touched the sand.

"Yes, please," she said, ever polite, and with that, he held a sketch pad and pencil out to her.

"What are you going to draw today? Mousse again? Now that you know how to do the hind legs, it should be easier," he said practically, and she looked pensive as she glanced up at his work.

"Do you think I could do a boat?" It seemed a stretch to her.

"I don't see why not. Do you want to try and copy mine? Or would you rather do a sailboat? I can sketch one for you, if you like."

"I can copy the ones in your painting, if that's

all right." She didn't want to put him to a lot of
trouble, which was typical of her. She was used
to being cautious not to make waves or cause
problems. She had always been careful with her
father, and it had served her well. He never got
as angry at her as he did at Chad. Although
most of the time, once they lived in a bigger
house, he didn't pay much attention to her at
all. He went to an office then, and came home
late, and traveled a lot. He had even learned to
fly his own plane. He had taken her up in it several times when he first got it, and even let her
bring the dog, with Chad's permission. And
Mousse had been very well behaved.

"Can you see from down there?" Matthew
asked, and she nodded, from where she sat near
his feet. He had brought a sandwich to the beach
with him, and unwrapped it. He had decided to
eat lunch on the beach that day, in case she came
by at lunchtime. He hadn't wanted to miss her,
and he offered half the sandwich to her, from his
perch on his stool. "Are you hungry?"

"No, thank you, Mr. Bowles. And yes, I can
see very well."

"Matt will do." He smiled at how polite and
formal she was. "Did you have lunch?"

"No, but I'm not hungry, thank you." And
then a moment later, as she sketched, out of

nowhere came a bit of information that surprised him. It was easier talking to him while
she wasn't looking at him, and was intent on
her sketch of the boat. "My mother never eats.
Or not very often anyway. She's gotten very
thin." It was obvious that Pip was worried
about her, and Matt was intrigued.

"Why is that? Has she been sick?"

"No. Just sad." They went on drawing for a
while, and he refused to pry. He figured she
would tell him as much as she wanted to, when
she was ready. And he was in no rush to press
her. Theirs was a friendship that seemed to float
in space, independent of time. And he felt as
though he had known her for a long time.

And then finally, it occurred to him to ask the
obvious. "Have you been sad too?" She nodded
silently, and never raised her eyes from the
sketch. And this time he purposely did not ask
why. He could sense painful memories wafting
around her, and he had to resist an urge to reach
out and touch her hair or her hand. He didn't
want to frighten her, or appear inappropriate by
being overly familiar. "How are you now?" It
seemed a safer question than other possibilities,
and this time she looked up at him.

"I'm better. It's been nice at the beach. I think
my mom is better too."

"I'm glad to hear it. Maybe she'll start eating soon."

"That's what my godmother said. She worries about my mom a lot too."

"Do you have brothers and sisters, Pip?" Matt asked her. It seemed a safe question to him, and he was totally unprepared for the look in her eyes as she turned her face up to him. The look of sorrow in her eyes seared him to his very soul, and nearly knocked him off his stool.

"I . . . yes . . ." She hesitated, unable to speak for a moment, and then she went on, still looking at him with those sad amber eyes that seemed to draw him into her world. "No . . . I mean sort of . . . well, it's hard to explain. My brother's name was Chad. He's fifteen. Well . . . he was . . . he had an accident last October. . . ." Oh God, he hated himself for asking her, and now he understood why her mother was so devastated and wasn't eating. He couldn't even fathom it, but there was nothing worse than the loss of a child.

"I'm so sorry, Pip. . . ." He didn't know what else to say.

"It's all right. He was very smart, like my father." And what she said next nearly finished him and explained everything. "My dad's plane crashed, and they were both . . . they both died. It exploded," she said with an audible lump in her throat, but she was glad she had told him. She wanted him to know.

Matt looked at her for an endless moment before he said a word, or could. "How terrible for all of you. I'm really sorry, Pip. How lucky for your mom that she has you."

"I guess so," Pip said thoughtfully, sounding unconvinced. "She's been pretty sad though. She stays in her room a lot." At times Pip had wondered if her mother was sadder because Chad had died and not Pip. It was impossible to know, but the question had inevitably come to mind. She had been so close to Chad and was so destroyed now that he was gone.

"I would be too." His own losses had damn near drowned him, but they were nothing like hers. His were far more ordinary, and the kind of thing you had to live with and accept. Losing a husband and son were far greater challenges than any he had weathered, and he could only imagine the blow it had been to Pip, particularly if her mother was depressed and withdrawn, which sounded as though it was the case from what Pip had said.

"She goes to a group in the city to talk about it. But I'm not sure it helps. She says everyone is really sad." It sounded morbid to him, but he knew it was the thing to do these days, to go to groups for whatever miseries you had. But a group of mourning bereft people struggling with their losses sounded grim to him, and hardly the right thing to cheer you up.

"My dad was an inventor, sort of. He did things with energy. I don't know what he did, but he was really good at it. We used to be poor, and when I was six, we got a big house and he bought a plane." It summed it up fairly succinctly, although it didn't entirely clarify what her father's profession was, but it was enough information for him. "Chad was really smart like him. I'm more like my mom."

"What does that mean?" Matt took exception to the implication of what she was saying. She was an exceptionally bright, articulate little girl. "You're smart too, Pip. Very smart. Both your parents must be. And you certainly are." It sounded like she had been pushed aside for a bright older brother, who was perhaps more interested in their father's field, whatever it was. It sounded like rank chauvinism to him, and he didn't like the impression it had obviously given her, of being second best, or worse yet, second rate.

"My dad and my brother used to fight a lot," she offered gratuitously. She seemed to need to talk to him, but if her mother was depressed, she probably had no one else to confide in, except maybe the godmother with the baby.

"Chad said he hated him, but he really didn't. He just said it when he got mad at my dad."

"That sounds about right for fifteen," Matt said with a gentle smile, although he didn't know that firsthand. He hadn't seen his own son in six years. The last time he had seen Robert, he was twelve. And Vanessa ten.

"Do you have kids?" Pip asked him, as though reading his mind and seeing them. It was his turn to share with her now.

"Yes, I do." He didn't tell her he hadn't seen them in six years. It would have been too hard to explain why. "Vanessa and Robert. They're sixteen and eighteen, and they live in New Zealand." They had been there for over nine years. It had taken him almost exactly three to finally give up. Their silence had convinced him.

"Where's that?" Pip looked puzzled. She'd never heard of New Zealand. Or maybe once, she thought, but she couldn't remember where it was. She thought it was in Africa maybe, or somewhere like that, but she didn't want to sound ignorant to Matt.

"It's a long way from here. It takes about twenty hours to get there by plane. They live in a place called Auckland. I think they're pretty happy there." Happier than he had been able to tolerate, or wanted to admit to her.

"That must be sad for you, having them so far away. You must miss them. I miss my dad and Chad," she said, and wiped a tear from her eye, which nearly tore his heart out. They had shared a lot in their second afternoon, and neither of them had drawn a thing in over an hour. It never occurred to her to ask him how often he saw them, she just assumed he did. But she was sorry for him anyway, for having them so far away.

"I miss them too." He got off his stool then, and came to sit next to her on the sand. Her small bare feet were dug into the sand, and she looked up at him with a sad smile.

"What do they look like?" She was curious about them, just as he had been about her. It was a reasonable thing to ask.

"Robert has dark hair and brown eyes like me. And Vanessa's blond with big blue eyes. She looks just like her mother. Does anyone else in your family have red hair like you?" Pip shook her head with a shy smile at his question.

"My dad had dark hair like you, and blue eyes, and so did Chad. My mom is blond. My brother used to call me carrot stick, because I have skinny legs and red hair."

"That's nice of him," Matt said, gently tousling the short curly red hair. "You don't look like a carrot stick to me."

"Yes, I do," she said proudly. She liked the name now, because it reminded her of him. She even missed his insults and his temper now that he was gone. Just as Ophélie missed even Ted's dark days. It was odd the things you missed about people once they were gone.

"Are we going to draw today?" he asked, deciding that they had shared enough painful confidences and both needed a break, and she looked relieved when he said it. She had wanted to tell him, but talking about it too much made her sad again.

"Yes. I want to," she said, picking up the sketch pad as he went back to his stool. And for the next hour or two they exchanged occasional non sequiturs and pleasantries that challenged neither of them. They were just comfortable being near each other, particularly knowing that they both knew more about their respective histories. Some of it was important information.

As she sat and worked on her drawings, and he on his painting, the clouds broke and the sun came out, and the wind died down. It turned out to be a beautiful afternoon. So much so that it was five o'clock before either of them realized how late it was. The time they had spent together had flown. And Pip looked suddenly worried when Matt told her it was after five.

"Will your mom be back by now?" he asked, looking concerned. He didn't want to get her into trouble over an innocent but productive afternoon. He was glad that they had talked. He hoped that it had helped her somehow.

"Probably. I'd better go back. She might get mad."

"Or worried," he said, wondering if he should go back with her to reassure her mother, or maybe that would make it worse if Pip came home with a strange man. He looked at the drawing she'd been working on then, and was impressed. "That looks great, Pip. You did a good job. Go on home now. I'll see you soon."

"Maybe I'll come back tomorrow, if she takes a nap. Will you be here, Matt?" There was a peculiar intimacy about the way she spoke to him, as though they truly were old friends. But they both felt that way now, after the confidences they'd exchanged. All that they had shared had brought them closer, as it was meant to.

"I'm here every afternoon. Don't get yourself in trouble now, little one."

"I won't." She stopped for a moment and smiled at him, like a hummingbird poised in midair, and then with a wave, clutching her drawing, and with Mousse at her heels, she dashed off toward home. And within instants, she was far down the beach. She danced around backward once and waved at him again, and he stood for a long time watching her, until she was a tiny figure far down the beach, and finally all he could see clearly was the dog running back and forth.

She was breathless when she got to the house. She had run all the way home. Her mother was sitting on the deck, reading, and Amy was nowhere in sight. Ophélie looked up with a frown.

"Amy said you'd gone down to the beach. I couldn't see you anywhere, Pip. Where were you? Did you find a friend?" She wasn't angry at the child, but she'd been concerned, and she had forced herself to stay calm. She didn't want her going to strangers' houses with them, it was a rule that Pip knew well, and conformed to. But Pip also knew that her mother worried more now than she had in the past.

"I was way down there," she waved vaguely in the direction from whence she'd come. "I was drawing a boat, and I didn't know what time it was. I'm sorry, Mom."

"Don't do it again, Pip. I don't want you wandering off that far. And I don't want you anywhere near the public beach. You never know who those people are." She wanted to tell her mother that some of them were nice, or Matt was at least. But she was afraid to tell her about her new friend. She sensed instinctively that her mother wouldn't understand. And she was right. "Stay around here next time." She was aware that the child was getting adventuresome. She was probably bored hanging around the house all day, or being alone on the beach with the dog. But nonetheless, Ophélie was concerned. She didn't ask to see the drawing, it never even occurred to her, as Pip went to her room, and laid it on the table next to the one of the dog. They were souvenirs of afternoons that were precious to her, and reminded her of Matt. She didn't have a crush on him, but there was no denying they had formed a special bond.

"How was your day?" Pip asked her mother when she came back to the deck. But she could see how it had been. Ophélie looked tired. She often did after her group.

"It was all right." She had been to the lawyer about Ted's estate. They still had some taxes to pay, and the last of the insurance money had come in. It was going to be a while before the estate was closed. Maybe even a long time. Ted had left everything in good order, and she had more money than she'd ever need. Hopefully most of it would go to Pip one day. Ophélie had never been extravagant. In fact, in some ways, she had always felt they'd been happier when they were poor. His success had brought headaches with it, and a lot of stress he had never had before. Not to mention the plane he had died in with Chad.

Ophélie spent hours every day fighting back the memories, particularly of that last day. That hideous call that had altered her life forever. And the fact that she had forced Ted to take Chad. He had had meetings in L.A., and wanted to go alone, but she had thought it would be good for both of them to spend some time together. Chad had been doing better than he had been in a while, and she thought they could both handle it. But neither of them had been enthused about sharing the trip. She blamed herself for selfish motives too. Their son required so much attention, and had been in such a precarious state for months, she had wanted a break from him, and to spend a quiet afternoon with Pip. With all the attention focused on Chad constantly, she never seemed to spend enough time with her. It was the first opportunity they'd had in a long time. And now it was all they had. Each other. Their life, their family, their happiness had been destroyed. And the fortune Ted had left meant nothing to Ophélie. She would have given all of it to spend the rest of her life with Ted, and to have Chad alive too.

There had been some tough times between her and Ted, but even then, her love for him hadn't faltered. But there was no question, it had been rocky between them at one point, and more than once because of Chad. But that was all over now. Their troubled son was at peace at last. And Ted, for all his brilliance and awkwardness and chemistry and charm, had vanished from her life. She spent hours at night rolling the film of their life backward in her head, trying to sort it out, trying to remember what it had really been like, savoring the good times, and trying to fast-forward past the bad. And as she did, she did some careful editing. What was left in the end was the memory of a man she had deeply loved, whatever his faults. Her love for him had been unconditional, not that it mattered now.

They solved the dinner dilemma with sandwiches, although Pip had barely eaten that day, and the silence in the house was deafening. They never put music on. They barely spoke. And as Pip sat eating the turkey sandwich her mother had made, she was thinking about Matt. She wondered again where New Zealand was, and felt sorry for him that he lived so far from his kids. She could imagine how hard that was. And she was glad she had told him about her father and Chad, although she hadn't explained how sick Chad had been. But it seemed disloyal to her to tell him that. She knew Chad's sickness had been a secret they kept to themselves. And there was no point telling him about it now. Chad was gone.

His illness had left a deep mark on her, on all of them. Living with him had been traumatic and difficult, and just as Chad had known how much his father resented him and the mental illness he refused to name, Pip had been aware of it herself. She had mentioned it to her father once, when Chad was in the hospital, and he had shouted at her and told her she didn't know what she was talking about, but she knew better than that. She understood full well, perhaps even better than he, how sick Chad was. And Ophélie did too. Only Ted clung to denial. It was essential to him. It was a matter of pride to Ted not to admit his son was sick. No matter what anyone said to him, or what doctors spoke to him, Ted insisted that if Ophélie handled Chad differently, and established stricter rules for him, there would be no problem at all. He always blamed Ophélie, and clung to the belief that Chad wasn't sick at all. No matter how severe the evidence, Ted's eyes remained firmly closed.

The weekend passed quietly. Andrea had promised to come to the beach again, but in the end, she didn't. She called and said the baby had a cold. And by Sunday afternoon, Pip was longing to see Matt. Her mother slept on the deck all afternoon, and after watching her quietly for an hour, Pip went down on the beach with Mousse. She wasn't intending to walk down to the public beach, she just headed that way, and before she knew it, she was far down the beach, and then she started running, hoping to see him. He was where he had been both times before, painting quietly, this time on a new watercolor. It was another sunset, with a child in it this time. She had red hair and was very small, and was wearing white shorts and a pink shirt. And in the far distance, there was a dark brown dog.

"Is that me and Mousse?" she asked quietly and startled him. He hadn't seen her approach, and when he turned to look at her, he smiled. He hadn't expected her until after the weekend, when her mother went to town again. But he was obviously pleased that she'd turned up.

"Could be, my friend. What a nice surprise." He smiled.

"My mom's asleep, and I had nothing to do, so I thought I'd come to visit you."

"I'm glad you did. Will she worry when she wakes up?"

Pip shook her head. He knew enough now to

understand. "She sleeps all day sometimes. I think she likes it better that way." There was no question that Pip's mother was depressed, but he was no longer surprised. Who wouldn't be, having lost both her husband and son. The only problem he could see, greater than that, was that her depression left Pip lonely and alone with no one to talk to but her dog.

She sat down on the sand next to him, and watched him paint for a while. And then she went down to the water's edge to look for shells. Mousse followed her, as Matt stopped painting and watched. He enjoyed just looking at her, she was so sweet, and seemed so other-worldly at times, like a wood sprite dancing along the beach. There was an elfin quality to her. And he was so intent on watching her that he didn't see a woman approach. She was stand-ing only a few feet from him, with a serious ex-pression, when he turned and gave a start. He had no idea who she was.

"Why are you watching my daughter? And why is she in your drawing?" Ophélie had in-stantly made the connection between the artist and the sketches Pip had brought home. She had come down to the public beach to find Pip and see what she was doing on her lengthy for-ays. And she didn't know how or why, but she knew this man was part of it somehow, and had no doubt once she saw the child and the dog in his painting.

"You have a lovely daughter, Mrs. Mackenzie. You must be very proud of her," he said calmly. More calmly than he felt actually. Her intense stare gave him considerable discomfort. He could almost sense what she was thinking, and wanted to reassure her, but he was afraid that doing so might arouse even darker suspicions.

"Are you aware that she is only eleven years old?" It would have been hard to mistake her for any older. If anything, she looked younger. But Ophélie couldn't imagine what this man wanted with her, and suspected him instantly of evil intentions. His seemingly innocent painting could have been, in her mind at least, simply a cover for something far more lurid. He could have been a kidnapper, or worse, and Pip was far too innocent to suspect that.

"Yes," he said quietly, "she told me."

"Why have you been talking to her? . . . and drawing with her?" He wanted to tell her that her daughter was desperately lonely, but didn't. By then, Pip had seen her mother standing, talking to him, and she approached quickly, with a handful of seashells. She searched her mother's eyes instantly to see if she was in trouble. And she realized almost as quickly that she wasn't, but Matt was. Her mother looked frightened and angry, and Pip wanted instantly to protect him.

"Mom, this is Matt," Pip said, as though trying to give some formality and respectability to the situation with an introduction.

"Matthew Bowles," he said, extending a hand to Ophélie, but she didn't take it, instead she looked directly at her daughter, with fire dancing in the amber eyes. Pip knew what that meant. It was rare for her mother to get angry at her, particularly lately. But now she was.

"I've told you never to talk to strangers. Never! Do you understand me?" And then she turned to Matt, with her eyes blazing. "There are names for this kind of thing," she said to him, "and none of them are pretty. You have no business picking up a child on the beach and befriending her, using your supposed artwork as a ruse to lure her. If you come near her again, I'll call the police. And I mean that!" she shot at him, and he looked wounded. Pip looked outraged, and was quick to defend him.

"He's my friend! All we did was draw together. He didn't try to take me anywhere. I came down the beach to see him." But Ophélie knew better, or thought she did. She knew that a man like him would lull Pip into feeling comfortable with him, and then God only knew what he would do to her, or where he would take her.

"You will not come down here again, do you hear me? *Tu entends? Je t'interdis!*" I forbid you. In her fury, her mother tongue betrayed her. She looked utterly Gallic as she raged at both of them. Her anger was born of fear, and Matt understood that.

"Your mother is right, Pip. You shouldn't talk to strangers." And then he turned to her mother. "I apologize. I didn't mean to upset you. I assure you, it has been an entirely respectable exchange between us. I understand your concerns, I have children who are only slightly older."

"And where are they?" Ophélie shot back at him, suspicious of him. She did not believe him.

"In New Zealand," Pip filled in for him, which didn't help the situation. Matt could see she didn't believe them.

"I don't know who you are, or why you've been speaking to my daughter, but I hope that you understand I'm serious. I'll call the authorities and report you if you encourage her to come and see you again."

"You've made yourself quite clear," he said, growing testy. In circumstances other than these, he would have said something harsher to her. She was being more than a little insulting, but he didn't want to upset Pip by being rude to her mother. And she deserved a little leeway given all she'd been through, but she had used almost all of it with her last words to him. No one had ever accused him of such vile motives. She was a very angry woman.

She pointed down the beach to Pip then, as the child looked sorrowfully over her shoulder. There were tears brimming in her eyes that spilled onto her cheeks, and all Matt wanted to do was hug her, but he couldn't.

"It's all right, Pip. I understand," he said softly.

"I'm sorry," she said, nearly sobbing, as her mother continued to point, and even Mousse looked subdued, as though he sensed that something awkward had happened. And with that, Ophélie took Pip's hand in her own, and led her firmly back down the beach, as Matt watched them. His heart went out to the child he had so quickly grown attached to, and for an instant, he wanted to shake her mother. He could understand her concerns, but they were unwarranted, and it was so obvious that Pip needed someone to talk to. Her mother may not have eaten much in the past nine months, but it was Pip who was starving.

He put his paints and drawing away then, and

folded up his stool and easel, and with his head down and a grim expression, he walked back to his cottage to drop them off. Five minutes later, he was on his way to the lagoon to take his boat out for a sail. He knew he needed to get out on the water to clear his head. Sailing always did that for him, and had all his life.

And on their way back to the part of the beach that belonged to the gated community, Ophélie interrogated her daughter. "Is that what you've been doing every time you disappear? How did you meet him?"

"I just saw him drawing," she said, still crying. "He's a good person. I know it."

"You don't know anything about him. He's a stranger. You don't know if what he told you is the truth. You know nothing. Did he ever ask you to go to his house?" her mother asked with a look of panic. The possibilities didn't even bear thinking.

"Of course not. He wasn't trying to kill me. He taught me how to draw Mousse's back legs. That's all. And a boat once." Killing her wasn't what Ophélie was worried about. She was an innocent child who could have easily been raped, kidnapped, or tortured. Once Pip trusted him, he could have done anything he wanted. The thought terrified her. And all of Pip's protests meant nothing to her. She was a child of eleven and didn't understand the potential dangers of befriending a strange man about whom she knew nothing.

"I want you to stay away from him," Ophélie said again. "I forbid you to leave the house without a grown-up. And if you don't understand that, we'll go back to the city."

"You were rude to my friend." Pip was suddenly angry, not just heartbroken. She had lost so many people she cared about, and now she had lost this one as well. He was the only friend she'd made all summer, or in a very long time.

"He's not your friend. He's a stranger. Don't forget that. And don't argue with me." They walked the rest of the way in silence, and once back at the house, Ophélie sent Pip to her room and called Andrea. She sounded distraught as her friend listened. Andrea heard the whole story, and then asked questions, sounding like an attorney.

"Are you going to call the police?"

"I don't know. Should I? He looked fairly respectable. He was decently dressed, but that doesn't mean anything. He could be an ax murderer for all I know. Can I get a restraining order against him?"

"You don't really have grounds to do that. He didn't threaten her, or molest her, or try to get her to go anywhere, did he?"

"She says he didn't. But he may have been trying to set the stage to do something dreadful later." Ophélie had a hard time believing his intentions had been innocent. In spite of everything Pip said, or maybe even because of it, she sensed danger. Why would he make friends with a child?

"I hope not," Andrea said, sounding thoughtful. "What makes you think it wasn't innocent? Did he look like a weirdo?"

"What does a weirdo look like? No . . . he looked relatively normal. And he says he has children. But he could be lying." Ophélie was convinced he was a child molester.

"Maybe he's just friendly."

"He has no business being friendly with a child that age, particularly a little girl. She's at exactly the right age for men like that to go after her, she's a total innocent, that's how they like them."

"That's true, of course. But maybe he isn't a pedophile. Was he cute?" Andrea grinned at her end, and Ophélie sounded outraged.

"You're disgusting!"

"More important, was he wearing a wedding ring? Maybe he's single."

"I don't want to hear this. The man was making friends with my daughter. He's four times her age, and he has no business doing that. If he is decent, then he should know better, particularly if he has children himself. How would he feel if some man were chatting up his daughter?"

"I don't know. Why don't you go back and ask him? Actually, he's beginning to sound interesting. Maybe Pip did you a favor."

"She did nothing of the sort. She put herself at great risk, and I'm not going to let her out of the house without me. And I mean it."

"Just tell her not to go back. She'll listen."

"I did. And I told him I'd call the police if he came near her."

"If he isn't a rapist, and he is a decent guy, he must have really liked that. Maybe we need to file down your fangs a little. I'm not sure you're quite ready for reentry." Matt was beginning to sound all right to her. She wasn't sure why, but her instincts told her the guy might actually be decent. If so, Ophélie's tirade must not have been appreciated or welcome.

"I'm not interested in 'reentry.' I'm not planning to reenter. I'm planning to stay out here. But I don't want anything terrible happening to Pip. I couldn't stand it." Her voice shook as she said it, and there were tears of terror in her eyes.

"I understand that," Andrea said gently. "Just keep an eye on her. Maybe she's lonely." After she'd said it, there was a silence, as Ophélie sat at the other end and cried.

"I know she is. But I can't seem to do anything about it. Chad is gone, her father's gone, and I'm a basket case. I'm barely functional. We don't even talk to each other." She knew it, she just couldn't get out of her own black hole enough to change it.

"Now maybe you've got the answer as to why she's picking up strangers," Andrea said gently.

"Apparently, they draw together," Ophélie said, sounding desperate. The entire episode had upset her immensely.

"There are worse things. Maybe you should invite him to the house for a drink and check him out. He might actually be a decent guy. You may even like him." As Ophélie listened, she shook her head.

"I don't think he'd speak to me after everything I said to him." But she wasn't sorry she had. They still had no idea who he was.

"You could go back and apologize tomorrow. Tell him you've been through a tough time and you're a little nervous."

"Don't be silly. I can't do that. And besides, what if I was right? Maybe he is a child molester, for all we know."

"In that case, don't go back and apologize. But my guess is that he's just a guy who was painting on the beach and likes kids. It sounds more like Pip went after him."

"And that is precisely why I sent her to her room."

"Poor kid. She didn't mean any harm by it, she was probably just having fun."

"Well, from now on she'll have to stay close to the house and have fun here." But after she hung up, Ophélie realized how little fun she provided for her. There were no children to play with, no activities, and they never did anything together anymore. The last time they'd been out somewhere together was the day that Ted and Chad had died. Ophélie had taken her nowhere since then.

After talking to Andrea, Ophélie went and knocked on the door of Pip's room. The door was closed, and when she tried to open it, she found it was bolted from inside.

"Pip?" There was no answer, and she knocked again. "Pip? May I come in?" There was another long silence, and then finally a small voice drowning in tears.

"You were mean to my friend. You were horrible. I hate you. Go away." Ophélie stood on the other side of the door, feeling helpless, but not guilty. She had an obligation to protect her daughter, even if Pip didn't agree or understand.

"I'm sorry. You don't know who he is," she said firmly.

"Yes, I do. He's a nice person. And he has children in New Zealand."

"Maybe he was lying," Ophélie persisted, but she was beginning to feel foolish trying to convince her through a locked door. And it was obvious that Pip had no intention of letting her in. Nor of coming out. "Come out and talk to me."

"I don't want to talk to you. I hate you."

"Let's have dinner and talk about it. We can go out if you want." There were two restaurants in town where they had never been.

"I don't want to go anywhere with you. Ever again." Ophélie didn't say it, but she was tempted to point out to Pip that her mother was all she had. Just as Pip was all she had now. All they had in the world was each other. They couldn't afford to be enemies or at each other's throats. They needed each other far too much.

"Why don't you just unlock the door? I won't come in if you don't want. You don't need to keep it locked."

"Yes, I do," Pip said stubbornly. She was holding the drawing of Mousse that she'd done with Matt, and still crying. She already missed him. And she wasn't going to let her mother keep her from him. She'd go to see him on the days when she was with Amy. And she hated the things her mother had said to him. She was mortified for him.

Ophélie continued to try to coax her out for a while longer, and then finally gave up, and went back to her bedroom. Neither of them ate dinner that night, and hunger finally drove Pip out of her bedroom the next morning. She came out for a piece of toast and a bowl of cereal and went back to her bedroom. She said not a single word to her mother, as she prepared her breakfast, and then left.

And at his house, Matt had lain awake all night, thinking of her, and worried about her. He didn't even know where they lived, so he could make a formal apology to her mother, in the hopes of softening her position. He hated to let Pip slip out of his life. He hardly knew her, but he already missed her a lot.

The war between Pip and her mother went on until early afternoon. And then they sat through one of their silent, painful dinners. It was the look on Pip's face that finally unnerved her mother.

"For heaven's sake, Pip, what's so special about him? You don't even know him."

"Yes, I do. And I like to draw with him. He lets

me sit there. Sometimes we talk, and sometimes we don't. I just like being with him."

"That's what worries me, Pip. He's old enough to be your father. Why would he want to be with you? It's not healthy."

"Maybe he misses his children. I don't know. Maybe he likes me. I think he's lonely or something," just as she was, but she didn't say that. She was remarkably stubborn, and ready to defend their cause.

"Maybe I could go with you sometime, if you really want to draw with him. I don't think he'd be very happy to see me." After everything she'd said, it would have been a miracle if he didn't throw his easel at her. And she wasn't sure she blamed him. She was beginning to wonder if she had been a little extreme in her position, or at least her expression of it. She had pretty much accused him of being a child molester. But at the time, she'd been startled to see them together, and frightened for her daughter. It was a somewhat normal reaction, although she had expressed it more than a little bluntly.

"Can I go back to see him, Mom?" Pip looked excited and hopeful. "I promise I'll never go to his house with him, and besides he never asked me." And she sensed correctly that he wouldn't. He would never have put her in that position, or himself.

"We'll see. Give me a little time to think about it. He may not want you there now," Ophélie said realistically, "after everything I said to him. I'm sure he didn't enjoy that."

"I'll tell him you're sorry." Pip beamed at her.

"Maybe you should take Amy with you. I'll walk down the beach with you later, and apologize. I hope he deserves it."

"Thank you, Mom," Pip said, with eyes filled with light again. She had won a major victory, the right to visit her only friend.

They walked down the beach together later that afternoon, and Pip could hardly contain herself as she ran along the water's edge with Mousse. Ophélie trailed far behind, she was trying to think of what she was going to say to him. She was doing this for Pip.

But when they got to the spot where Pip had always seen him before, there was no one there this time. There was no sign of Matt, the easel, or the folding stool. He had been so disheartened by the events of the day before, that he had stayed inside, despite Wedgwood blue skies, and was quietly reading a book. He wasn't even in the mood to sail, which was rare for him. Ophélie and Pip sat on the sand together for a long time, talking about him, and finally they went back up the beach, hand in hand. For the first time in a long time, Pip felt closer to her mother again. And she was glad that she had at least tried to apologize to Matt.

And from his living room, Matt stood and gazed out the window for a long time. He saw birds, and a fishing boat, and some new driftwood on the beach. He never saw Pip and her mother sitting there, or walking hand in hand. They were gone by the time he looked, and the beach was empty and deserted, like his life.

5

SHORTLY BEFORE NOON THE NEXT DAY, PIP told Amy she was going down the beach to see a friend. She took sandwiches with her this time, and an apple, in an effort to make amends for her mother's behavior. Amy thought to ask if it was okay with her mother, and Pip assured her it was. She left with her offering for him in a small brown bag, and hoped he would be back in his usual spot after his absence of the day before. She wondered what had happened to him, since he said he went there every day, and hoped his absence wasn't her mother's fault. But as soon as she saw him and looked into his eyes, before he said a single word, she knew it was. Even two days later, he looked distant and hurt. She got straight to the point.

"I'm sorry, Matt. My mom came to apologize yesterday, but you weren't here."

"That was nice of her," he said noncommittally, wondering what it had taken to get her
there. Pip, obviously. She would have moved
mountains for him, and had. And he was
touched by that. "I'm sorry she got so upset
about us. Was she very angry with you when
you left?"

"For a while," Pip said honestly, and was relieved to see him relax again. "She said I could
come to see you today, and whenever I want. I
just can't go to your house."

"That makes sense. How did you get her to
agree to that?" he asked with interest, as he sat
comfortably on his folding stool, pleased to see
her again. He had been depressed all the night
before at the prospect of her no longer being
able to draw with him. He was going to miss
their conversations and her confidences. She
had come to mean a lot to him, in a remarkably
brief time. She had landed like a bright little
bird, right on his heart. But there were also
deep emotional holes in each of them that the
other filled. She had lost a father and brother, he
both his children. And Matt and Pip each filled
a need for the other.

"I locked myself in my room, and refused to
come out," Pip said with a grin. "I think she felt
bad afterward. She was so rude to you. I'm
sorry . . . she's different than she used to be. She

worries about everything, and she gets mad about stupid, little stuff sometimes. And other times she doesn't seem to care about anything. I think she's confused."

"Or suffering from post-traumatic stress," he said sympathetically. He hadn't liked her much the day before, for obvious reasons. But he could also understand her point of view. He just thought she had expressed it a little too stridently. There had been something faintly hysterical about her pitch.

"What's that?" Pip asked, as she opened the bag of sandwiches and handed one to him. It was so comfortable being back with him. She loved talking to him, and watching him paint. "The post office thing you just talked about . . . what is it?"

"Thank you," he said for the carefully wrapped sandwich, and then took a bite. "Post-traumatic stress. It's when something very shocking happens to someone, it's what happens to them afterward. It's kind of like they're in shock. Your mom probably still is. She had a terrific blow to her system when your brother and father died."

"Do people like that ever get better again? Can they be fixed?" She'd been worried about it for nine months and had no one to ask. She had never felt as comfortable talking to Andrea, as she did with Matt. He was her friend, and Andrea was her mother's.

"I think so. It takes time. Is she any better than she was when it first happened?"

"Sort of," Pip said pensively, but didn't sound convinced. "She sleeps a lot more now, and she doesn't talk as much as she used to before it happened. She almost never smiles. But she doesn't cry all the time either. She did at first," and then she looked sheepish. "Me too . . ."

"So would I in your shoes. It would have been weird if you didn't, Pip. Half your family disappeared." And what was left didn't even feel like one, but out of loyalty to her mother, she didn't say anything.

"My mom was really sorry about the things she said the other day." Pip was still embarrassed about the way her mother had behaved.

"It's all right," he said calmly, "she was right in some ways. I really am a stranger, and you don't know much about me. I could have been trying to fool you or do something bad to you, just as she said. She was right to be suspicious of me, and you should have been too."

"Why? You were nice to me, and you helped me draw Moussy's hind legs. That was a nice thing to do. I still have the picture of him in my room."

"How does it look?" he teased.

"Pretty good." She grinned. And when he finished his sandwich, she handed him the apple. He cut it in half, and handed the better half back to her. "I always knew you were a good person, right from the first time I saw you."

"How did you know?" He looked amused.

"I just knew. You have nice eyes." She didn't tell him that she was touched when he looked sad, when he talked about his kids being so far away. She liked that about him too. It would have been worse if he didn't care about them.

"You have nice eyes too. I'd like to draw you one day. Maybe even paint you. What do you think of that?" He had been thinking about it since they met.

"I think my mom would like it a lot. Maybe I could give it to her for her birthday."

"When's that?" He wasn't her mother's greatest fan yet, but he would have done it for Pip. Besides, he wanted to do a portrait of her. She was a remarkable little girl, and now his friend.

"December tenth," she said solemnly.

"And when's yours?" he asked with interest. He always wanted to know more about her. She reminded him so much of his daughter Vanessa. And aside from that, he admired her, she was a spunky little kid. Even more than he had first thought, if she had managed to convince her mother to let her come back down the beach to visit him, and even dragged her along to apologize the day before. That was a major feat. The woman he had seen on Sunday looked like she never apologized, except at gunpoint maybe. In this case, Pip had held the gun.

"My birthday is in October." Not long after her brother and father died.

"How was your last one?" he asked conversationally.

"My mom and I went out to dinner." She didn't tell him it was abysmal. Her mother had almost forgotten it, and there had been no party or cake. It was her first birthday since her father and Chad had died, and it had been horrible. She couldn't wait for it to end.

"Do you and your mom go out a lot?"

"No. We used to. Before. My dad liked taking us to restaurants. But it always takes too long. I get bored," she admitted easily.

"That's hard to believe. You don't look bored to me."

"I'm not when I'm with you," she said graciously. "I like drawing with you."

"I like drawing with you too." And with that, he handed her pencil and sketch pad, and she decided to draw a bird, one of the bold seagulls that swooped down next to them whenever possible, and then flew away instantly as Mousse began to chase them. It was hard doing a seagull, she discovered. And after a while, she switched to boats again. But just in the few times she'd been with him, her drawing had improved. She was getting good, as long as she liked what she was drawing, but that was true for him too.

They sat for hours in the sunshine, it was another golden day at Safe Harbour. And she was in no rush to go home. She was glad she didn't have to lie about it anymore. She could tell the truth, that she'd been drawing with him on the beach. It was four-thirty when she finally got up. Mousse had been lying quietly next to her for once, and he got up too.

"Are you two heading back?" Matt asked with a warm smile, and as she looked at him, she realized that he looked more like her father than ever when he smiled, although her father hadn't smiled very often. He'd been a very serious man, probably because he was so smart. Everyone said he was a genius, and Pip suspected it was true. It made people accept the way he behaved, which was nice for him. Sometimes it seemed to her that her father was allowed to say and do anything he wanted.

"My mom comes home around this time.

She's usually pretty tired after she goes to group. Sometimes she just walks in, and falls asleep on her bed."

"It must be pretty rough."

"I don't know. She doesn't talk about it. Maybe people cry a lot." It was a depressing thought. "I'll come back tomorrow or Thursday, if that's okay with you." She had never asked him before, but they had more leeway now.

"I'd like that, Pip. Whenever you like. Say hello to your mother for me." She nodded, and thanked him, waved, and then like a butterfly she flew off and was gone. And he watched her and Mousse disappear down the beach, as he always did. She was like a rare gift that had happened into his life. A little bird who came and went, her wings fluttering, her huge eyes so full of mysteries. Their conversations touched him and made him smile. He couldn't help wondering, as he thought about her, what her mother was really like. And the father she said was a genius. He sounded difficult, from things she'd said, and a little dark. And the boy sounded unusual too. Not the typical family. And she was certainly no ordinary child. Nor were his. They had been great kids. The last time he'd seen them anyway. It had been a long time. But he didn't let himself dwell on that.

It occurred to him as he walked over the dune to his cottage that he would have liked to take her sailing with him, and even teach her how to sail, as he had his own kids. Vanessa had loved it, Robert hadn't. But out of respect for Pip's mother, Matt knew he wouldn't take her out on the boat. She didn't know him well enough to trust him on the water, and there was always the faint possibility that something could go wrong. He didn't want to risk that.

When Pip got home, she found her mother just walking through the door. As usual, she looked drained, and asked where Pip had been.

"I went to see Matt. He said to say hi. I drew boats today. I couldn't do birds, they were too hard." She dropped several pages on the kitchen table, and as she glanced at them, Ophélie saw that the drawings were good. She was surprised to find how much Pip had improved. Chad had been something of an artist too, but she tried not to think of that. "I'll cook dinner tonight, if you want," Pip offered, and for once, Ophélie smiled.

"Let's go out."

"We don't have to." Pip knew how tired she was, but she looked a little better tonight.

"It might be fun. How about it? Why don't we go now?" It was a major step for Ophélie, which Pip knew and acknowledged.

"Okay." Pip looked pleased and surprised. And half an hour later, they were seated at a table for two at the Mermaid Café, one of the two restaurants in town. They both had hamburgers, and chatted amiably. It was the first night out they'd had. And when they got back to the house, they were both happy, full, and tired.

Pip went to bed early that night, and went back to see Matt the next day. Her mother offered no objection when she left, and looked relaxed when Pip got back. As usual, she dropped her drawings on the table. And by the end of the following week, there was a sizable collection of them, most of them pretty good. She was learning a lot from Matt.

It was on a Friday morning, when she had brought him lunch again, that she walked off with Mousse for a few minutes to look for shells, as she sometimes did, and he saw her jump back from the water's edge. He smiled, thinking she had seen a jellyfish or a crab, and he waited to hear Mousse bark. But this time he heard Mousse whine, and saw Pip sitting on the sand, holding her foot.

"Are you okay?" he called out to her, wondering if she'd hear, she was a good distance away. But she shook her head, and he put down his brush and watched her for a minute. She didn't move or stand up. She just sat there and held her foot. And he couldn't see her face. Her head was bent as she looked down at her foot, and the dog continued to whine. Matt walked over to her to see what had happened, and hoped she hadn't stepped on a nail. There were a lot of rusty ones on the beach, loose in the sand or sticking out of pieces of wood that had washed up on shore.

But as soon as he got to her, he saw that it wasn't a nail she'd stepped on, but a jagged piece of glass, and she had an ugly gash on the sole of her foot.

"How did that happen?" he asked as he sat down next to her, there was a considerable amount of blood in the sand, and her foot was still bleeding profusely.

"It was under a piece of seaweed I stepped on," she said bravely, but he saw instantly that her face was pale.

"Does it hurt a lot?" he asked solicitously, reaching out gently for her foot.

"Not too much," she lied.

"I'll bet it does. Let me have a look at it." He wanted to make sure there was no glass left in it. It looked like a clean slice, but it was a deep gash. And she looked up at him with worried eyes.

"Is it okay?"

"It will be, after I cut off the foot. You won't miss it a bit." In spite of how much it hurt, she laughed. But she looked frightened too. "You can still draw with one foot," he said, as he scooped her up. She was light as a feather and even smaller than she looked. He didn't want her to get sand in it, and was afraid she already had. And he instantly remembered her mother's admonitions not to go to his house. But he couldn't let her walk home with a gash in her foot, and he was almost certain she'd need stitches, although he didn't mention it to Pip. "Your mom may get mad at both of us, but I'm going to take you inside, and clean this up a bit."

"Will it hurt?" She looked anxious, and he smiled at her reassuringly, as he carried her toward his house, and Mousse followed. He left all his painting equipment on the beach without a thought.

"It won't hurt as much as your mom yelling at both of us," he said, distracting her. But they both noticed that they were leaving a trail of blood along the sand as he walked over the dune with Pip in his arms. And in a few strides, he had reached his front door, and walked straight into the kitchen, still carrying her. And they left a trail of blood on his floor too. He sat her on a kitchen chair, and lifted her foot gently to rest it on the sink. And within seconds, it looked like there was blood everywhere, and all over him as well.

"Will I have to go to the hospital?" she asked nervously. Her eyes looked enormous in the pale face. "Chad cut his head open once, and he bled all over the place and had to have a lot of stitches." She didn't tell him it was because he had had a tantrum, and had banged his head into the wall. He had been about ten at the time, and she was six, but she remembered it perfectly. Her father had shouted at her mother about it, and at Chad too. And their mother cried. It had been an ugly scene.

"Let's take a look." It didn't look any better to him than it had on the beach. He lifted her up and sat her on the edge of the sink, and ran some cold water on it, which made it feel better, but the water looked bright red as it ran down the drain. "Well, my friend, let's wrap this in a towel." He took a clean one from a rack, and she noticed that he had a warm, cozy kitchen, although everything in it looked worn and old. But it seemed friendly that way. "And after we wrap it in the towel, I think I should get you home to your mom. Is she at the house today?"

"Yes, she is."

"Good. I'm going to drive you up to the

house, so you don't have to walk. How does that sound to you?"

"Pretty good. And then will we have to go to the hospital?"

"Let's see what your mom says. Unless you want me to chop the leg off right here. It'll only take a minute, unless Mousse gets in the way." He was sitting obediently in the corner, watching them both quietly. And Pip giggled at what he'd said, but she still looked pale to him, and he suspected that the foot hurt a lot. He was right, but she didn't want to admit it to him. She was trying very hard to be brave.

He wrapped the foot in a towel, as he'd promised, and picked her up again, grabbing his car keys on the way, and Mousse followed them out behind the house, and got into the back of the station wagon as soon as Matt opened the door. By the time he set her down on the front passenger seat, there was a large spot of bright red blood soaking through the towel.

"Is it really bad, Matt?" she asked on the way home, and he tried to look unconcerned.

"No, but it's not terrific. People shouldn't leave glass like that on the beach." It had sliced through her like a knife. And felt that way too.

They were at her house in less than five minutes, and when they got there, he carried her inside, with Mousse at his heels. Her mother was in the living room, and was startled when she looked up and saw them both, and Pip in Matt's arms.

"What happened? Pip, are you all right?" Ophélie looked instantly worried as she came toward them.

"I'm okay, Mom. I cut my foot." Matt's eyes met her mother's. It was the first time he had seen her since the day she had implied he was a child molester when she met him on the beach.

"Is she all right?" Ophélie asked him, noticing how gently he set her down, and carefully unwrapped the foot.

"I think so. But I thought you should have a look." He didn't want to tell her in front of Pip that he thought she should have stitches, but as soon as she saw it, she came to the same conclusion.

"We'd better go to the doctor. I think you need stitches, Pip," her mother said calmly, as Pip's eyes filled with tears and Matt patted her shoulder.

"Maybe one or two," he said, gently touching the child's head, and feeling the silky curls. But the disquieting event got the best of her then, and she started to cry, in spite of wanting to be brave for him. She didn't want him to think she was a sissy. "They'll make it numb first. I did the same thing last year. It won't even hurt."

"Yes, it will!" she shouted at both of them, sounding eleven years old for once. She had a right to. It was a nasty cut, and had bled a lot. "I don't want stitches!" she said, burying her face against her mother.

"We'll do something fun afterward, I promise," Matt said, looking at Ophélie, and wondering if he should leave. He didn't want to intrude. But she seemed grateful to have him there, and so was Pip. He had a calming influence on both of them. He was a patient, easygoing person, and it showed at times like this.

"Is there a doctor here?" Ophélie asked, looking worried.

"There's a clinic behind the grocery store. With a nurse. She sewed me up last year. How do you feel about that? Otherwise, we can drive her into the city. I don't mind taking you if you'd like."

"Why don't we take her to the clinic, and see what the nurse says."

Pip whimpered a little on the way there, and Matt told her funny stories and distracted them both, which was a relief. And as soon as the nurse saw it, she agreed with Matt and Ophélie. And she did just what Matt had said she would. She gave Pip a shot to numb it, and then neatly stitched it up. She had seven stitches, and a huge bandage to cover it, and she had to stay off the foot for several days, and come back to get the stitches out in a week. Matt carried her back to the car afterward, and she looked worn out from the ordeal.

"Can I take you both out to lunch?" Matt offered, as they drove through the tiny town, but Pip said weakly that she felt kind of sick, and they decided to drive home. Once there, he laid her gently on the couch. Her mother turned on the TV for her, and five minutes later, she was sound asleep.

"Poor kid, that was a nasty one. I knew it the minute I saw it. She was very brave."

"Thank you for being so good to us," Ophélie said gratefully, as Matt thought it was hard to believe she was the same woman who had read him the riot act on the beach. This one was a gentle soul, with the saddest eyes he'd ever seen, much like Pip's. There was the same waiflike quality to her. And it made him want to put his arms around her too. Everything she had been through and suffered was in her eyes and on her face. But in spite of it, he couldn't help noticing that she was a beautiful woman, and looked surprisingly young for her age.

"I have to confess," he said with a look of concern, but he wanted to tell her first, and take the brunt of her anger, if there was any. "I took her into my house to clean the foot. We were only there for five minutes, and then I brought her back to you. I wouldn't have done it otherwise, but I wanted to get some water on the foot, and she was bleeding all over the place, so I needed something to wrap it up."

"It's lucky you were there. I understand. Thank you for telling me."

"I thought about bringing her straight here, knowing how you'd feel about it, but I wanted to take a good look at the cut. It was uglier than I thought."

"Yes, it was." She had felt sick herself as she watched the nurse stitch it up. She had felt that way when Chad had cut his head too. And that had been such an upsetting day. This had been far simpler, and thanks to Matt, they had gotten her to the clinic quickly, and he had kept Pip amused and distracted all the way. She could see now what Pip saw in him. He was a remarkably nice person. "Thank you for being so kind. You made it a lot easier for her. And for me."

"I'm just sorry it happened. It's so dangerous to leave glass on the beach. I always pick it up when I see it. It leads to things like this." He glanced over at Pip, and smiled as he watched her sleep.

"Can I offer you something to eat?" she asked graciously, and he hesitated. They had been through enough that morning.

"You must be tired. It's always hard to watch when kids get hurt." He was feeling a little worn out too. It had been an emotional morning.

"I'm fine. Why don't I make some sandwiches? It won't take me a minute."

"Are you sure?"

"Totally. Would you like a glass of wine?" He declined and settled for a Coke, and she put out a plate of sandwiches a few minutes later. In spite of her constant lethargy these days, she seemed calm and efficient. And they sat down facing each other at the kitchen table.

"Pip tells me you're French, although you can't even hear it. You speak amazingly good English."

"I learned it as a child in school, and I've been here for more than half my life. I came here to college as a foreign student, and married one of my professors."

"What did you come to study?"

"I was a pre-med student. But I never went on to med school. I got married right after graduation." She didn't mention that she'd gone to Radcliffe, which would have seemed pretentious to her.

"Are you sorry you didn't go on to med school? " he asked with interest. Like her daughter, she was an intriguing woman.

"Never. I don't think I'd have been a very good doctor. I got squeamish just now watching the nurse sew up Pip's foot."

"It's different when it's one of your own children. I felt the same way when I watched her, and she's not even my daughter."

It reminded her of one of the few facts she knew about him. "Pip tells me your children are in New Zealand," but as soon as she said it, she knew it was a painful subject. His eyes looked pained. "How old are they?"

"Sixteen and eighteen."

"My son would have been sixteen in April," she said sadly, and then for both their sakes, he changed the subject.

"I studied at the Beaux Arts in Paris for a year when I was in college," he said. "What a spectacular city. I haven't been back in a few years, but I used to go at every opportunity. The Louvre is my favorite place on the planet."

"I took Pip there last year and she hated it. It's a bit too serious for her. But she loved the international cafeteria in the basement. She almost liked it better than McDonald's." They both laughed at the culinary and cultural perversities of children.

"Do you go back often?" He was curious about her. And she about him now.

"Usually, every summer. But I didn't want to

this year. This seemed easier, and more peaceful. I used to go to Brittany as a child, and this reminds me a little of it." Matt was surprised to admit it to himself as he chatted with her, but he liked her. She seemed simple, warm, and honest, and not like the wife of a man who had made an enormous fortune and flown his own plane. She seemed down-to-earth and unpretentious. Although he couldn't help noticing that peeking through the mane of long wavy blond hair were tiny diamond studs on her ears, and she was wearing a beautiful black cashmere sweater. But the luxuries seemed inconsequential and were outshone by her gentleness and beauty. She was a very pretty woman. And he noticed that she was still wearing her plain gold wedding ring, and that touched him. Sally had thrown hers away, she said, the day she left him. At the time, it had been a piece of information that nearly killed him. He liked the fact that Ophélie still wore hers. It seemed like a gesture of love and respect for her late husband. And he admired her for it.

They chatted quietly as they finished lunch, and were both surprised by how long they'd talked when they finally heard Pip stirring. But she only whimpered a little, and turned on her side on the couch, as Mousse lay on the floor near her.

"That dog adores her, doesn't he?" Matt commented, and she nodded.

"He was my son's originally, but he's adopted Pip now. She loves him."

A little while later, Matt got up to leave, thanked her for lunch, and suggested she come down the beach with Pip one day. He had told her about his sailboat too, and had offered to take her sailing when Ophélie said how much she loved the ocean.

"I don't suppose she'll be walking anywhere for the next week," he said almost sadly. He would miss her.

"You can come and visit her here, if you'd like. I know she'd love to see you." It was hard to believe, as he looked at her, that this was the same woman who, almost two weeks earlier, had forbidden her daughter to see him. But things had changed in the meantime. Because of Pip's staunch loyalty to him, Ophélie had come to trust him. And after the morning they had just shared, more than that, she was grateful to him, and even liked him. She could see why Pip had befriended him. Everything about him suggested that he was a decent person. And she noticed, as Pip had, that he looked ever so slightly like her husband. It was more in size and shape and the way he moved, and coloring, than in any great similarity of features, but there was something that made Ophélie feel comfortable with him.

"Thank you for lunch," he said politely. She gave him the phone number, and he promised to call before coming by. He said he would give Pip a few days to recover before he called them.

And Pip was vastly disappointed when she woke up to discover that he had left and she had missed him. She had slept for nearly four hours, and the anesthetic had worn off by then. The foot hurt a lot, as the nurse had warned it might for a day or two. Ophélie gave her some aspirin and tucked a blanket over her in front of the TV, and Pip was sound asleep again before dinner.

She was still asleep when Andrea called them, and Ophélie told her what had happened. And she commented on Matt's involvement.

"He doesn't sound like a child molester to me. Maybe you should molest him," Andrea suggested with a chuckle. "And if you don't, I will." She hadn't had a date since the baby, and she was getting antsy. Andrea enjoyed male companionship, and she had her eye on a single father at the playground. She had always dated the men in her office, many of them married. "Why don't you invite him to dinner?"

"We'll see," Ophélie said vaguely. She had enjoyed having lunch with him, but she had no desire to pursue him, or anyone, for that matter. As far as she was concerned, she still felt married. She had talked about it in her group frequently, and couldn't imagine feeling otherwise. The thought of being single again made her shudder. She had been in love with Ted for twenty years, and even death hadn't changed that. In spite of everything that had happened, her love for him had never wavered.

"I'll come out to see you this week," Andrea promised. "Why don't you invite him to dinner when I come? I want to see him."

"You're disgusting." Ophélie laughed at her old friend. They chatted for a few minutes, and after they hung up, she carried Pip into her room and tucked her in. And as she did, she realized she hadn't done it in ages. She felt as though she were slowly waking from a deep sleep. Ted and Chad had been gone for ten months now. It was hard to believe. Nearly a year since her life had been utterly and totally shattered. She hadn't picked up the pieces yet, but ever so slowly she was finding them here and there, and one day, maybe, she would get her life back together. But she wasn't there yet. And she knew she still had a long way to go before she got there. It had been nice having company that afternoon, and talking to Matt. But she still felt like a married woman entertaining a guest. The thought of dating was inconceivable to her, if not to Andrea.

But it was that which had impressed Matt as he sat across the table from her. He had liked her dignity, and gentle grace. There was nothing sharp or pushy about her. He had had the same feelings as Ophélie about dating at first. It had taken him years and years and years to get over Sally. And now where those feelings had been, he was numb finally. He didn't love her anymore, and he no longer hated her. He felt nothing for her. And where his heart had been, there was empty space. All he was capable of, in his own mind at least, was a friendship with an eleven-year-old girl.

6

PIP'S WEEK OF CONVALESCENCE WAS FRUSTRATING for her. She sat on the couch in the living room watching television and reading books, and when Ophélie felt up to it, playing cards. But most of the time, Ophélie was still too distracted to play with her. Pip did little sketches on random pieces of paper she found, but what irked her most of all was that she couldn't go down on the beach, or visit Matt, she wasn't supposed to get sand in her stitches. And ever since the day she'd cut her foot, the weather at the beach had been terrific, which made her incarceration seem that much worse.

Pip had been home for three days, under house arrest, when Ophélie decided to take a walk down the beach, and turned without thinking toward the public end. She kept walking, and after a while, much to her surprise, she saw Matt at his easel. He was hard at work and deeply engrossed in what he was doing. She hesitated, as Pip had at first, staying at a distance. And after a time, Matt sensed her, turned, and then saw her. She was standing hesitantly, and looked strikingly like her daughter. And when he smiled at her, she finally approached him.

"Hello, how are you? I didn't want to interrupt you," she said, smiling shyly.

"No problem," he smiled reassuringly, "I welcome the interruptions." He was wearing a T-shirt and jeans, and she could see that he was in good shape. He had strong arms and broad shoulders, and an easy way about him. "How's Pip?"

"Bored, poor thing. Having to stay off the foot is driving her crazy. She misses coming down to see you."

"I'll have to come and visit, if that's all right with you," he asked cautiously. He didn't want to intrude on child or mother.

"She'd love that."

"Maybe I'll give her some assignments."

Ophélie noticed that he was working on a view of the sea, with tall, rolling waves on a stormy day, and a tiny sailboat being buffeted by them. The painting was powerful, and somehow touching. It gave off a sense of loneliness and isolation, and the relentlessness of the ocean.

"I like your work." And she meant it. The painting was lovely, and very good.

"Thank you."

"Do you always work in watercolors?"

"No, I prefer oils. And I enjoy doing portraits." It made him think of the one he had promised to do of Pip for her mother's birthday. He wanted to get started before she left Safe Harbour, but since her accident, he hadn't had time to do the preliminary sketches of her. Although he had a clear picture in his head of how he would paint her.

"Do you live here all year round?" she asked with interest.

"Yes, I do. I have for almost ten years."

"It must get lonely in the wintertime," she said quietly, not sure if she should sit down in the sand, or just stand near him. She felt as though she should wait for an invitation, as if this part of the beach was his private province. Like an office.

"It's quiet here. I like that. It suits me." Almost all of the residents of the beach community were summer visitors. There were a few more people who lived there year-round in the section between the public beach and the gated community, but not many. The beach and the town were all but deserted in winter. He seemed like a lonely man to Ophélie, or solitary at least, but he didn't look unhappy. He seemed peaceful and very much at ease in his own skin, as the French would say.

"Do you go into the city much?" she chatted with him, curious about him. It was easy to see why Pip liked him. He was not overly talkative, he had a way of making people feel comfortable with him.

"Almost never. I have no reason to anymore. I sold my business ten years ago when I moved here. I thought I was just taking a break before getting back into it again, and as things turned out, I stayed here." Selling the ad agency at the top of the market had allowed him to do that, even after he split the proceeds with Sally. And a small inheritance he'd gotten from his parents after that had allowed him to stay. All he had wanted originally was a year off before he started something else, but then she'd left for New Zealand, and he had tried commuting to see the kids. By the time he stopped doing that four years later, he had lost interest in starting another business. And all he wanted to do now was paint. He had had a few one-man shows over the years, but he didn't even do that anymore. He had no need to show his work, only to do it.

"I love it here," Ophélie said quietly, sinking down into the sand eight or ten feet away from him. It was close enough to see what he was doing and talk to him, but not so close that either of them felt encroached on or invaded. They were mindful of each other's space, and as Pip did sometimes, Ophélie sat watching him in silence, until he finally spoke again.

"It's good for kids here," he said, squinting at his work, and then looking into the distance. "It's pretty safe, and they can run around on the beach. It's a lot simpler than life in the city."

"I like how close it is. I can go back and forth easily, and leave her here. We don't have to go anywhere, just be here."

"I like that too." He smiled at her. And then he decided to inquire further about her. He was curious, despite what he knew, she was obviously bright, but at the same time, haunted and quiet. "Do you work?" He didn't think so. She hadn't mentioned it at lunch, and Pip had never said anything about it.

"No. I did a long time ago, when we lived in Cambridge, before we moved out here and the kids were born. I didn't work then, because whatever I would have made wouldn't have been enough to pay a baby-sitter, so there didn't seem to be much point. I worked as a TA in the biochemistry lab at Harvard. I loved it." Ted had gotten her the job, and it had fit into her pre-med plans then, until she'd shelved her own dreams completely. In the end, and almost since the beginning, Ted had been the only dream she wanted or needed. He and their children had been her entire world.

"Sounds very lofty. Do you think you'd ever go back to it? I mean med school." Ophélie laughed in answer to the question.

"I'm way too old. Between med school and residency and studying for boards and certifying, I'd be fifty by the time I was a doctor." At forty-two, her dreams of med school had long since vanished.

"Some people do it. It might be fun."

"It would have been then, I guess. But I was happy standing behind my husband." In many ways, she was still very French, and had been happy to play second fiddle to him. She didn't see it that way, she saw herself as his support system and cheering team to encourage him through the hard times, and she had been. It was the main reason their marriage had lasted. Ted needed her as his link to the real world. She was the one thing that had kept him going when things were hardest. And now there was no one to do the same for her, except her daughter. "I've been thinking about getting a job lately. Or to be honest, other people have been thinking of it for me. My group and my closest friend mostly. They think I need something to keep me busy. Pip is in school all day, and I don't have a lot to do." With Ted and Chad gone, her job seemed to be almost over. Chad had kept her more than occupied, with his many challenges and problems. And Ted had also required a fair amount of attention. But Pip didn't, she was busy during the day and after school and with her friends on weekends. She was surprisingly well occupied and self-sufficient. And Ophélie felt as though she had lost not only half her family but her job along with it. "I don't know what I'd do though. I have no formal training."

"What do you like to do?" he asked with interest, glancing over at her from time to time. Most of the time he talked while he painted, and Ophélie liked that. They could talk to each other without her feeling overly focused on or scrutinized. It was almost like therapy as she opened up to him, just as Pip did.

"You know, it's embarrassing, but I'm not sure. I haven't done anything for myself, or that I wanted to do, in such a long time. I was always busy with my children and my husband. And

Pip seems to need me much less than Ted and Chad did."

"Don't be so sure," Matt said quietly. He wanted to tell her that the child was obviously lonely, but he didn't. "What about some kind of volunteer work?" It was obvious from the house they were renting, and the fact that her husband had flown his own plane, that she didn't need the money.

"I've been thinking about that," she said, looking pensive.

"I used to teach a drawing class in a mental hospital. It was wonderful. One of the best things I've ever done. They taught me more than I taught them, about life, and patience, and courage. They were terrific people. I stopped doing it when I moved here." It was more complicated than that, he had stopped when he had been overwhelmed by depression himself, when he stopped seeing his children. And by the time he'd come out of it, or felt better at least, he was happier here alone, and rarely went into the city.

"People with mental illnesses are sometimes extraordinary people," she said softly, and the way she said it made him turn to look at her. He could see instantly in her eyes that she knew more than a little about what she was saying. Their eyes met, and then he turned back to his painting. He was suddenly afraid to ask her why she had said it, but she sensed his question.

"My son was manic-depressive . . . bipolar . . . it was a struggle for him, but he was very brave. He tried to commit suicide twice in the year before he died." It was an enormous gesture of trust that she had shared that with him, but she knew from what she had seen of him with Pip that he was compassionate and understanding.

"Does Pip know that?" He looked shaken.

"Yes. It was very hard for her. I found him the first time, and she found him the second. It was very traumatic."

"Poor kid . . . both of them . . . how did he do it?" His heart went out to her as he watched her and listened.

"The first time he slashed his wrists, and made a botch of it, thank God. The second he tried to hang himself, and Pip went into his room to ask him something, and she found him. He was already blue, and he had nearly done it. But she came and got me, we got him down, and his heart stopped. I kept him going with CPR until the paramedics came, and they saved him. They had to defibrillate him, and it was a close call, a very close call. It was terrifying." She seemed almost breathless herself as she said it. The memory of it was still haunting.

Even now sometimes, she had dreams about it. "He was doing much better when he died, which is why I had sent him to L.A. with his father that day. Ted had meetings, and I thought it would be fun for Chad to go with him. They didn't spend a lot of time together. Ted was very busy." And had almost total denial about Chad's problems, although she didn't say that. Even after the suicide attempts, Ted steadfastly insisted it had been a play for attention, and not something far worse.

But Matt knew men, and children. "How did he relate to your son? Was it hard for him to accept his illness?"

She hesitated, and then nodded. "Very. Ted always thought he'd outgrow it. He refused to accept how ill Chad was, no matter what the doctors said. Every time things got better, he thought the war was over. And so did I, at first. Ted never even thought there was a war, he kept saying it was growing pains, or that I was spoiling him, or he needed a girlfriend. I think it's hard for parents to admit sometimes that they have a sick child, and it's never going to go away, or get better. It gets better for a while, with the right medication, and a lot of work and effort, but it doesn't go away. It's going to be there forever." She seemed to have a good grip on it, but she had learned her lessons at a high

price, and had never had denial about it. She
had believed since Chad was small that he had
serious problems, no matter how bright and
charming he was. He was brilliant, like his father, but also very, very sick. It was Ophélie who
had been relentless in ferreting out the problem, until they had a diagnosis. And even then,
Ted refused to believe it. He said the psychia-
trists were quacks, and the tests inconclusive.
There had been nothing inconclusive about
Chad's suicide attempts, his manic episodes,
sleepless nights, or crippling depressions. And
for him, medication and therapy had taken the
edge off, but never solved the problem ade-
quately. By the time he died, Ophélie had accepted that Chad would be sick forever. Only
Ted hadn't. He had resisted facing it to the end.
Having a mentally ill son was unacceptable to
him.

And her greatest grief, her biggest sin, as far as
she was concerned, was that she had sent him to
L.A. with his father. She had wanted a break,
and to spend some quiet time with Pip, without
worrying about Chad for a change, or being
distracted by him. He needed so much attention. Only she knew that she had sent the boy
away for two days, not so much to foster the relationship between Ted and him, as to get a
breather herself. She knew that, however long

she lived or how many groups she went to, she would never forgive herself for it. But she said nothing of that to Matt. She had to live with it now, whatever it cost her.

"You've all been through a lot, not just the tragedy of the accident. It must be particularly hard knowing you saved the boy twice, and then lost him to a fluke accident like that."

"Destiny," she said quietly. "We are all in the hands of fate, and can do nothing to control it. Thank God I didn't send Pip too," although it had never been an issue. Ted hadn't even wanted to take Chad, the boy always irritated him and made him nervous, and Chad hadn't been enthused about the trip either. They'd both agreed finally, at Ophélie's insistence. But Ted would never have taken Pip. She was too young to go on a trip with him, in his estimation, and he rarely paid attention to her. He had in their early days of poverty, but since then, he had been far too busy. The only better solution to what had happened, barring the accident not happening, which would have been the best of all worlds, would have been if they had all been on the plane, and died together. There were many, many times now when Ophélie wished that that had happened. It would have been so much simpler.

"Would you want to do volunteer work with

mentally ill kids?" Matt asked kindly, trying to get off the immediate subject of the son she'd lost and her late husband. Inevitably, he could see in her eyes that it was excruciatingly painful.

"I don't know," Ophélie said, looking out to sea and thinking about it, as she stretched her legs into the sand. "I had so many years of it with Chad, and it was so intense at times, in some ways I'd like to use what I learned, to help others maybe, or it might just be better to do something else. I don't want to fight that war forever. For me anyway, it's over. It may be better to do something different. I suppose that sounds selfish, but it's honest." She seemed to be that above all, and wise, caring, and wounded. Who wouldn't have been after what she'd been through? Matt had nothing but compassion and respect for her, and more for Pip now. She had been through a lot too, particularly for a child her age.

"You could be right. Maybe you need a break from all that, and to do something a little more cheerful. What about some kind of work with kids? Runaways, homeless kids or families? There's a lot of good work to be done there."

"That would be interesting. It's amazing how many lost people you see now on the streets, even in France, not just here. It's a problem all around the world." They talked about home-lessness for a while then, and the political and economic issues they both felt had caused it. For the moment at least, the problem seemed insoluble, but it made for an interesting conversation between the two of them, and it was obviously far more adult than the things he discussed with Pip, while he taught her to draw. He liked both of them, and felt lucky that their paths had crossed and he had met them both.

Ophélie got up eventually, and said she had to get back, and he told her to say hello to Pip for him, and then she had a thought.

"Why don't you do that yourself?" She smiled. She had enjoyed the time she'd spent talking to him, and she wasn't sorry she had told him about Chad. It was an insight into Pip as well for him, she liked him so much, it seemed important to Ophélie to let him know how brave her daughter had been, how much she'd been through, and what she had lost. Heavy baggage for a child to carry, and for Ophélie too, and he had his too, far more than she knew. At a certain age, no matter who it was, people had baggage and wounds and scars and lives that had hurt or sometimes even broken them. No one ever went unscathed, sometimes even a child Pip's age. Ophélie liked to think that it would make Pip stronger in the

end, and more caring perhaps, she just wasn't
sure anymore what it would do to her. The pat-
tern of scars on anyone's soul determined who
they were. Sometimes it enriched the spirit, and
sometimes it broke it. The secret of life seemed
to be surviving the damage, and wearing the
scars well. But in reality, no heart went unscathed. Life itself was all too real. And in order
to love someone, whether lover or friend, one
had no choice but to be real.

"I'll give Pip a call," Matt said in response to
what she'd said. He felt badly that he hadn't
called yet. But he didn't want to intrude on
Ophélie.

"Why don't you come to dinner tonight? The
food is terrible, but I know she'd enjoy seeing
you, and so would I." It was the nicest invitation
he'd had in years, and he smiled.

"I'd like that. Are you sure it's not too much
trouble?"

"On the contrary. We'd love it. In fact, I think
I'll keep it a surprise for Pip, if you can come.
How about seven o'clock?" The invitation was
entirely innocent and ingenuous. She liked
talking to him, just as Pip did.

"That sounds perfect. Can I bring anything?
Pencils? Wine? An eraser?" She laughed at him,
but it gave him an idea.

"Just bring yourself. Pip will be thrilled." He

didn't add "me too," but he wanted to, and felt
like a kid. They were nice people, two very nice
people, who'd survived an incredible lot of
heartache, tragedy, and grief. He had all the
more respect for both of them the more he
knew, especially after today. What she had told
him about her son sounded like an agonizing
ordeal.

"See you later, then," he said with a smile, and
she waved as she headed back up the beach, and
as he watched her, he couldn't help thinking
again how much she reminded him of Pip.

7

PIP WAS LYING ON THE COUCH LOOKING BORED, with her foot on a pillow, when the doorbell rang. Ophélie went to answer it, she knew who it would be. He was right on time, and when she opened the door, Matt was standing there in a gray turtleneck and jeans, holding a bottle of wine. Ophélie put a finger to her lips and pointed toward the couch. And with a broad smile, he walked in. And when Pip saw him, she squealed with delight and hopped off the couch on one foot.

"Matt!" She looked from him to her mother, immensely pleased, with no idea how the surprise had come about. "How did . . . what . . ." She was delighted and confused.

"I ran into your mom on the beach today, and she was nice enough to invite me to join you for dinner. How's the foot?"

"Really dumb. It's a stupid foot, and I'm tired of it. I miss drawing with you." She had done a lot of sketches on her own, but she was getting tired of that too, and felt as though her new-found skills had regressed. She had had trouble with the hind section on a drawing of Mousse just that afternoon. "I forgot how to do back legs."

"I'll show you again," and as he said it, he handed her a brand-new sketch pad, and a box of colored pencils he had found in a drawer. It was just what the doctor ordered, and she pounced on them with glee.

As they chatted, Ophélie set the table for the three of them, and opened the bottle of very nice French wine. Although she seldom drank, it was one that she liked and reminded her of France.

She had put a chicken in the oven, and in a very short time, cooked some asparagus and wild rice, and made hollandaise. It was the most elaborate culinary effort she'd made in a year. And she'd enjoyed doing it.

Matt was impressed when they sat down to dinner, and so was Pip. She laughed at her mom.

"No frozen pizza tonight?"

"Pip, please! Don't give away all my secrets." Ophélie smiled at her.

"It's the mainstay of my diet too. That and instant soup." Matt grinned. He looked handsome
and well groomed as he sat with them, there
was a faint whiff of male cologne, and more
than anything, he looked fresh and wholesome
and real. Ophélie had combed her hair for him,
and was wearing a black cashmere sweater and
jeans. She hadn't worn makeup or color all year
and didn't tonight. She had been wearing formal mourning for Ted and Chad. But for the
first time, she wondered if she should have at
least put on lipstick. She hadn't even brought
any to the beach. It was all in a drawer somewhere at home. For the last ten months, she
hadn't cared if she never wore it again. It
seemed irrelevant now. Or had, until tonight.
Not that she was wooing him, but she at least
felt like looking like a woman again. The robot
she had become in the past year was slowly
coming back to life.

The three of them enjoyed a lively conversation through dinner. They talked about Paris,
and art, and school. Pip said she wasn't looking
forward to going back. She was turning twelve
in the fall and entering seventh grade. And
when asked, she told Matt she had a lot of
friends, but she felt weird with them now. A lot
of her friends' parents were divorced, but no

one had lost a father. She didn't want people to feel sorry for her, and she knew some of them did. She said she didn't want them to be "too nice," because it made her sad. She didn't want to feel different. And he knew it was inevitable that she would. "I can't even go to the father-daughter dinner," she said plaintively. "Who would I take?" Her mother had thought of it too, and had no solution to the dilemma. She had taken Chad once when her father couldn't go. But now she couldn't take him either.

"You can take me, if you want," Matt offered sincerely, and then glanced at Ophélie. "If your mother doesn't object. There's no reason why you can't take a friend, unless you can take your mom. You could do that too, you don't have to follow the rules. A mom is as good as a dad."

"They won't let you do that, someone else tried last year," which seemed pathetically limited to him. But she looked delighted at the prospect of taking Matt, and her mother nodded approval.

"That would be very nice of you, Matt," she said quietly, and then brought out dessert. All they had was ice cream in the freezer, and she had melted some chocolate and poured it on the vanilla bean ice cream Pip loved. It had been Ted's favorite too. She and Chad were ad-

dicted to Rocky Road. It was odd how even favorite ice cream flavors were sometimes dic-
tated by genes. She had noticed that before.

"When is the father-daughter dinner?" Matt
inquired.

"Sometime before Thanksgiving." Pip looked
thrilled.

"Tell me when, and I'll be there. I'll even
wear a suit." He hadn't done that in years either.
He lived in jeans and old sweaters, and the occasional worn tweed jacket left over from the
old days. He didn't need suits anymore. He
didn't go anywhere, and hadn't had or wanted a
social life in years. Once in a while, an old
friend came over from the city to have dinner
with him, but less and less. He had been out of
the loop for a long time, and liked it that way.
He was enjoying being a recluse. And no one
argued with him about it anymore. They just
figured that was who he was, and had become.

Pip stayed and chatted with them until long
after her bedtime, and finally she began to
yawn. She said she could hardly wait to get her
stitches out at the end of the week, but was annoyed that she would have to wear shoes on the
beach for another week afterward.

"Maybe you could ride Mousse," Matt teased,
and she came back in her pajamas a few minutes later to say goodnight to them both. They

were sitting on the couch, and Matt had lit a fire. It was a warm, cozy scene, and Pip looked happy when she left them and went to bed, happier than she had been in a long time. And so did Ophélie. There was something very comfortable about having a man around. His male presence seemed to fill the entire house. Even Mousse looked up from time to time, and wagged his tail, where he lay by the fire.

"You're very blessed," he said quietly to Ophélie, after she had gently closed Pip's door so they didn't keep her up. The house had only a large living room, an open kitchen and dining room, and their two bedrooms. It all seemed to blend together, no one wanted privacy or grandeur at the beach. But the decor was very nice. The owners had some lovely things, and some very handsome modern paintings, which Matt said he liked. "She's a terrific kid." He was crazy about her, and she always reminded him of his own. But he wasn't even sure his own children would have been as open, as wise, or as adult. And he had no idea who they were now. They were Hamish's now, and no longer his. Sally had seen to that.

"Yes, she is. We're very lucky we have each other." She thanked God again that Pip hadn't been on the plane too. "She's all I have. My parents died years ago, and so did Ted's. We were both only children. All I have are some second cousins in France, and an aunt I never liked and haven't seen in years. I like taking Pip back there, to keep her in touch with her French roots, but there's no one we're really close to. It's just us."

"Maybe that's enough," he said quietly. He didn't even have that. And like her, he was an only child, and had become solitary over the years. He didn't even have close friends anymore. During the bad years after the divorce, the friendships had been too hard to maintain, and like Pip, he didn't want people feeling sorry for him. What had happened with Sally had just been too tough. "Do you have a lot of friends, Ophélie? In San Francisco, I mean."

"Some. Ted wasn't very sociable. He was very much a loner, and completely engrossed in his work. And he expected me to be there for him. I wanted to be. But it made it hard to keep friendships. He never really wanted to see people, only work. I have one woman friend I'm very close to, but other than that, I lost touch with a lot of people over the years, because of Ted. And Chad became all-consuming in the last few years. I never knew what was going to happen, if he would be bouncing off the walls, or too depressed for me to leave. He became a pretty full-time job at the end." She had had her hands full between him, Ted, and Pip. And now her hands were emptier than they had been for years, except for Pip, who didn't need much from her. Although the little she did need, Ophélie hadn't been able to deliver. She felt a little better now, after the summer at the beach, and she was hoping she would improve further in the coming months. She had felt utterly disconnected for the past ten months, but the connections were slowly forming again. The robot she had become was nearly humanoid again, but not quite. But there were clearly indications of returning life, and even the fact that she had invited Matt to dinner, and was willing to extend a hand of friendship to him, and take his in exchange, was a good sign.

"What about you?" she asked him with curiosity. "Do you see a lot of friends in town?"

"None," he said with a small smile. "I've been very bad at that, for nearly ten years. I ran an ad agency in New York with my wife, and we got tangled up in a pretty ugly divorce. We sold the business, and I decided to come out here. I lived in the city then, and I took a little bungalow out here to paint on the weekends. And then, just when you think things won't get worse, they did. She was living in New Zealand, and I was trying to commute to see my kids, which is pretty hard to do. I had no home turf there. I stayed at a hotel, I even got an apartment at one point, but I was very much the fifth wheel. She married a great guy, a friend of mine, who loved my kids, about nine years ago, and they were crazy about him. He's very much a man's man, lots of money, lots of toys. Four kids of his own, they had two more. My kids got completely absorbed in their combined family, and they loved it. I can't blame them, it was pretty appealing.

"After a while, whenever I got to Auckland, they didn't have time to see me, they wanted to be with their friends. As they say in your country, I felt like hair on the soup." She smiled at the familiar expression, and understood the feeling. Sometimes she had felt like hair on the soup in Ted's busy, scientific life. Out of place. Superfluous, except as a possession he owned but didn't need. Obsolete.

"That must have been hard for you," she said sympathetically, touched by the look of loss in his eyes. He was a man who had known pain, and had survived. He had made his peace with it, but like everyone else, at a price. A high price.

"It was hard," he said honestly. "Very. I kept at it for four years. The last few times I went out there, I hardly saw them, and Sally explained that I was disrupting their life. She thought I should only come out when they wanted to see me, which of course was almost never. I called a lot, and they were busy. And eventually, I wrote and they didn't answer. They were only seven and nine when she remarried, and she had the other babies in the first two years they were married. My kids got swept up in her new family. I felt in a way as though I was making things harder for them. I did a lot of soul-searching, and it was probably stupid, but I wrote to them and asked them what they wanted. They never answered. I didn't hear from them for a year, but I kept writing. I figured, if they wanted to see me, they'd ask me to come out. And I have to confess, I drank a lot that year. I wrote to them for three years and heard nothing. And Sally told me in no uncertain terms that they no longer wanted to see me and were afraid to say so. That was three years ago, and I haven't written since. I finally gave up. And I haven't seen or heard from them in six years. My only contact with them is the support checks I still send Sally. And the Christmas card she sends me every year. I never wanted to confront them about seeing me. They know where I am if they want me. But sometimes I've thought that I should have gone out there and discussed it with them. I didn't want to put them on the spot. Sally was so emphatic about how they felt.

They were only ten and twelve the last time I saw them, more or less Pip's age, that's a tough age to have to be brave enough to tell your father to get lost. Their silence did that. It was enough. I understand. So I bowed out.

"I wrote them some pretty pathetic letters for years before I gave up. And they never answered. And sometimes I write to them now, but in the end, I never send the letters. It doesn't seem fair to put pressure on them. I miss them like crazy. I don't think I exist for them anymore. I've talked to their mother and she says it's for the best. She tells me they're happy and don't want me in their life. I never did anything wrong, from my perspective, they just don't need me anymore. Their stepfather is a great guy. I like him myself, or did. We were good friends for years before he and Sally got together. Anyway, that's the story of my kids, and the last ten years. The last six without my kids. She sends me photographs with the Christmas card so I know what they look like. I'm not sure if that's better or worse. Sometimes better, sometimes worse. I feel like one of those poor women who've given birth to a baby, and for whatever reason, given it up. And all they get are pictures once a year. She sends me Christmas cards with all eight kids on it, his, mine, and theirs. I usually cry when I look at it," he said, barely looking embarrassed. They knew a lot about each other now. "But I stepped back for them. I think it's what they need, or want, or so she tells me.

"Robert is eighteen now. He'll be going to college soon, probably over there. They have a great life in Auckland. Hamish owns the biggest ad agency in that part of the world. Sally runs it with him, just as she did ours with me. She's a very capable woman. Not a lot of heart, but enormously creative. And a good mother, I think. She knows what the kids need. Better than I do probably. I don't even know them anymore. I'm not even sure I'd recognize them on the street, which is an agonizing admission. That's the worst of it. I try not to think of it. I let go for their sakes. Sally wrote to me a few years ago and asked how I felt about Hamish adopting my kids. It damn near killed me. I don't care how much they don't want me in their lives, they're still my kids. And always will be. I wouldn't agree to it. I've hardly heard from her since, except at Christmas. Before that, we'd talk once in a while. I think they just wish I'd go away quietly and disappear somewhere, and I pretty much have. Out of their lives and everyone else's. I lead a very quiet life here, and it's taken me a long time to get over everything that went wrong between me and Sally, and losing my kids to Hamish." It was an agonizing story, but explained a lot of things to her as she listened, and said much about him. Like her, he was a man who had lost nearly everything that mattered to him, his business, his wife, and his children. And he had retreated into the life of a hermit. At least she had Pip, and was grateful for it. She couldn't even begin to imagine her life without her.

"Why did the marriage break up?" She knew it was impertinent, but it was a piece she didn't have yet of the total picture, and she knew that if he didn't want to tell her, he wouldn't. After all that they had told each other, they were friends now.

He sighed for a moment before he answered. "It's a pretty classic story. Hamish and I went to grad school together. He went back to Auckland afterward. I stayed in New York. We both opened ad agencies, and formed a sort of loose alliance with each other. We shared some clients with international interests, referred business to each other, consulted on some big accounts together. He came to New York several times a year. We went there. Sally was the creative director of our agency, she was the brain of the outfit, and also handled the business side, and brought in most of the clients. I was the art director. We were a fairly unbeatable combination, and we had some of the biggest clients in the business. Hamish and I stayed friends, and he and his wife and Sally and I went on a number of vacations together. Mostly to Europe. A safari in Botswana once. We rented a château in France one fateful summer. I had to go back early, and Hamish's wife's mother died unexpectedly and she went back to Auckland. He stayed in France. So did Sally, with our kids. In as few words as possible, Hamish and Sally fell in love. Four weeks later she came home and told me she was leaving me. She was in love with him, and they were going to see what happened. She needed to get away from me to figure it out. She needed space, and time. Those things happen, I guess. To some people. She told me she'd never really been in love with me, we were just a great business team, and she had had the kids because it was expected of her. Hell of a thing to say about our children, and about me, but I actually think she meant it. She's not known for her sensitivity about other people's feelings, which is probably why she's so successful.

"Anyway, Hamish went home and delivered the same piece of news to his wife, Margaret, and the rest is history. Sally moved out of the apartment in New York with the kids, and stayed in a hotel. She offered to sell me her half of the business, but I had no desire to run it without her, or find a new partner. I just didn't have the heart to do it. She knocked me flat on my ass, and I couldn't get up for a long time. We sold the whole shebang, lock, stock, and barrel, to a major conglomerate. It was a terrific deal for both of us, but all I had left after fifteen years of marriage was a hell of a lot of money, no wife, no job, and kids who had moved nine thousand miles away to Auckland. She left me on Labor Day, and she and the kids moved to Auckland the day after Christmas. They got married as soon as the ink on our divorce was dry. I'd been hoping that if I let her be, and didn't push her, she'd come back to me. Crazy of me to think that, I guess. But we're all crazy, and stupid sometimes.

"By the time she left, my head was still spinning. And I guess that, my friend, answers your question about my marriage. The worst of it is I still think Hamish Greene is a great guy. Not a great friend, mind you, but he's an all-around bright, fun, amusing person. And from all I can gather, I think they've been very happy with each other. And their business is booming." From the outside, all Ophélie could see was that Matt had been screwed royally, by his wife, his best friend, and maybe even by his children. She'd heard stories like it before over the years,

but none as totally ruthless. He had lost everything, except his money, and it didn't look like
that mattered much to him. All he seemed to
want was a quiet life in a bungalow on the
beach at Safe Harbour. Other than that, and his
talent, he had absolutely nothing left. It was dis-
graceful what they had done to him. The
thought of it left her speechless and grief-
stricken on his behalf.

"That is a horrible story," she said, frowning.
"Absolutely awful. I hate them both, just listening to you. But not the children. They are the
victims of all this, as you have been. They've obviously been manipulated into shutting you out
and forgetting you. It was your wife's responsibility to help them maintain their relationship
with you," she said sensibly, and he didn't disagree with her. And amazingly, he had never
blamed his children for their defection. They
were too young to know what they were doing, and he knew how convincing Sally could
be. She could turn anyone around in a hot
minute, and confuse them forever.

"That's not Sally. She wanted a clean break
from me, and she got one. Sally always got what
she wanted, even from Hamish. I'm not sure
whose idea their children were, but knowing
Sally, she thought it was a smart thing to do to
lock him in. Hamish is a little naïve in some

ways, it was one of the things I always liked about him. Sally isn't. She's as clear and calculating as it gets, and she always does what's best for Sally."

"She sounds like a very evil woman," Ophélie said loyally, and it touched him. Telling her about his life had been somewhat emotional for him, and as he stoked the fire again, they were both silent for a moment.

"And what about since then? Has there been no one important to you?" It would have been the only possible consolation, but there was no evidence of a woman in his life. He seemed to lead a very solitary existence, or at least that was her impression of him. There could have been someone, of course, but she didn't think so.

"Not really. I was in no condition to get involved with anyone else for the first few years after Sally left. I was a basket case. And after that, I was commuting to Auckland to see my kids, and I wasn't in the mood. I didn't trust anyone, and I didn't want to. I swore I never would again. There was a woman I liked very much about three years ago, but she was a lot younger than I, and she wanted to get married and have kids. I just couldn't see myself doing that again, or trusting anyone enough to put myself in that position. I didn't want to get married and have kids, and risk getting divorced again and losing them. I couldn't see the point. She was thirty-two years old, and I was forty-four at the time, and she gave me an ultimatum. I don't blame her. But I couldn't make a commitment to her either. I bowed out gracefully, and she got married about six months later, to a very nice guy. They just had their third baby this summer. I just couldn't go there. I hope I'll get back in touch with my own kids again someday, when they get a little older. But I have no desire to start another family, or open myself up to that kind of disappointment. Going through that once in a lifetime has done it for me." Ophélie had to admit that very few people would have survived what he'd been through. And in some ways he hadn't. As gentle and caring as he was, he was emotionally shut down, and not willing to open up again, but she couldn't really blame him. It also explained why he had opened up to Pip so much and reached out to her. She was almost the same age as his children the last time he saw them. And he was obviously hungry for some kind of human contact, even from a little girl of eleven. And she was safe for him. He had no real investment in her, other than friendship. There was nothing wrong with it, and it met Pip's needs at the moment as well. But it was hardly enough emotional sustenance for a man of forty-seven. He deserved so much more than that, in Ophélie's eyes at least, but he wasn't brave enough at this point to share more than he did with a child on the beach, whom he could teach to draw a few times a week. For a man of his caliber and abilities, it seemed a paltry existence. But clearly, it was all he wanted.

"What about you, Ophélie? What kind of marriage did you have? I get the feeling that your husband wasn't entirely an easy person. Geniuses usually aren't, or so they say." Ophélie looked gentle and accommodating to him. And from what she had said about her husband's relationship with his sick son, he had the feeling that her late husband hadn't given her an easy time. He wasn't far from wrong, although she didn't often admit it to anyone, and hadn't over the years, sometimes even herself.

"He was a brilliant man. With incredible vision. He always knew what he wanted to do, from the beginning. He was single-minded in his purpose, and he refused to let anything stop him. Absolutely nothing. Not even me, or the children, not that we wanted to stand in his way. We did everything we could to support him, or I did at least. And he finally got what he wanted, and achieved what he'd always dreamed of. He was a huge success in the last five years of his life. It was wonderful for him."

But not necessarily for her or their kids, other than materially.

"And how was he to you in all that?" Matt asked persistently. It was obvious that he'd been a success, even from the little Matt knew of him. He had achieved greatness in his field. But the real question, in Matt's mind, was how was he as a human being and a husband? Ophélie seemed to have dodged the question.

"I always loved him. From the very first moment I met him. I had a huge crush on him as a student. I always admired him, his brilliant mind, his single-mindedness of purpose. He was a man who never lost sight of his dreams. You have to admire someone like that." Whether or not he had been difficult had never been the issue for her. She accepted that about him. She thought he was entitled to be.

"And what were your dreams?"

"Being married to him." She smiled sadly at Matt. "It was all I ever wanted. When he married me, I thought I'd died and gone to Heaven. And it was difficult certainly at times. There were years, many of them, when we had absolutely no money. We struggled for about fifteen years, and then he made so much we didn't know what to do with it. But that was never what was important to us, or me anyway. I loved him just as much when we were poor. His money never mattered to me. He did." He had been the sun and the moon to her, along with their kids.

"Did he spend time with you and the children?" Matt asked quietly.

"Sometimes. When he could. He was always incredibly busy, doing far more important things." It was obvious to Matt that she had worshiped him. Probably far more than he deserved.

"What's more important than your wife and kids?" Matt said simply, but he was very different than Ted, in a lot of ways. And she was light-years from Sally. Ophélie was everything Sally wasn't. Gentle, kind, decent, honest, compassionate. She was locked in her own miseries at the moment, but even with that, he could tell she wasn't a selfish person. She was lost and grieving, which was different. He knew it well. He had been there himself. And grief could be all-absorbing when you were in the midst of it, which was why she was less attentive than she had previously been with Pip. But she was aware enough to berate herself for it.

"Scientists are very different people," Ophélie explained tolerantly. "They have different needs, different perceptions, different emotional abilities than the rest of us. He wasn't an ordinary person." But in spite of her excuses for him, Matt didn't like what he was hearing. He suspected that the late Dr. Mackenzie had been narcissistic and egocentric, and possibly even a lousy father. And he wasn't at all sure he'd been a decent husband to her. But if not, Ophélie was clearly not prepared to see it, or admit it to him. Death was different from divorce, Matt knew too, with a deceased spouse came early sainthood. It seemed to be hard to remember the flaws and failings of someone you loved who had died. In divorces, all you remembered was what had been wrong with them. And over time the remembered flaws just seemed to get bigger and worse. When they died, all you remembered was the best part, and then you improved on it. It made the deceased spouse's absence seem that much more cruel. And Matt felt genuinely sorry for her.

They talked for a long time that night, about their childhoods, their marriages, their kids. Her heart ached every time she thought of Matt's estrangement from his children, and as he spoke of it, from the look in his eyes, she could see easily what it had cost him. Nearly his sanity at one point, and eventually, his faith in the human race, and desire to be with people, a woman especially. It was a high price to pay for two children, and a marriage he had lost ten years before. Ophélie suspected his ex-wife had stolen the kids from him, more than likely by some kind of manipulation. It was hard to believe that without prodding or prejudice from her, children that age would decide not to see their father. There had to be some foul play in there somewhere, although Matt didn't say much more about it, and didn't seem to want to wage war with her. As far as he was concerned, he had lost the war, and for now at least, it was over. All he could hope was to see his children again someday. A distant hope he thought of at times, but no longer lived for. He lived day to day, and was content with his spartan existence at the beach. Safe Harbour was a refuge for him.

Matt was about to leave when it occurred to him to ask her something. He had been meaning to mention it all evening.

"Do you like to sail, Ophélie?" he inquired cautiously, looking hopeful. Along with art, it had always been one of his passions. And it suited his solitary nature.

"I haven't in years, but I used to love it. I sailed as a child, when we went to Brittany in the summer. And in Cape Cod, when I was in college."

"I have a little sailboat in the lagoon that I take out from time to time. I'd be happy to take you with me, if you'd like that. It's very simple, it's an old wooden boat I restored myself when I first moved here."

"I'd love to see it, and it would be fun to go out with you sometime," Ophélie said, looking enthusiastic about it.

"I'll call you the next time I go sailing," he said, pleased to hear that she liked sailing. It was one more thing they had in common, and he could easily imagine she would be fun to sail with. She was lively and bright, and energetic, and her eyes had lit up when he mentioned his sailboat. She and Ted had gone out on the bay a couple of times with friends and he'd never enjoyed it. He complained bitterly about the cold and the wet, and always got seasick. She didn't, and although she didn't say it to Matt, she was an excellent sailor.

It was after midnight when he left, and it had been a good evening for both of them. It had been the human contact and warmth that they both so desperately needed, although neither of them was aware of it. If nothing else, they each needed a friend, and they had found that. It was the one thing they both still trusted. Friendship. Pip had done them a great favor by bringing them together.

Ophélie turned off the lights after he left, walked softly into Pip's bedroom, and smiled as she saw her there. Mousse was asleep at the foot of her bed, and never stirred as Ophélie approached them. She smoothed back Pip's soft red curls, and bent to kiss her. Another piece of the robot had been dismantled that night, and little by little the woman she had once been was emerging.

8

WHEN OPHÉLIE WENT BACK TO HER GROUP later that week, she mentioned seeing Matt, and what a nice evening it had been, which brought up the issue of dating among some of the others. There were twelve people in the group, ranging in age from twenty-six to eighty-three. Their common bond was having lost someone dear to them. The youngest member of the group had lost her brother in a car accident. The oldest had lost his wife of sixty-one years. There were husbands and wives and sisters and children. Age-wise, Ophélie was somewhere in the middle, and some of the stories were truly heart-wrenching. A young woman had lost her husband to a stroke at thirty-two, eight months after they were married, and she was already pregnant. She had just had the baby, and spent most of her time in the group crying. A mother had watched her son choke on a peanut butter sandwich in front of her, and had been unable to do anything to reverse it. The wad of peanut butter had been too soft to respond to the Heimlich, and too far down his throat for her to reach it. Along with her own grief, she was wrestling with the guilt she felt over not being able to save him. All of the stories were deeply touching. And Ophélie's was no different. Hers was not the only double loss. A woman in her sixties had lost two sons to cancer, within three weeks of each other, her only children. There was a woman there who had lost her five-year-old grandson when he died in his parents' pool. She had been baby-sitting, and had found him. She also blamed herself for what had happened, and her daughter and son-in-law had not spoken to her since the funeral. Tragedies in abundance. The stuff of which real lives are made, and destroyed. None of it was easy, for any of them. Their common bonds were grief, loss, and mutual compassion.

Ophélie had talked about losing Ted and Chad for the past month, but she had said little about their marriage, except that from her perception, it had been perfect. And she had talked a little about Chad's mental illness, and the stress it had put on all of them, particularly Ted, since he was so unwilling to accept it. She barely saw the strain his denial had put on her, trying to bridge the gap between father and son, while keeping Pip happy.

She found the subject of dating of no interest to her when they discussed it. She had said for the past month that she had no interest in marrying again, or even in dating.

The eighty-three-year-old man had commented that she was too young to give up on a romantic life, and in spite of his intense grief over his wife, he said he was hoping to go out with other women, as soon as he met one who appealed to him. He wasn't embarrassed to admit he was looking.

"What if I live to be ninety-five, or even ninety-eight?" he said optimistically. "I don't want to be alone until then. I want to get married." All feelings were fair game here. Nothing was shocking or taboo. The hallmark of the group was that they were all honest, and tried to be. As honest as they were with themselves at least. And some of them admitted that they were angry at their loved ones for dying, which was a normal part of the grief process. They each had to work through whatever aspect of their grief they were wrestling with at the moment. Until then, Ophélie had been deadlocked in depression. But they all noticed this week that she seemed better. She said she thought she was, but she was afraid she would slip back again. And she talked about wanting to find a job after the summer, which she thought might help her.

When Ophélie mentioned it, Blake, the leader of the group, questioned her about what kind of job she wanted, and she admitted she didn't know. Ophélie had been referred to the group by her doctor, when she told him she wasn't sleeping at night right after Ted and Chad died. She had been reluctant to come at first, and it had taken her eight months to do it. She was sleeping too much by then, and eating far too little. Even she knew that she was seriously depressed, and it was unlikely to get better unless she did something about it. It had been hard at first to get over her own sense that she had failed somehow because she couldn't solve her own problems. But no one else in the group had been able to either, and most people couldn't. The smart ones tried to reach out at least, and despite her initial skepticism, even Ophélie had to admit it had made some slight difference in her life, even after a month. At least she had others in the same boat to talk to. It made the process just a little bit less lonely, and she felt less like a freak for the things she was experiencing and thinking. She was able to share with them, without shame, how disconnected she felt from Pip, and that she sneaked into Chad's room more often than she should, just to lie on his bed and smell his pillow. The others had all done similar things, and were experiencing varying degrees of the same problems, with spouses, or children, or even parents. One woman had admitted to the group that she hadn't had sex with her husband in a year since her son died, she just couldn't. Ophélie was always impressed by the things they were willing and able to say to each other, without shame. She felt safe in their midst.

The goal of the group was to heal the wound, bind the broken heart, and deal with the practical issues of daily living. The first questions Blake asked each of them every week were "Are you eating? Are you sleeping?" And in Ophélie's case, he often asked her if she had gotten out of her nightgown since their last meeting. Sometimes their progress was measured in such tiny increments that no one outside of the group would have been impressed with what they had accomplished. But each of them knew how hard the baby steps were, and what a difference it made when you finally achieved one. They celebrated each other's victories, and sympathized with each other's anguish. And you could tell early on who the successes would be, those who were willing to go through the agony of moving forward. It was by no means an easy process, and even making the commitment to be there meant something. And the wounds that were touched on were so raw that sometimes when they left after a meeting, the pain was worse rather than better. But dealing with it was part of the healing process. At times, saying something out loud was exhilarating, and at other times just getting it out was exhausting. Ophélie had experienced both ends of the spectrum in the past month, and most of the time, afterward she was exhausted, but also grateful. And when she thought about it, she knew that it had helped her, far more than she had hoped.

Her doctor had recommended this particular group because Ophélie had resisted the idea of antidepressants, and the group itself was less formal than some. And the doctor had a profound respect for the man who ran it, Blake Thompson. He had a Ph.D. in clinical psychology, had done grief work for nearly twenty years, and was somewhere in his mid-fifties. He was a warm, practical man, who was open to trying anything that worked, and reminded the group often that there was no one right way to go through the grief process. As long as they were doing whatever worked for them, he was more than happy to support it. And when it wasn't working, he was tireless in his efforts, encouragement, and creative suggestions. He often felt that when people left the group, they had broadened their lives to something more than the life they'd been living prior to their loss. And to that end, he had just suggested singing lessons to a woman who had lost her husband, scuba diving lessons to a man who'd lost his wife in a car accident, and a religious retreat to a woman who had been a confirmed atheist, and was finding deep religious feelings for the first time since the death of her only son. All he wanted for the people in the group was for their lives to be better than they had been before he met them. And for twenty years, his results had been fairly impressive. The group was challenging, and painful at times, but much to everyone's surprise, not depressing. All he asked from them when they began was to be open-minded, kind to themselves, and respectful of each other. What they discussed in the group was to be kept only among themselves. And he was adamant about a four-month commitment.

And although some people had met their new spouses in his groups, he strongly discouraged people from dating each other while they were in it. He didn't want people either showing off, or hiding things, in order to impress each other. That request and the privacy of the group he

had borrowed from the twelve-step model, and
he had found them helpful, although now and
then there were people in the group who grew
attached to each other and started dating before
the group ended. Even there, he reminded people that there was no "right model" for new re-
lationships or even marriage.

Some people waited years to find a new mate,
others never did, nor wanted to. Some felt they
needed to wait a year before dating or remarry-
ing, others married literally weeks after they lost
a spouse. In his opinion, it didn't mean you
hadn't loved your late husband or wife, it meant
that you felt ready to move on and make another commitment. And no one else had a right
to judge if that was right or wrong. "We are not
the grief police here," he reminded the group
from time to time. "We're here to help and support each other, not judge each other." And he
always shared with each group that he had
come into this particular line of work when he
lost his wife, and a daughter and son, his only
two children at the time, in a car accident on a
rainy winter night that he had thought at the
time had been the end of his life. And when it
happened, he wished it had been. Five years
later he had remarried, to a wonderful woman,
and they had three children. "I would have married earlier, if I'd met her sooner, but she was

worth waiting for," he always told them, with a smile that never failed to touch the people with whom he shared the story. The focus of the group was not on remarriage, but it was an issue that came up, and was a focal point for some, and of no interest to others, many of whom had lost siblings, parents, or children, and were married. But they all agreed that the loss of a loved one, particularly a child, put an enormous strain on an existing marriage. In some cases, there were couples in the group, but more often than not, one spouse was willing to reach out earlier than the other, and it was actually rare for couples to attend together, although Blake always wished that people did that more often.

For some reason, the issue of dating had come up a lot that day, and Blake never got around to discussing Ophélie's wanting to find a job. It was the second time she had mentioned it, and he stopped to talk to her after the group. He had an idea that he wanted to suggest to her. He didn't know why, but he had the feeling it might be right up her alley. She had been doing well in the group so far, although he had the impression that she didn't think so. She was consumed with guilt over what she was still not able to do for her daughter, and might not be able to do for a long time. More than anything, he didn't want her beating herself up over it.

What she was experiencing, in the disconnect from all other loved ones, was entirely normal, according to him. If she were attuned to them, or to her daughter in this case, her feelings would be wide open, and all the pain she felt over her loss would come rushing in to drown her. The only way her psyche could keep the agony at bay was to put itself on hold for a while, so she felt nothing at all, for anyone. The only problem was that it left her surviving child out in the cold in the meantime. It was a fairly typical problem, and an even more disruptive one when it happened between spouses, as it often did. The divorce rate was high among people who had lost children. Often, by the time they recovered to a significant extent, they had lost each other and the marriage.

When Blake spoke to Ophélie after the group, he asked her if she'd be interested in volunteering at a homeless shelter. Matt had suggested something like that too, and she thought it might be meaningful to her, and less emotionally charged for her than volunteering in the field of mental illness. She had always had a keen interest in the welfare of the homeless, and no time to pursue it, while Ted and Chad were alive. She had far more disposable time now, with no husband and only one child at home.

She responded with considerable warmth and interest, and Blake promised to get some referrals for her, of volunteer projects dealing with the homeless. This was exactly what he was good at. She was thinking about it as she drove back to Safe Harbour. She had to take Pip to get her stitches out that afternoon. And as soon as they did, Pip chortled with glee, and put on a pair of sneakers when she got home.

"How does that feel?" Ophélie asked, watching her. She was beginning to enjoy her again, and they seemed to talk more than they had in a long time. Not as much as they used to, but things were definitely a little better. And even she wondered if talking to Matt had helped her. He was a very kind, soothing person. And very caring. He had been through so much himself that he was full of empathy for others, without being sappy. And there was no question that the group was helping too, and she liked the people in it.

"It feels pretty good. It only hurts a little."

"Well, don't overdo it." She knew what Pip had in mind. She was dying to walk down the beach to see Matt. She had a load of new drawings to show him. "Why don't you wait till tomorrow. It's probably too late today anyway," Ophélie said wisely. She could read Pip's mind sometimes. It was just that for months, she hadn't tried to. She was starting to tune in again, and Pip liked it.

The next day Pip set out with the sketch pad and pencils he had given her, and two sandwiches in a brown bag. Ophélie was tempted to go with her, but she didn't want to intrude on them. Their friendship had been the primary one, hers with him had been an offshoot of it and came later. She waved as Pip set off down the beach in her sneakers, to protect the newly healed foot. And she didn't run, as she usually did. She was being a little more circumspect, and respectful of the foot, and as a result, it took her longer to reach him. And when she did, he stopped painting and beamed at her.

"I was hoping you'd come today. If you didn't, I was going to call you tonight. How's the foot?"

"Better." It was a little tender after the long walk down the beach, but she would have walked on nails and ground glass to see him. She was so happy to be there. And he looked equally pleased to see her.

"I've really missed you," he said happily.

"Me too. I hated being home all week. Mousse didn't like it either."

"Poor guy, he probably needed the exercise. I had a nice time with you and your mom the other night by the way. That was a delicious dinner."

"A lot better than pizza!" She grinned at him. He had brought out the best in her mother, and even since then. She had seen her mother rooting around in her purse the day before, and she had finally come up with an old lipstick, and put some on before she went into the city. It made Pip realize how long it had been since she'd worn any. And it made her happy to see that she was getting better. It had been a good summer in Safe Harbour. "I like your new painting," she commented to Matt. He had done a sketch of a woman on the beach, with a haunted expression. She was looking out to sea, as though she had lost someone there. There was something anxious and uncomfortable about it, almost tragic. "It looks very sad though, but she's pretty. Is that my mom?"

"A little maybe. She might have inspired it, but it's just a woman. It's more about a thought process and a feeling, than a person. It's a little bit in the spirit of a painter called Wyeth." Pip nodded solemnly, fully aware of what he was saying. She always enjoyed their conversations, particularly about his paintings. And a few minutes later, she sat down with her own sketch pad and pencils, close to him. She liked being next to him.

The hours flew by as they had before, and they were sorry to leave each other at the end of the afternoon. He wanted to sit there with her forever.

"What are you and your mom doing tonight?" he asked casually. "I was going to call her, and ask if you wanted to go into town for a hamburger. I'd cook for you, but I'm a rotten cook and I ran out of frozen pizza." Pip laughed at their comparable menus.

"I'll ask Mom when I go home, and tell her to call you."

"I'll give you time to get home, and then call her." But as she got up, and he saw her start down the beach, he saw that she was limping, and called after her. "Pip!" She turned when she heard him, and he waved her back. It was a long walk for someone who had just had stitches taken out, and the sneakers had rubbed where the scar was. She walked slowly back to him as he beckoned. "I'll give you a ride home. The foot doesn't look too great."

"I'm okay," she said gamely, but he was no longer worried about her mother.

"Don't wear it out, you won't be able to come back tomorrow."

It was a good point, and she followed him willingly over the dune, to where his car was parked behind his cottage. He had her home five minutes later. He didn't get out of the car, but Ophélie saw him from the kitchen window and came out to greet him.

"She was limping," he said by way of explanation. "I figured you wouldn't mind my driving her." He smiled easily at her.

"Of course not. That was sweet of you. Thanks, Matt. How are you?"

"Fine. I was going to call you. Can I lure the two of you to dinner in town tonight? Hamburgers and indigestion. Or maybe not, if we're lucky."

"That sounds nice." She hadn't thought about what to cook yet. And although her spirits had improved somewhat, her culinary interest hadn't. She had given it her best shot the night he'd come to dinner. "Are you sure that's not too much trouble?" Life was so easy at the beach, and so casual, meals were never formal, and didn't seem terribly important. Most people barbecued, but Ophélie wasn't very good at it.

"I'd enjoy it," Matt said. "How about seven?"

"Perfect. Thank you." He drove off with a wave, and was back, punctually, two hours later. Pip had shampooed her hair, at her mother's urging, to get the sand out of it, and Ophélie's hair looked pretty too. It hung in long soft waves and a few graceful curls to below her shoulders. And as a symbol of her slowly reviving spirit, she had worn lipstick. And Pip loved it.

They had dinner in one of the two local restaurants, the Lobster Pot, and all three of them ate clam chowder and lobster. They decided en masse to make a real feast of it, and forget the hamburgers, and all of them complained on the way out that they could hardly move. But it had been a fun evening. No serious topics were introduced, and they exchanged funny stories and bad jokes, and laughed a lot. Ophélie asked Matt if he wanted to come in afterward, but he only stayed for a few minutes. He said there was some work he wanted to do. And after he left, Ophélie commented to Pip again how nice he was, and she turned to her mother with an impish grin.

"Do you like him, Mom? You know . . . like a guy, I mean." Ophélie looked startled by the question, and then smiled as she shook her head.

"Your father was the only guy for me. I can't imagine ever being with anyone else." She had said as much to the group, and many of them had challenged her, but Pip didn't dare. She was disappointed to hear it. She liked Matt. And she didn't want to make her mother mad, but her father hadn't always been nice to her. He used to yell at her, and was mean to her sometimes, especially when they argued over Chad, or other things. She loved her father, and always would, but she thought Matt was a lot friendlier and easier to be with.

"Matt's really nice though, don't you think?" she asked hopefully.

"Yes, I do." Ophélie smiled again, amused that Pip was trying to matchmake for her, but it was obvious that Pip had a crush on him, or a serious case of hero worship at least. "He's going to be a good friend to us, I hope. It would be nice to see him after we leave the beach."

"He said he'd come to town to visit us. And he's going to take me to the father-daughter dinner at school. Remember?"

"Yes, I do." She just hoped he would. Ted had never been good about that. He hated going to his children's sports events, or anything at their schools. It wasn't his thing, although he did it when he had no other choice. "He's probably pretty busy though, Pip." They were the same excuses she had always made for Ted, and that his children hated hearing. There was always some excuse why he couldn't be there for them.

"He said he'd be there for sure," Pip said fiercely, looking at her mother with huge, trusting eyes, and Ophélie hoped she wouldn't be disappointed. It was impossible to know at this point if their friendship would last, but she hoped it would.

9

ANDREA CAME OUT AND VISITED THEM AGAIN two weeks before they left the beach. The baby was fussy and had a cold again, and she said he was getting teeth. This time, he cried whenever Pip held him. He wanted his mommy and no one else. So after a while, Pip took off down the beach. She was going to sit for Matt that day. He wanted to have plenty of sketches of her for the portrait he'd promised to do, as a gift for Ophélie.

"So what's new? Anything?" Andrea asked as the baby finally fell asleep.

"Nothing much," Ophélie said, looking relaxed as they sat in the sun. The last golden days of summer had set in, and they were loving their final days at the beach. And Andrea thought Ophélie looked better than she had in months. The three months at Safe Harbour had done her a world of good. She hated to see her go back to the city, and her sad memories in the house.

"How's the child molester?" Andrea asked casually, she knew they had befriended him finally, and she was still curious about him. They hadn't met. And from Pip's description, he sounded like a hunk. Ophélie had said very little, which Andrea thought was suspicious. But Andrea saw nothing secretive in her eyes. No magic. No carefully hidden agenda. No guilt. She looked very relaxed.

"He's so good with Pip. We had dinner with him the other night."

"That's odd for a man with no kids," Andrea commented.

"He has two."

"Then that makes sense. Did you meet them?"

"They live in New Zealand, with his ex-wife."

"Uh-oh. How's that? Does he hate her? How bad is the damage?" She was an expert in the field, and by now she had seen it all. Men who'd been cheated on, ripped off, abandoned, lied to, screwed over, left, and hated every woman in their life from then on. Not to mention the ones who were sexually confused, still in a relationship, had lost wives who had been absolutely perfect, men who'd never married and were middle-aged, and those who forgot to mention that they were still married. Older, younger, same age. Andrea had dated them all. And she was willing to cross a number of boundaries, when she found a man she liked. Even damaged, they were sometimes fun for a while. But she at least preferred knowing what the damage was.

"I'd say there's a fair amount of damage," Ophélie said honestly, "and I feel bad for him. But it's not my concern. He got pretty badly screwed over by his ex-wife. She walked off with his best friend, and married him. She forced Matt to sell their business, and seems to have estranged him from his kids."

"Oh my God, what else did she do? Slash his tires and set fire to his car? What else was left?"

"Not much, from the sound of it. He got a lot of money for their ad agency, I suspect, but I don't think he really cares."

"At least that explains why he was so friendly with Pip. He must miss his kids."

"He does," Ophélie said, thinking about the things they'd said the night he came to dinner. It had definitely touched her heart.

"How long ago was the divorce?" Andrea had a clinical look on her face, and Ophélie laughed.

"About ten years ago, I think. Give or take. He hasn't seen his kids in six, or heard from them. They cut him off."

"Maybe he is a child molester, then. Either that, or his ex is a piece of work. More likely that. Has he had a serious relationship since?"

"One. She wanted to get married and have kids. He didn't. I think he's too wounded to try again, and I can't say I blame him. What he describes is about as bad as it gets."

"Forget it," Andrea said in a matter-of-fact tone of voice, shaking her head. "Trust me. Too much baggage. This guy's a mess."

"Not as a friend," Ophélie said calmly. She didn't want anything from Matt, other than his friendship. She didn't want a relationship either. She had Ted, in her head and heart. She didn't want anyone else.

"You don't need a friend," Andrea said practically. "You have me. You need a man in your life. And this one is too damaged. I've seen guys like that. They never get their shit together again. How old is he?"

"Forty-seven."

"Too bad. But I'm telling you. You'd be wasting your time."

"I'm not wasting anything," Ophélie said with quiet determination. "I don't want a man in my life. Now or ever again. I had Ted. I don't want anyone else."

"You had problems with him, Ophélie, and you know it. I don't want to bring up ugly memories, but there was a little incident about ten years ago, if you'll recall. . . ." Their eyes met and Ophélie looked away.

"That was a one-time thing. It was an accident. A mistake. He never did it again."

"You don't know that. He might have. And whether he did or not is irrelevant. He wasn't a saint, he was a man. A very, very difficult man who gave you a tough time sometimes, like with Chad. Everything was about him. You're the only woman I know who could have put up with him for as long as you did. He was a genius, I concede that, but no matter how much I liked him, and you loved him, he was a sonofabitch at times. The only person he really cared about was himself. He wasn't exactly a gift."

"He was to me," Ophélie said stubbornly, upset by what Andrea had said, whether true or not. He had been difficult, but men of his caliber and genius were entitled to be, or she thought so anyway. Andrea didn't agree. "I loved him for twenty years. That's not going to change overnight, or ever."

"Maybe not. And I know he loved you too, in his own way," Andrea said gently, afraid she had gone too far. But Andrea didn't pull any punches with her friend, and never had. And if nothing else, Andrea felt Ophélie needed to free herself of Ted now, and her delusions about him, in order to have a life. Ophélie and Ted had had their differences over the years, and the incident she had been referring to, which Ophélie said was a "mistake," was an affair he had had one summer while Ophélie and the children were in France. And it had been a total mess. He had nearly left Ophélie over it, and she had been heartbroken. Andrea had never been sure if things were quite the same between them again. It was hard to say. After that Chad got sick, and things got worse between them anyway. But the affair couldn't have helped. Despite the fact that Ophélie had been willing to forgive him. It was a liberty he had not only taken, but allowed himself. Ted had had a sense of entitlement on all fronts.

"The real issue here is not how good or bad he was, but that he's gone. He's never coming back. You're here, and he's not. You can take as long as you need to recover, but you can't stay alone forever."

"Why not?" Ophélie looked sad as she asked. She didn't want another man in her life. She was used to Ted. Familiarity was part of it. She couldn't even imagine herself with another man. She had been with him since she was twenty-two, and married since she was twenty-four. At forty-two, she couldn't even begin to imagine starting all over again. She didn't want to. It was easier to be alone. Which was Matt's conclusion too. They were both the walking wounded, which was another thing they had in common.

"You're too young to stay alone," Andrea said quietly. She was the voice of reason, and of the future. Ophélie was steadfastly clinging to the past. And in some ways, a past that had never existed, except in her heart and imagination. "You have to let go eventually. Maybe not now. But sooner or later. You're only halfway through your life. You can't even begin to think of being alone forever. That's ridiculous, and a terrible waste."

"Not if it's what I want," Ophélie said stubbornly.

"You don't want that. No one does. You just don't want the pain of exploring. And I don't blame you. It's rotten out there. I've lived there all my adult life. I hate it. But someone is bound to turn up eventually. A good one. Maybe even better than Ted." There was no one better in Ophélie's estimation, but she didn't argue the point with Andrea. "But I don't think your child molester is the answer. He sounds pretty screwed up, or maybe just screwed over. But either way, I don't think he's the guy you want, except as a friend. I think you're right there. But that means that eventually, you're going to have to find someone else."

"I'll let you know when I'm ready, and you can leave my name on bathroom walls, or hand out leaflets. Come to think of it, there's a man in my group who's desperate to get remarried. He might be just the thing."

"Stranger things have happened. Widows meet guys on cruises, at art classes, in grief groups. At least you'd have a lot in common. Who is he?"

"Mr. Feigenbaum. He's a retired butcher, he loves opera and the theater, is a gourmet cook, has four grown children, and he's eighty-three."

"Perfect." Andrea grinned. "I'll take him. I can tell you're not taking this seriously."

"No, I'm not, but I appreciate your concern."

"You ain't seen nothing yet. I intend to stay on your back."

"That," Ophélie said with a very Gallic raised eyebrow, "I believe." And with that, the baby woke up with a scream.

And while they were chatting on the deck, far down the beach, Matt was making careful sketches of Pip, and he took two rolls of black-and-white film. He was excited about doing the portrait, and had promised her it would be ready in time for her mother's birthday, and probably long before.

"I'm going to miss you when we leave," Pip said sadly after he'd taken the photographs of her. She loved coming down to sit with him, and talk and draw for hours. He had become her best friend.

"I'm going to miss you too." He was being honest with her. "I'll come into the city to visit you and your mom. But you're going to be busy with your friends once you go back to school." Her life would be far fuller than his, he knew. And it startled him to realize how much he had come to depend on seeing her nearly every day. She had kept him company for most of the summer.

"That's not the same thing," Pip chided him. Their friendship was special, and she relied on him too. He had become her confidant and best friend, and in some ways, a substitute for her father. He was the father Ted had never been. In many ways, Pip felt he was nicer to her than her father had been. Her father had never spent as much time with her as Matt did, nor been as kind to her. Or her mother. He had always had an edge to him, and got angry easily, especially at her mom or Chad, not as much with her. Because Pip had always been careful with him. He scared her a little. Although he'd been nicer to her when she was very young, she had pleasant memories of that, and less so in recent years. "I'm going to miss you a lot," she said, near tears as she thought about it. She was going to hate leaving him at the beach. And Matt hated to see her go.

"I promise I'll come in whenever you want. We can go to the movies, or lunch, whatever you like, as long as it's all right with your mom."

"She likes you too," Pip said comfortably, not divulging any secrets. Her mother had said so openly, and agreed that he was a very nice man.

For a crazy instant, he was tempted to ask her what her father had really been like. In spite of everything Ophélie had said, he couldn't get a clear picture of Ted. The only portrait of him he could paint in his mind's eye was of a difficult, probably selfish tyrant, who may have been a genius, but more than likely wasn't very nice to his wife. Yet Ophélie had clearly worshiped him and made him sound like a saint now. But pieces of the puzzle didn't seem to fit. Particularly in his relationship with his son. And Matt didn't have the feeling he'd spent much time with Pip, she had almost said as much, in incidents she talked about, and stories she told. And it didn't sound as though he'd spent much time with his wife either. It was hard to get a clear picture. Particularly now that he was dead, and the normal tendency was to forget the unpleasant parts, and improve the rest. But he didn't want to put Pip on the spot.

"When do you go back to school?" he said finally.

"In two weeks. The day after we go back."

"You'll be busy then," he said reassuringly, but she looked sad anyway.

"Can I call you sometimes?" Pip asked, and he smiled.

"I'd like that very much." She had been a gift to him, and she soothed a place in him that had been raw for a long time. She did something magical to fill the gaping hole in him his own kids had left. And he did the same for her. He was, in some ways, the father she had never had, and wished she did. Ted was an entirely different beast.

She left him after he packed up his things, and she walked back up the beach. Andrea was just leaving when she got home.

"How was Matt?" her mother asked pleasantly, as Pip kissed Andrea and the baby goodbye.

"Fine. He said to say hello to you."

"Remember what I said," Andrea reminded her, and Ophélie laughed.

"I told you. Mr. Feigenbaum is the answer."

"Don't count on it. Guys like that marry their wives' sisters or best friends within six months. You'll still be trying to decide what to do long after he's remarried. It's a shame he's so old."

"You're disgusting," Ophélie said as she hugged her friend and kissed the baby, and then they left.

"Who's Mr. Feigenbaum?" Pip asked, curious. She'd never heard his name before.

"A man in my group. He's eighty-three years old and he's looking for a new wife."

Pip's eyes opened wide. "Does he want to marry you?"

"No, he doesn't. And I don't want to marry him either. So everything's fine." Pip had a sudden urge to ask her if she would ever marry Matt. She wished she would one day, but after what her mother had said recently, she knew there wasn't much chance of it. Probably none at all. But at least he had said he would visit them in town, and she really hoped he would.

Pip and her mother had a quiet dinner that night, and Pip mentioned to her that Matt had said he might call sometimes.

"He wanted to know if it was all right with you."

"I don't see why not," Ophélie said quietly. He seemed trustworthy and had proven himself as a friend. She had no qualms about it now, even though Andrea still referred to him as "the child molester," but she had no concerns about that. "I think that would be nice. Maybe he'd like to have dinner with us sometime."

"He said he'd take us out to dinner and a movie when he comes to the city."

"That sounds like fun," Ophélie said, not thinking about it much as she put the dishes in the dishwasher and Pip turned on the TV. Friendship with Matt wasn't what Andrea wanted for her, but it suited Ophélie. Their summer in Safe Harbour had been a success, and she and Pip had made a new friend.

10

IT WAS THE BEGINNING OF THEIR LAST WEEK
when Matt called Ophélie about sailing with
him, on a brilliantly sunny day. They had just
had two days of fog, and everyone was relieved
to see a last burst of summer. As it turned out, it
was the hottest day of the year. So much so that
Pip and Ophélie had both gotten too hot, and
had decided to go inside for lunch. They were
just finishing the sandwiches Ophélie had made
when Matt called. And Pip looked half asleep in
the heat. She had been thinking about walking
down to see Matt, but it was almost too hot to
go, and the sun was blazing overhead. It was going to be the first day in a long time that she'd
missed with him. But she didn't think he'd be
outside painting either. It was a good day to
swim, or sail, as Matt said himself when he
called Ophélie.

"I've been meaning to ask you for weeks," Matt said apologetically. He couldn't explain to her that he'd been too busy sketching Pip for her portrait. "It's so hot, I thought I'd take the boat out this afternoon. Can I interest you in a sail?" It sounded like a great idea to her too. It was too hot to sit on the deck, or the beach, and at least on the ocean, there would be a breeze. The wind had started to come up in the last hour, which was what had given him the idea. He'd been in the house all day, drawing Pip, from memory, photographs, and sketches he'd made of her on the beach.

"That sounds great," Ophélie said enthusiastically. She still hadn't seen his boat, although she knew he was immensely fond of it, and had promised to take her sailing before she left. "Where do you keep her?"

"I have her moored at a private dock at a house on the lagoon side, just down from you. The owners are never there, and they don't mind the boat. They say it adds charm to the place when they're here. They moved to Washington last year. It worked out well for me." He gave her the house number, and told her he'd meet her there in ten minutes. She told Pip what she was doing, and was surprised when Pip looked upset.

"Will you be okay, Mom?" Pip asked worriedly. "Is it safe? How big is the boat?" Listening to her, and seeing the look in her eyes, Ophélie was touched. It was exactly how she felt about her. Everything seemed more ominous now, which was why she'd been so upset earlier in the summer, when Pip disappeared down the beach. All they had now was each other. And danger was no longer an abstract concept to them. It was real. And tragedy a possibility they both knew existed. It had changed life forever for both of them. "I don't want you to go," Pip said in a frightened voice, as Ophélie tried to decide what to do. They couldn't live in fear forever either. Maybe it was a good idea to show her that they could lead normal lives, and nothing terrible would happen. She felt no danger whatsoever about going out on the boat with Matt. And she was certain he was a supremely competent sailor. They had talked a lot about sailing. And he'd done a lot of it since he was a boy. Far more so than she. She hadn't been sailing herself in at least a dozen years. But she had some experience too, in far more treacherous waters than these.

"Sweetheart, I really think it will be fine. You can watch us from the deck." Pip did not look reassured, but more like she was going to cry. "Do you really not want me to go?" It was an element she hadn't even considered when she

told him she would. And she was going to ask
Amy to come over. She had just seen her go
into her house, so she knew she was home. Or
Pip could even go there for a few hours, if Amy
had things to do.

"What if you drown?" Pip asked in a stran-
gled voice, and Ophélie sat down and pulled
her gently onto her lap.

"I'm not going to drown. I'm a good swimmer. And so is Matt. I'll ask him for a life vest if
you want." Pip considered it for a moment and
then nodded, reassured.

"Okay." She looked slightly mollified and
then visibly panicked again. "What if a shark attacks the boat?" Ophélie couldn't deny that
there were shark sightings in those waters now
and then, but there hadn't been one all summer.

"You've been watching too much TV. I
promise. Nothing is going to happen. You can
watch us. I just want to go out with him for a
little while. Do you want to come with us?"
Ophélie hadn't really wanted her to go, for
some of the same reasons, which seemed foolish now. And Pip wasn't all that crazy about the
water. She didn't want to scare her. Sailboats
were her thing and not her daughter's. Pip
shook her head the moment her mother asked
her. "I'll tell you what. I'll tell Matt I want to be
back in an hour. It's a beautiful day, and we'll be

back before you know it. How does that sound?"

"Okay, I guess." She looked forlorn as she said it, and Ophélie felt guilty. But she really wanted to sail with him, and see his boat, even if only for a few minutes. She was torn now, but it was beginning to seem important to prove to Pip that she could go and come back, and nothing untoward would happen. It was going to be part of the healing process for her.

She went to put shorts over a bathing suit, and called Amy to come and sit with Pip. The teenager had promised to be over in a few minutes, and by the time Ophélie was ready to leave, she was there. But before her mother left, Pip threw her arms around her and held her tight. It brought home to Ophélie just how hard hit Pip had been by her father and brother's deaths. She had never behaved this way before. But Ophélie hadn't gone anywhere either. She had spent most of the last ten months lying on her bed in tears.

"I'll be back soon, I promise. If it's not too hot, you can watch us from the deck. Okay?" She kissed Pip, and walked out the door in as swift and clean an exit as she could manage, while Mousse stood by and wagged his tail. But Ophélie was pensive as she walked down the road to the house where Matt kept his boat. His

car was already there. And she found him a moment later, putting some things away on his
boat. She was a lovely little sailboat in immacu-
late condition. It was easy to see how much he
loved her by how beautifully he kept her.
Everything on deck had been varnished, the
brass shone, and the hull had been freshly
painted white that spring. She had one mast,
which rose forty feet in the air, with a mainsail
and a jib, and a fair amount of sail for her size.
She had a short bowsprit that made her look
longer than her thirty feet, a small engine, and a
tiny cabin with ceilings too low for Matt to
stand up. And her name was *Nessie II,* named
for the daughter he hadn't seen in six years. The
elegant little sailboat was a gem, and Ophélie
stood back with a smile as she admired her
from the dock. "What a little beauty she is,
Matt." She meant every word of it and couldn't
wait to sail with him.

"Isn't she?" He looked pleased. "I really
wanted you to see her before you left." And
sailing on her was better yet. He was anxious to
get under way. Ophélie took off her sandals, and
he helped her on board. He started the engine,
and she helped him get the lines off the dock.
And a moment later, they were moving at a
good clip down the lagoon toward the ocean. It
was a perfect day for a sail.

"What a lovely boat!" Ophélie said again, admiring all the little details that he so lovingly
tended to in his spare time. The pretty little sailboat was one of the joys of his life, and he was
happy to be sharing it with her. "When was she
built?" Ophélie asked with interest as they
reached the mouth of the lagoon, and he
moved into the ocean and turned off the engine, as they felt the breeze pick up. For a moment, Ophélie savored the delicious silence of
the sailboat, as they felt the ocean beneath
them, and the wind overhead as he put up the
sails. She was easy for him to manage on his
own, but without asking, Ophélie began to
help him.

"She was built in 1936," he said proudly. "I've
had her for about eight years. I bought her from
a man who had owned her since just after the
war. She was in great shape, but I did a fair
amount of restoration on her myself."

"She's a jewel," Ophélie said, and then remembered her promise to Pip. She stuck her
head in the cabin, and grabbed a life vest that was
hanging on a peg. Matt looked faintly surprised
when he saw her put it on. She had told him she
was a strong swimmer, and she loved to sail. "I
promised Pip," she answered the question in his
eyes. And he nodded, as the wind caught their
sails and they got under way. It was an exquisite

feeling as the sailboat cut through the water with delicious grace. They exchanged the long, slow smile of two sailors enjoying the pleasure of the boat on a perfect day.

"Do you mind if we head out a bit?" he asked, as Ophélie shook her head, looking positively blissful. She didn't mind at all, as they left the beach and its row of houses far behind. She wondered if Pip was watching them, and hoped she was. They were a lovely sight. And then, as she sat beside him at the tiller, Ophélie told him about Pip's reaction before she left.

"I guess I didn't realize how anxious she's gotten since . . ." She didn't finish her sentence, and he understood, as Ophélie sat with her face up to the sun and closed her eyes. He wasn't sure which was the prettier sight, the sailboat that he loved, or the woman at his side.

They sailed for a long time in silence until the beach had all but disappeared. She had promised Pip they wouldn't stay out for long, but it was too tempting to just sail away and leave the world behind. She had almost forgotten what a relief it was to be sailing on a lovely boat. It was the most peaceful thing she knew. And she didn't mind at all when the wind came up. He was pleased to see that she really was a sailor, and was enjoying it as much as he had hoped she would. For a moment, she wished that they could sail away forever and never go back. It was such an extraordinary feeling of freedom and peace. She hadn't felt this happy or content in years, and it was lovely sharing it with him.

They passed a number of fishing boats, and waved at them, and in the distance there was a freighter on the horizon, heading in. They were heading in the direction of the Farallones, when Matt leaned to the side and seemed to be looking at something. Ophélie glanced in the same direction but saw nothing. She wondered if he'd seen a seal or a big fish, hopefully not a shark. He handed the tiller to her, and went below, grabbed a pair of binoculars, and came back up. He looked through them with a frown.

"What's up?" She wasn't worried, just curious, and wished she could take off the cumbersome vest, but she had promised Pip, and wanted to keep her word, on principle, not out of any need.

"I thought I saw something a minute ago," he answered her. "I guess not." The waves had come up a bit, which didn't bother her, but it made it harder to see. She had never gotten seasick in her life, she loved the movement of the boat, no matter how rough it got.

"What did you think you saw?" she asked with interest, sitting next to him. He was thinking about turning back, they had come very far, and had been sailing for over an hour, nearly two, with a good wind at their backs.

"I'm not sure . . . it looked like a surfboard, but it's too far out for that, unless it fell off a boat." She nodded, and he adjusted the sails, and just as they turned, she saw it this time and shouted to him in the wind, and pointed. She grabbed the binoculars, and this time saw not only the board, but a man clinging to it. She waved frantically at Matt, and he quickly grabbed the binoculars from her, nodded, and together they maneuvered the sails down, and he started the engine and headed toward what they'd seen as fast as he could. Getting the sails down in the brisk wind was harder to do than it looked.

It took them several minutes to reach the board, and when they did they both saw that the man clinging to it was barely more than a boy, he was nearly unconscious, his face was gray and his lips were a deep blue. It was impossible to guess where he'd come from or how long he'd been there. He was miles and miles from shore. Ophélie helped Matt steady the boat, while he disappeared into the cabin for a length of sturdy rope. The water was getting rougher, and Ophélie felt her throat tighten as she realized what an impossible task it was going to be to get the boy on the boat. Pulling him out of the water was going to be a Herculean feat, but getting the rope around him before that was going to be even harder. As they approached him, they could see that he was shaking violently, and he looked at them with desperate eyes.

"Hang on!" Matt shouted at him, realizing that as long as he clung to the board they couldn't get the rope around him, and if he let go, he might drown. He was wearing an abbreviated wetsuit, which had probably saved his life thus far, and looking at him with a lump in her throat the size of a fist, Ophélie guessed him to be about sixteen, the same age as Chad. All she could think of was that somewhere there was a woman who was about to lose her son and suffer untold grief. She didn't see how they could save him either. Matt had a small radio onboard, but other than the freighter, which was miles away, there were no boats in sight, and even the Coast Guard would take too long to arrive. If he was to live, they had to save him themselves. And there was no telling how far gone he was, or how long he'd been in the water. It was obvious to both of them they didn't have much time. Matt reached into the cabin and grabbed a life vest, and asked Ophélie a question before he dove in. "Can you get the boat back yourself if you have to?" She nodded without hesitating. She had sailed alone in Brittany for years as a young girl, often in rough weather, and conditions far more adverse than this. But he needed to know before he left her alone on-board.

Matt made a loop in the rope, and took it with him when he dove in, and instinctively the boy grabbed on to him and clung to him, and almost drowned Matt as he fought to get the rope around the boy. He managed to get behind him somehow, as the boy flailed his arms weakly, and Ophélie watched the grim scene. It seemed to take forever to get the rope under his arms, and for Matt to drag him back toward the boat. She could see then how powerful Matt was, it was an inhuman effort he was making, and when he approached the boat with the boy, he shouted to her, and she understood. He threw the end of the rope back up to her, and miraculously she caught it, and attached it to the winch. She knew what she had to do. The only question now was if she could do it and save them both. It took five attempts and she was beginning to panic as the rope held finally, and the winch brought the boy slowly up. He barely had the strength to hang on, but it didn't matter, the rope was holding him under his arms, and she caught him as he spilled nearly lifelessly onto the deck. He was barely conscious and shaking violently, as she looked back at Matt, got the rope from around the boy, and threw it to Matt.

Despite the movement of the water, he caught it effortlessly, and the winch hauled him up. It seemed a miracle that they had both managed to get out of the water and into the boat. And as Matt assessed the situation, he decided it would be faster to sail. The wind had turned and come up powerfully, and he thought he could get to shore faster under sail. He put the sails back up, while she got a blanket from the cabin and covered the boy, as he looked at her with dying eyes. She knew that look, and had seen it twice on Chad when he'd attempted suicide. But with every ounce of her being, she vowed to save this child. He'd obviously gone out on a surfboard and been swept away, on a riptide probably, and gone out so far there was no hope of his getting back. Only a miracle had brought them to just the right spot at just the right time. And Matt looked intent as he sailed toward shore, and after a moment he shouted to her that there was a bottle of brandy in the cabin, and told her to give some to the boy. But Ophélie was quick to shake her head, and he didn't understand. He told her again, thinking she hadn't heard him. Not knowing what else to do, she got under the blanket with the trembling boy and held him close to her, hoping that her own body warmth might help keep him alive until they got to shore. Matt pointed to the tiller then and went inside to the radio. He reached the Coast Guard in less time than he had hoped, and told them that he had a major medical emergency on-board, and was heading to land. He believed he would get back to shore before they could reach him, and asked them to have paramedics waiting for him on shore, or to try and catch up with him by boat if they could.

They were halfway back when the wind began to die down, and he took down the sails again and started the engine back up. It was a straight shot back to the beach by then, and land was in plain sight, as Matt looked intent, and kept glancing at Ophélie with the boy in her arms. He had been unconscious for the last twenty minutes and looked nearly dead. Ophélie's face was white.

"Are you okay?" he shouted at her, and she nodded, but it was an all-too-familiar scene for her, and reminded her excruciatingly of Chad. All she wanted now was to save this boy, so his mother would never have to live all that she had. "How is he?"

"Still alive." She had him pressed against her, and she was soaking wet underneath the blanket, but she didn't care or notice. The sun was beating down on them, and their lazy pleasure sail had become a race against death.

"Why didn't you give him the brandy?" Matt asked, trying to force the engine to go faster. He had never pushed the boat this hard, nor had to, but she hadn't let him down yet.

"It would have killed him," she said, looking frantic, he was so limp and cold in her arms, but she could still feel the slightest pulse. He wasn't gone yet. "It would have pulled all his circulation to his extremities, he needs the blood in his trunk, for his heart." Despite the fact that his limbs now felt like ice, but whatever circulation he still had was where he needed it most.

"Thank God you knew that," Matt said, as he prayed silently to get the boy back in time. They were nearly at the mouth of the lagoon by then. They were only minutes away from help, and as they came out of the ocean into the lagoon, they could hear sirens and see lights at the end of the beach nearest to them. Without hesitating, Matt pulled the boat up to a stranger's dock. There were people gathered, watching, as half a dozen paramedics jumped onboard and Ophélie rolled back and struggled to her feet on the deck. She was sobbing as she watched them check him and then take him on a gurney, as one of the paramedics looked back at her and held a thumb of victory in the air with a smile. He was still alive. She was shaking violently as Matt took a step across the deck to her and held her in his arms. She was sobbing as he did and two men off a fire truck stepped gingerly onboard.

"You saved that kid's life," the senior officer said with admiration. "Did anyone get his name?" All Ophélie could do was shake her head, as Matt explained to them what had happened and they took down a report, and congratulated them again. It was another half-hour before the fire trucks left, and Matt put the engine on again, and motored slowly toward his dock. Ophélie was too shaken to even speak, and she sat next to him trembling, as he kept an arm firmly around her shoulders.

"I'm sorry, Ophélie." He knew without effort what it must have reminded her of, and done to her. "I just thought we'd have a nice sail."

"We did. We saved his life, and his mother's heart." If he lived. No one could be sure yet, but at least he had a chance. He had none whatsoever out where they found him, clinging to his board, which they had abandoned. Matt hadn't wanted to waste time trying to get it onboard.

They were both exhausted when they tied up the *Nessie II,* put everything away, locked the cabin, and left the boat. He still needed to hose down the deck to get the salt off her, but he

would have to come back later. By the time it
was all over, they'd been out for five hours. She
barely had the strength to walk when they left
the dock, and Matt drove her back to her
house. But neither of them was prepared for
what they found there. Pip was sobbing on her
bed, and Amy looked distraught as she tried to
comfort her. She had watched them sail away,
and when they didn't come back in an hour or
two, Pip was convinced that the worst had happened and the boat had sunk or her mother had
drowned. She was inconsolable when Ophélie
walked into her room and Matt stood looking
aghast from the doorway.

"It's okay, Pip . . . it's okay . . . I'm back . . ."
Ophélie cooed gently, horrified to find her in
this condition, and suddenly feeling guilty for
ever having left her. Everything had turned out
so differently than expected, but a life had been
saved. It appeared to be destiny that they had
gone out that day on Matt's boat.

"You said you'd be back in an hour!" she
shouted at her mother as she turned to look at
her with eyes filled with accusation and terror.
Just as Ophélie had been distraught over the
sight of the dying boy who reminded her of
Chad, Pip's own fears had convinced her that
she had lost her mother.

"I'm so sorry . . . I didn't know . . . some-thing happened."

"Did the boat turn over?" Pip looked even more frightened, as Matt walked into the room and joined them, and Amy discreetly left. She had run out of things to say to reassure Pip hours before, and she had never been as grateful as she was to see the child's mother appear.

"No, the boat didn't capsize," Ophélie said gently, as she held Pip close to her. It was just what she needed. Words were no longer enough. "And I wore a life vest, just like I promised."

"Me too," Matt said, not sure whether he was welcome, or an intruder in the scene between mother and anguished child.

"We found a boy in the water far out from shore, on a surfboard, and Matt saved him." Pip's eyes grew wide when she told her.

"We both did," Matt corrected. "Your mom was terrific." Thinking back on it now, he was even more impressed than he had been when it happened. She had been calm and efficient and effective. He couldn't have saved the boy with-out her help.

They told Pip all about what had happened, and Ophélie managed to marshal her forces to reassure her. And a little while later, while they all sipped hot tea, Matt called the hospital, and they told him that the boy's condition was serious, but stable for the moment. He wouldn't be out of the woods for a while, but it looked like he might make it, and his family was with him at Marin General. There were tears in Matt's eyes when he told them, and Ophélie closed her eyes for a long moment. All she could think of was the tragedy that had been averted, and she was deeply grateful for it. A woman she would never know had been spared tragedy and heartbreak. Ophélie was thankful they had been able to save the boy.

By the time Matt left an hour later, Pip had calmed down considerably, but she said she never wanted her mother to go sailing again, ever. It was obvious to all concerned how traumatic the afternoon had been for Pip, without even knowing what had happened. She said she had heard the sirens go past the house, on their way to the spit at land's end, and she had been convinced then her mother and Matt were dead. It had been a hideous day for her, and Matt apologized again to both of them for their respective traumas. It hadn't been easy for him either, and Ophélie knew with perfect clarity how easy it would have been for Matt to drown while attempting to save the boy in the water.

They might have both died, and she would have been able to do nothing to help him. It had been a narrow escape from tragedy, too narrow for anyone's comfort. And shortly after Matt got home, he called her.

"How is she?" he asked, sounding concerned and exhausted. He had gone back to hose off the boat, and could barely lift his arms to do it, and then he had gone home and soaked in a hot tub for an hour. He hadn't even realized till then how cold he was, or how badly shaken.

"She's fine now," Ophélie said calmly. She had taken a hot bath too, and she felt better, though she was every bit as tired as he was. "I guess I'm not the only one around here who worries more than I used to." For Pip, the fear of losing her mother had become her worst nightmare, and she knew better than anyone how easily it could happen. She would never feel entirely safe again. In an important sense, the innocence of her childhood had ended ten months before.

"You were amazing," Matt said gently.

"So were you," she said, still in awe of what he'd done, and the determination with which he'd done it. He hadn't hesitated for a moment to risk his life for the unknown boy.

"If I'm ever planning to fall overboard, I'm going to take you with me," he said admiringly.

"And thank God you knew about the brandy, I'd have killed him. I'd have poured it right down his throat."

"A lot of first aid, and a little pre-med, or I wouldn't have known either. It turned out fine, that's all that matters." It was their teamwork that had saved him in the end.

Matt called to check on him again later that night, and then called Ophélie to tell her the boy was doing well, and by the next morning he was in satisfactory condition, and his parents had called both Matt and Ophélie to thank them profusely for their heroic act. They were horrified by what had happened, and his mother had sobbed when she thanked Ophélie. She had no idea how well Ophélie knew the tragedy that had been averted. Better than she did.

The newspapers carried an account of it, which Pip read to her mother over breakfast. And then she looked at Ophélie with huge eyes that pierced her mother's like knives.

"Promise you won't ever do anything like that again. . . . I can't . . . I couldn't . . . if you . . ." She couldn't finish, and Ophélie's eyes filled with tears as she looked at her and nodded.

"I promise. I couldn't live without you either," she said softly. She folded the newspaper then, and gave Pip a hug, and a moment later the child walked out to the deck, and sat down next to Mousse, lost in her own thoughts, and staring out at the ocean in silence. The day before had been too terrifying to even think of. Ophélie stood in the living room, crying softly as she watched her, and said a silent prayer of thanks that everything had turned out as it had.

11

MATT TOOK PIP AND OPHÉLIE TO DINNER ON their last night in Safe Harbour. They had all recovered from the trauma of saving the boy by then, and all three of them looked relaxed. He had gone home from the hospital the day before and had called Ophélie and Matt to thank them himself. Ophélie had been right in guessing how it had happened. He had been swept away for miles by the tide.

They went to the Lobster Pot in town again for dinner, and they had a nice time. But for most of the evening, Pip looked sad. She hated saying good-bye to her friend. She and her mother had packed their bags that afternoon, and they were going home the next morning. Pip had a few things to do at home before starting school.

"It's going to be awfully quiet around here

without you two," Matt said pleasantly as they finished dessert. Most of the summer residents were leaving that weekend. The next day was Labor Day. And Pip was starting school on Tuesday.

"We're going to rent a house here again next year," Pip said firmly. She had already extracted a promise from her mother, although Ophélie thought that the following summer they should go back to France again, at least for a few weeks. But she liked the idea of renting at Safe Harbour again too, and if possible the same house, or another. The one they had worked well for them, although it had been too small for others. But it suited them.

"I can check the market for you if you like, as things come up. I'm here anyway. In case you want something bigger next year."

"I think we like the one we had," she said, smiling at him. "If they rent it to us again. I'm not sure they're crazy about letting us bring Mousse." But he hadn't done any damage fortunately. He was very well behaved. All he did was shed. And there was a cleaning service coming to scrub the place the next day. But she and Pip were fairly neat.

"I'll be expecting to see lots of drawings when I come into the city to visit. And don't forget the father-daughter dance," he reminded

Pip, and she grinned. She loved the fact that he remembered it, and she actually believed he would come. Her own father never had. He had to work. She had brought her brother once. And a friend of Andrea's another time. Ted hated events at their schools, and he and her mother had argued about it. They had argued about a lot of things, although her mother didn't like to be reminded of it now. But it was true anyway, whether she admitted it or not. But Pip was convinced Matt would keep his word about the dance, and even make it fun for her.

"You'll have to wear a tie," Pip said cautiously, hoping that wouldn't make him change his mind, and he smiled.

"I think I might have one dragging around somewhere. It's probably holding back my curtains." In fact, he had many of them, he just didn't have a lot of occasions to wear them anymore, although he could have if he wanted to. But he didn't. The only things he did in the city were visit his dentist, or see his banker or attorney. But he had every intention of visiting Ophélie and Pip. They were important to him. And after the drama he and Ophélie had shared earlier that week, he felt closer than ever to her.

He took them back to the house, and Ophélie invited him in for a glass of wine. And he accepted with pleasure. She poured a glass of red wine for him, as Pip went to put on her pajamas. He liked the domesticity of it, and asked Ophélie if she wanted him to light a fire. The evenings were cool, as they always were, and despite the hot September days, the nights already smelled of autumn.

"That would be nice," she said about the fire, as Pip came out to kiss them both goodnight, and promised to call him soon. He had already given her his number. And Ophélie had it too, in case Pip lost it. He gave Pip a hug then, and bent down to light the fire, as Mousse watched him, and he realized he would even miss the dog. He had forgotten what it was like to have the accoutrements of a family around him, and he hated to admit even to himself how much he liked it.

The fire was already blazing by the time she came back from tucking Pip in. It was a tradition she had revived over the last few weeks. And as she sat looking into the fire, she realized how much had changed in the three months since they'd been there. She felt almost human, although she still missed her son and husband. But the pain of their absence was a little more bearable than it had been three months earlier. Time did make a difference, albeit a small one.

"You're looking very serious," he said, as he

sat down next to her and took a sip of the wine she had poured him. It was the last of the bottle he had brought her. She wasn't much of a drinker, particularly for a French woman.

"I was just thinking how much better I feel than I did when I got here. It's done us both good. Pip seems happier too. In great part, thanks to you. You've made her summer." She smiled gratefully at him.

"She's made mine too. And so have you. We all need friends. Sometimes I forget that."

"You lead a solitary life out here, Matt," she said, and he nodded. For the past ten years it had been what he wanted. But now, for the first time in years, it seemed lonely to him.

"It's good for my work, or something like that. At least that's what I tell myself. And it's close enough to the city. I can always go in if I want to." And he would now, to see them, but he was startled to realize that, in spite of its proximity, it was over a year since he'd been there. The time just slipped away sometimes, while you weren't looking, as did the years.

"I hope you'll come and see us often. In spite of my cooking," she laughed.

"I'll take you out to dinner," he teased her, but he meant it. He was enjoying the prospect. It was something to look forward to and soften the blow of their leaving, which he knew would hit him like a sledgehammer the next morning. "What are you going to do with yourself when Pip goes back to school?" he asked, looking concerned about her. He knew it would be lonely for her. She wasn't used to having as much time on her hands as she did now with only Pip to care for. She was used to having two children, and a husband.

"I may take your advice and look into some volunteer work at a homeless shelter." She had fun reading the material Blake Thompson, the leader of the group, had given her. It seemed interesting and appealed to her.

"That would be good for you. And you can always come out here and have lunch with me, if you have nothing else to do. It's pretty here in the winter." She liked it too. She loved the beach at all times of the year, and it was an appealing invitation. She liked the idea of maintaining their friendship. And whatever Andrea thought of it, it suited both of them, and was what they wanted.

"I'd like that." Ophélie smiled at him.

"Are you happy to be going back?" he asked, and she stared into the fire and looked pensive, thinking about it.

"No, I'm not. I hate going back to the house, although until now, I've always liked it. But it's so empty now. It's too big for the two of us, but it's familiar. I didn't want to make any hasty decisions last year that I'd regret later." She didn't tell him that their bedroom closets were still full of Ted's clothes, and all of Chad's things were in his bedroom. She had touched nothing, and knowing that they were there depressed her. But she couldn't bring herself to part with them. Andrea had already told her it was unhealthy, but for now at least, it was what Ophélie wanted. She wasn't ready to make changes, or she hadn't been. She wondered if she'd feel differently now, after the summer. She didn't know yet.

"I think you were smart not to do anything too quickly. You can always sell the house, if you really want to. It's probably good for Pip not to have the trauma of moving. That would be a big change for her, if you've lived there for a long time."

"Since she was six, and she loves it. More than I do."

They sat quietly then for a while, enjoying each other's company, even in silence. And when he finished his wine, he stood up, and she joined him. By then, the fire was slowly dying.

"I'll call you next week," he said, and it reassured her. He was a solid, reliable male presence in her life, like a brother. "Call if you need anything, or if there's anything I can do for you or Pip." He knew he'd worry about them.

"Thank you, Matt," she said gently. "For everything. You've been a wonderful friend, to both of us."

"I intend to stay that way," he said, and put an arm around her as she walked him to his car.

"So do we. Take care of yourself. Don't be too lonely out here, it's not good for you. Come to see us in the city, it will distract you." Now that she knew more about his life, she could imagine how alone he must feel at times, just as she did. So many people they had loved and cared about had left their lives, through death and divorce, and circumstances that neither of them had wanted. The tides of life that swept away people and places and cherished moments all too quickly, just as the ocean had swept away the boy they'd saved only days before.

"Goodnight," he said softly, not knowing what else to say to her. He waved as he drove away, and watched her walk back into the house, and then he drove back to his bungalow down the beach, wishing that he were braver, and that life were different than it was.

12

"GOOD-BYE, HOUSE," PIP SAID SOLEMNLY AS they left it. Ophélie locked the door, and dropped the keys in the mail slot at the realtor's on the way out. The summer was over. And as they drove past the narrow winding street that Matt lived on, Pip was strangely silent. She didn't speak until they were on the bridge, and then she turned to her mother. "Why don't you like him?" she said almost angrily. Her tone was an accusation. Ophélie had no idea who she was talking about.

"Like who?"

"Matt. I think he likes you." Pip was glaring at her, and totally confusing her mother.

"I like him too. What are you talking about?"

"I mean like a man . . . you know . . . like a boyfriend."

They were nearly at the tollbooth, and Ophélie was fumbling for her money, and then glanced at her daughter. "I don't want a boyfriend. I'm a married woman," she said firmly, as she found the money.

"No, you're not. You're a widow."

"That's the same thing. Nearly. Whatever brought this on? And no, I don't think he likes me 'as a girlfriend.' And if he did, it wouldn't make a difference. He's our friend, Pip. Let's not spoil that."

"Why would it spoil it?" She sounded stubborn. She had been thinking about it all morning. And she already missed him.

"It just would. Trust me. I'm a grown-up. I know. If we got involved, someone would get hurt or upset about something, and then it would be all over."

"Does someone always get hurt?" Pip looked disappointed. This was not encouraging information.

"Almost always. And then you don't like each other anymore, and you don't get to stay friends. And he wouldn't see you. Think how sad that would be." Ophélie was very definite in her opinion on the subject.

"What if you got married? Then none of that would happen."

"I don't want to get married again. And neither does he. He got very badly hurt when his wife left him."

"Did he tell you that? About not wanting to get married again?" Pip sounded suspicious. It didn't sound likely to her.

"More or less. We talked about his marriage and divorce. It sounded very traumatic."

"Did he ask you to marry him?" She looked suddenly hopeful.

"Of course not. Don't be silly." It was a ridiculous conversation, from Ophélie's perspective.

"Then how do you know that's how he feels?"

"I just know it. Besides, I don't want to get re-married. I still feel married to your father." It sounded noble to her, but it made Pip angry, which surprised her mother.

"Well, he's dead, and he's not coming back. I think you should marry Matt, and then we could keep him."

"He may not want to be 'kept,' never mind how I feel. Why don't you marry him? I think he would suit you." She was teasing her, in order to end the awkward moment. She didn't like being told that Ted was dead and never coming back. It was all she thought about, and had for the last eleven months. It was hard to believe it was almost a year now. In some ways it felt like forever, in others like only minutes.

"I think he would suit me too," Pip said sensibly, "which is why you have to marry him."

"Maybe he'd like Andrea," Ophélie said to distract her, but crazier things had happened. She suddenly wondered if she should introduce them, but Pip had an instant and very negative opinion. Besides, she didn't want to lose him. She wanted Matt for them.

"No, he wouldn't," Pip said firmly. "He'd hate her. She's too strong for him. She likes to tell everyone what to do, including men. That's why they always leave her." It was an interesting assessment, and Ophélie knew her daughter wasn't entirely mistaken. Pip had overheard a lot of conversations between her parents about Andrea over the years, and had figured some of it out herself. Andrea had a way of emasculating men, and she was too independent, which was why she'd had to go to a sperm bank for a baby. No man so far had wanted to get that closely entangled with her. But it was an amazing perception for a child Pip's age, and Ophélie didn't disagree with her, although she didn't say it. But she was impressed by her wisdom. "He'd be much happier with you, and me," Pip said modestly, and then giggled. "Maybe we should ask him the next time we see him."

"I'm sure he'd love that. Why don't we just tell him. Or order him to marry us. That would do it." Ophélie smiled too.

"Yeah," Pip grinned, "I like that." She squinted her eyes in the sun, thinking about it. She looked delighted.

"You're a little monster," her mother teased her, and a few minutes later, they got home, and Ophélie unlocked the door. She hadn't been to the house in three months. She had purposely avoided it whenever she came into the city, and had had their mail forwarded all summer to Safe Harbour. It was the first time she'd been back since they left it. And the reality of their situation hit her like an express train as they entered. She had somehow allowed herself to believe, in the back of her mind, that when they came back, Ted and Chad would be there, waiting for them. As though this had been a trip, and the agony of the last year had been a bad joke. Chad would come down the stairs, grinning at her, and Ted would be standing in their bedroom doorway, waiting for her with that look that still turned her stomach upside down and her knees to jelly. The chemistry between them had been powerful for their entire marriage. But the house was empty. There was no escaping the truth. She and Pip were alone forever.

They both stood in the front door, as the same realization hit them at the same time, and their eyes filled with tears as they held each other.

"I hate it here," Pip said softly, as they clung to each other.

"So do I," her mother whispered.

Neither of them wanted to go upstairs or to their respective bedrooms. The reality of it was just too awful. And for the moment, Matt was forgotten. He had his own life, his own world. And they had theirs. There was no hiding from it.

Ophélie went out to the car and unloaded the bags, and Pip helped her drag them up the stairs. Even that was hard for them. They were both small and the bags were heavy, and there was no one to help them. Ophélie was breathless as she set both of Pip's bags down in her bedroom.

"I'll unpack for you in a minute," Ophélie said, trying to hang on to the steps she'd made over the summer, but she felt down a black hole again the moment they were back in the house she had once shared with her son and husband. It was as though the healing months at Safe Harbour had never happened.

"I can do it myself, Mom," Pip said sadly. She felt it too. In some ways it was worse now.

Ophélie was more alive again, and had feelings. The year of the robot had been better.

Ophélie dragged her own bags upstairs then, and her heart sank as she opened the closet. It was all still there. Every jacket, every suit, every shirt, every tie, all the shoes he had worn, even the old battered loafers he wore on weekends, that he'd had since Harvard. It was like reliving a nightmare. And she didn't even dare go into Chad's room, she knew it would kill her. This was bad enough, and as she unpacked her things, she could feel herself slipping backward. It was frightening.

By dinnertime, they were both silent and pale and exhausted, and they both jumped when the phone rang. They had just decided not to eat dinner for the moment, although Ophélie knew the child had to eat at some point, hungry or not. In her own case, she never hesitated to miss a meal.

Ophélie didn't move, there was no one she wanted to speak to, so Pip answered. And her face brightened slowly when she heard his voice.

"Hi, Matt. It's okay," she said in answer to his question, but he could hear in her voice that it wasn't, and then as her mother watched, she started crying. "No, it isn't, it's awful. It's horrible here. We hate it." She included her mother in the statement, and Ophélie thought of stopping her, and then didn't. If he was to be their friend, he might as well know how bad it was.

Pip listened for a long time and kept nodding, but at least the tears had stopped. She sat down on a kitchen chair as she listened. "Okay. I'll try. I'll tell my mother . . . I can't . . . I have to go to school tomorrow. When are you coming?" Whatever he had said at the other end, Ophélie saw that she looked pleased with the answer. "Okay . . . I'll ask her . . ." She turned to Ophélie then with her hand discreetly over the mouthpiece. "Do you want to talk to him?" But Ophélie shook her head and whispered.

"Tell him I'm busy." She didn't want to talk to anyone. She was too unhappy. And she knew she couldn't fake being cheerful. It was one thing for Pip to cry on his shoulder, but she couldn't. It didn't seem appropriate for her to do that, and she didn't want to.

"Okay," Pip said to Matt again, "I'll tell her. I'll call you tomorrow." Ophélie was beginning to wonder about the wisdom of daily contact with Matt, but maybe there was no harm in it. Whatever gave Pip comfort. And as soon as she hung up, Pip reported the conversation to her. "He said it's normal that we feel this way because we lived here with my brother and father, and pretty soon we'll feel better. He said to do

something fun tonight, like order Chinese
food, or a pizza or go out. And turn on some
music. Happy music. Real loud. And if we're
too sad, we should sleep together. He said we
should go shopping together tomorrow and
buy something silly, but I told him I couldn't, I
have to go to school. But his other ideas
sounded pretty good. Do you want to order
Chinese food, Mom?" They hadn't had it all
summer, and they both liked it. It was something different at least, which was Matt's plan.

"Not really, but it was sweet of him to suggest
it." Pip particularly liked the idea of the music.
And then Ophélie suddenly thought about it.
Why not, after all? It might help. "Do you want
Chinese food, Pip?" It seemed foolish since nei-
ther of them was hungry.

"Sure, why don't we just order egg rolls? And
fried wontons."

"I'd rather have dim sum," Ophélie said pensively, and then started looking on the counter
for the number they used for Chinese takeout,
and found it.

"I want shrimp fried rice too," Pip said, as her
mother called them and placed the order. And
half an hour later, the doorbell rang and all of it
appeared, and they sat in the kitchen and ate it.
By then, Pip had put on some truly awful music, as loud as they could tolerate. But they both

had to admit, they felt better than they had an hour before.

"It was kind of a silly idea," her mother smiled at her sheepishly, "but it was sweet of him to suggest it." And it had worked, better than she wanted to admit. It was embarrassing that some Chinese food and one of Pip's CDs could actually soothe some of the pain of the horrifying grief they had to live with. But even from the distance, he had cheered them both.

"Can I sleep with you tonight?" Pip asked hesitantly, as they walked upstairs, after they'd cleaned up the kitchen and put the leftovers in the fridge. Alice, the cleaning woman, had left them enough groceries for breakfast the next day, and Ophélie was going to buy more in the morning. And she looked startled at Pip's request. In the whole last year, she'd never asked her mother once if she could sleep with her. She had been afraid to intrude on her mother, and in her own intense grief, Ophélie had never offered.

"I guess so. Are you sure you want to?" It had been Matt's idea, but Pip thought it another good one.

"I'd like to." They each took baths in their own bathrooms, and then Pip turned up in her mother's bedroom in pajamas. It suddenly felt like a slumber party, and Pip giggled as she got into her mother's bed. Somehow, by remote control, Matt had changed the entire texture of their evening. And Pip looked blissful as she snuggled in the big bed next to her mother, and was asleep in minutes. And Ophélie was startled at how much comfort it gave her to hug the little body close to hers. She wondered why she hadn't thought of it sooner. They couldn't do it every night, but it was certainly an appealing option on nights like this one. And within minutes, she was sleeping as soundly as her daughter.

They both woke with a start when they heard the alarm ring. They had forgotten where they were, and why they were sleeping together, and then they both remembered. But they didn't have time to get depressed again, they had to hurry to get ready. Pip went to brush her teeth while Ophélie ran downstairs to make breakfast. She saw the Chinese food in the fridge, and with a smile, cracked open a fortune cookie and ate it.

"You will have happiness and good fortune all year," the fortune said, as Ophélie smiled to herself. "Thank you. I need it." She poured milk into cereal for Pip, orange juice for both of them, and dropped a slice of bread in the toaster. And then made herself a cup of coffee. Pip was down the stairs five minutes later in her school uniform, as Ophélie reached outside the front door for the morning paper. She had hardly read it all summer, and barely missed it. There was nothing exciting happening, but she glanced at it anyway, and then ran upstairs to dress so she could drive Pip to school. The mornings were always a little hectic, but she liked that, it kept her from thinking.

Twenty minutes later, she was in the car, with Mousse, driving Pip to school, and the child was smiling as she looked out the window, and then back at her mother.

"You know, that stuff Matt suggested really worked last night. I liked sleeping with you."

"I liked it too," Ophélie admitted. More than she'd expected. It was so much less lonely than sleeping in her big bed all alone, mourning her husband.

"Can we do it again sometime?" Pip looked hopeful.

"I'd love to." Ophélie smiled at her as they approached the school.

"I'll have to call and thank him," Pip said, and with that, the car stopped, and Ophélie kissed her hastily, wished her luck in school, and with a wave, Pip was gone to her friends, her day, and her teachers. Ophélie was still smiling to herself as she drove home to the much-too-big house on Clay Street. She had been so happy when they moved into it, and now it made her so un-happy. But she had to admit, last night had turned out better than she'd expected. And she was grateful for Matt's input, and creative ideas.

She walked slowly up the stairs with Mousse, and sighed as she unlocked the front door. She still had a few things to unpack, and groceries to order, and that afternoon she wanted to go by the homeless shelter. It was enough to keep her busy until she picked Pip up at three-thirty. But as she walked past Chad's room, she couldn't help herself. She opened the door and looked in. The shades were drawn and it was dark, and so empty and sad, it nearly tore her heart out. His posters were still there, and all his treasures. The photographs of him with his friends, the trophies from when he'd played sports when he was younger. But the room looked different than when she last saw it. It had a dry quality, like a leaf that had fallen and was slowly dying, and a musty smell. And as she always did, she went to his bed, and put her head on his pillow. She could still smell him, although more faintly. And then, as always happened when she walked into this room, the sobs engulfed her. And no amount of Chinese food or loud music would change that. They only postponed the inevitable agony, as she realized once again that Chad was never coming home.

She had to tear herself away finally, and went back to her bedroom, feeling drained and exhausted. But she refused to give in to it. She saw Ted's clothes hanging there, and it was almost too much for her. She lifted a sleeve to her face, and the rough tweed felt incredibly familiar. She could still smell his cologne and almost hear him. She almost couldn't bear it. But she forced herself not to give in to it. She couldn't. She knew that now. She couldn't afford to become a robot again, to stop feeling, or to let the feelings destroy her. She had to learn to live with pain, to go on in spite of it. If nothing else, she had to keep going for Pip's sake. She was grateful she had group that afternoon and could talk to them. The group was about to end soon, and she wasn't sure what she was going to do without them, and their support.

When she went to group, she told them about the night before, the Chinese food and the loud music, and Pip sleeping in her bed with her. And they saw nothing wrong with that. They saw nothing wrong with any of it, even with dating, although she insisted she wasn't ready for that, and didn't want to. They were all at different stages of their grieving. But at least it was comforting to share it with them.

"So, do you have a girlfriend yet, Mr. Feigenbaum?" she teased him as they left the building together. She liked him. He was honest and open and kind, and willing to make an enormous effort to recover, more than most.

"Not yet, but I'm working on it. What about you?" He was a warm roly-poly old man with pink cheeks and a shock of white hair. He looked like one of Santa's helpers.

"I don't want a boyfriend. You sound like my daughter." She laughed at him.

"She's a smart girl. If I were forty years younger, young lady, I'd give you a run for your money. What about your mother? Is she single?" Ophélie just laughed at him again, and they waved as they left each other.

And after that, Ophélie stopped at the shelter. It was in a narrow back street South of Market, in a fairly dicey neighborhood, but she told herself that she could hardly expect it to be in Pacific Heights. But the people she saw at the desk and wandering in the halls were all friendly. She told them she wanted to make an appointment to sign up as a volunteer, and they asked her to come back the next morning. She could have called to make the appointment, but she wanted to see it. And as she left, two old men were standing outside with shopping carts full of everything they owned, as a volunteer handed them styrofoam cups full of steaming coffee. She could see herself doing that. It didn't seem very complicated, and it might do her good to feel useful. Better than sitting at home crying, and smelling Ted's jackets and Chad's pillow. She just couldn't let herself do that, and she knew it. Not again. Not for yet another year. The year before, of mourning them, had been a nightmare and nearly killed her. Somehow she had to make this year better. The anniversary of their death was coming up in four weeks, and although she was dreading it, she knew that in the second year of their grief, she had to make it better. Not just for herself, but for Pip as well. She owed it to her. And maybe working at the shelter would help her. She hoped so.

She was on her way to pick Pip up at school, and was stopped at a light, when she glanced into the window of a shoe store. She wasn't paying attention at first, and then she smiled to herself when she saw them. They were giant fluffy slippers for grown-ups, that were made of *Sesame Street* characters. There were giant blue ones of Grover, and a red pair of Elmo. They were perfect, and without thinking, she pulled over and double-parked, and ran into the shoe store. She bought Grover for herself, and Elmo for Pip, and then she ran back out to the car with them in a shopping bag. She made it to school just in time to see Pip come out of the building and head for the corner where she always waited for her mother. Pip saw her as soon as she got there. She looked tired and a little disheveled, but delighted.

She hopped into the car with a big grin on her face, happy to see her mother. "I've got great teachers. I like all of them except one, Miss Giulani, who's a dork and I hate her. But the others are all really cool, Mom." She sounded not a minute older than eleven when she said it, and Ophélie grinned at her in amusement.

"I'm very glad they're cool, Mademoiselle Pip," she said, lapsing into French, and then pointed at the bag in the backseat. "I bought us a present."

"What is it?" Pip looked pleased as she pulled the bag into the front seat and looked inside, and then she squealed and looked at her mother in amazement. "You did it! You did it!"

"Did what?" Ophélie looked confused for a moment.

"Bought something silly! Remember? That's what Matt said last night. He said to go shopping today and buy something silly. And I told him I had to go to school and couldn't. But you did it anyway! Mom, I love you!" She put the Elmo slippers on right over her school shoes and looked ecstatic, as Ophélie stared at her in amazement. She didn't know if it had been a subliminal message or just serendipity, but she had never thought of what he'd said, or of him, when she bought them. She just liked the slippers. But they were certainly silly. And Pip loved them. "You have to put them on when we get home. Promise?"

"I promise," Ophélie said solemnly, smiling as they drove home. It had actually been a very decent day after all. And she was excited about her appointment at the shelter. She told Pip about it on the drive home, and she was impressed and pleased to see her mother doing better. It had been horrible coming home the day before, but things seemed to be improving. The black holes didn't seem to be quite as dark, or as deep, and Ophélie was able to get out of them more quickly. It was what they had told her at the group would happen eventually, and she hadn't believed them. But things were slowly getting better after all.

Pip made Ophélie put the Grover slippers on when they got home, and after she had a glass of milk, an apple, and a cookie, she called Matt, before she went to do her homework. He was just coming in from the beach, and her mother was upstairs somewhere, probably in her room, Pip thought, as she sat on a kitchen stool and waited for him to answer. He was just on his way in, and he sounded a little breathless, as though he'd been running to the phone.

"I called to tell you how smart you are," she announced, and he smiled the minute he heard her.

"Is that you, Miss Pip?"

"Yes, it is. And you're a genius. We ordered Chinese food, and I put on my best CD, as loud as Mom would let me. And I slept with her last night, and we loved it . . . and today she bought us both *Sesame Street* slippers. She got Grover, and I got Elmo. And I really like my teachers, except for one, who's disgusting." He could hear in her voice how much better things were than they'd been the night before, and he felt as though he'd just won a national award. She made him embarrassingly happy.

"I want to see the slippers. I'm jealous. I want some."

"Your feet are too big, otherwise I'd ask Mom to buy some."

"That's too bad. I always liked Elmo. And Kermit."

"Me too. I like Elmo better." She rattled on then about school, and her friends, and her teachers, and after a while, she told him she had to do her homework.

"You do that. Give your mom my love, I'll call you tomorrow," he promised, feeling the way he used to when he called his children. Happy and sad, excited, and hopeful, as though there was something to live for. He had to remind himself that she wasn't his daughter. They were both smiling when they got off the phone, and Pip stuck her head in her mother's door on her way to her bedroom.

"I talked to Matt and told him about the slippers. He said to send you his love," Pip gloated, as Ophélie smiled at her from across her bedroom.

"That's nice of him." Ophélie didn't look excited, just happy and peaceful.

"Can I sleep with you again tonight?" Pip asked, almost shyly. She was wearing the Elmo slippers, and had taken her shoes off. And Ophélie was wearing the Grovers, as she'd promised.

"Is that Matt's idea?" she asked curiously.

"No, mine." Pip was being honest. He hadn't made any suggestions this time. He didn't need to. He had helped them the night before, and they were doing fine now, for the moment.

"Sounds good to me," Ophélie said, as Pip hopped and skipped to her room to do her homework.

It was another good night for both of them. Ophélie wasn't sure how long the new sleeping arrangement would go on, but they both liked it. She couldn't imagine why she hadn't thought of it before. It solved a myriad of problems and gave comfort to them both. She couldn't help thinking then of the positive changes Matt had made in their life.

13

OPHÉLIE'S APPOINTMENT AT THE WEXLER Center was at nine-fifteen. She dropped Pip off at school first, and headed for the area South of Market immediately after. She had worn an old beaten-up black leather jacket and jeans, and Pip commented on the way to school that she looked nice.

"Are you going somewhere, Mom?" she asked, in her white middy and navy blue pleated skirt, which were her school uniform. She hated wearing it, but Ophélie had always thought it solved a multitude of fashion decision problems at that hour of the morning. It made Pip look sweet and young. She wore a navy tie for important school events, and her red curls seemed like the perfect accent to it.

"Yes, I am," Ophélie said with a quiet smile. She loved the nights they had been sharing in her bed. It dimmed the pain of the loneliness, and quelled the agony of mornings. She didn't know why she hadn't thought of it before, mostly because she didn't want to lean on Pip for comfort, but it was turning out to be a blessing for them both. And she was grateful to Matt for the suggestion. She had slept really well next to Pip for the first time in months, and waking up to Pip hugging her and looking into her eyes nose to nose was the happiest thing that had happened to her since Ted died. He hadn't been nearly as cozy and friendly in the morning, and hanging around in bed and cuddling, or telling her he loved her as he woke, had never been his thing.

She told Pip about the Wexler Center then, what they did and the fact that she hoped to volunteer.

"If they want me." She had no idea what they would want her to do, or if she could really be useful to them. Maybe if nothing else, they would let her answer phones.

"I'll tell you all about it when I see you this afternoon," she promised as she dropped Pip off on the corner, and watched her head into the school driveway with her friends. She was so busy talking to them, she didn't even turn to wave.

Ophélie parked in a space on Folsom Street,

and walked into the alley where the Wexler Center was, and she saw a cluster of drunks, sitting against a wall as she went past. They didn't have far to go to the Center, but it seemed to be too much trouble for them even to move. She glanced at them, and they seemed not to notice her, they appeared to be lost in their own private world, which was more a private hell. Ophélie walked past them with her head down, feeling silently sorry for them.

She walked into the same lobby she'd seen the day before. It was a large open room hung with posters, and paint chipping off the walls. There was a long desk and a different receptionist than she'd seen. She was a middle-aged African American woman who was manning both the desk and the phones. She looked competent and pleasant, and had tightly braided salt-and-pepper hair, and she looked up expectantly at Ophélie. In spite of the simple clothes she'd worn, she looked well kept and beautifully groomed, and she looked out of place in the threadbare room. None of the furniture matched and it all seemed beaten up. It was easy to guess they'd gotten it at Goodwill, and there was a coffeemaker with styrofoam cups in the corner.

"May I help you?" the woman at the desk asked pleasantly.

"I have an appointment with Louise Anderson," Ophélie said quietly. "I think she's the head of volunteers." And with that, the woman at the desk smiled.

"That and the head of marketing, donations, ordering groceries, supplies, PR, and hiring new talent. We all wear a lot of hats around here." It sounded interesting to Ophélie, as she walked around the room, looking at posters and literature, while she waited. She didn't have long to wait. Two minutes later, a young woman seemed to burst into the room. She had bright red hair like Pip's and wore it in two long braids down her back, one hanging over the other. She obviously had a huge mane of hair. She was wearing combat boots and jeans, and a lumberjack shirt, but in spite of it, she was obviously pretty, and looked utterly feminine. She had a lithe grace, like a dancer, and was small like Ophélie and Pip. But she exuded energy, and kindness, enthusiasm and power. She had a take-charge style about her that suggested confidence and ease.

"Miss Mackenzie?" she asked with a warm smile, as Ophélie stood up to greet her and nodded that she was. "Will you follow me?" She walked with a quick, sure step to a back office, with a bulletin board that covered an entire wall. There were bits of scrap paper, bulletins, announcements, messages from government agencies, photographs, and an endless list of projects and names. It was overwhelming just looking at all she presumably had on her plate. On the opposite wall were photographs of people at the Center, and her small desk and chair and two chairs for visitors, nearly filled the small, sunny room. Like her, the room was tiny, cheerful, chock full of information, and blatantly efficient.

"What brings you to us?" Louise Anderson asked, smiling warmly straight into Ophélie's eyes. She was clearly not the normal profile of their volunteers, who were usually college students, or grad students accruing hours toward a social work degree, or people who were somehow related to their field.

"I'd like to volunteer," Ophélie said, feeling shy.

"We can sure use all the help we can get. What are you good at?" The question stumped her for a minute. She had no idea, and even less of what they needed from her. She felt totally out of her league. "Or maybe I should say what do you like to do?"

"I'm not sure. I have two kids." She winced as she said it, but correcting it would have sounded pathetic, she thought, so she didn't. "I've been married for eighteen years . . . or was . . ." She was brave enough to say that at least. "I can drive, shop, clean, do laundry, I'm fairly good with kids, and dogs." It sounded ridiculous even to her own ears, but she hadn't thought for years about what her real skills were. And it all sounded so foolish and limited now. "I was a biology major in college. And I know a fair amount about energy technology, which was my husband's field," another useless bit of knowledge they wouldn't need, "and I have some experience with dealing with family members of people who have mental illness." She thought of Chad. It was all she could think of as she looked into Louise Anderson's eyes.

"Are you going through a divorce at the moment?" She had picked up the reference to having been married, and the "was."

Ophélie shook her head, trying to look normal, and not scared, but she was. It was intimidating being here and feeling so useless and unskilled. But the woman across the desk from her was gazing at her with openness and respect. She just needed to know more.

"My husband died a year ago," she gulped nearly audibly, "and my son. I have an eleven-year-old daughter. And a lot of time on my hands."

"I'm sorry about your son and your husband," she said sincerely, and went on. "Your experience with mental illness could be very useful to you here. A lot of the people who come through here are mentally ill. It's just a simple fact of homelessness much of the time. If they're too sick, we try to refer them to the right agencies and clinics. But if they're relatively functional, we let them in. Most of the shelters have criteria that eliminate people who exhibit bizarre behavior, which makes many of the homeless population ineligible for the shelters. It's a pretty crazy rule, but it makes things easier for the shelters. We're a little soft on that here, but as a result, we see some pretty sick people."

"What happens to them?" Ophélie asked, looking concerned. She liked this woman, and hoped she would get to know her better. She had a peaceful but powerful positive energy that seemed to fill the room. And her passion for what she did was contagious. Ophélie was excited about being there and the prospect of working for them, even as a volunteer.

"Most of our clients go back on the street after a night or two. The family units stay, but most of them move on to permanent shelters. We're not permanent. We're a temporary facility. We're a Band-Aid on the face of homelessness. We let them stay as long as we can, we try to find them referrals to agencies, or long-term shelters, or foster care for kids. We try to meet their needs in every way we can, clothe them, house them, get them medical assistance when they need it, apply for government benefits when that's appropriate. We're kind of like an emergency room. We give them lots of TLC and information, a bed, food, a hand to hold. We like it because we serve more people this way, but there are also a lot of problems we can't solve. It breaks your heart sometimes, but there's only so much we can do. We do what we can, and they move on."

"It sounds like you're doing a lot as it is," Ophélie said with eyes full of admiration.

"Not enough. This is a business that breaks your heart. You're emptying an ocean with a teacup, and every time you think you've made a difference, the ocean fills up again faster than you can look. The ones that kill me are the kids. They're in the same boat with everyone else, and more liable to drown, and it's not their fault. They're the victims in all this, but so are a lot of the adults."

"Can the children stay with their parents?" Ophélie ached thinking about them. She couldn't even imagine Pip homeless on the streets at her age, and many of them were younger, or even born there. It was a tragedy of our age, but as she listened, Ophélie was glad she had come. It had been the right choice for her, and she was grateful to Blake for suggesting it. She was excited about coming to work at Wexler.

"The kids can only stay with their parents, or parent, as the case may be, if they're accepted into a long-term family shelter, or some kind of safe house, like for abused mothers and kids. They can't stay out on the street, the minute the cops see them they take them into protective services and foster them out. It's no life for a kid on the streets. A quarter of our population dies on the street every year, from weather, disease, accident, trauma, violence. A kid wouldn't survive half as long as an adult. They're better off in foster homes," which seemed sad to Ophélie too. "Do you have any idea what hours you'd like to work? Days? Nights? Probably days, if you're a single mother with a kid in school." The term "single mother" hit her like a punch in the solar plexus. She had never thought of herself that way, but she was now, much as she hated it.

"I'm available from nine to three every day. I don't know . . . maybe two or three days a week?" It seemed like a lot, even to her, but she had nothing else to do, and far too much time on her hands. She could only spend so much time in the park with Mousse. This might give some purpose to her days, and do someone else some good. She liked that idea.

"What I like to do with volunteers," Louise said honestly, flipping one of her braids back over her shoulder, "is give them a good honest look at us first. No frills. The real thing. You can spend a few days with us, and see how you feel. If you think it's what you're looking for and what you want to do. And after that, if we both think it's a match, we train you for a week, two at the most, depending on which area appeals to you, and then we put you to work. Hard, hard work," she warned, and meant it. "Nobody here messes around. The full-time staff works a twelve-hour day most of the time, sometimes more if we have some kind of crisis, and we often do. Even the volunteers work their asses off while they're here." She grinned. "How does that sound to you?"

"Terrific, actually." Ophélie smiled back at her, suddenly hopeful. "It sounds like just what I need. I just hope I'm what you need."

"We'll see." Louise stood up and smiled broadly. "I'm not trying to scare you off, Ophélie. I just want to be honest. I don't want you to get the impression that it's easier than it is. We have a lot of fun here, but some of what we do is just plain awful, dirty, depressing, grueling, dangerous, exhausting. You may go home feeling great some days, or cry yourself to sleep other days. We see just about everything there is to see on the streets. And I don't know if you'd be interested, but we have an outreach program too."

"What do they do?" Ophélie was intrigued.

"They drive around in two vans that were donated to us, and they look for people on the streets, people who are too sick, mentally or physically, in body and spirit, to come to us. So we go to them. We take them food, clothing, medical supplies, if they're too sick, we try and get them into a hospital, or a program, or a shelter. There are a lot of people out there who are too disoriented to make it here. No matter how accessible we try to make ourselves, there are some people out there who are too scared, or broken, or disenfranchised to reach out. We have at least one outreach van on the street every night to find them. Two vans if we can staff them. They go to the clients who need us most of all. The ones who can get to us here are at least thinking a little more clearly and on their feet. Some of the people out there are actually doing okay, but they need help and may be too scared to try and get it. They don't trust us, even though they may have heard about us. Sometimes all we do on the streets at night is sit and talk to them. And personally, I always try to get the runaways off the streets. But a lot of what they're running away from is worse than what they run into on the streets. There's some pretty ugly stuff that goes on in this world. We see most of it, or the results of it, every day, particularly at night. The days are a little more tame. But that's why we go out there at night, that's when they need us most."

"It sounds like fairly dangerous work," Ophélie said sensibly. She didn't think she should risk that because of Pip. Besides, she wanted to be home at night with her.

"It is dangerous. We go out around seven or eight o'clock at night, and we stay out late, doing whatever needs to be done. They've had a few close calls. But so far, none of our outreach staff have gotten hurt. They're pretty aware of what goes on on the streets."

"Are they armed?" Ophélie asked, impressed. These were brave people, doing miraculous work.

Louise laughed and shook her head. "Only with their heads and hearts. You have to want to be out there. Don't ask me why or how, but personally, deep in your heart and gut, it has to be worth the risk. You don't need to worry about that. There's plenty you can do for us here at the house." Ophélie nodded, the street work sounded dangerous to her. Too much so

for a single mother, as Louise put it, solely responsible for a child. "When do you want to
start?"

Ophélie thought about it for a moment. Her
time was her own, and she didn't have to pick
up Pip till after three o'clock. "Whenever you
like. My time is free."

"How about now? You can give Miriam a
hand at the desk. She can introduce you to people as they come in and out, and she can explain a lot of what happens here. How does that
sound?"

"Great." Ophélie was excited as she followed
Louise back to the front desk, and Louise explained to Miriam what she had in mind. The
woman with the gray hair looked thrilled.

"Boy, can I use your help today." She beamed.
"I've got a stack of filing back here, all our caseworkers dumped everything on my desk last
night. They do that every time I go home!"
There were files, case folders, brochures about
programs and other shelters that they kept in reference files. There was a mountain of stuff. More
than enough to keep Ophélie busy until three
o'clock, and for days after that.

She hardly stopped all day, and it seemed like
every five minutes, someone came either in
or out, and always passed the desk. They
needed reference material, caseload informa-

tion, referral numbers, documents, entry forms for intake clients, or sometimes they just stopped to say hi. And Miriam introduced Ophélie to staff members every chance they got. They were an interesting-looking group of people, mostly young, although there were a number of them who were as old as, or older than, Ophélie. And just before she left, two young men came in, who looked different from all the rest, and between them a slight young Hispanic woman. Miriam smiled the moment she saw them. One of the men was African American, and the other was Asian. Both were handsome, young, and tall.

"Here come our *Top Gun* guys, or at least that's what I call them." And then she turned to them with a broad grin. It was obvious that she liked them. And Ophélie was struck by the fact that the young woman was unusually pretty, she looked like a model. But when she turned her head, Ophélie could see that she had a nasty scar that ran the length of her face. "What are you guys doing here so early?"

"We came to check out one of the vans, we had trouble with it last night. And we need to load some stuff for tonight." Miriam introduced her to them then as a new volunteer checking them out. "Give her to us," the Asian man said with a grin. "We're a man short since Aggie left." Aggie didn't sound like a man to her, but all three of them were open and friendly to Ophélie. The Asian man's name was Bob, the African American was Jefferson, and the Hispanic girl's name was Milagra, but the two men called her Millie. They left after a few minutes, and went behind the building to the garage where the vans were kept.

"What do they do?" Ophélie asked with interest as she went back to work at the file cabinets behind Miriam's desk.

"That's our outreach team. They're heroes around here. They're all a little crazy, and a lot wild. They're out there every night, five nights a week. We have a weekend crew that takes over when they're not here. But these guys are incredible. All of them. I went out with them once, it damn near broke my heart . . . and scared me to death." Her eyes were filled with affection and respect.

"Isn't it dangerous for a woman to go with them?" Ophélie looked impressed. They seemed like heroes to her too.

"Millie knows her stuff. She's an ex-cop. She's on permanent disability, she got shot in the chest and lost a lung, but she's as tough as the guys. She's a martial arts expert. Millie can take care of herself, and the guys."

"Is that how she got the scar, doing police

work?" Ophélie asked with growing respect for all of them. They were the bravest people she'd ever met, and the most caring. And the Hispanic woman was remarkably beautiful, in spite of the scar. But Ophélie was curious about her now.

"No, she got that as a kid. Child abuse. Her father. He cut her when she defended herself when he tried to rape her. I think she was eleven." A lot of them had stories like that, but it shocked Ophélie to realize that Milagra had been the same age as Pip when it happened. "Maybe that's why she went into the department."

It was an amazing day for Ophélie. And throughout the day, homeless people of varying sizes, ages, and genders came in to take showers, have a meal, sleep, or just get off the streets and shuffle around the lobby for a while. Some of them looked remarkably coherent and responsible, and even clean, and others looked confused and had glazed eyes. A few were obviously inebriated, and one or two looked like they were on drugs. The Wexler Center was extremely generous in their criteria for admission. No one could use alcohol or drugs on the premises, but if they were in less-than-ideal condition when they got there, they were still allowed to stay.

Ophélie's head was reeling by the time she left and promised to be back the next day. She could hardly wait to come back, and she told Pip all about it on their way back to the house after school. Pip was understandably impressed, not only by what she heard of the Center, but by the fact that her mother had gone there and wanted to volunteer.

She told Matt all about it when he called that afternoon. Ophélie was upstairs having a shower, she felt filthy after working at the Center all day, and she was starving when she came downstairs with her hair in a towel. She hadn't even stopped for lunch. Pip was still talking to Matt on the phone.

"Matt says hi," Pip said, and then went on speaking to him as Ophélie made herself a sandwich. In the past few weeks, her appetite had improved.

"Say hi to him too," Ophélie said, taking a bite of her sandwich.

"He thinks you're very cool for what you're doing," Pip transmitted, and then told him all about the sculpture project she was doing in art. And she had volunteered to help with the layouts of the yearbook too. She loved talking to him, although it wasn't as good as sitting with him on the beach. But more than any-thing, she didn't want to lose touch, and neither did he. And then finally, she handed her mother the phone.

"It sounds like you're up to some interesting doings," he said admiringly. "What's it like?" Matt asked her.

"Scary, exciting, wonderful, smelly, touching, sad. I love it. The people who work there are terrific, and the ones who come to the shelter for help are really nice."

"You're an amazing woman. I'm impressed." And he meant it. She had impressed him from the first.

"Don't be. All I did was file papers, and look lost. I have no idea what I'm doing, or if they'll want me by the end of the week." She had promised them three days, and had two left. But so far, she loved it.

"They'll want you. Just don't do anything dangerous, or put yourself at risk. You can't afford to, with Pip."

"Believe me, I know." The fact that Louise Anderson had referred to her as a single mother had made the point, uncomfortably so. "So, how's the beach?"

"Absolutely dead without the two of you," he said sadly. Although the weather had been terrific in the two days since they left. It was hot and sunny and there were bright blue skies every day. September was one of the warmest

months at the beach, and Ophélie was sorry not
to be there, as was Pip. "I was thinking of coming in this weekend to see you, if that suits you,
unless you'd rather come out here."

"I have a feeling Pip has soccer practice on
Saturday morning . . . maybe we could come
out Sunday . . ."

"Why don't I come in? If that works for you,
I don't want to intrude."

"You won't be intruding. Pip will be thrilled.
And I'd love to see you too," she said, sounding
enthusiastic. She was in a great mood, despite
her long day. Being at the Center had been in-
vigorating for her.

"I'll take you both out to dinner. Ask Pip
where she'd like to go, and you can tell me all
about your work. I'm dying to hear about it."

"I don't think I'm going to be doing anything
important. They have to train me for a week,
and then I guess I'll just be a spare pair of hands
for anyone who needs them. Mostly referrals
and phones. But at least it's something." It was
better than sitting in Chad's room, crying at
home. And he knew that too.

"I'll come in around five on Saturday. See you
then."

"Thanks again, Matt," she said, and handed
the phone back to Pip so she could say good-
bye to him. And then Ophélie went upstairs to

read some material they'd given her at the Center. Articles, studies, data about homelessness, and the Center. It was fascinating and heart-wrenching stuff.

And as Ophélie lay on her bed, in a pink cashmere robe, with clean sheets under her, she couldn't help thinking how lucky they were. Their house was large and comfortable and beautiful, filled with antiques Ted had insisted she buy. The rooms were sunny, the colors bright. Their bedroom was done in bright yellow-flowered chintz, and Pip's room was done in pale pink silk, it was a dream for a little girl. Chad had had a typical teenage boy's room, in dark blue plaids. There was a study for Ted in brown leather, which she never went into anymore, and a small sitting room off her bedroom in pale blue and yellow watered silk. And downstairs there was a large, inviting living room filled with English antiques, with a big fireplace, a formal dining room, and a den. The kitchen was state of the art, or had been when they remodeled the house five years before. And in the basement, there was a large playroom with a billiards table and a Ping-Pong table, video games, and a maid's room they'd never used. There was a small pretty garden out back, and the front of the house was a dignified stone facade, with manicured trees in big stone pots on either side of the front door, and a trimmed hedge. It had been Ted's dream house, and never hers. But there was no question, it was beautiful, and light-years away from the agony of the people who went to the Wexler Center, or even worked there. As Ophélie sat staring into space, Pip appeared in the doorway and looked at her.

"Are you okay, Mom?" She had that same glazed look she'd had for the entire year before, and Pip was worried about her.

"I'm fine. I was just thinking how fortunate we are. There are people out there on the streets who never sleep in a bed, who have no bathroom, can't shower, are hungry, and have no one to love them and nowhere to go. It's hard to imagine, Pip. They're only a few miles away from here, and they might as well be somewhere in the third world."

"It's so sad, Mom." Pip looked at her with big eyes, but she was relieved that nothing was wrong with her mom. She was always afraid her mother would slip back into the dark depths of despair, and she didn't want her to go there again.

"Yes, it is, sweetheart."

Ophélie made dinner for them that night. There were lamb chops, which she burned a little, and they each ate one. Neither of them was a big eater, but she thought she should make an effort at least to improve their diet. She made a salad, and warmed tinned carrots, which Pip said were disgusting. She said she preferred corn.

"I'll keep it in mind." Ophélie smiled at her.

And that night, without even asking, Pip went to sleep in her mother's bed. When the alarm went off in the morning, they both hurried to shower, dress, and have breakfast. Ophélie looked excited as she dropped Pip off at school, and headed for work at the Wexler Center. It was exactly what she had wanted, and what she needed. For the first time in years, there was a purpose to her life.

14

THE REST OF THE WEEK FLEW BY FOR BOTH OF them, as Pip settled into school, and Ophélie tried out at the Wexler Center. And by Friday afternoon, there was no doubt in her mind, or anyone else's. She was ready to volunteer three days a week, and they wanted her.

She was going to work Mondays, Wednesdays, and Fridays, and the following week they were going to train her, by having her follow various staff members for several hours each. She had to give them a medical certificate, showing that she was in good health, and clear a criminal check, which they said they'd take care of for her. They fingerprinted her on Friday before she left. And they needed two personal references as well. Andrea said she would supply one, and Ophélie called her attorney and asked him to send the second. Everything was all set.

She wasn't sure yet exactly what she'd be doing for them, it sounded like an assortment of everything, helping whoever needed a spare pair of hands on the days she was in. They were also going to train her to do intakes. She still felt relatively inadequate, but she was more than willing to learn. And she had gotten a glowing recommendation from Miriam at the end of the week. Ophélie thanked her warmly as she left.

"Well, I made the grade," Ophélie said proudly when she picked Pip up at school on Friday afternoon. "They want me as a volunteer at Wexler." She was truly pleased. It gave her a sense of accomplishment and being needed, and maybe even making some small difference in the world.

"That's cool, Mom! Wait till we tell Matt tomorrow!" He had offered to watch Pip play soccer, but she said she'd rather he came another time to see a game. Saturday was just going to be a practice and their first day. She was small and delicate, but she was also fast, and played well. She had been playing for two years as part of her PE requirement at school. And she liked it a lot better than ballet.

Pip finished her homework on Friday, and had a friend over to spend the night, and Andrea came over to have dinner with them. She picked up from Pip that Matt was coming to take them to dinner the following day, and raised an eyebrow at Ophélie.

"You're holding out on me, old friend. The child molester's coming here?" She looked amused.

"He wanted to see Pip," Ophélie said benignly, and believed it was true, although she was pleased to see him too, and considered him a friend. "Maybe we should stop calling him that one of these days."

"Maybe the term 'boyfriend' would suit him better," she said, as Ophélie objected instantly with a shake of her head.

"Hardly. I have no interest in having a boyfriend. Only a friend." And she knew from their conversations that Matt felt the same way. She had decided that romance was no longer in the cards for her, nor did she want it to be. Ever again.

"That's what you're interested in. What about him? Guys don't come into town to take women to dinner, just to see their little girls. Trust me on that one. I know men." That she did, as they both knew.

"Maybe some do." Ophélie held firm.

"He's just biding his time," Andrea said confidently. "As soon as he thinks you're comfortable, he'll make a move."

"I hope not," Ophélie said, looking sincere, and then, to change the subject, she told Andrea about her week at Wexler. Andrea was impressed, and glad she'd found something to do.

But the following afternoon, when the doorbell rang, and Ophélie went to answer it, Andrea's assessment of her friendship with Matt crossed her mind as she opened the door. And she ardently hoped Andrea was wrong.

He was standing there in a leather jacket and gray slacks, a plain gray turtleneck, and a well-shined pair of loafers. It was the kind of outfit Ted would have worn, only better. Ted never remembered to shine his shoes, nor cared. He was too concerned with more important things. Ophélie shined them for him.

Matt smiled the moment he saw her, and as soon as Pip bounded down the stairs and he saw her, Ophélie knew her friend was wrong, however well she thought she knew men. Andrea was wrong about this one, there was no doubt in Ophélie's mind, and she was immensely relieved. He exuded fatherly kindness to Pip, and brotherly concern for her. After Pip had shown him her room and her treasures, and her latest drawings, and had finally calmed down, Ophélie told him a little about the Wexler Center, and he sounded impressed and intrigued. She even told him about the out-reach team.

"I hope you're not planning to join them," he said quietly, with a look of concern. "That's an important aspect of their work, I'm sure, and a good thing, but it sounds dangerous to me."

"I'm sure it is. They're all very skilled. The woman on the team is an ex-policewoman, one of the men is an ex-cop and a martial arts expert, and so is she, and the third one is an ex–Navy SEAL. They don't need any help from me!" She smiled, and Pip joined them again then. She was thrilled to have Matt visiting them, and when her mother left the room to get Matt a glass of wine, Pip whispered to him about the portrait of her he was doing.

"How's it coming? Did you work on it this week?" She knew it was going to be the best present her mother had ever gotten, and she could hardly wait to see her face when she did.

"I'm just getting started." He smiled at his young friend. He hoped she wouldn't be disappointed in the end result, but he liked the work he had done on it so far. His own feelings for Pip made it easier to capture her, it was as much about her spirit and her soul as it was about the bright red hair and gentle brown eyes with the amber lights in them. He would have liked to paint a portrait of Ophélie too, although he hadn't done one of an adult in a long time. But he would have liked to try.

Shortly before seven, they got up to leave and go to dinner, and as they reached the front door, Matt stopped in his tracks.

"You forgot something," he said, looking down at Pip, and she looked surprised.

"We can't take Mousse to a restaurant," she said in a serious voice. She was wearing a little black skirt and a red sweater, and she looked very grown-up. She had dressed carefully for him, and her mother had done her hair with a brand-new barrette. "We can only take Moussy to restaurants at the beach," she explained.

"I wasn't thinking of him, although I should have. We'll bring him a doggy bag. You didn't show me the Elmo and Grover slippers," he said reproachfully, and Pip laughed.

"Do you want to see them?" She looked pleased. He remembered everything she told him. He always did.

"We're not leaving till I do," he said firmly. He took a step back and crossed his arms, with an expectant look as Ophélie smiled at them both. And then he looked at her too.

"I'm serious. Both of you. I want to see Elmo and Grover. I think you should model them for me." He looked as though he meant it, and Pip ran up the stairs to get them, looking ecstatic. She returned a minute later with both pairs, and handed the Grover ones to her mother.

Feeling silly, Ophélie put them on, as Pip put on hers, and they both stood there in the over-size fuzzy slippers as Matt smiled approval. "They're terrific. I love them. Now I'm really jealous. I want a pair too. Can't you find them in my size?"

"I don't think so," Pip said apologetically. "Mom said she could barely get a pair for her, and she has pretty small feet."

"I'm crushed," he said, as they changed shoes again and he followed them out of the house, and down the steps to his car.

They had a lovely time at dinner, chatting about assorted things. And it occurred to Ophélie again as she watched him with Pip, what a blow it must have been to him to lose contact with his kids. He was obviously a man who loved children, and had a way with them. He gave a lot of himself, was open and caring, and interested in everything Pip had to say. There was an irresistible warmth about him, and at the same time just the right amount of respectful reserve. Ophélie never felt pushed or crowded, or invaded by him. He approached just enough to be friendly, and never enough to be invasive. He was truly a kind man, and a wonderful friend for both of them.

And when they got back to the house at nine-thirty, everyone was in great spirits. Matt had even remembered to ask for some scraps for the dog. And Pip went out to the kitchen to put them in his bowl.

"You're too good to us, Matt," Ophélie said quietly, as they sat down in the living room, and he lit a fire, just as he had done at the beach. Pip came back a few minutes later and Ophélie sent her to put on her pajamas, under mild protest. But she yawned as she objected, and Matt and Ophélie both laughed.

"You deserve to have people be good to you, Ophélie," Matt said sincerely, as he sat back on the couch next to her, having just declined her offer of a glass of wine. He was hardly drinking at all these days. He was having a lot of fun with Pip's portrait, and he really enjoyed coming into town to see them. He only seemed to drink more, he noticed, when he was lonely or depressed, and he was neither these days, thanks to them. "We all deserve good people in our lives," he said to her, without greater motive than to enjoy her friendship. "Your house is beautiful," he commented honestly, admiring the room they were sitting in, and the handsome antiques she had used to furnish it. It was a little formal for his taste, but not unlike the apartment he and Sally had had in New York. They had bought a duplex on Park Avenue, and one of the city's best decorators had done it for them, and Matt couldn't help wondering if a decorator had done Ophélie's house, or if she had done it herself. And after another glance around, he asked.

"I'm flattered that you'd even ask." She smiled at him gratefully. "I bought all of this myself over the last five years. I enjoy doing it. I love antiquing and decorating. It's fun, although this house is too big now for me and Pip. But I don't have the heart to sell it. We've loved it here, it seems a little sad with just the two of us. Eventually, I'll have to figure something out."

"You don't need to rush. I always felt we sold the apartment in New York too fast. But there was no point in my keeping it after Sally and the kids left. We had some lovely stuff," he said nostalgically.

"Did you sell it?" Ophélie asked.

"No. I gave it all to Sally, and she took it to Auckland. God knows what she did with it there, since she moved in with Hamish almost instantly. I didn't realize at that point that that was her plan, or that she'd move that fast. I thought she was going to get her own place, and check it out for a while. But she didn't lose any time. That's Sally. Once she makes up her mind, it's done." It had made her a great business partner, but a lousy wife in the end. He would have greatly preferred the reverse. "It doesn't really matter." He shrugged and looked surprisingly relaxed. "You can always replace things, not people. And I hardly need a houseful of antiques at the beach. I lead a very simple life, and that's all I want." She knew from having seen his place briefly that that was true, but it still seemed sad to her anyway. He had lost so much. But she had to admit, in spite of everything, he appeared to be at peace, and fairly content. His life suited him, and his house was comfortable. He enjoyed his work. The only thing that appeared to be missing in his life was people, and he didn't seem to miss them either. He was a very solitary being. And now he had Pip and Ophélie, whenever he wanted to see them.

He stayed until eleven, and then said he'd better leave. It got foggy on the road to the beach at night, and would take him a while to get back. But he assured her how much fun he'd had with them, he always did. And he stuck his head in Pip's door to say goodnight to her again, but she was sound asleep, with Mousse at the foot of her bed, and the Elmo slippers on the floor beside it.

"You're a lucky woman," he said with a warm smile, as he followed Ophélie down the stairs. "She is one great kid. I don't know how I got lucky enough to have her find me on the beach, but I'm glad she did." He couldn't imagine what he'd do without her in his life anymore. She was like a gift from God, and Ophélie was the added bonus he had gotten with Pip.

"We're lucky too, Matt. Thank you for a lovely evening." She kissed him on both cheeks, and he smiled. It reminded him of the year he had spent in France as a student twenty-five years before.

"Let me know when she has a soccer game. I'll come in again. Anytime, in fact. Just give me a call."

"We will." She laughed. They both knew Pip would be on the phone to him by the next day, but Ophélie saw no harm in it. She needed a man in her life in some form, and Ophélie had no others to offer. Theirs was a relationship that suited all three of them, and served them well, even the adults.

Ophélie watched him drive away in his old station wagon, closed the door, and turned off the lights. Pip had slept in her own bed that night, which was rare these days, and Ophélie lay in her too-big bed for a long time, in the dark, wide awake, thinking of the evening, and the man who had become Pip's friend, and then hers. She knew they were lucky to have him, but thinking of him somehow led to thoughts of Ted. The memories she had of him seemed so perfect in some ways, and so disturbing in others. There was a deep, silent dissonance there when old agonies crept into her head, and in spite of that, she still missed him unbearably, and wondered if she always would. Her life as a woman seemed to be over, and even her role as a mother would be short-lived. Chad was gone, and Pip would be off to her own life in a few years. She couldn't even imagine what her life would be like then, and hated to think of it. She would be alone, inevitably. And in spite of friends like Andrea, and now Matt, once Pip went off to college and a life of her own, any semblance of purpose and usefulness in her life would be over. The thought of it filled her with panic, and longing for Ted again. The only direction she seemed to be able to look on nights like that was backward, to a life that was now over, and looking ahead filled her with terror and dread. It was at moments like that, of deep soul-searching, that she understood all too well how Chad had felt. Only her responsibilities to Pip still kept her going, and from doing something truly foolish. But at times, in the dark of night, undeniably, the temptation was there. However wrong she knew it was, given her responsibilities to Pip, death would have been a sweet release.

15

THREE DAYS AFTER THEIR COZY DINNER WITH
Matt, Ophélie had to face a challenge she had
been dreading for a while. After four months of
regular support and attendance, her grief group
was about to end. They treated it as a "graduation," and talked of "re-entry" into the world at
one's own pace, and tried to give their last
meeting a celebratory air. But the reality of losing each other and the support and intimacy
they'd shared brought most of them to tears on
the last day, and Ophélie as well.

They hugged each other and promised to stay
in touch, exchanged phone numbers and ad-
dresses, and each discussed their future plans.
Mr. Feigenbaum was dating someone, a sev-
enty-eight-year-old woman he had met while
taking bridge lessons, and he was excited about
her. And a few of the others had started dating,

some had travel plans, one of the women had decided to sell her house, after agonizing endlessly, another woman had agreed to move in with her sister, and a man Ophélie didn't like much had finally made peace with his daughter after his wife's death, and after a family feud of nearly thirty years. But for the most part, they still had a long road to travel, and many adjustments to make.

Ophélie's main accomplishment, visibly at least, was her volunteer job at the Wexler Center. Her attitude was better, the black hole she still fell into at times, that they all talked about and dreaded, was not quite as deep, and the dark periods not quite as long. But she knew, as they each did about their own lives, that her struggles to adjust to her losses were by no means over. They were just better than they had been, and she had acquired more effective tools to cope. It was all she could hope for, and in some ways seemed enough.

But she felt overwhelmed with sadness, and a sense of loss again, as she said good-bye to Blake, and she looked grief-stricken when she picked Pip up at school.

"What's wrong, Mom?" Pip looked frightened. She had seen that look too often before, and was always worried now that the robot would return again and replace her mom, as it had for nearly a year. She didn't want it back again. Pip had felt abandoned for ten months after her brother and father's deaths.

"Nothing." Ophélie felt foolish admitting it to her. "It's stupid, I guess. My group ended today. I'm going to miss it. Some of the people were nice, and even though I complained about it, I think it actually helped."

"Can you go back?" Pip was still concerned. She didn't like the way her mother looked. It was all too familiar to her. And she remembered when Chad had looked that way too. That glazed, dark, vague, nameless misery that seemed bottomless and left its victim paralyzed with lethargy, indifference, and grief. Pip wanted to do something to stop it before it took hold, but she didn't know what. She never did.

"I can go to a different group, if I need to. But that one is gone." She sounded hopeless as they drove home, and Pip felt panic take her in its grip.

"Maybe you should."

"I'll be okay, Pip. I promise." Her mother patted her arm, and they drove home in silence. And as soon as they got there, Pip slipped into the upstairs den that no one used anymore, and called Matt. It was raining that day, and he was working on her portrait, instead of painting on the beach. As winter advanced, he would do that less and less, but the weather was still pretty good, except for today.

"She looks terrible," Pip reported in a low voice, praying that her mother wouldn't pick up the phone elsewhere in the house. There was a privacy button she had hit, but she wasn't sure if it worked. "I'm scared, Matt," she said honestly, and he was glad that she'd called. "Last year, I thought . . . she just . . . she didn't even get out of bed sometimes, or comb her hair . . . she never ate . . . she was awake all night . . . she wouldn't even talk to me . . ." Tears filled her eyes as she talked to him, and her words struck his heart like a blow. He was so sorry for them both.

"Is she doing any of those things now?" he asked with genuine concern. She had seemed all right to him the Saturday before, but you never knew. People could hide those things. Sometimes those most in despair kept it to themselves with dire results, and he didn't know if Ophélie was one of those. Pip would know better than he, despite her age.

"Not yet," Pip said, foreseeing doom everywhere. "But she looks really sad." There were tears in her eyes as she said it.

"She's probably a little scared to lose the support of the group. And saying good-bye is hard for her now. You've both lost a lot," he said, feeling awkward about reminding her, but it was true, and she sounded so adult, he thought he could take certain liberties with her. On the phone just then, she sounded more parent than child. It was the kind of conversation he would have expected to have with Ophélie about Pip, instead of the reverse. She had grown up fast in the last year. The anniversary of her brother's and father's deaths was in a month. "I think you should keep an eye on her, but I think she's going to be okay. She seemed fine the other night, and the last few times I saw her at the beach. It's probably kind of an up-and-down thing, but she'll probably pull out of it soon. If she doesn't, I'll come and visit, and see what I think." Not that there was really anything he could do. In the context of the relationship he had with them, it wasn't his role. But even as a friend, he might have been able to help, or at least to support Pip. She hadn't even had that the previous year, and was grateful to him now. More than he knew, or she could say.

"Thanks, Matt," she said, and meant it from the bottom of her heart. Just calling him and talking about it helped.

"Call me tomorrow and tell me how it's going. And by the way, your portrait is looking pretty good," he said modestly.

"I can't wait to see it!" She smiled, and got off the phone a few minutes later. They had no plans to see each other again at the moment, but she knew he was there if she needed him, and that gave her an immeasurable feeling of love and support from him. It was what she needed from him.

Ophélie was feeling forlorn about the group and cooking dinner that night when the doorbell rang. She looked startled, and couldn't imagine who it was. They weren't expecting anyone, she knew Matt wasn't in town, and Andrea never came by without calling first. All she could imagine was that it was a delivery of some kind, or maybe Andrea had decided to stop by unannounced. And when she opened the door, Ophélie saw a tall, bald man standing there, wearing glasses, and she didn't recognize him at first. It took her a full minute to place the face. His name was Jeremy Atcheson, and he had been a member of the group that had ended only that afternoon. Away from the group, his face didn't register at first, and then it quickly did.

"Yes?" she said, looking blank, as he peered over her shoulder into the silent house. And then she realized who he was. He seemed nervous as he stood facing her, and she couldn't imagine what he was doing there. He was one

of those faceless people who spoke infre-
quently, and in her opinion had always con-
tributed less than the rest. She had never had
any particular affinity for him, and she couldn't
remember ever speaking to him, in or out of
group.

"Hi, Ophélie," he said, as sweat broke out on
his upper lip, and she had the distinct impression that she could smell liquor on his breath.
"May I come in?" He smiled nervously, but it
struck her as more of a leer. And she realized, as
she looked more closely, that he seemed somewhat disheveled and unsteady on his feet.

"I'm cooking dinner," she said awkwardly,
unable to figure out what he wanted. But she
knew he had her address from the group list
they'd distributed that day so those who wanted
to could stay in touch.

"That's great," he said boldly with an unpleasant grin, "I haven't eaten yet. What's for
dinner?" Her jaw nearly dropped at his pre-
sumptuousness, and for a minute, he looked like
he was going to just walk in, as she started
slowly closing the door and narrowing the gap
through which he could enter. She had no intention of inviting him in. She sensed something unpleasant about to happen, and wanted
to avoid it at all cost.

"I'm sorry, Jeremy. I've got to go. My daughter's starving, and a friend of mine is coming by in a few minutes." She started to close the door, and he stopped it with a hand, and she realized instantly that he was faster and stronger than she'd expected. She wasn't sure whether to kick him, or scream. But there was no one in the house to help her but Pip. And the "friend coming by" was one she had made up to discourage him. It was, in every way, an unpleasant scene, and a violation of the respect that had been fostered in the group.

"What's your hurry?" he said, leering at her, wanting to push past her, but not quite daring to do it. Fortunately, the liquor he had obviously consumed was slowing him down. But as he stood facing her, only inches from her, she could smell the fumes. "Got a date?"

"Yes, as a matter of fact, I do." And he's six feet ten, and a karate expert, she wanted to add, but she couldn't come up with anyone scary enough, or fast enough, to stop him. And as she realized the situation she was in, she was frightened.

"No, you don't," he called her on it. "You kept saying in group that you don't want to date, and never will. I thought maybe we could have dinner together, and you might change your mind." It had been a ridiculous thing for him to do, and rude beyond words. Besides which, he was frightening her, and she wasn't sure how to handle it. She hadn't faced a situation like this since she'd married Ted. There had been a couple of drunks in her college dorm once, and they had scared her to death until the floor monitor saw them and had security throw them out. But there was no floor monitor to rescue her now, only Pip.

"It was nice of you to come by," Ophélie said politely, wondering if she could muster enough force to slam the door on him, although she realized that it might break his arm. "But you're going to have to leave."

"No, I'm not. And you don't want me to. Do you, sweetheart? What are you afraid of? The group is over, we can date anyone we want now. Or are you just scared of men? Are you a dyke?" He was drunker than she had thought at first, and suddenly she realized that she was in real danger. If he got into the house, he might hurt her or Pip. Knowing that gave her the strength she needed, and without warning, using her full force, she shoved him backward with one hand, and slammed the door with the other, as Mousse appeared at the top of the stairs and began to bark as he came bounding toward her. He had no idea what was happening, but something told him it was not good, and he was right. She was shaking as she slipped the chain on the door, and she could hear him cursing her from the other side and shouting obscenities at her. "You fucking bitch! You think you're too good for me, don't you?" She stood on the other side of the door, shaking in her shoes, and feeling more frightened and vulnerable than she had in years. She remembered suddenly that he had come to the group because of the death of his twin brother, and he couldn't seem to get past his anger over it. His brother had been killed by a hit-and-run driver. When she paid attention to him in the group, which had been rare, she had the feeling that he had come unglued over his twin's death, and adding booze to it hadn't helped. She had the distinct impression that if he'd gotten into her house, he might have done something terrible to her or Pip.

And not knowing what else to do, she did exactly what Pip had done earlier, and went to the phone and called Matt. She told him what had happened, and asked him if he thought she should call the police.

"Is he still out there?" He sounded upset by what he'd heard.

"No, I heard him drive off while I was dialing."

"Then you're probably okay, but I would call the leader of the group. Maybe he can call and say something to him. He was probably just drunk, but that's a pretty rotten thing to do. He sounds like a lunatic." Or worse, a rapist. But he didn't want to scare her.

"He's just a drunk, but he scared the hell out of me. I was afraid if he got in, he might hurt Pip."

"Or you. For heaven's sake, don't open the door to strangers like that." She suddenly seemed so vulnerable and unprotected to him. She was capable certainly, as she had proven during the rescue of the boy at sea, but she was also beautiful and living alone with a little girl. It brought home the risks of her situation not only to her, but to him as well. "Have the group leader read this guy the riot act, tell him next time you'll call the police and have him arrested for stalking you. And if he comes back tonight, call the police immediately, and then call me. I can sleep on the couch if you're worried about it, I don't mind coming in."

"No," she said, sounding calmer again, "I'm okay. It was just weird, and scary for a minute. He must have been having strange ideas about me the whole time we were in group. That's an unpleasant feeling, to say the least."

Being single again was hard enough, but having people like Jeremy trying to push their way into her house was more than a little unsettling.

Her vulnerability now was one of the evils of her situation, but all she could do was be careful about it, and aware, now that it had happened. She knew she couldn't expect Matt to be her bodyguard, or anyone else for that matter. She had to learn to deal with things like that herself. She was sorrier than ever that group was over. She would have liked to discuss how to handle things like that with them. Instead, she thanked Matt for his sympathy and concern and good advice, and as soon as she hung up, she called Blake Thompson, and he was deeply upset about it too.

He promised to call Jeremy the next day, when he sobered up, and talk straight to him about not only violating the sacred trust of the group, but being abusive about it. And she sounded calm again when Matt called to check on her after dinner. She hadn't said anything more to Pip because she didn't want to frighten her. She had reassured her that the man was harmless and it meant nothing, which was probably true. Ophélie was convinced it was an isolated incident, but it had rattled her none-theless. But even Pip was relieved to see her looking more engaged again during dinner, and by the next morning, she seemed fine when she left the house to drive Pip to school, and go to work at the Wexler Center.

Blake called her there later that morning, and he told Ophélie that he had spoken to Jeremy and said there would be a restraining order taken out against him if he went near her again. He said Jeremy had cried over it, and admitted he'd gone straight to a bar when the group ended and had been drinking all afternoon right up until he appeared on her doorstep. He was going to have some private therapy sessions with Blake, and he had asked Blake to apologize to her. Blake said he felt confident it wouldn't happen again, but it had been a good lesson to her to be cautious and wary of strangers, even those she knew slightly. There was a whole new world out there, waiting for her, full of evils she had never encountered before, as a married woman. It was not a cheering thought.

She thanked Blake for handling it, and went back to work, and forgot about it. And when she went home that afternoon, there was a letter of apology from Jeremy on her doorstep. He assured her he wouldn't bother her again. Apparently, they all had their own ways of dealing with the destabilizing effect of losing the support of the group. His had just been scarier than most. But it showed her that she wasn't the only one depressed and shaken up by it. It was a major adjustment, and a loss of sorts, to no longer have the group. Now she had to go out in the world, as they all did, and try to use what she'd learned.

As soon as Ophélie set foot in the Center, she forgot her own troubles. She was so busy until three o'clock, she hardly had time to breathe. She loved what she was doing, and everything she was learning. She did two intakes that day. One a couple with two children, who had come from Omaha, and lost everything. They didn't have enough to eat, live, pay rent, take care of the kids, and both husband and wife had lost their jobs. They had no one to turn to, but were valiantly trying to get on their feet, and the Center did everything they could to help, including get them on food stamps, signed up for unemployment, and the kids enrolled in school. They were due to move into a permanent shelter within a week, and it looked as though, with the Center's help, they were going to be able to keep their kids with them, no small feat. It nearly brought Ophélie to tears, as she listened to them, and talked to the little girl, who was exactly Pip's age. It was hard to imagine how people reached that point, but it reminded her again of how lucky she and Pip were. Imagine if Ted had died and left them homeless on top of it. It defied thinking.

The second intake Ophélie did was a mother

and daughter. The mother was in her late thir-
ties and alcoholic, the daughter was seventeen
and on drugs. The daughter had been having
seizures, either as a result of drug use, or for
some other reason, and they had been on the
streets together for two years. Things were
complicated further by the daughter's admission to Ophélie that she was four months pregnant. None of it happy stuff. And Miriam and
one of the professional caseworkers stepped in
to get them both into rehab, with medical benefits, and prenatal care for the daughter. They
were out of the Center and in another facility
by that night, and on the way to rehab by
morning.

By the end of the week, Ophélie felt as though
her head was spinning, but she loved it. She had
never felt as useful in her life, or as humble. She
was seeing and learning things that were hard to
even imagine until you saw and heard them. A
dozen times a day she wanted to put her head
down and cry, but she knew she couldn't. You
couldn't let on to the clients how tragic you
thought their situation was, or how hopeless.
Most of the time, it was hard to imagine their
ever getting out of their desperate situations, but
some did. And whether they did or not, like the
others at the Center, she was there to do everything she could to help them. She was so moved

by everything she was experiencing that her biggest regret, when she went home at night, was that she couldn't tell Ted about it. She liked to believe that he would have been fascinated by it. Instead, she shared as much as seemed reasonable with Pip, without frightening her unduly. Some of the stories were too depressing, or fairly hairy. A homeless man had died on their doorstep that week, on his way into the Center, of alcoholism, kidney failure, and malnutrition. But she didn't tell Pip about him either.

By Friday afternoon, it was clear to Ophélie that she had made the right decision. And that opinion was strongly reinforced by her advisers, those who directed her, and her co-workers. She was obviously going to be an asset to the Center, and she felt as though, for the first time in a year, she had found some purpose and direction that was fruitful.

She was just about to leave when Jeff Mannix of the outreach team breezed past her, and stopped to grab a cup of coffee.

"How's it going? Busy week?" he asked with a grin.

"Seems like it to me. I don't have anything to compare it to, but if it gets any busier around here, we may have to lock the doors so we don't get trampled."

"Sounds about right." He smiled at her, taking a sip of the steaming coffee. He had come by to check their provisions, they were adding some new medical and hygiene supplies to their usual offerings. Most of the time, he didn't come to work till six o'clock, and usually stayed on the streets until three or four in the morning. And it was easy to see that he loved what he was doing.

They both talked for a minute about the man who had died on the doorstep on Wednesday. Ophélie was still shaken by it.

"I hate to say it, but I see that out there so often, it no longer surprises me. I can't tell you how many guys I try to wake up, and when I turn them over . . . they're gone. Not just men, women too." But there were far fewer women on the streets. Women were more likely to go to the shelters, although Ophélie had heard horror stories about that too. Two of the female intakes she had done that week had told her that they'd been raped at shelters, which was apparently not unusual. "You think you'll get used to it," he said somberly, "but you never do." And then he looked at her appraisingly. He'd been hearing good things about her all week. "So when are you coming out with us? You've worked with everyone else around here. I hear you're a whiz with intakes and provisioning. But you ain't seen nothing yet till you come out with Bob, Millie, and me. Or is that a little too real for you?" It was a challenge to her, and he meant it to be. As much as he respected his co-workers, he and the others on the outreach team felt as though theirs was the most important work the Center did. They were at greater risk, and provided more hands-on care in a night than the Center itself did in a week. And he thought Ophélie should see that too.

"I'm not sure how helpful I'd be," Ophélie said honestly. "I'm pretty cowardly. I hear you guys are the heroes around here. I'd probably be too scared to get out of the van."

"Yeah, maybe for about five minutes. After that you forget, and you just do what you have to do. You look pretty ballsy to me." There was a rumor around that she had money, no one knew it for sure, but her shoes looked expensive, her clothes were too neat and clean and fit too well, and her address was in Pacific Heights. But she seemed to work as hard as anyone else, harder according to Louise. "What are you doing tonight?" he pressed her, and she felt both pushed and intrigued. "You gotta date?" he asked fairly bluntly, but as aggressive as he was, she liked him. He was young and clean and strong, and he cared desperately about what he did. Someone had told her he'd nearly been stabbed once on the streets, but he went right back out there the next day. Foolhardly probably, but she thought admirable too. He was willing to risk his life for what he did.

"I don't date," she said simply. "I have a little girl, I'll be home with her. I promised to take her to a movie." They had no other plans that weekend, except Pip's first soccer game the next day.

"Take her tomorrow. I want you to come out with us. Millie and I were talking about it last night. You should see it, at least once. You'll never be the same once you do."

"Particularly if I get hurt," she said bluntly, "or killed. I'm all my daughter has in the world."

"That's not good," he said, frowning. "Sounds like you need a little more in your life, Opie." He found her name pretty but impossible to pronounce, and had teased her about it when he met her. "Come on, we'll keep an eye on you. How about it?"

"I don't have anyone to leave her with," Ophélie said thoughtfully, tempted, but scared too. His challenge was difficult to resist.

"At eleven?" He rolled his eyes, and his vast ivory grin lit up the deep brown face. He was a beautiful man, and roughly six feet five. He was the ex–Navy SEAL. He'd been a Navy commando for nine years. "Shit, at her age, I was taking care of all five of my brothers, and haulin' my mama's ass out of jail every week. She was a prostitute." It sounded stereotypical, but it was real, and what he didn't tell her but she had heard from others was what a remarkable human being he was, and the family of siblings he had raised. One of his brothers had gone to Princeton on a scholarship, another had gotten into Yale. Both were lawyers, his youngest brother was studying to be a doctor, yet another was a lobbyist, speaking out on inner-city violence, and the fifth had four kids of his own and was running for Congress. Jeff was an extraordinary man, and fiercely persuasive. Ophélie was seriously considering going out on the streets with them, although she had sworn she never would. It seemed far too dangerous to her. "Come on, Mama . . . give us a chance. You ain't never gonna wanna sit behind that desk again, after you been out with us! We're what's happening around here . . . and why we all do this work. We leave at six-thirty. Be here." It was more a command than an invitation, and she said she'd see what she could do. She was still thinking about it, half an hour later, when she picked Pip up at school. And she was quiet on the way home.

"You okay, Mom?" Pip asked, with the usual concern, but Ophélie reassured her that she was. And as Pip looked her over, she decided to agree. Pip knew most of the danger signs now of her mother taking a bad turn. She just looked distracted this time, but not depressed, or disconnected. "What did you do today at the Center?"

As usual, Ophélie told her an edited version, and then made a phone call from her bedroom. The woman who cleaned for her several times a week said she could baby-sit that night, and Ophélie asked her to be there by five-thirty. She wasn't sure how Pip would feel about it, and she didn't want to disappoint her, but as it turned out, Pip said it would be better to go to the movies on Saturday anyway. She was playing soccer the next morning, and didn't want to be too tired. Ophélie explained that there was something planned at the Center that she wanted to be part of. And Pip said she didn't mind at all. She was happy that her mother was doing something she enjoyed. It was a lot better than watching her sleep her days away in her room, or stalk the house all night looking anxious, the way she had the year before.

As promised, Alice, the cleaning lady, appeared promptly at five-thirty, and when Ophélie left, Pip was watching TV. Ophélie was wearing jeans and a heavy sweater, a ski parka she had found at the back of her closet, and some hiking boots she hadn't worn in years. And she'd brought a little knitted cap and gloves in case it got cold. Jeff had warned her that it would. No matter what time of year it was in San Francisco, the nights got cold, sometimes in summer most of all. And there had been a distinct chill in the air at night for the past few weeks. They carried with them doughnuts and sandwiches and thermoses of coffee, she knew, and Jeff had said that they stopped at McDonald's sometimes halfway through the night. Whatever they had planned, she was prepared, as best she could be. But as she parked near the Center, she had a definite feeling of trepidation. If nothing else, she knew it would be an interesting night. Maybe the most interesting of her life. And she knew that if either Matt or Andrea knew, or Pip, they would have tried to talk her out of it, or been scared to death on her behalf. And she was scared too.

As she walked into the garage behind the Wexler Center, she saw Jeff, Bob, and Millie loading up. They were putting boxes and duffel bags in the back of one van, and a stack of sleeping bags and donated clothes in the other. Jeff turned with a grin as he saw her, and looked pleased.

"My, my, my . . . Hello, Opie . . . welcome to the real world." She wasn't sure if it was a compliment or a put-down, but whatever it was, he seemed happy to see her, and Millie smiled at her too.

"I'm glad you could make it," she said quietly, and went back to work. It was another half-hour before they were loaded up, as Ophélie helped. It was a backbreaking job, and the real work hadn't even begun. And as soon as they were through, Jeff told her to ride with Bob in the second van.

The tall quiet Asian man waved at the passenger seat, the rest of the seats had been removed to make room for their supplies.

"You sure you want to do this?" he asked calmly as he turned the key in the ignition. He knew Jeff and the way he strong-armed people into doing things, and he admired her for coming. She had guts. She didn't need to do this, didn't have to prove anything to anyone. She looked as though she came from a different life. But he had to give her credit for showing up, for being willing to stick her neck out, and even risk her life. "This isn't required, you know. They call us the cowboys of the outfit, and we're all a little crazy. No one is going to think you're a sissy if you back out." He was giving her a chance to leave now, before it was too late. He thought it only fair to her. She had no idea what was in store.

"Jeff will think I'm a sissy." She smiled at him, and he laughed.

"Yeah. Maybe. So what? Who gives a shit. You wanna go, Opie? Or you wanna bag it? Either way. No shame. Call your shot." She thought about it for a long moment, and looked at Bob long and hard. She took a breath then, for the smallest of seconds ready to change her mind, and then as she looked at him, she realized she felt safe with him. She didn't know him from Adam, but she sensed that she could trust him, and she was right. The other van honked then. Jeff was getting impatient and couldn't understand the delay, as Bob waited for Ophélie to decide. "You in or out?"

She exhaled slowly as she looked at him, and the word came out of her mouth of its own accord. "In."

"All right!" he said, with a grin, as he stepped on the gas, and the convoy of loaded vans lumbered out of the garage. It was seven o'clock at night.

16

FOR THE NEXT EIGHT HOURS, OPHÉLIE SAW
things that she had never dreamed existed, and
surely not within only a few miles of her house.
They went to areas she had never known, down
back alleys that made her shudder, and saw people so far beyond her ken that it nearly ripped
out her heart. People with scabs on their faces,
covered with sores, with rags on their feet instead of shoes, or without even that, barefoot
and sometimes half-naked in the cold. At other
times, there were clean, neat, decent-looking
people hiding in corners under bridges and
sleeping under cardboard and newspaper on
dirt. And everywhere they went, there were
thank-yous and God-bless-yous when they left.
It was a long, slow, agonizing night. And yet at
the same time, Ophélie had never felt such

peace, or joy, or a sense of purpose to equal it, except maybe the nights she had given birth to Chad and Pip. This was almost like that.

And for most of the night, she and Bob moved as one. He didn't need to tell her what to do. All you had to do was follow your heart. The rest was obvious. Where sleeping bags were needed, you gave them, or warm clothes. Jeff and Millie were dispensing the medicines and hygiene supplies. And when they found a camp of runaways near the loading docks far South of Market, Bob wrote the location down. He explained to Ophélie that there was another outreach program for juvenile runaways. He was going to give them the address in the morning, and they would come out and try to talk them in. Only a few were ever willing to leave the streets. Even more than the adults, they distrusted the shelters and programs. And they didn't want to be sent home. More often than not, what the young ones were fleeing from was worse than what they encountered on the streets.

"A lot of them have been out here for years. It's safer for them most of the time than where they've been. The programs try for reunification with their families, but a lot of times no one gives a damn. Their parents don't even care where they've been. They come here from all over the country, and they just wander around, living on the streets till they grow up."

"And then what?" Ophélie asked with a look of despair. She had never seen so many people in such desperate need, with so little means for relief. They were almost, or appeared to be, a lost cause. The forgotten people, as Bob called them. And she had never seen people so grateful for the little help they got. Some of them just stood there and cried.

"I know," Bob said once, when she got back in the van in tears. "I cry sometimes myself. The young ones really get to me . . . and the old ones . . . you can't help but know that they're not going to be alive out here for long. But this is all we can do for them. It's all they want. They don't want to come in. It may not make much sense to us, but it does to them. They're too lost, or too sick, or too broken. They can't exist anywhere but here. Since federal funds got cut back years ago, we don't have the mental hospitals anymore to house them, and even the ones who look relatively okay probably aren't. There's a lot of mental illness out here. That's all the substance abuse is, a lot of self-medication just to survive. And who can blame them? Shit, if I were out here, I'd probably be on drugs myself. What else have they got?"

Ophélie learned more that night about the human race than she had in the whole rest of her life. It was a lesson she knew she would never forget. And when they stopped at McDonald's for hamburgers at midnight, she felt guilty eating them. She could hardly swallow the food and hot coffee, knowing that in the streets around them were people starving and cold, who would have given all they had for a cup of coffee and a burger.

"How's it going?" Jeff asked her, as Millie peeled off her gloves. It had gotten cold, and Ophélie was wearing hers as well.

"It's amazing. You really are doing God's work out here," Ophélie said in awe of all three of them. She had never been so moved in her life. And thus far, Bob was impressed. She had a gentle, compassionate way about her, without condescending to them or being patronizing. She treated each person they encountered with humanity and respect, and she worked hard. He said as much to Jeff on the way out, and Jeff nodded. He knew what he had been doing when he asked her. Everyone had said she was great, and he wanted her for the outreach team before she got bogged down in a lot of paperwork at the Center. He had sensed almost instantly that she would be a valuable member of the outreach team, if he could get her to sign up. The risks they dealt with every night, and the long hours, were what kept most people out. And most volunteers and even staffers were too scared. Even the guys.

They headed for Potrero Hill after their break, and into Hunters Point after that. And the Mission was going to be their last stop. And as they approached it, Bob warned her to stay behind him and be careful. He told her that among the aggressive and the hostile, dirty needles were the weapon of choice. And as he said it, all she could think of was Pip. She couldn't afford to get injured or killed. It reminded her, even if only for an instant, that she was crazy to be out here. But being there was like a drug. She was already addicted to it before the night was out. What they were doing was the single greatest act of giving and caring that she could imagine. These people were putting their lives on the line every night. Unaided, unarmed, unsupported, they went out there on a mission of mercy that in turn risked their lives. And yet everything about it made sense. She was surprised that she wasn't even tired when they finally drove the vans back into the garage. She was energized, and felt totally alive, maybe more so than ever in her life.

"Thanks, Opie," Bob said kindly as he turned

off the ignition. "You did a great job." He truly meant it. She had.

"Thank you," she said, with a smile. From him, it was high praise. She liked him even better than Jeff. Bob was quiet and hardworking and kind to the people they dealt with, and respectful to her. She had learned in the hours they'd spent together that his wife had died of cancer four years before. He was bringing up three children on his own, with his sister's help. And working at night allowed him to be with his kids during the day. The risks didn't seem to faze him, they had been worse as a cop. He had a pension from the force, so he could afford the low pay he made at Wexler. More than anything, he loved the job. And he was less of a cowboy than Jeff. He had been incredibly nice to her all night, and she was dismayed to discover that they had devoured nearly an entire box of doughnuts together. She wondered if the stress had made her hungry, or maybe just the work. Whatever, it had been one of the most remarkable and meaningful nights of her life. And she knew that in those magical hours between seven P.M. and three A.M., she and Bob had become friends. And when she thanked him, it was heartfelt.

"See you on Monday?" Jeff asked her, looking

her straight in the eye, as they stood in the garage. He was as bold as ever, and Ophélie looked surprised.

"You want me to come again?"

"We want you on the team." He had decided halfway through the night, based on what he'd observed and Bob had said about her.

"I have to give it some thought," she said carefully, but was flattered anyway. "I couldn't come every night." And shouldn't at all. It wasn't fair to Pip. But all those people, all those faces, those lost souls sleeping near railroad tracks and under underpasses and on loading docks. It was as though she heard a call, and knew it was what she was meant to do, no matter how great the risk. "I couldn't do it more than twice a week. I've got a little girl."

"If you were dating, you'd be out more than that, and you said you're not." He had a point. Jeff didn't pull any punches, nor hold back.

"Can I think about it?" She felt pressed, but that was what he wanted. He wanted her on the team, in no uncertain terms.

"Do you need to? Really? I think you know what you want." She did. But she didn't want to do anything hasty or foolish, out of the emotions of the night. And emotions had run high, particularly for her, because it was all new to her. "Come on, Opie. Give it up. We need you . . . so do they . . ." His eyes pleaded with her.

"Okay," she said breathlessly. . . . "Okay. Twice a week." It meant she would be working Tuesday and Thursday nights instead of Monday, Wednesday, and Friday.

"You got it," he said, beaming at her, and slapped her a high-five as she laughed.

"You're a hard man to resist."

"Damn right," he said, "and don't you forget it. Good work, Opie . . . see you Tuesday night!" He waved and was gone. Millie got into a car parked next to the garage, and Bob walked her to her car and she thanked him again.

"Anytime you want to quit," he said gently, "you can. You're not signing in blood here," he reminded her, which made it a little less scary for her. She had just made a hell of a commitment, and she couldn't even imagine what people would say if she told them. She wasn't sure she would. For now.

"Thanks for the out."

"Anything you do, for however long you do it, is valid and appreciated. We all do it for as long as we can. And when we can't, then that's okay too. Take it easy, Opie," he said, as she got into her car. "See you next week."

"Goodnight, Bob," she said gently, finally starting to feel tired. She was coming down from the high of the night, and wondered how she'd feel about it in the morning. "Thanks again . . ."

He waved, put his head down, and walked down the street to his truck. And as he did, she realized with a feeling of elation that she was one of them now. She was a cowboy. Just like them. Wow!

17

WHEN OPHÉLIE WENT BACK TO HER HOUSE late that night, she looked around as though seeing it for the first time. The luxury, the comforts, the colors, the warmth, the food in the refrigerator, her bathtub, and the hot water as she got in it. It all seemed infinitely precious suddenly, as she lay there soaking for nearly an hour, thinking back on what she'd seen, what she had done, what she had just committed to. She had never felt so fortunate in her life, or so unafraid. In confronting what she had feared most, her own mortality on the streets, other things no longer seemed as menacing anymore. Like the ghosts in her head, her guilt over urging Chad to go with Ted, and even her seemingly bottomless grief. If she could confront the dangers on the street, and survive them, the rest seemed so much easier to deal with. And as she got into bed next to Pip, who had opted to sleep in her mother's bed again that night, she had never in her life been as grateful for her child, and the life they shared. She went to sleep with her arms around her daughter, giving silent thanks, and woke with a start when she heard the alarm. For a minute, she couldn't even remember where she was. She had been dreaming of the streets and the people she'd seen there. She knew she'd remember those faces for the rest of her life.

"What time is it?" she asked, turning off the alarm and dropping her head back on her pillow next to Pip's.

"Eight o'clock. I have a game at nine, Mom."

"Oh . . . okay . . ." It reminded her that she still had a life. With Pip. And that maybe what she had done the night before was more than a little crazy. What would happen to Pip if she got hurt? Yet it no longer seemed as likely. The team seemed very efficient, and as best they could, they took no obvious risks. The risks were inherent on the streets, but they were sensible people who knew what they were doing. But it was still more than a little scary anyway. She had a responsibility to Pip, which she was deeply sensitive to.

She was still thinking about it when she got

up and dressed, and went downstairs to make breakfast for Pip.

"How was last night, Mom? What did you do?"

"Some pretty interesting stuff. I worked with the outreach team on the streets." She told Pip a modified version of what she'd done.

"Is it dangerous?" Pip looked concerned, and then finished her orange juice, and dug into her scrambled eggs.

"To some extent." Ophélie didn't want to lie to her. "But the people who do it are very careful, and they know what they're doing. I didn't see anyone dangerous out there last night. But things do happen on the street." She couldn't deny the risk to her.

"Are you going to do it again?" Pip looked concerned.

"I'd like to. What do you think?"

"Did you like doing it?" she asked sensibly.

"Yes, a lot. I loved it. Those people need so much help."

"Then do it, Mom. Just be careful. I don't want you to get hurt."

"Neither do I. Maybe I'll just try it a couple more times, and see how it feels. If it looks too risky after a few times, I'll stop."

"That sounds good. And by the way," she said

over her shoulder as she headed upstairs to get her cleats, "I told Matt he could come to the game if he wanted to. He said he wanted to come."

"It's pretty early. He might not make it." Ophélie didn't want her to be disappointed, and she didn't know how serious Matt's offer was. "I told Andrea she could come too. You have a whole cheering team."

"I hope I play okay," she said, putting on a sweatshirt. She was ready to roll. And Ophélie let Mousse get into the backseat. Within minutes, they were headed for the polo field in Golden Gate Park, where they played. It was still foggy, but looked like it would be a nice day eventually. As they drove along, and Pip put the radio on, a little too loudly, Ophélie found herself thinking again of what she'd seen the night before, the poor people living in camps, and boxes, sleeping on concrete with rags over them. In the clear light of day, it seemed even more incredible than it had the night before. But she was glad now that she had agreed to go again, and be part of the team. It was a powerful pull she felt. And she could hardly wait to be out there again. She smiled to herself as she thought of it, and as they got out of the car at the polo field, she was surprised to see Matt. Pip gave a whoop of glee and threw her arms around him. He was wearing a heavy sheepskin jacket that looked like it had been through the wars, running shoes, and jeans, and he looked suitably rugged and fatherly, as Pip ran off to the field.

"You really are a faithful friend. You must have left the beach at the crack of dawn," Ophélie said with a grateful smile.

"No, just around eight. I thought it would be fun." He didn't tell her that he had gone to every one of Robert's games before the divorce, and many in Auckland after that. Robert had learned to play rugby there too.

"She was hoping you'd come. Thank you for not disappointing her." Ophélie meant it. He had never disappointed Pip once since they'd met, nor her. He was the one person they both knew they could rely on.

"I wouldn't miss it for the world. I used to coach."

"Don't tell her. She'll sign you up for the team." They both laughed, and stood for ages watching the game. Pip was playing well and had scored a goal, when Andrea arrived with the baby in a stroller in a little down bag to keep him warm. Ophélie introduced her to Matt, and they stood chatting for a while. She tried not to feel the vibes of Andrea's questions and opinions and assumptions directed at her when she saw Matt. Ophélie looked artfully unruffled, and after the baby had cried for half an hour because he wanted to be fed, Andrea left. But Ophélie felt certain that she would hear from her later on. She could count on it. And she ignored all of Andrea's meaningful looks when she left, and continued chatting with Matt.

"She's Pip's godmother and my oldest friend out here," Ophélie explained.

"Pip told me about her, and the baby. If Pip's description of the situation is correct, it was a brave thing to do." He was discreetly referring to the sperm bank story that Pip had told him, and Ophélie understood. She liked his delicacy and discretion.

"It was brave, but she thought she'd never have children otherwise, and she's thrilled with the baby."

"He's very cute," he said, and then went back to watching Pip. He and Ophélie were both pleased and proud when her team won the game, and she came off the field with a broad grin of victory, as they praised her.

He offered to take them to lunch afterward, and they went to a pancake house at Pip's request, had a nice brunch together, and then Matt went back to the beach. He wanted to work on the portrait, and said as much to Pip in a whisper as they left, and she winked. And after that, she and Ophélie went home. The phone was ringing as soon as Ophélie opened the door, and she could guess who it was.

"My, my . . . now he's coming to Pip's soccer games?" Andrea's voice was full of innuendo, as Ophélie shook her head at her end. "I think you're holding out on me."

"Maybe he's in love with her, and he'll be my son-in-law one day," Ophélie said, laughing. She had expected this. "I am not holding out on you."

"Then you're crazy. He's the best-looking man I've seen in years. If he's straight, grab him, for chrissake. Do you think he is?" Andrea said, suddenly sounding concerned.

"Is what?" Ophélie hadn't gotten the gist of what she said. It hadn't even occurred to her, and either way, she didn't care. They were just friends.

"Straight. Do you think he's gay?"

"I don't think so. I never asked him. He was married, for heaven's sake, and had two kids. But what difference does it make?"

"He could have become gay after that," Andrea said practically, but she didn't think he was gay either. "But I don't think so. I think you're nuts if you don't grab him while you've got the opportunity. Guys like that get snatched off the market before you can sneeze."

"Well, I'm not sneezing, and I don't think he's on the market any more than I am. I think he wants to be alone."

"Maybe he's depressed. Is he on medication? You could suggest it, that might get the ball rolling. Of course, then you could have the issue of side effects to deal with. Some antidepressants depress men's sex drives. But there's always Viagra," Andrea said optimistically while Ophélie rolled her eyes.

"I'll be sure to suggest it to him. He'll be thrilled. He doesn't need Viagra to have dinner with us. And I don't think he's depressed. I think he's wounded." That was different.

"Same thing. How long ago did his wife leave? Ten years? It's not normal for him to still be alone. Or to be so interested in Pip, if he's not a child molester, which I don't think he is either. He needs a relationship, and so do you."

"Thank you, Dr. Wilson. I feel better already. The poor man, he should only know that you're reorganizing his life, and mine. And prescribing Viagra."

"Someone has to. He's obviously incapable of organizing this himself, and so are you. You can't just sit there for the rest of your life. Besides, Pip'll be gone in a few years."

"I've already thought about that myself, and it makes me hysterical, thank you. I just have to get used to it. Fortunately, I still have time before she leaves." But it was the one thing that frightened her most now, she couldn't conceive of living alone without Pip, once she grew up. The thought of it depressed her so badly, it took her breath away. But Matthew Bowles wasn't the answer to her problems. She just had to get used to being alone. And enjoy Pip as much as she could while she was still there. Ophélie wasn't looking for anyone to fill the void Chad and Ted had left, nor the one Pip would leave when she went. She was going to have to fill it with work, friends, and whatever else she could find, like the work she was doing with the homeless. "Matt's not the answer," she reiterated to Andrea.

"Why not? He looks pretty good to me." Better than that, in fact.

"Then you go after him, and give him Viagra. I'm sure he'll be grateful to you," Ophélie said, laughing again. Andrea was outrageous, but she always had been. It was one of the things Ophélie liked about her. And they were very different.

"Maybe I will go after him. When is Pip's next soccer game?"

"You're impossible. Why don't you just drive to Safe Harbour and beat his door down with an ax. It might impress him with how determined you are to save him from himself."

"Sounds like a great idea to me." Andrea sounded undaunted.

They chatted for a few minutes, and Ophélie didn't tell her about the remarkable night she'd had on the streets the night before. Late that afternoon, she and Pip went to a movie, and then came home and had dinner. And by ten o'-clock, they were both in Ophelie's bed, sound asleep.

At Safe Harbour at that hour, Matt was still working on Pip's portrait. He was wrestling with her mouth that night, and thinking about how she had looked when she came off the field from the soccer game. She had been wearing the most irresistible grin. He loved looking at her, and painting her and being with her. And he enjoyed Ophélie's company too, but probably not as much as he enjoyed Pip's. She was an angel, a wood sprite, an elf, a wise little old soul in a child's body, and as he painted her, all of those qualities began to emerge. He was pleased with the painting by the time he went to bed that night. And he was still asleep the next morning when Pip called. She was apologetic when she realized she had woken him up.

"I'm sorry I woke you, Matt. I thought you'd be up by now." It was nine-thirty, which seemed late enough to her. But he hadn't gone to bed till nearly two.

"That's fine. I was working on a certain project of ours last night. I think I've nearly got it." He sounded pleased, and so did she.

"My mom is going to love it," Pip assured him. "Maybe we can go to dinner one night and you can show me. She's going to be working two nights a week."

"Doing what?" He sounded surprised. He didn't even know she had a job, other than volunteer work she'd been planning to do with the homeless at the Wexler Center. This somehow sounded more serious, and somewhat official.

"She's going to work in a van, visiting the homeless on the street, on Tuesdays and Thursdays. She'll be out all night almost, and Alice is going to spend the night here, because it'll be too late for her to go home when my mom gets back."

"That sounds pretty interesting," he said to Pip. But also very dangerous, he thought to himself, but he didn't want to worry her. "I'll be happy to come and take you to dinner. But maybe we should wait until a night when your

mom will be there too. She might feel left out."
He enjoyed Ophélie's company, but also never
lost sight of the proprieties, of seeing a child
Pip's age without her mother, except on an
open beach, as he had all summer. That was different, in his view at least. And he suspected that
Ophélie would have agreed. Most of their ideas
about children seemed to be fairly similar, and
he had great respect for how Ophélie had
raised Pip, and was continuing to do so. The results had been extremely good, from all he
could see.

"Maybe you can come visit us next week."

"I'll try," he promised, but as it turned out, his
plans and theirs didn't mesh for the next few
weeks. He was working on the portrait, and had
some other things to do, and business to attend
to. Ophélie was busier than she'd ever expected.
She had decided to work three days a week at
the Center, and two nights a week on the
streets with the outreach team. It was a heavy
schedule for her. And Pip had a lot more homework than she wanted to admit.

It was the first of October, when he called
Ophélie and invited her to the beach for the
day the following weekend, but Ophélie
seemed to hesitate, and then explained it to
him.

"Ted and Chad's anniversary date is the day before that," she said sadly. "I think it's going to be kind of a tough day for both of us. I'm not sure how we're going to feel so soon after, and I'd hate to come out and be gloomy and depressed. It might be better to wait another week. Actually, Pip's birthday is the following week." He remembered it vaguely, but she hadn't said much about it to him, which he thought very adult of her, and discreet.

"We could do both. Let's play the day after the anniversary by ear. It might do you both good to come out to Safe Harbour for a change of scenery. You don't have to tell me till you wake up that morning. And if it wouldn't be an intrusion, I'd love to take you and Pip to dinner for her birthday, if you think that would be fun for her."

"I'm sure she'd love it," Ophélie said honestly, and in the end agreed to call him the morning after the anniversary. She suspected correctly they'd be talking to him before that anyway. And even busy as she was these days, she enjoyed hearing his voice on the phone.

She told Pip about both invitations, and she was visibly pleased, although she herself was nervous about the anniversary. She was mostly afraid it would be hard on her mother and set her back again. She had been doing so well lately, and the anniversary date seemed like a major threat to them both.

Ophélie was having a mass said at Saint Dominic's, and other than that, they had nothing planned. There had been no remains after the plane exploded and burned, and Ophélie had purposely not put up headstones in a cemetery over empty graves. She didn't want to have a place to go or mourn. As far as she was concerned, she had explained to Pip the year before, they carried them in their hearts. All that had been left in the rubble were Chad's belt buckle, and Ted's wedding ring, both twisted almost beyond recognition, but she had saved both.

So all they had to do that day was go to mass. They were planning to spend the rest of the day quietly at the house, thinking about the loved ones they had lost. Which was exactly what Pip was worried about. And as the day drew closer, so was Ophélie. She was anticipating the anniversary of their death with dread.

18

As it turned out, the day of the anniversary dawned sunny and beautiful. The sun was streaming through Ophélie's bedroom windows when she and Pip woke up in her bed. Pip had been there almost every night since the beginning of September. It had afforded Ophélie great comfort, and she was still grateful to Matt for the suggestion. But they were both silent when they woke up that day.

Ophélie thought instantly, as did Pip, of the day of the funeral, which had been equally sunny, and agonizing for all concerned. All of Ted's colleagues and associates over the years, and their friends, had come, as well as all of Chad's friends, and his entire class. Mercifully, Ophélie scarcely remembered it, she had been in such a daze. All she remembered was the sea of flowers, and Pip holding her hand so tightly it hurt. And then from somewhere, like a choir from Heaven, the *Ave Maria,* which had never sounded as beautiful or as mesmerizing as it had that day. It was a memory she knew she would never get out of her head.

They went to mass together, and sat silently next to each other. At her request, Ted's and Chad's names were read off during the special intentions, and it brought tears to Ophélie's eyes, and once again she and Pip held hands. And after that, they went home, after stopping for a moment to thank the priest. They each lit a candle, Ophélie's for her husband, and Pip's for Chad, and then they drove home in silence. You could have heard a pin drop all day in the silent house. And it reminded them both of the day of Ted's and Chad's deaths. Neither of them ate, neither of them spoke, and when the door-bell rang that afternoon, they both jumped. It was flowers from Matt, he had sent a small bou-quet to each of them. And Ophélie and Pip were equally touched. The cards said simply, "Thinking of you today. Love, Matt."

"I love him," Pip said simply as she read the card. Things were so simple at her age. So much simpler than they would ever be again.

"He's a nice man, and a good friend," Ophélie said, and Pip nodded in answer, and took the flowers upstairs to her room. Even Mousse was quiet, and seemed to sense that neither of his owners was having a good day. Andrea had sent them flowers too, which had arrived the previous afternoon. She was not religious or she'd have gone to mass with them, but they knew that she would be thinking about them both, as was Matt.

By nightfall, they were both anxious to go to bed. Pip turned the television on in her mother's room, and Ophélie asked her to turn it off, or go watch it somewhere else. But Pip didn't want to be alone, so she stayed in the silent room with her mother, and it was a mercy when they both finally went to sleep in each other's arms. Ophélie hadn't told her, but Pip knew that her mother had spent several hours that day crying in Chad's room. It had been an utterly awful day for them in every way. There was nothing good about the anniversary, no obvious blessing, no compensation for what they'd gone through. It was a day, like most of the last year, that was entirely about loss.

And in the morning, when the phone rang, they were both at the kitchen table, where Ophélie was silently reading the paper, while Pip played with the dog. It was Matt.

"I don't dare ask how yesterday was," he said cautiously, after he had said hello to Ophélie.

"Don't. It was as bad as I thought it would be.

But at least it's over. Thank you so much for the flowers." It was hard to explain, even to herself, why anniversaries were so meaningful. There was no reason it should be so much worse than the day after or the day before, but it was. It was like a celebration of the worst day of their lives. There was not a single benefit in it. The entire day was the anniversary of the worst day that had ever dawned, and it was flooded with memories of an agonizing time. He sounded infinitely sympathetic, but had no wisdom to offer, having never been through it himself. His own losses had stretched over time, and finally become evident. They hadn't happened all at once in a single hideous instant like theirs.

"I didn't want to intrude, so I didn't call," he apologized.

"It was better that way," she said honestly. Neither of them had wanted to talk to anyone, although Pip probably would have liked to talk to him, she realized. "Your flowers were beautiful. We were very touched."

"I was wondering if you'd like to come out today. It might do you both good. What do you think?" She really didn't want to, but she thought Pip might, given the opportunity. And she felt guilty just rejecting the invitation out of hand.

"I'm not very good company." She still felt

utterly worn out by the previous day's emotions, especially the hours she had spent sobbing on Chad's bed, muffling the sounds of her crying in his pillow, which still smelled faintly like him. She had never washed the sheets or the pillowcase, and knew she never would. "I can't speak for Pip though. She might like to see you. Why don't I talk to her and call you back," but Pip was already waving frantically when her mother hung up.

"I want to! I want to!" she said, looking instantly revived, and Ophélie didn't have the heart to disappoint her, although she wasn't in the mood to go anywhere herself. It was hardly a long journey. It only took half an hour, and if it turned out to be too difficult, Ophélie knew they could come back in a couple of hours. She knew Matt would understand. She wasn't much in the mood herself. "Can we go, Mom? Please???"

"All right," Ophélie conceded. "But I don't want to stay long. I'm tired." Pip knew it was more than that, but she hoped that once she got her there, her mother would perk up. She knew her mother liked talking to Matt, and she had the feeling she'd feel a lot better walking along the ocean on the sand.

Ophélie told Matt they would be there by noon, and he was pleased. She offered to bring

lunch, and he told her not to worry about it.
He said he'd make an omelette, and if Pip hated
it, he had bought peanut butter and jelly for her
the day before. It sounded like just what the
doctor ordered, and was.

He was waiting for them outside when they
drove up, sitting in an old deck chair on his
deck, and enjoying the sun. He looked pleased
to see them, and Pip threw her arms around
him, and then, as always now, Ophélie kissed
him on both cheeks. But he noticed instantly
how sad she was. She looked as though there
was a thousand-pound weight on her heart,
which there was. He sat her in his deck chair,
and put an old plaid blanket over her, insisting
she stay there and relax, and then he enlisted
Pip to help him make mushroom omelettes and
help him chop herbs. She liked helping him,
and set the table, and by the time Matt sent her
to call her mother in, Ophélie was more relaxed, and felt as though the ice block on her
chest was thawing a little in the sun. She was
quiet during lunch, but by the time he served
strawberries and cream, she was actually smiling, and Pip was immensely relieved. Ophélie
went to get something out of the car, while he
made tea, and Pip whispered to him with a
worried look.

"I think she looks a little better, don't you?"

He did, and was touched by Pip's obvious concern.

"She'll be okay. Yesterday was just hard on her, and on you. We'll go for a walk on the beach in a little while and it will do her good."

Pip silently patted his hand in gratitude as her mother came back in. She had gone to get an article on the Wexler Center that she wanted to show Matt. It essentially explained all the things they did, and was very informative.

He read it carefully, nodding, and then looked at Ophélie with renewed respect. "It sounds like a remarkable place. What exactly do you do for them, Ophélie?" She had talked to him about it before, but she had always been intentionally vague.

"She works on the street with the outreach team," Pip jumped in instantly, and Matt looked at both of them, shocked. It was not what Ophélie would have said, but it was too late to change it now.

"Are you serious?" He looked directly at her, and she nodded, trying to look unconcerned, but she shot a look at Pip, who realized she'd put her foot in it, and pretended to be playing with the dog. It was rare for Pip to make a faux pas, and she was embarrassed, and a little worried that her mother might be annoyed. "It says in the article that they spend their nights on the streets, bringing assistance to those who are too disabled or disoriented to come to the Center, and that they cover all the most dangerous neighborhoods in the city. Ophélie, that's a crazy thing for you to do. You can't do that." He sounded horrified and looked worried as he stared at her. As far as Matt was concerned, this was not a piece of good news.

"It's not as dangerous as it sounds," Ophélie said quietly, for once ready to strangle Pip, but she recognized that it wasn't her fault. It was natural for him to react that way. She was well aware of the risks herself, and they had in fact had a close call the week before, with a man on drugs brandishing a gun, but Bob had calmed him down, and convinced him to put the gun away. They had no right to take it away from him and hadn't. But it had reminded her again of the dangers that they confronted every time they went out. It was hard to tell Matt they didn't exist, when they both knew that they did. "The crew is very good, and highly trained. Two of the people I work with are ex-cops, both are martial arts experts, and the third one is an ex–Navy SEAL."

"I don't care who they are," he said bluntly, "they can't guarantee to keep you safe, Ophélie. Things can go sour in an instant on the streets. And if you've been out there, you know that

too. You can't afford that risk." He glanced
meaningfully at Pip, and then Ophélie suggested they all take a walk on the beach.

Matt still looked upset when they went out,
and Pip ran ahead with the dog, while Matt and
her mother walked more sedately down the
beach. He was quick to bring the subject up
again with her.

"You can't do this," he said, objecting strenu-
ously. "I don't have the right to tell you that you
can't, but I wish I did. This is a death wish on
your part, or some subliminal suicide wish, you
can't take a risk like that, as Pip's only parent.
But even disregarding that, why take a risk that
you'll get hurt? Even if you don't get killed, all
sorts of things could happen to you out there.
Ophélie, I am begging you to reconsider." He
looked extremely somber as he spoke.

"I promise you, Matt, I know it could be dangerous," she said calmly, trying to calm him as
well. "But so are a lot of things. So is sailing, if
you think about it. You could have an accident
when you're alone on your boat. I honestly feel
comfortable doing it. The people I work with
are enormously skilled and good at what they
do. I don't even feel at risk out there anymore."
It was almost true. She was so busy getting in
and out of the van with Bob, and the others, she
hardly thought of the potential dangers during

their long nights. But she could see that she wasn't convincing Matt. He looked frantic.

"You're crazy," he said unhappily. "If I were related to you, I would have you committed, or lock you in your room. But I'm not, unfortunately. And what's wrong with them? How can they let an untrained woman go out there on the streets with them? Don't they have any sense of responsibility for the people whose lives they risk?" He was nearly shouting into the wind as they walked, and Pip danced on ahead, happy to be back on the beach, as was Mousse, who was bounding and leaping and chasing birds and running up and down with driftwood in his teeth, but for once, Matt paid no attention to Pip or the dog. "They're as crazy as you are, for God's sake," he said, furious with the people at the Center.

"Matt, I'm an adult. I have a right to make choices, and even to take risks. If I ever get the feeling it's too dangerous, I'll stop."

"You'll be dead by then, for chrissake. How can you be so irresponsible? By the time you figure out that it's too dangerous, it'll be too late. I can't believe you can be so foolish." As far as he was concerned, she had taken leave of her senses, and was clearly out of her head. He admitted that it was admirable, but thought it far too foolhardy for her to do, particularly in light of Pip, and her responsibilities to her.

"If something happens to me," she said, trying to tease him out of his worries a little bit, "you'll just have to marry Andrea, and you can both take care of Pip. It would be great for her baby too."

"I don't find that amusing," he said, sounding almost as stern as Ted had from time to time, and it was very much unlike Matt, who was always easygoing, and kind. But he was extremely worried about her, and felt totally helpless to make her change her mind. "I'm not going to give up on this," he warned her on the way back toward his house. "I am going to hound you until you give up this craziness. You can still work at the Center, and do whatever you do for them in the daytime. But this outreach program is for cowboys and lunatics, and people who have no one depending on them."

"My partner in the van is a widower with three small children," she said quietly, with a hand tucked into Matt's arm as they walked.

"Then he has a death wish too. And maybe if my wife had died and I had three small children to raise, I would too. All I know is that I can't let you do this. If you're looking for approval from me, don't. I won't give it to you. And if you're trying to worry me sick, I am. I'm going to be panicked every time I know you're going out on the streets, for your sake and Pip's," and he almost added "and my own," but he stopped himself and didn't.

"Pip shouldn't have told you," Ophélie said calmly, and he shook his head in despair.

"I'm damn glad she did. Otherwise I never would have known. You need someone to talk sense into you, Ophélie. You have to give this some more thought. Promise me you will."

"I will. But I swear to you, it's not as bad as it sounds. If I feel uncomfortable, I'll stop doing it. But if anything, I feel more comfortable about it now. The people on the outreach team are extremely responsible." What she didn't tell him, though, was that the group was small, they often spread out, and in simple fact, if someone shot one of them, or lunged at them with a knife or gun, it was unlikely that the others could move fast enough to save someone, particularly as they weren't armed. You just had to be smart and fast and keep your eyes open, which they all did. But beyond that, for the most part, they had to rely on their own wits, the benevolence of the homeless they served, and the grace of God. There was no question in anyone's mind, at any given time, something bad could happen. And Matt had no problem whatsoever figuring that out.

"This conversation isn't over, Ophélie, I promise you that much," he said, as they walked back to his house.

"I didn't plan to do this, Matt," she said by way of explanation, "it just happened. They took me out with them one night, and I fell in love with it. Maybe you should come with us and see it for yourself," she invited him, and he looked horrified.

"I'm not as brave as you are, or as crazy. I'd be scared to death," he said honestly with a look of horror, and she laughed. She didn't know why, but she felt right being out there, and was no longer scared. She hadn't even been as frightened as she would have expected to be when the addict pulled the gun on them, but she didn't say anything about it to Matt. He would have had her locked up, as he'd threatened to earlier. And nothing she had said so far had reassured him in any way.

"It's not as scary as you think. Most of the time, it's so touching, you just want to sit down and cry. Matt, it rips out your heart."

"I'm a lot more worried that someone is going to put a bullet in your head." It was blunt but expressed everything he felt. He hadn't felt as shaken by anything in a long time. Maybe not since Sally had told him that she was moving to Auckland with the kids. He was suddenly convinced that his newfound friend was going to die. And he didn't want that to happen to her, to Pip, or to him. He had a lot at stake now, and hadn't in a long time. He cared about both of them. His heart was at risk now too.

He put a log on the fire when they got back to his house. Ophélie had helped him wash the lunch dishes before they went out, and he stood staring into the fire for a long time, and then he looked straight at her. "I don't know what it's going to take to stop you from doing this crazy thing, Ophélie. But I'm going to do everything I can to convince you that it's a bad idea." He didn't want to frighten Pip so he stopped talking about it, but he looked worried and upset for the rest of the afternoon, and he still was when they left. They already had a dinner date for Pip's birthday the following week.

"I'm sorry I told him about the homeless thing, Mom," Pip said with obvious remorse as soon as they drove away from his house, and Ophélie glanced over at her with a rueful smile.

"It's okay, sweetheart. I guess secrets aren't a good thing."

"Is it as dangerous as he says it is?" Pip looked worried.

"Not really," Ophélie tried to reassure her, and believed what she said. She wasn't lying to Pip. She truly felt safe with the team. "We have to be careful, but if we are, it's fine. No one on the team has ever been hurt, and they want to keep it that way, and so do I." Hearing that reassured Pip, and she looked over at her mother again.

"You should tell Matt that. I think he's really scared for you."

"That's nice of him. He cares about us." But the truth was that there were a lot of things that were dangerous in life. Nothing in life was entirely without risk.

"I love Matt," Pip said quietly. It was the second time in two days she had said that about him, and Ophélie was silent on the way home. It had been a long time since anyone had cared about her in that protective way. Not even Ted. He hadn't paid much attention to her in recent years. He was too preoccupied with his own doings to worry much about her, but there was no reason to. The one Ophélie had always worried about, particularly after his suicide attempts, was Chad, and Ted hadn't worried about him either. He was for the most part extremely self-involved. But she loved him anyway.

Pip called Matt that night to thank him for

the nice day at the beach, and after a few minutes, he asked to speak to Ophélie. She was almost afraid to pick up the phone, but she did.

"I've been thinking about what we talked about, and I've decided I'm angry at you," he said, sounding almost fierce. "It's the most irresponsible thing I've ever heard, for a woman in your position, and I think you should see a shrink. Or go back to your group."

"My group leader referred me to the Center," she said sensibly, and he groaned audibly.

"I'm sure he never thought you'd join the outreach team. He probably thought you'd pour coffee, or roll bandages, or whatever it is they do." He knew what they did. He had read the article she had given him. But he was obviously extremely upset.

"I promise you, I'll be fine."

"You can't promise anyone that, not even yourself, or Pip. You can't predict or control what could happen out there."

"No, but I could be hit by a bus crossing the street tomorrow too, or die in my bed of a heart attack. You can't control everything in life, Matt. You know that as well as I." She was far more philosophical about life, and even dying, than she had been before Ted's and Chad's deaths. Dying no longer held the terror for her it once had. She knew that death was the one thing you could not control.

"That's less likely and you know it." He sounded desperately frustrated, and after a few minutes they both got off the phone. She was not about to resign from the outreach team, and he knew it. He just didn't know what to do about it. But he stewed about it all week, and brought it up at Pip's birthday dinner again, after she went to bed.

He had taken them to dinner at a little Italian restaurant Pip had loved. The waiters had all sung "Happy Birthday" in Italian in resounding baritones, and he had given her some art supplies she'd been longing for, and a sweatshirt with "You're My Best Friend" painted on it. He had done the artwork himself, and she was thrilled. It had been a lovely evening, and as always, Ophélie was grateful to him. But she also knew what was coming next. She could see it on his face, and he knew she did. They were getting to know each other well.

"You know what I'm going to say, don't you?" he asked, looking serious, and Ophélie nodded, almost sorry that Pip had gone to bed.

"I suspect." She smiled at him. It touched her that he cared about them so much. She cared about him too, and she realized each time she saw him how increasingly attached to him she was. She had come to expect him to be part of her life, and Pip's, in whatever form.

"Have you given it any more thought? I truly think you should resign from the outreach team." He looked at her intently.

"I know you do. Pip said I should tell you that no one on the team has ever been hurt. They're careful and smart, and they know what they're doing out there. They're not fools, Matt, and neither am I. Does that reassure you at all?"

"No. All it means is that they've been lucky so far, and it hasn't happened yet, but it could, at any time. And you know that just as well as I do."

"Maybe we have to have a little more faith than that. Maybe it sounds hokey to you, but I don't think God would let me get hurt doing something so worthwhile."

"What if He's busy somewhere else on a night when you run into trouble? He has famines and floods and wars to take care of, not just you," Matt said, and she couldn't help laughing, and finally he smiled.

"You're going to drive me crazy, you know. I've never known anyone as stubborn as you. Or as brave," he said quietly, "or as decent. Or as foolish, unfortunately. I just don't want you to get hurt," he said almost sadly. "You and Pip mean a great deal to me."

"You mean a great deal to us too. You gave Pip a wonderful birthday," she said gratefully. Her birthday the year before had been ghastly, only a week after her father's and brother's deaths. This one had been fun and as nice as Matt could make it. She was having a slumber party with four friends from school the following weekend, and she was looking forward to that too. But the dinner with Matt, and his gifts to her, had been a high point to her, and to Ophélie. She was just sorry that the outreach team and her work with them had become a bone of contention between them. She had no intention of resigning from the team, and Matt knew it. But he had every intention of continuing to reason with her about it, and put pressure on her to resign.

They finally got onto other subjects for the first time in a week, and they both seemed to relax over a glass of wine as they sat by the fire. It was so easy and comfortable being with him. She had never felt as at ease with any man in her life, not even Ted. And Matt was equally at ease with her. He looked happier when he finally left. He hadn't given up his pitched battle about her homeless work, and had no intention of doing so, but he also realized that he could have only so much influence on her, and for the moment it wasn't much. But he was doing the best he could, given the limitations of his role in her life.

And as she walked slowly up the stairs in the dark, to find Pip in her bed, as usual, she was thinking of him. He was a nice man, and a good friend, and she was lucky that someone cared about them. It had been a nice evening with him. Nicer than she wanted it to be in some ways. She worried sometimes that she was getting too attached to him, but she stopped herself from thinking of it. The situation between them seemed to be well in hand. He was her friend, and nothing more.

As he drove back to Safe Harbour, Matt was smiling to himself. He was a little shocked at what he had done before he had left her house, but it was for a good cause. The idea had only come to him as he sat next to her and happened to look past her at a photograph on the table. He had waited until she had gone to check on Pip, and then made his move. And as he drove home, thinking of the evening, and Pip's face when the waiters sang, there was a photograph of Chad in a silver frame lying on the seat, smiling up at him.

19

PIP AND OPHÉLIE DIDN'T SEE MATT AGAIN UN-
til the father-daughter dinner nearly three
weeks later. He was busy, so were they. He
called to talk to Pip nearly every day. Ophélie
tried to stay off the subject of the Wexler Center with him. She knew only too well how he
felt about the outreach team. He wasn't angry
at her, she knew, just frustrated that she refused
to agree with him. And he worried about her,
and Pip too.

He arrived for the father-daughter dinner in a
blazer, gray slacks, a blue shirt, and red tie, and
Pip looked proud when they left for the dinner,
held in the gym at her school. Ophélie had dinner with Andrea that night, at a small sushi
restaurant nearby. Andrea had hired a sitter, and
was enjoying a few hours of being free.

"So what's happening?" she asked pointedly.

"I'm busy at the Center, Pip seems to be happy in school. That's about it for us. Everything's fine. How about you?" Ophélie looked well these days. Her work at the Center had done her good. Andrea could see it too.

"Your life sounds as boring as mine," she said, with a disgusted look. "That's not what I meant, and you know it. What's happening with Matt?"

"He took Pip to the father-daughter dinner tonight," Ophélie said innocently, teasing her friend beyond belief.

"I know that, you dope. What's happening with you and him? Anything?"

"Don't be ridiculous. He's going to marry Pip one day and be my son-in-law." She looked pleased.

"You're sick. He must be gay."

"I doubt it. But if he is, it's none of my business." Ophélie looked unconcerned, and Andrea sat back with a frustrated look. She had recently started going out with one of her colleagues from the office, although Ophélie knew he was married. But that never seemed to bother Andrea. She'd been out with a lot of married men over the years, and said the arrangement suited her. She didn't want to get married, and didn't want a man underfoot all the time. But Ophélie had long since suspected that wasn't true. Especially now, with the baby, it would have been nice for her to get married. She just didn't have much faith that she'd find anyone anymore, and was willing to settle for whatever she could have, even if it was on loan and belonged to someone else.

"Don't you even want to go out with him?" It sounded unnatural to her. Ophélie was a beautiful woman, and she was only forty-two, nearly forty-three, but far too young to give up on men, and spend the rest of her life mourning Ted.

"Nope," Ophélie answered quietly. "I don't want to go out with anyone. I still feel married to Ted." And whatever she felt, or didn't, for Matt was irrelevant. They both liked the relationship as it was. Expecting more from it, or even allowing it to go there, if it did, was too high-risk for her. And she never wanted to spoil what they had now. But she said none of that to Andrea. Ophélie knew she would never have understood. She was far more given to self-indulgence than restraint, which Ophélie preferred.

"What if Ted didn't feel as married to you? What do you think he would have done if you had died instead? Do you think he would have carried a torch for you for the rest of his life?" Ophélie looked unhappy at the question. It

brought up some old painful memories that
Andrea was aware of. But it irked her to see
Ophélie wasting her life. She didn't think Ted
was worth it, no matter how much Ophélie had
loved him. It just wasn't healthy for her to be
alone forever because of him. And Ophélie was
clearly determined to stay on the path of the
celibate grieving widow for the rest of her life.

"It doesn't matter what he would have done,"
she said quietly. "This is what I'm doing, and
how I feel. It's what I want to do." She had
made a choice for herself, and was comfortable
with it, no matter how kind and attractive Matt
was.

"Maybe Matt just doesn't turn you on. What
about the homeless place you work? Is there
anyone there? What's the director like?" She
was clutching at straws for her friend's benefit,
and Ophélie laughed at her.

"I like her very much. And she's a woman."

"I give up. You're hopeless." Andrea threw up
her hands.

"Good. How about you? What's this new guy
like?"

"Just my cup of tea. His wife is having twins
in December. He says she's brain dead, and the
marriage has been in trouble for years, which is
why she got pregnant. Dumb thing to do, but
people do it. He's not the love of my life, but we

have a good time together." Until the babies came, and he fell in love with his wife again, or didn't. But it was no solution for Andrea, and they both knew it. She claimed she didn't want a "solution," just an occasional roll in the hay to prove to herself she wasn't dead yet.

"He doesn't sound like the answer," Ophélie said sympathetically, sorry for her. Andrea had made so many poor choices in her life, for such a long time.

"He isn't. It'll do for now. He'll be too busy when the babies come anyway. Right now, she's on bed rest, and they haven't had sex since June." Just listening to her was depressing. Everything she described was all that Ophélie had never wanted. It was all about expediency and convenience and settling for less than she deserved, just to have a warm body in her bed.

As difficult as Ted may have been, Ophélie loved their marriage. Loved being married to him and loving him, and supporting him emotionally in their years of poverty, celebrating with and for him when he made it. She loved their loyalty, and the fact that they'd been together forever. She had never cheated on him, nor wanted to. And even if he had slipped once, she knew he loved her, and had forgiven him. It horrified her now to think that she was single again, and the dating world terrified her. She was much happier at home with Pip, than out carousing with men who were cheating on their wives, or even bachelors who wanted to stay that way, and were just looking to get laid. She couldn't think of anything worse. And she had no desire to spoil her friendship with Matt, hurt him, or get hurt again. She cherished what they had, just as it was. They were much better off as friends, no matter what Andrea thought.

He and Pip came home at ten-thirty that night. She looked happy and disheveled, her shirt had come untucked from her skirt, and he had his tie in his pocket. They had eaten fried chicken, and danced to rap music the girls had selected. And they both said they'd had a great time.

"I'm not so sure about their music," he said, laughing with Ophélie, as she poured him a glass of white wine, after Pip went to bed. "Pip seems to love it. And she sure can dance."

"I used to love to dance too," Ophélie said with a happy smile. She was glad they had had a good time. As usual, he had saved the day for them. And Pip had gone to bed beaming from ear to ear. Ophélie suspected she had a crush on him, but it seemed harmless and reasonable to her. Matt wasn't even aware of it, which seemed a good thing. If he had known, it might have embarrassed Pip.

"And now? You don't love to dance any-more?" he asked with a broad grin as they sat down.

"Ted hated to dance, although he was a fairly decent dancer. I haven't danced in years." And she realized now that she wasn't likely to again. Not the way she chose to live. Pip was going to have to do all the dancing in the family from now on. She told herself she was over the hill. The Widow Mackenzie was in seclusion, and intended to stay that way. It was one of the many things she accepted about her situation. She would never make love again either. She didn't even allow herself to think about it.

"Maybe we should go dancing sometime, just to keep your hand in. Or your feet," he teased, and she smiled. She knew he was just being silly with her. He was in high spirits after his evening with Pip.

"I think my feet are pretty much past it by now. Besides, I agree with you about Pip's mu-sic. Pretty scary stuff. She puts on the radio every day on the way to school, and nearly deafens me."

"I thought about that tonight too. Industrial injury at seventh-grade dance. It's okay, as an artist, it's no great loss. It would be tough if I were a composer or a conductor." They went on chatting for a while, and for once, he didn't

mention the outreach team, and she was relieved. Her work with them had been going
well, and there had been no untoward events in
recent weeks. More than ever, she felt safe and
comfortable with them. And she and Bob had
become good friends. She gave him gratuitous
advice about his kids, although he seemed to be
doing fine on his own, and she talked a lot
about Pip. He had just started dating his wife's
best friend, which she thought was sweet, and
probably good for his kids, who were crazy
about her. She was happy for him.

It was nearly midnight when Matt left. It was
a beautiful starry night, and she knew it would
be peaceful and lovely on his drive home. She
envied him. She missed the beach. And then,
just before he drove off, she waved and ran
down the steps. She had wanted to ask him
something.

"I almost forgot. What are you doing for
Thanksgiving?" It was in three weeks, and she
had been meaning to ask him for weeks.

"Same thing I do every year. Ignore it. I am
the original Bah Humbug person. I don't believe in turkeys. Or Christmas. They're against
my religion." It was easy for her to guess why.
Since his children had gone out of his life, she
was sure the holidays were painful for him, but

maybe with her and Pip, it would be all right, and a little more appealing to him.

"Do you have any desire to change that? Pip and Andrea and I are going to have it here. What do you think?"

"I think you're sweet to ask me. But I'm not very good at all that anymore. Too much water under the bridge, or under the turkey, as it were. Why don't you and Pip come out for the day, the day after? I'd like that, if you want to come."

"I'm sure Pip would, and so would I." She didn't want to press him about Thanksgiving. She could only imagine how hard it must be for him. Just as it was for her now. The holidays had been hateful the year before. "I just thought I'd ask." She was slightly disappointed, but concealed it from him. He had already done more than enough for them. He didn't owe them anything.

"Thank you," he said, looking touched in spite of his refusal of her invitation.

"Thank you for taking Pip to her dance," she said, smiling at him.

"I loved it. I'm going to listen to rap music every day, and see if I can learn to dance. I don't want to embarrass her next year." It was nice that he even thought that way, Ophélie thought to herself, as he drove off. He was indeed a nice man. It was funny how people learned to survive, she mused. One learned to make do, and to make shift, and substitute and rely on friends instead of mates and spouses. They became family to each other, huddled together like people in a lifeboat in a storm. It wasn't what she had expected to do with her life, but it worked. It gave them each what they needed. It wasn't the kind of family unit she'd once had, but it was all they had now, and what worked for them. Like it or not, they had no other choice, and she was grateful for the kind hands that appeared in the dark, and held theirs, like Matt's. She was infinitely grateful to him as she locked the front door, walked upstairs, and went to bed in the silent house.

20

THANKSGIVING WAS EVEN HARDER THAN SHE'D expected. There was something brutal about the holidays without Ted or Chad. There was no way to dress it up, soften it, or pretend it was less painful than it was. And when she said grace to the small group at her kitchen table, expressing gratitude for all they had to share, and asking for God's blessing on her lost son and husband, she broke down and sobbed. Pip cried with her. And watching them, Andrea began to cry, and seeing all the misery around him, her baby William began to howl too. Even Mousse looked unnerved. It was so awful that after a minute Ophélie started to laugh. And they spent the rest of the day alternating between hysterical laughter and tears.

The turkey was respectable, but no one really wanted to eat it, and the stuffing was somewhat dry. It just wasn't a meal that anyone enjoyed. They had decided to eat in the kitchen, because at almost seven months, waving his chubby arms in his high chair, they knew Willie would make a mess. Ophélie was grateful they weren't in the dining room, where all she would have been able to imagine was Ted carving the turkey, as he had done every year, and Chad dressed in his suit, complaining bitterly about having to wear a tie. The memories and the loss were too fresh.

Andrea went home at the end of the afternoon with her baby, and Pip went to her room to draw. It had not been an easy day. She came out of her room just in time to see her mother about to slip into Chad's room, and she looked at her with pleading eyes.

"Please don't go in there, Mom, it'll just make you sad." She knew what she did in there, lying miserably on Chad's bed, smelling what was left of his scent, and feeling his aura around her. She just lay there and cried for hours. Pip could always hear her through the closed door, and it broke her heart. There was no way she could take his place in her mother's eyes. And it was impossible for Ophélie to explain to her that it wasn't that she was inadequate or meant less than he had, it was simply a loss that no one could dim, a loss that nothing could replace, an unfillable void. No other child could fill it, but that didn't mean she loved Pip any less.

"I'll just go in for a minute," Ophélie looked at her pleadingly as tears filled Pip's eyes, and then silently she went back into her room and closed the door. The look in Pip's eyes made Ophélie feel guilty for going into Chad's room, and instead she walked into her own room, and stood in her closet, staring at Ted's clothes. She needed something, someone, one of them, any-thing, an object, a touch, one of his jackets, a shirt, something familiar that still smelled of him, or of his cologne. It was an insatiable need that no one could understand unless they had suffered a similar loss. All that was left were their possessions and their clothes, the things they had touched or worn, or carried, or handled. She had worn his wedding ring for the past year, on a thin chain around her neck. No one knew it was there, but she did, and her hand went to it from time to time, just to reassure herself that he had in fact existed, that they had been married, and she had once been loved. It was almost hard to remember that now. It was an overwhelming feeling of panic at times, real-izing yet again that he was gone, and would never return. She felt a wave of panic overwhelm her as she clutched one of his jackets to her face, as it hung in the closet next to her, and as though she could feel his arms around her, she took it off the hanger and put it on.

She stood in the closet, feeling like a lost child, as the sleeves hung down, and she wrapped her arms around herself. She could feel something rustle in one of the pockets as she did, and without thinking she reached inside. It was a letter, and for an insane moment, she wanted it to be a letter from him to her, but it wasn't. It was a single typed sheet someone had written on a computer, with an initial at the bottom of the page. She felt uncomfortable reading it since it hadn't been written to her, but it was something, some piece of him, something that he had once touched and read. And her eyes traveled slowly down the page. For a moment, she almost wondered if she'd written it herself, but she knew she hadn't, and she felt her heart begin to pound as she read what it said.

"Darling Ted," it began, and it did not get better, but worse. "I know this has come as a shock to both of us, but sometimes the greatest blows turn out to be life's greatest gifts. This isn't what I intended either. But I believe it's what is meant to be. I'm not as young as I used to be, and to be honest, I'm afraid I won't get another chance, with you or anyone else. This baby means everything to me, more than anything in this world, because it's yours.

"I know this isn't what you planned, nor I. This started out as a little fun, a harmless thing between the two of us. We've always had so much in common, and I know how hard these last few years have been at home for you. No one knows better than I. I think she's mishandled things, for you, and for Chad, and more importantly between the two of you. I'm not even convinced he would have attempted suicide, if in fact he did, if she hadn't alienated you from him. I know only too well how hard this has been for you. And like you, I'm not all that convinced he really has problems. I have never truly believed the diagnosis, and I think it's possible that the so-called suicide attempts were only bids for your attention, maybe even asking you to save him from her. I think she has misjudged this whole thing since the beginning. And maybe the answer, if we wind up together as I hope we will and you say we might, is for her to keep Pip, and you and I to have Chad with us. He might be a lot happier than he is now, with her buzzing around him like a hornet, in a constant panic about him. That can't be good for him either. And he is a lot more like us, you and me, than he is like her. It's obvious to both of us that she doesn't understand him. Maybe because he's smarter than she is, maybe even smarter than we are. In any case, if it's what you want, I'd be willing to try it, and have him live with us, if that's what you decide.

"As for us, I firmly believe that this is only the beginning. Your life with her is over. It has been for years. She doesn't see it, or want to. She can't. She is completely dependent on you and the children. She has no life. She doesn't want one. She feeds off of you, and them, in order to give her life meaning. It doesn't have one. She'll have to find a life of her own, sooner or later. Maybe in the long run, this is what she needs, to jolt her into realizing how pointless her life is, how empty, and how little she has come to mean to you. She drains you. She sucks all the life from you, and has for years.

"This baby, whoever he or she will be, is our bond to each other, our link to the future. I know that you have made no firm decision yet, but I think I know what you want, as you do. All you have to do is reach out and claim it, as you claimed me. As you reached out nearly a year ago now. This baby would never have happened if it wasn't meant to be, if you didn't want us as badly as I do.

"We have six months to figure it out, to make the right moves, until the baby comes. Six months to end the old life, and start a new one. I can't think of anything more important, or better, or that I want more. You have my faith in you, my loyalty, my love for you, my admiration and respect for all that you are, and have been to me.

"The future is ours. Our baby is coming. Our life will begin soon, just as his will, or hers, although I feel sure it is a boy, just like you. God is offering us a new life, a fresh start, the life we have always wanted, between two people who understand and respect each other, two people who are in fact one now in this child.

"I love you with all my heart, and I promise you that if you come to me, when you come to me, because I believe you will, you will be happy as you've never been. The future, my darling, is ours. As I am yours, with all my love. A."

The date on it was a week before his death, and Ophélie felt as though she were going to have a heart attack, and she fell to her knees as she read, and reread it yet again. She couldn't believe what she was reading, and she couldn't imagine who it could be. It was unthinkable. This couldn't have happened. It was a lie. A cruel trick someone had played on them. She wondered if it was a blackmail letter, as the coat slipped off her shoulders and fell to the floor as she held the letter in her trembling hand.

She clung to the wall to help herself up, and stared blindly ahead, still holding the letter. And then as she knew, as she thought of it, as it came to her, she wanted to die. The baby spoken of in the letter had been born, if it had been, six months after he died. William Theodore. She hadn't dared name him Ted, but she had come close enough. And it was not the honor she had claimed it was for her dead friend. The baby had been named for his father. Ted's middle name was William. All she had done was reverse the names. The baby was his, not from a sperm bank. And the letter could only be Andrea's. The single signed letter "A" was her initial, and she had even manipulated him about Chad, played into his desperate need for denial, and criticized her. The letter had been written by the woman who had claimed for eighteen years to be her best friend. It was beyond belief, beyond thinking, beyond bearing. Andrea had betrayed her. And so had he. All it could mean was that when he died, he hadn't loved her. He had been in love with Andrea, and had fathered her baby. Ophélie was still holding the letter when she went into the bathroom and got violently ill. She was standing over the sink, looking deathly pale when Pip found her. And she could see that her mother was shaking violently.

"Mom, are you okay?" Pip looked panicked. "What's wrong?" Her mother looked frighteningly ill, and so pale she looked green.

"Nothing," she croaked, rinsing her mouth out. All she had thrown up was bile and a little bit of turkey. She had eaten almost nothing. But she felt as though she had retched up all her insides along with her heart and her soul and her marriage.

"Do you want to lie down?" Pip offered. It had been a horrible day for all of them, and now she was desperately worried about her mother. She looked like she was going to die, and wished she would.

"I will in a minute. I'll be fine." Even she knew it was a lie. She would never be fine again. And what if he had left her? What if he had done that and not died? And taken Chad with him. It would have killed her, and maybe Chad, if they both had denial. But he was dead anyway. They both were. It no longer mattered. And now he had killed her, as surely as if he had shot her. The letter made a travesty of their marriage, not to mention her friendship with Andrea. She couldn't understand how anyone

could do that to her, how she could be so insid-
ious and so treacherous, so dishonest and so
cruel.

"Mommy, go lie down, please . . ." Pip was
nearly crying. She hadn't called her mother
Mommy since she was a baby. And she was very
frightened.

"I need to go out for a minute." Ophélie
turned to look at her daughter, and this time
the robot had not returned, she looked like a
vampire, with icy white face and red-ringed
watering eyes. Pip almost didn't recognize her,
and didn't want to. She wanted her mother
back, wherever she had gone to in the last hour.
Whoever this was didn't even look like her
mother. "Can you stay here alone?"

"Where are you going? Do you want me to
come with you?" Pip was shaking now too.

"No. I'll only be gone for a few minutes. Just
keep the doors locked, and keep Moussy with
you." She sounded like her mother, but she
didn't look it. And suddenly Ophélie had a sin-
gleness of purpose, and a power she never knew
she had. She could understand suddenly how
people committed crimes of passion. But she
didn't want to kill her. She just wanted to see
her, to take one last look at her, the woman
who had destroyed their marriage, who had

turned her memories of Ted and what they had shared to ashes. She couldn't even allow herself to hate him. Everything she felt, all the agony and horror of the last year was now focused on Andrea in a single moment of time, like a bullet. But the bullet had struck Ophélie and run straight through her. And there was nothing she could do to them to equal what they had done to her.

Pip stood at the top of the stairs looking frightened as her mother left. She didn't know what to do, or who to call, or what to say. She just sat on the steps, and pulled Mousse close to her. He licked her face, and her tears, as they sat there and waited for Ophélie to come back.

She drove the ten blocks to Andrea's house without stopping. She drove through crosswalks and stop signs, and one stoplight, and left her car parked on the sidewalk. She had made no call of warning, and she ran up the stairs and rang the doorbell. She had worn no coat over her thin shirt, not even a sweater, and she felt nothing. It took Andrea only a moment to answer the doorbell. She was holding the baby in his pajamas, and they both smiled the minute they saw her.

"Hi . . ." Andrea started to greet her warmly, and saw instantly that she was shaking. She had put the letter in her pocket. "Are you okay? Did something happen? Where's Pip?"

"Yes, something happened." Ophélie stood in the open doorway, and pulled the letter from her pocket with hands that shook so violently, she could hardly control them. "I found your letter." Her face got even paler, and was instantly matched by Andrea's. She made no attempt to deny it. They looked like two chalk women standing in the doorway, with the wind blowing in around them.

"Do you want to come in?" There were things to say, but Ophélie didn't want to hear them, and did not move from where she stood.

"How could you? How could you do that for a year, and pretend to be my friend? How could you have his baby and pretend it was from a sperm bank? How dare you say what you did about Chad to manipulate his father? You knew how Ted felt about him. It was all a manipulation, you probably didn't even love him. You don't love anyone, Andrea. Not me, not him, probably not even that poor baby. And you would have taken Chad from me, just to impress Ted, and he would have killed himself while you were playing games, using him as a lure. You're beyond pathetic. You're evil. You are the worst kind of human being. I hate you . . .

you destroyed the only thing I had left . . . the belief that he loved me . . . he didn't . . . and you didn't love him either. I did. I always always loved him, no matter how rotten he was to me, or how much he wasn't there for me, or for his children . . . you don't love anything . . . my God, how could you do this?" She felt as though she were going to die standing there, but she no longer cared. They had destroyed her. It took them a year after his death, but even after his death, they had done it. Both of them. She couldn't even begin to understand why. "I want you to stay away from me . . . and from Pip . . . don't ever call us. Don't contact me. You're dead as far as I'm concerned. Forever. Just as dead as he is . . . do you hear me . . ." Ophélie's voice broke in a sob.

Andrea didn't argue with her, and she was shaking too, as she held the baby. They were both cold and in shock, and badly shaken, and Andrea knew she deserved it. She had worried endlessly about what he had done with the letter, but when it never surfaced, she assumed he had destroyed it, and hoped he had. But there was one last thing she wanted to say to the woman who had been her friend and never betrayed her.

"I want you to listen to me . . . I only have

one thing to say to you other than that I am so sorry . . . I'll never forgive myself either, but at least the baby is worth it . . . it wasn't his fault."

"I don't give a damn about you or your baby." But the trouble was she did, about both of them, which was why this was so exquisitely painful, and even more so knowing that the baby was his . . . he even looked like him, she saw now . . . more than Chad had.

"Listen to me, Ophélie. And hear me. He hadn't made up his mind yet. He told me he didn't see how he could ever leave you, you had been so good to him in the beginning, and always, he knew that . . . he was a selfish man, he only did what he wanted to, and he wanted me, but I think he was only playing. We had a lot in common. I wanted him. I always did. And when I saw my chance, when you and the kids were in France, I took it. I grabbed it. He didn't. He walked right into it, but I'm not even sure he loved me. Maybe he didn't. He might never have left you. He hadn't decided. You have to know that. He did not die, having decided to leave you. He wasn't sure. That's why I wrote him the letter. I was trying to convince him. You can see that. He may well have decided to stay with you. I'm not sure he ever loved either of us, to tell you the truth. I'm not even sure he was capable of it. He was brilliant and narcissistic. I don't know if he loved me. But if he loved either of us, if he loved anyone, it was you. He said so. And I think he believed it. I always thought he was a shit to you, and you deserved better. But I do think, to the extent that he could, he loved you. And I want you to know that now."

"Don't ever speak to me again." Ophélie spat the words at her, and then turned, and on trembling legs she walked back down the stairs to her car. She had left it running on the sidewalk. She didn't look back at Andrea. She never wanted to see her again, and Andrea knew she wouldn't. Andrea was sobbing as she watched her drive off erratically, but at least she had told Ophélie the truth, as she knew it. Ted hadn't been sure what he was going to do. And he may have loved neither of them, but at least Ophélie deserved to know that he felt he owed her something, and might have stayed with her. Ophélie might well have been the winner and not the loser. But in the end, they had all lost. Ted, Chad, Ophélie, Andrea, and even her baby . . . all losers. He had died with the decision unmade, and instead of destroying the letter, he had left it for her to find it. Maybe he wanted her to. Maybe he expected her to. Maybe it was his way of manipulating the solution. Neither of them would ever know. But all Andrea had left to give her was the truth, that he wasn't sure, that he didn't know when he died . . . and that maybe . . . only maybe . . . he had loved her, as best he could.

21

OPHÉLIE NEVER KNEW HOW SHE DROVE BACK to the house, or how she got there. She parked the car in their driveway, and went inside. Pip was still sitting where she had left her on the steps, clinging to the dog.

"What happened? Where did you go?" If humanly possible, her mother looked even worse than she had half an hour earlier, and she felt sick again as she crawled up the stairs, and walked into her bedroom looking dazed.

"Nothing happened," she said, with eyes that only stared, and a heart that had been gouged out with a single letter. They had done it together. He and Andrea. It had taken them a year, but they had finally killed her. Ophélie turned to look at Pip as though she couldn't see her. As though she was blind suddenly. The robot had returned, and it was utterly, totally broken, with sparks shooting everywhere, a system that had misfired and was self-destroying as Pip watched. "I'm going to bed now" was all she said to Pip, and then turned off the lights and lay there, staring into space. Pip would have screamed if she had dared, but she was afraid to make things even worse. She ran to her father's den then and dialed the phone. She was crying when he answered. He couldn't understand her at first, and he sounded unusually happy.

"Something happened . . . there's something wrong with my mother." Matt came sharply to earth as he listened. He had never heard Pip sound like that, not even close. She was panicked, and he could hear the tremor in her voice.

"Is she hurt? Tell me quickly, Pip. Do you need to call 911?"

"I don't know. I think she's gone crazy. She won't tell me." She described everything that had happened, and he asked to speak to her mother. But when she went back to her mother's room, the door was locked and she wouldn't answer. Pip was crying harder when she came back to speak to him on the phone. He didn't like the sound of any of it, but he was afraid to make matters worse by calling the police and having them break down the door. He told Pip to go back and knock again, and tell her he was on the phone.

Pip knocked for a long time, and she could finally hear a sound in the room. It sounded as though something had fallen down, like a lamp or a table, and then slowly she opened the door. She looked like she'd been crying, and still was, but she didn't look as crazed as she had half an hour before.

Pip looked at her in despair, and touched her hand as though to make sure she was real, and spoke in a shaking voice. "Matt's on the phone. He wants to talk to you."

"Tell him I'm tired," she said, looking down at her now-only child, as though seeing her for the first time. "I'm so sorry . . . I'm so sorry . . ." She finally understood what she was doing to her child, it was what they had done to her. "Tell him I can't talk right now. I'll call him tomorrow."

"He says if you don't talk to him, he's coming in." Ophélie wanted to tell her that she shouldn't have called him, but she knew Pip had no one else to call.

Ophélie didn't say another word, she walked back into her bedroom and picked up the phone. It was dark, but Pip could see the lamp she'd knocked over on the floor. It was the noise she had heard. She had stumbled in the dark.

"Hello." It sounded like a voice from the dead, and Matt was as worried as Pip had been.

"Ophélie, what's happening? Pip is scared to death. Do you want me to come in?" She knew he would, all she had to do was ask, but she didn't want him or anyone else. Not even Pip. Not yet. Not right now. Or maybe ever. She had never felt so alone in her life, not even on the day he died.

"I'm all right," she said unconvincingly. "Don't come in."

"Tell me what happened." He was firm, and strong.

"I can't." It was the voice of a waif. "Not now."

"I want you to tell me what's wrong." She shook her head, and he could hear her sob. He was worried sick. "I'm coming in."

"Please don't. I want to be alone." She sounded saner again. She was coming in and out of some kind of hysteria, or panic, and he had no idea what it was.

"You can't do this to Pip."

"I know . . . I know . . . I'm sorry . . ." She couldn't stop crying.

"I want to come in, but I don't want to intrude on you. I wish I knew what the hell is happening."

"I can't talk about it now."

"Do you think you can pull yourself together?" It sounded like she had snapped, and at that distance, he couldn't assess how bad it was. It sounded pretty bad to him. And he had no idea what had caused it. Maybe the holiday. Maybe she couldn't stand the reality of her double loss. What he didn't know was that it was now a treble loss, she had lost not only Ted and Chad, but all her illusions about their marriage as well. It was almost more than she could bear.

"I don't know," she said in answer to his question.

"Do you want me to get help?" He was still thinking of calling 911. He thought of calling Andrea, she was closer, but a sixth sense he didn't quite trust told him not to call anyone.

"No, don't call. I'll be all right. I just need time."

"Do you have anything you can take to calm down?" Although he didn't like that idea either. He didn't want her sedated and alone with Pip. That would be upsetting for her too.

"I don't need anything to calm down. I'm dead. They killed me." She was crying harder again.

"Who killed you?"

"I don't want to talk about it. Ted is gone."

"I know he is. I know . . ." It was worse than he thought, and for a minute he wondered if she was drunk.

"I mean really gone. Forever. And so is our marriage. I'm not even sure it ever was." Andrea's reassurances meant nothing now.

"I understand," he said, mostly to calm her down.

"No, you don't. And neither did I. I found a letter."

"From Ted?" He sounded shocked. "Like a suicide note?" He suddenly wondered if he had killed himself and Chad. It would have explained how she sounded. Not much else would.

"A homicide note." Ophélie was not making sense. But clearly, something terrible had happened.

"Ophélie, do you think you can get through the night?"

"Do I have a choice?" She sounded dead.

"No, you don't, not with Pip there. The only choice you have is whether I come into town or not." But for once, he didn't want to leave the beach. He wanted to explain it to her, but not now. It had to wait.

"I can get through the night." What difference did it make now? Nothing did, from her perspective.

"I want you and Pip to come out tomorrow." It was what they had planned, and now more than ever, he wanted her there, or he would come in.

"I don't think I can." She was being honest with him. She couldn't imagine driving to Safe Harbour. And he didn't like the idea either. She was in no condition to drive.

"If you're not up to it, I'll drive in. I'll call you in the morning. And I'll call you in an hour to see how you are. Maybe you should sleep alone tonight, if you're too upset. It sounds like you need some time to yourself, and this might be hard on Pip." It already was.

"I'll ask her what she wants. You don't have to call me back. I'll be fine."

"I'm not convinced yet," he said, sounding strained, he was worried about both of them. "Let me talk to Pip." She called Pip to the phone, and Pip took it in the den. Matt told her to call him if anything happened, and if things got too bad, to call 911.

"She looks a little better," Pip reported, and when she went back to see her mother, Ophélie had turned the lights on in her room. She still looked deathly pale, but she was trying to reassure Pip.

"I'm sorry. I just . . . I think I got scared." It was all she could say to explain what had happened to her. She was not going to tell her the story. Ever. Or that Andrea's baby was her half brother.

"Me too," Pip said quietly, and crawled onto her mother's bed and into her arms. She felt icy cold, and Pip gently put a blanket on her to keep her warm. "Do you want anything, Mom?" She brought her a glass of water, and Ophélie took a sip, just to please the child. She felt terrible that she had frightened her so badly. She had nearly lost her mind, and had for a while.

"I'm okay. Why don't you sleep here tonight?" Ophélie took her clothes off and put her nightgown on, and Pip came back in her pajamas with the dog. They lay holding each other for a long time, and then Matt called. Pip assured him that everything was all right, and she sounded better, so he had to assume they were. It sounded as though it had been a rotten night for both of them. And before he hung up, he assured Pip that one way or another, he would see her the next day. And for the first time that night, Matt told Pip he loved her. He knew she needed to hear it, and he needed to say it to her.

Pip snuggled up to her mother then, and nei- ther of them slept for a long time. Pip kept glancing up to check on her mother, and when they finally fell asleep, they slept with the lights on that night, to keep the demons away.

Matt's Thanksgiving had been at the opposite end of the spectrum from theirs. He had been prepared to ignore it, as he always did, or had for the past six years. He worked on Pip's portrait, and was pleased with the results. And then made himself a tuna fish sandwich. He liked doing everything he could to prove to himself it wasn't Thanksgiving Day. Even a turkey sandwich by coincidence would have been an affront. And he was washing the plate he'd eaten the sandwich on when he heard a knock at the door. He couldn't imagine who it was. He was expecting no one, and his neighbors never bothered him. It had to be a mistake. He thought of ignoring it, but the knock was persistent. So he finally strode to the door and pulled it open, and stared at the unfamiliar face. There was a tall young man standing there with brown eyes and dark hair, and he had a beard. The odd thing was that the face wasn't entirely unfamiliar to him. He realized with consternation that he had seen that face, in the mirror, years before. The experience was entirely surreal. It was like looking at himself. He had even had a beard at the same age. It was like looking at the ghost of Christmas past. And then the man spoke, and Matt felt a lump rise in his throat.

"Dad?" It was Robert. The boy who had been twelve the last time he saw him. His only son. Risen from the ashes of his life. Matt said not a word, but pulled him close to him and held him so tight he could hardly breathe. He had no idea how he had found him, or why he was there. Matt was just grateful he was.

"Oh my God," Matt said, loosening his grip on him, unable to believe it had finally happened. He had always believed they would see each other again one day. He didn't know how or when, but he had always sensed that they would. "What are you doing here?"

"I go to Stanford. I've been looking for you for months. I lost your address, and Mom said she didn't have it."

"She said what?" They were still standing in the doorway, and Matt waved him in with a puzzled expression. "Sit down." He waved him at the weathered leather couch, and Robert sat down and smiled. He was as pleased as his father. He had promised himself he would find him, and he had.

"She said she lost track of you when you stopped writing," Robert said quietly.

"She sends me a Christmas card every year. She knows where I am." Robert looked at him strangely, and Matt suddenly felt sick.

"She said she hadn't heard from you in years."

"I wrote to both of you for four years after you stopped writing, you and Vanessa," Matt said, looking stricken.

"We didn't stop writing, you did." Robert looked shocked.

"No, I didn't. Your mother said you didn't want me in your lives anymore, you only wanted Hamish. I'd been writing to you for three years by then, with no response. Eventually, she asked me if I'd let him adopt you, and I wouldn't. You're my children, and you always will be. But after three years of silence from you, I finally gave up. It's been another three years since then. But your mother and I always stayed in touch. She said you were both happier without me in your life, you and Vanessa, and wanted it that way. So I let you be."

It took the entire afternoon to piece all of it together, but it was obvious what had happened, once each told the other their part of the story. It was obvious that Sally had withheld his letters, and told them he'd stopped writing.

She had told Matt that his children no longer
wanted contact with him. She had seen to it
that Hamish replaced him, and possibly even
lied to her new husband about it. She had cleverly and maliciously cut Matt out of their lives,
she thought, forever, and cheated him of his
children, and them of their father, for six years.
It had been cleverly done, almost brilliantly, and
had succeeded for the past six years. Robert
said he had been looking for him since September, and finally found him three days before. It had been his Thanksgiving gift to
himself to drive over and surprise him. His only
fear was that Matt would refuse to see him. He
had never understood why his father had abandoned them, and was afraid that he wouldn't
want to see him now. He had never expected
the reception he got or the story he had just
heard. They both cried when they realized
what had happened, and they embraced each
other again and again as they sat beside each
other on the couch. It was dark outside by the
time all the mysteries were solved. And Robert
showed him a picture of Vanessa, who was a
beautiful, blond sixteen-year-old girl. They
called her a few minutes later, Robert knew
where she was, and for her it was three in the
afternoon.

"I have a surprise for you," Robert said mysteriously, overwhelmed by what he was about to do, and there were tears in Matt's eyes, as they held hands. "I've got a lot to tell you, and we'll talk about it later. I'll explain everything. But there's someone here who wants to say hello to you."

"Hi, Nessie," Matt said gently, and for an instant, there was silence on the other end of the phone, as tears rolled down his cheeks.

"Dad?" She still sounded like a little girl to him. She sounded just as she always had, only a little more grown up. And in a minute she was crying too. "Where are you? I don't understand. How did Robert find you? . . . I was always so scared you had died and no one knew. Mom never knew anything. She said you just disappeared off the face of the earth." But not as far as she would have liked. What a vicious thing to do. And all the while, she'd been cashing his support checks and sending Christmas cards.

"We'll talk about it sometime. I didn't go anywhere. I thought you did. Robert will explain later, and so will I. I just wanted to tell you I love you . . . I've wanted to tell you that for the last six years. It looks like Mom played a little game with all of us. I wrote to you guys for three years and never got any answers." He at least wanted her to know that.

"We never got your letters," she said, sound-

ing confused. It was a lot for any of them to absorb. A heinous crime had been committed by
the mother they trusted, and the woman he had
once loved.

"I know. Don't say anything to your mother.
I'll talk to her about it myself. I'm just glad to
talk to you. I want to see you," he said hungrily.
"I'll come over soon. Maybe we can all spend
Christmas together."

"Wow! That would be so cool." She still
sounded like an American kid, and a slightly
older version of Pip. He wanted Pip and
Ophélie to meet them too.

"I'll call you in a few days. We have a lot of
catching up to do. You look gorgeous in the
picture Robert showed me. You've got Mom's
hair." But fortunately not her heart. Or her
twisted mind. He couldn't believe that the
woman he had loved and been married to had
cheated him out of his own children for six
years. He couldn't think of anything worse. He
couldn't even begin to imagine what had gone
through her head. He had a lot to say to her, but
he wanted to cool off first, or he knew he
wouldn't even be coherent. He was going to
call Hamish too. He assumed he'd been part of
her plot, but Robert didn't seem to think he
was, and still insisted he was a nice guy. At least
he'd been decent to them. But what Sally had

done was unforgivable. And he knew he never would.

He and Vanessa talked for a few more minutes and then she talked to Robert, and he tried to explain as much as he knew. It sounded incredible to them too, but Robert believed his father. He could see in his eyes that it was the truth, and he could also see what it had cost him. There was a depth of pain that Matt hadn't been able to hide in years, even from his son now. Seeing that, and knowing what had happened put Robert's relationship with his mother on the line, which was hard for him too.

Matt and Robert talked for hours and were still talking when Pip called about her mother. Robert listened intently to the exchange.

"What was that all about?" he asked, wanting to know everything about him now, including who his friends were and what his life was like.

"A widow and her daughter. Apparently, something's wrong."

"Is she your girlfriend?" Robert asked with a smile as Matt shook his head.

"No, she's not. We're just friends. She's had a tough time. Her husband and son died last year."

"That's too bad. Do you have a girlfriend?" Robert asked with a grin. He was so happy just being there, he wanted to soak it all in. Matt had given him a sandwich and a glass of wine by then, but Robert was too excited to eat or drink.

"No, I don't have a girlfriend." Matt laughed. "Or a wife. I'm a recluse."

"And you still paint." He saw the portraits of himself and his sister, and then stared at the one of Pip. "Who's that?"

"The little girl on the phone."

"She looks like Nessie," Robert said, looking intently at the painting. There was something mesmerizing about her eyes, and touching about her smile.

"Yes, she does. I painted that as a surprise for her mother, for her birthday next week."

"It's good. Are you sure her mother's not your girlfriend?" There was something about the way he talked about her that made Robert suspicious.

"Absolutely sure. Now what about you? Do you have a wife or a girlfriend?" Robert laughed in answer and told him about his current love, his classes at Stanford, his friends, his passions, and his life. They had six years to cover, and cruised through midnight as they sat talking for most of the night. It was four A.M. when Robert fell into Matt's bed, and Matt slept on the couch. Robert hadn't intended to spend the night, but couldn't bring himself to leave.

And when he woke up in the morning, they started talking again. Matt cooked him bacon and eggs, and at ten o'clock Robert said he had to go, but he promised to come back the following week. He had plans for the weekend. Matt said he'd come down to see him at Stanford during the week.

"You'll never get rid of me now," Matt warned, looking happier than he had in years. And so did Robert.

"I never wanted to, Dad," he said gently. "I thought you'd forgotten us. The only way that I could explain it to myself was I thought you had died. I didn't think you'd stop writing for any other reason. I knew you wouldn't just walk away, no matter what. But I just had to know for sure." He had used all kinds of ingenious means to find him, and his efforts had finally borne fruit.

"Thank God you found me. I was going to contact you and Nessie in a few years, and find out if you'd had a change of heart, and wanted to see me again. I hadn't given up, I was just waiting." And there was the whole issue of what to say to Sally. But more importantly, what could she possibly say to him to explain what she had done? And what could she say to her children? She had deprived them of their father, and lied to all of them. It seemed an unforgivable sin, not only in Matt's eyes, but in her son's. She had a lot of reckoning to do. And justifiably, they would never trust her again.

Robert left reluctantly, finally, at ten-thirty on Friday morning. It had been the best Thanksgiving of Matt's life, and he couldn't wait to tell Ophélie and Pip. But he had to see what had happened to Ophélie first, and how she was. He dialed their number only seconds after Robert left. Matt felt like a new man, or the man he had once been. He was a man with children again. There was no feeling like it in the world. And he knew Ophélie and Pip would be happy for him.

Pip answered the phone on the second ring. She sounded serious, but not upset, and reported to him in an undertone that her mom seemed okay, or at least better than the night before. And then she went to tell Ophélie Matt was on the phone and wanted to talk to her.

"How are you?" he asked calmly when she came to the phone.

"I don't know. Numb, I think." She didn't offer more.

"You had a hell of a night. Are you coming out?"

"I'm not sure." She sounded indecisive and still shaken. But he was fully prepared to come into town if she wanted, it would have been harder the night before, with Robert there. But he would have, if necessary, and even brought his son with him. He could hardly wait to tell Ophélie and Pip what had happened.

"Do you want me to come in? It might do you good to come out here. We can take a walk on the beach. Whatever you prefer."

She hesitated as she thought about it, and she had to admit, the idea appealed to her. She wanted to get out of the house, and away from everything that reminded her of him. She wasn't even sure yet what she was going to tell Matt. The whole thing was degrading, so shameful and humiliating. Ted had betrayed her, with her best friend. It had been the cruelest of all tricks, and Andrea had even been prepared to use Chad to destroy her. Ophélie knew it was a blow she would never recover from, nor for-give. And she knew Matt would understand that too. He had the same feelings about loyalty that she did.

"I'll come out," she said softly. "I don't know if I want to talk. I just want to be there, and breathe." She felt as though she couldn't breathe in the house, as though her lungs and her chest and her ribs had been crushed.

"You don't have to say anything if you don't want to. I'll be here. Drive carefully. I'll make lunch."

"I'm not sure I can eat."

"That's all right," he said gently. "Pip will. I have peanut butter." And pictures of his children to show them. Robert had left all the pictures he had in his wallet. They were the best gifts Matt had had in years. He felt as though someone had returned his soul. The soul his ex-wife had tried to destroy. But she never could. And for him, the healing had already begun. He couldn't wait to go down to Stanford to see him again the following week.

It took Ophélie longer than usual to dress and drive over. She felt as though she was moving under water, and it was noon before he heard them drive up. Things were worse than he thought, or maybe they just looked worse. Pip looked solemn, and Ophélie was visibly shaken and pale. She didn't even look as though she'd combed her hair. It was exactly the way she had looked when Ted first died. It was a familiar sight to Pip, who ran to Matt and threw her arms around him. She clung to him like a drowning child.

"It's okay, Pip . . . it's okay . . . everything's fine." She clung to him for a long time, and then walked into the house with the dog. He looked at Ophélie then, and saw her eyes. She didn't move. She just stood there, without saying a word. And he walked over to her and put an arm around her shoulders, and together, they walked inside. He had put the portrait away, and Pip was looking around, wondering where it was, with a shy smile. Their eyes met conspiratorially, and he nodded, as though to tell her that it was all in good order, and done.

He made sandwiches for all three of them, and Ophélie never said a word all through lunch. And then sensing that she was ready to talk to him, he suggested to Pip that she take Mousse for a walk on the beach. She understood, and a minute later, she put on her jacket and they left. Matt didn't say anything. He just handed Ophélie a cup of tea.

"Thank you," she said quietly. "I'm sorry I was such a mess last night. It was a rotten thing to do to Pip. I felt like Ted had died all over again." He had figured out that much, he just didn't know why it had happened.

"Was it the holiday?" She shook her head. She didn't know what to say to him, but she knew now that she wanted to share it with him. She walked over to where she had left her handbag, pulled out Andrea's letter, and handed it to him. He hesitated, holding it, wanting to ask her if she was sure she wanted him to read it, but he could see that she was. She sat down across from him at the table, with her head in her hands, as he began to read. It didn't take him long.

And when he had finished, he looked at her, and said not a word. Her eyes were bottomless pools of pain, and now he knew why. He reached out and took her hand, and they sat that way for a long time. As she had, he had figured out that the letter was from Andrea, and the baby was Ted's. It wasn't hard to figure out. But a great deal harder to live with, and understand. The cruelty of the timing was excruciating, that she should find out now after his death, and to learn that Andrea had used Chad to coerce Ted, if he even needed to be coerced.

It took Matt a long time to speak. "You don't know what he would have done. The letter makes it pretty clear that he hadn't made up his mind." It was small consolation now. He had still had the affair with her best friend, and fathered her child.

"That's what she said," Ophélie said, feeling wooden again. Her whole body felt like it was made of lead.

"You talked to her?" He looked stunned.

"I went to see her. I told her I never wanted to lay eyes on her again, and I don't. I never will. She's dead to me now, just like Ted and Chad. And I guess our marriage was dead too. I just didn't want to see it, just like he didn't want to know that Chad was sick. I had denial too. We were all stupid and blind, each in our own way."

"You loved him. That's allowed. And in spite of this, he probably loved you too."

"I'll never know now." That was the worst of it. The letter had robbed her of the belief that Ted had loved her. It was a cruel trick.

"You have to believe he did. A man doesn't spend twenty years with a woman if he doesn't love her. He may have been flawed, but I'm sure he loved you, Ophélie. In spite of this."

"He might have left me for her." Although, knowing Ted, she wasn't sure, not even because he had loved her, but he didn't love anyone that much. Except himself. He might have left Andrea with his baby, and done nothing for her. It would have been possible for him. But it still did not mean that he had loved his wife. Perhaps he had loved neither of them, that was entirely possible too. "He had another affair years ago," she told Ted in a stifled voice. She had for-

given him. She would have forgiven him anything. Until now. And this time they could not
fix it, or talk about it, or explain. She had to live
with it this time, all by herself. There would be
no repairing it this time. The fabric of their entire life together had been torn to shreds in a
single night, with one letter, and a betrayal by a
friend. Damage beyond repair. "He had the affair when Chad first got sick. I think he hated
me for that. That was his revenge. Or his escape.
Or the only way he could cope. He did it while
I was in France with Pip. I don't think he cared
about the woman. But it nearly killed me. It
was a lot happening at once. But he stopped
seeing her. I forgave him. I always did. I forgave
him everything. All I ever wanted was to love
him and be his wife." And all he had ever loved
was himself. Matt could see it clearly, but didn't
say a word to her. She had to come to her own
conclusions and be able to live with them. Matt
didn't want to wound her any more than she
was. And the damage to her was so great, he
didn't want to hurt her more. The last thing he
wanted was to hurt Ophélie or Pip.

"You may have to let this go," Matt said
wisely. "It's only going to hurt you. He's out of
it now. This isn't about him anymore, it's about
you."

"They destroyed everything, the two of them. Even from the grave, he managed to destroy our life." It had been stupid of him to keep the letter and to leave it where she might find it. It made Matt wonder if he had wanted to get caught. Maybe he was counting on that to make her leave him. It was painful to imagine the drama that would have caused, and had, finally.

"What are you going to say to Pip?"

"Nothing. She doesn't need to know. This is between Ted and me, even now. At some point, I'll tell her that we won't be seeing Andrea anymore. I'll have to think of some reason to give her, or maybe just tell her that it's something I'll explain to her later on. She knows something terrible happened last night, but she doesn't know that Andrea was part of it. I didn't tell her where I went when I went out."

"That was a good thing." He was still holding her hand, and he wanted to put his arms around her, but he was afraid that she couldn't even tolerate that. She looked so broken and frail, like a little bird with both its wings broken, not even one.

"I think I lost my mind last night, or nearly did. I'm sorry, Matt. I didn't mean to burden you with this."

"Why not? You know how much I care about you and Pip." Or maybe she didn't. He had only just begun to realize it himself, and he knew it now as he looked at her. He had never cared about anyone as much in his life, except his kids. Which reminded him of what he hadn't told her yet. "Something happened to me yesterday," he said softly, still holding her hand. "Although I unearthed a terrible betrayal too. I had a visitor yesterday, for Thanksgiving. It's the first real Thanksgiving I've had in years."

"Who was it?" She tried to emerge from her misery to listen to him.

"My son." He told her what had happened then as her eyes grew wide.

"I can't believe she did that to you, and her own kids. Didn't she think they'd ever find out?" She looked horrified. They had both been betrayed horrifyingly by people they had trusted and loved. It was the worst kind of betrayal of all. And she wasn't sure which was worse. It was a close match.

"Apparently not. She must have thought they'd forget me, or assume I was dead. They nearly did forget me. Robert and Vanessa both said they thought I was dead. He tried to find me, to be sure. And was amazed to find me very much alive. He's a great kid. I want you and Pip to meet him soon. Maybe we could spend

Christmas together," he said hopefully. He was already making plans.

"No more Bah Humbug?" she said with a smile, and he laughed.

"Not this year. And I'm going to fly over to see Vanessa in Auckland very soon."

"How wonderful for you, Matt," she said, squeezing his hand, and with that, Pip walked in, and smiled when she saw them holding hands. She took it to mean something other than it did, but was pleased.

"Can I come back yet?" she asked, as Mousse bounded in and got sand all over Matt's living room, but he insisted he didn't mind.

"I was just going to suggest to your mom that we go for a walk on the beach. Do you want to come?"

"Do I have to?" she asked, installing herself on the couch, looking tired. "I'm cold."

"That's fine. We won't be long." He looked at Ophélie then, and she nodded. She wanted to go for a walk too.

They put on their coats and went outside, and he put an arm around her and pulled her close. She suddenly seemed even smaller and so frail. They walked down the beach, and she leaned against him, as though for support. He was the only friend she had left, the only person she still trusted, and knew she could. She no longer

knew what to believe about her marriage or
her late husband. She no longer knew what to
think or believe about anyone, but him. And
she was so distressed over all that had happened,
and what it meant, that they walked all the way
down the beach together, with his arm tightly
around her, and said not a word. It was enough
just being with him.

22

MATT WENT TO SEE HIS SON THE MONDAY AF-
ter Thanksgiving, and stopped in to see Pip and
Ophélie on the way home. Pip had just come
home from school, and Ophélie had taken the
day off from work. She was too upset to think.
And she felt as though her whole life had
changed. She had made a decision that morning to get rid of Ted's clothes. It was her way of
throwing him out of the house, and punishing
him posthumously for what he'd done. It was
the only revenge she had left, but she also knew
it would be good for her. She had to move on.
She couldn't hang on forever to a man who had
betrayed her and fathered another woman's
child. She knew now that she was hanging on
to her illusions and a lifetime of dreams. It was
time to wake up, no matter how alone it made
her feel.

She told Matt when Pip went to her room to do her homework, and he was afraid to say too much. He didn't want to tell her that he thought her late husband was a sonofabitch. It didn't seem fair. She had to come to those conclusions herself. And it was hard to let go now in death, after she had been willing to forgive him so much in life. She had been willing to tolerate almost anything from him. But Matt was pleased to see her making different decisions now, and silently approved.

And while he was there, he made a date with her for her birthday the following week. And as always, he included Pip. He always did. And always had, right from the first. After all, he and Pip had been friends first, as she often pointed out, which made him smile. It was true.

But he had picked a slightly more grown-up restaurant than usual for her birthday night. He wanted to take her somewhere special. She deserved a reward for all the misery Ted and Andrea had just put her through. And she told him that she'd had a letter from Andrea, which had been delivered by messenger that afternoon. It was a letter of abject apology, in which Andrea told her that she didn't expect to be forgiven, but wanted her to know how much she had loved her, and how sorry she was. For Ophélie, it was too late, and she said as much to Matt.

"I suppose that makes me an awful person. But I just can't. I never want to see or hear from her again."

"That sounds reasonable to me." He told Ophélie he was planning to call Sally that night, if she would talk to him.

"It sounds like we're both settling our accounts," she said sadly.

"Maybe it's time." He had been thinking all day about what he was going to say to his ex-wife. What did you say to someone who had stolen your children and six years of your life, not to mention the marriage and life she had destroyed before that? There was no restitution possible for that. Ophélie knew it too.

They talked for so long that Ophélie invited him to stay for dinner with her and Pip. He accepted, and helped her cook. And as soon as dinner was over, he left. But they had a date for her birthday the following week. Pip could hardly wait.

And he called Ophélie late that night, after he had called Sally. He sounded drained.

"What did she say?"

"She tried to lie about it," he said, sounding amazed. "But she couldn't. I know too much now. So she just cried. For about an hour. She told me she was doing it for the children, that she thought it would be better for them to feel part of one family with Hamish, and to hell with me, I guess. I became dispensable. She decided to play God. There wasn't much she could say to clean it up, nothing in fact. I'm going to fly over and see Vanessa after your birthday next week. I'll only be there for a few days. And she said she'd send her over for Christmas if I like. I said I would. I'll have both of my kids with me." He sounded deeply moved, and she was pleased for him. "I'm thinking of renting a house in Tahoe, to take them skiing. Maybe you and Pip would like to come. Can she ski?"

"She loves it."

"What about you?" He sounded hopeful.

"I ski, but I'm not great. I hate the chair lifts. I'm afraid of heights."

"We can ride them together. I'm not a fabulous skier either. I just thought it would be fun. I hope you and Pip will come." He sounded sincere, but Ophélie was concerned.

"Won't your kids object to having strangers with them after not seeing you for so long? I don't want to intrude." She was always cautious about his feelings, as he was with hers, unlike the people they'd been married to, who had been selfish and self-serving in the extreme.

"I'll ask them, but I can't imagine they'd mind, especially after they meet you and Pip. I told Robert about both of you the other day." And he almost slipped and said he'd seen Pip's portrait, which was Pip's big birthday surprise for her.

And then Matt inquired if she was going out with the outreach team, as usual, the following night, and she said she was.

"You've had a tough few days. Why don't you give yourself some time off?" Like forever, he wished. He still hated her doing it, but she refused to listen to him.

"They'll be shorthanded if I don't go. And it will take my mind off of things." They both knew that she now had a far deeper wound to heal, the loss not only of her son and husband, but now of her marriage and best friend as well. It compounded everything, and made it all seem much worse. But she seemed to be holding up, and Matt was relieved. The only thing he didn't like was that she was going out with the outreach team, particularly when she was distracted and tired, and more likely to get hurt.

But all went well. She had an uneventful night, as she told Matt when he called to check on her on Wednesday, and it was another quiet night when she went out with them on Thursday. They had come across several camps of kids and young people, some of them still decently dressed from when they left home, which tugged at her heart. And a camp of clean-cut-looking men, all of whom said they were employed but wound up homeless anyway. There were a lot of heart-wrenching stories on the streets. And Saturday was her birthday, which turned out even better than planned. It was everything Pip had dreamed. They celebrated at the house before they went out to dinner, and Pip was so excited she couldn't sit still. She and Matt went out to his car to get the portrait. Pip made Ophélie close her eyes, and then with a kiss and a flourish, she handed it to her. And Ophélie gasped. And then cried.

"Oh my God . . . it's so beautiful . . . Pip! . . . Matt . . ." She kept holding it and staring at it. It was a beautiful portrait, and he had captured not only her elfin face, but also her spirit. Each time Ophélie looked at it, she cried. And she hated to leave it when they went out to dinner. She could hardly wait to hang it up. Her reaction was everything Matt had hoped, and she didn't stop thanking him for it all night.

They had a lovely time at dinner, and he had arranged a birthday cake for her at the restaurant. It was a perfect birthday, and Pip was yawning when they got home. It had been a big night for her too. She had waited months for the presentation of the portrait, and her excitement and anticipation had worn her out. Ophélie was still holding it when Pip kissed her mother and Matt and went up to bed, and he was thrilled to see how happy Ophélie was with the gift.

"I don't know how I can ever thank you. It's the most beautiful present I've ever had." It was truly a gift of love, not only from Pip, but from Matt.

"You're an amazing woman," he said gently, as he sat next to her on the couch. And an honorable one, he knew, which had come to mean a great deal to him, particularly in light of what Sally had done to him, and what he now knew had been done to Ophélie. She was very rare, and so was he. But the people they had loved had also been unusually cruel.

"You're always so good to me and Pip," she said gratefully, as he looked down at her and took her hand. He wanted her to trust him, and he thought she did, but he didn't know how much. And what he wanted to say to her was going to require a great deal of trust.

"You deserve to have people be good to you, Ophélie. And so does Pip." He felt as though they were part of his family, and he was the only family she and Pip still had. It seemed as though all else had been lost.

And as he looked at her, he leaned toward her gently, and kissed her on the mouth. She was the first woman he had kissed in years, and she hadn't been touched by a man since her husband died. They were two fragile, cautious beings, like stars, floating gently through the skies. Ophélie was startled, she hadn't expected him to kiss her, but much to his relief, she didn't resist or pull back. She just seemed to hang there in the moment with him, and when he stopped, they were both out of breath. He had been afraid she would be angry at him, and he was immensely relieved that she was not, but she looked scared, as he pulled her into his arms and held her close.

"What are we doing, Matt? Is this crazy?" More than anything, she needed to feel safe. And she no longer did, anywhere in her life, except with him. And he felt safe with her too.

"I don't think it is," he reassured her. "I've felt this way about you for a long time. Longer than I knew. I was just afraid to frighten you away if I said anything. You've been so badly hurt."

"So have you," she whispered, touching his face with a gentle hand, and thinking how pleased Pip would be. The thought of it made her smile, and she said as much to him.

"I'm in love with her too. I can't wait for you both to meet my kids."

"Neither can I," she said, sounding happy, and he kissed her again.

"Happy birthday, my darling," he said, as he kissed her, and when he left that night, she thought that, without a doubt, it had been the best birthday of her life.

23

THE TUESDAY AFTER HER BIRTHDAY, OPHÉLIE was out with the outreach team, and Bob reminded her that she was being careless while they were checking what they called "cribs," the boxes and structures people were sleeping in. They walked up to them, checked if people were inside and awake, and asked what they needed, but they needed to be vigilant while they did it, to avoid surprises. She had been dreamy eyed, and more than once turned her back on groups of young men who approached them. People on the streets were always curious about who they were, where they came from, and what they were doing. But being alert and cautious was vital to the team. The rules of the jungle applied at all times, no matter how friendly people appeared. For the most part, the homeless they encountered were gentle and kind, and grateful for whatever they got. But threaded among them were the inevitable dissidents, the troublemakers, and the predators who preyed on them, and wantonly took the little they had. It was painful to realize that for everything the outreach team distributed, a third or even half of it would be stolen by someone else. It was a world in which the honor code was survival, and little else. Ophélie knew that, as the others did. And all you could do, in helping them, was give it your best shot, and hope it made a difference.

"Hey, Opie! Watch your back, girlfriend. What's up?" Bob asked her with a look of concern as they headed back to the van after their second stop. He wanted to make her aware of it, so no one got hurt. The safety of the entire team rested on each one of them. And although they were casual at times, and joked with each other, and even those they helped, they still had to keep their wits about them and remain aware of the players. They had to anticipate the worst in order to prevent it happening to them. There were the inevitable stories of cops and volunteers and social workers who'd been killed on the streets, usually doing something they shouldn't have done, like going out to work on the streets alone. They knew better, but there was always the temptation to believe that they were exempt and couldn't be touched. Safety, for all of them, lay in being, and staying, alert.

"I'm sorry. I'll be more careful next time," she promised apologetically, focusing more diligently again. She had been thinking about Matt.

"You better be careful. What's happening with you? You look like you're in love." He knew, because he was. He was having a great time with his late wife's best friend. Ophélie looked at him and smiled as she swung into the van. He was right. She'd been out of it all night. She'd been thinking about Matt. And had been all day. Their kiss the night before had both delighted and rattled her. It was everything she wanted in some ways, and in others the one thing she didn't want at all. Vulnerability. Openness. Love. Pain. All of which had brought her to her knees when Ted died, and nearly killed her when she found Andrea's letter. For a moment, she thought it had. Now, more than anything, she was numb, as she tried to sort out what she felt. About Ted, Andrea, herself, and now Matt. It was a lot to absorb and try to understand. And at the same time it was so tempting to let herself free-fall into his arms and life.

"I don't know. Maybe," she said honestly, as they headed toward Hunters Point. It was late in their night, when it was usually safer there.

By then, a lot of the troublemakers had gone to bed, and the neighborhood had calmed down.

"There's a news flash," he said with a look of interest. He had come to respect her and like her a lot in the nearly three months they'd worked together. She was smart and honest and solid and real, without artifice or arrogance. There was a simplicity and earnestness about her that had won his heart.

"I hope he's a good guy. That's what you deserve," he said sincerely.

"Thanks, Bob," she said, and smiled. She seemed uninclined to talk about it, and he didn't press her. They had an easygoing relationship and solid understanding of each other's rhythms. Sometimes they talked about serious matters. Sometimes they didn't. They were like police partners, they were compatible, respectful of each other, and trusted each other completely. Their lives depended on it. But she paid closer attention, and "watched her back," as he put it, at the next stop and for the rest of the night.

But she realized as she drove home that night that she was worried about Matt. About what she was doing, and the door that had opened. More than anything, she didn't want to jeopardize their friendship, and a romance, if it went awry, might. She didn't want to risk that for

him, or herself, or even more importantly for
Pip. If she and Matt got involved romantically,
and made a mess of it, it could spoil it all, and
that was the last thing she wanted.

Even Pip noticed that she looked quiet and
pensive the next morning in the car on the way
to school.

"Something wrong, Mom?" she asked as she
turned the radio on, and Ophélie winced at the
volume, as she always did. It was a raucous way
to start the morning. Pip worried less about her
mother's moods these days. Whatever else happened, she seemed to recover from the bad days
sooner. Although she still didn't know what
had happened on Thanksgiving. All she knew
was that it had something to do with Andrea.
Her mother had told her that they wouldn't be
seeing her again. Pip was shocked. But Ophélie
refused to answer any questions. And when Pip
asked her, "Ever?" Ophélie confirmed it. Ever.

"No, I'm okay," Ophélie answered, but she
didn't look convincing. And she had to struggle
for concentration all that day at the Center.
Even Miriam at the front desk commented on
it. And when Matt called, he could hear it.

"Are you okay?" he asked, sounding worried.

"I think so," she said honestly, which didn't
reassure him. Her uncertainty was unnerving.

"What does that mean? Should I panic?" She smiled in answer.

"No, don't panic. I'm just scared, I think." She wasn't sure if it was a timing or adjustment issue for her, or something deeper.

"What are you scared of?" He wanted to air it with her, so she'd feel better. He had been floating on air since he kissed her on her birthday. It was just exactly what he wanted, and hadn't known it. Although for a while now he'd been aware of his growing feelings for her, which were not by any means as casual as he'd pretended.

"Are you kidding? I'm scared of you, me, life, fate, destiny, good things, bad things . . . disappointment, betrayal, your dying, my dying . . . do you want me to go on?"

"No, that ought to do it. For now at least. You can save the rest till you see me. We can spend all day on it then." It sounded like it was going to take that long. And then he got serious with her. He was sorry that she was so afraid, and wanted to share his sense of confidence with her. "What can I do to reassure you?" he asked gently, and she sighed.

"I'm not sure you can. Give me time. I just lost the last of my illusions about my marriage. I'm not sure I can handle much more than that.

This may not be the right time." His heart sank at her words.

"Will you at least give us a chance? Don't make any decisions yet. We have a right to be happy, both of us. Let's not blow it to bits before we start. Will you do that?"

"I'll try." It was all she could do. In her heart of hearts, she thought he might be better off with someone else. Someone simpler, and who had been less brutally hurt than she had been, and again recently. At times, she felt so damaged. Yet with him she always felt peaceful, whole, and safe, which said a lot.

He came to town and had dinner with her and Pip that weekend, and on Sunday she and Pip drove out to the beach to see him. Robert had come up for the day from Stanford, and Matt was anxious for them to meet. Ophélie was enormously impressed. He was a lovely boy, and in spite of the years they had missed together, he was remarkably like Matt. As they often do, genes had won out, and in this case for the best. He spoke very openly about his mother's perfidy at one point, and he was obviously upset about it. But he seemed to accept, and even love her as she was. He had a very forgiving heart. Although he referred to the fact that Vanessa was furious with her, and hadn't spoken to her since she found out.

And by the time she and Pip went back to town, Ophélie felt better again. Matt had put an arm around her several times, and held her hand when they walked on the beach, but he didn't press her, or make it obvious to Pip that something was happening. He wanted to give Ophélie time to adjust. Their relationship, past, present, and future, was of vital importance to him, and he wanted to treat it cautiously, and give her all the time and space she needed to make room for him in her heart.

He was just about to pick up the phone on Monday night to call her, when it rang before he did. He was hoping it was her. She had looked happy and relaxed the day before, and sounded fine when he called her on Sunday night. He wanted to tell her that he loved her, but he didn't. He wanted to tell her in person the first time he said it, and not on the phone. But it wasn't Ophélie when he answered, or even Pip. It was Sally, calling from Auckland, and he was terrified when he heard her voice. She was crying. And he thought instantly of his daughter, and was deathly afraid something had happened to her.

"Sally?" He could hardly understand her, but even after all these years, he knew her voice too well. "What is it? What's wrong?" All he could make out was "keeled over . . . tennis court . . ." and then with a sense of relief that was almost sinful, he realized she was talking about her husband, and not their younger child.

"What? I can't understand you. What happened to Hamish?" And why was she calling him?

She gave a horrible wrenching sob and then shot the words into the phone. "He's dead. He had a heart attack an hour ago on the tennis court. They tried to revive him, but . . . he was gone." She started sobbing again, as Matt listened and stared into space, as the last ten years flashed before his eyes. Her telling him that she was leaving him, and then moving to Auckland. The realization that she had been having an affair with his friend, and had left their marriage for him . . . and then moving to Auckland with his kids . . . "Hamish and I are getting married, Matt," the cannonball she had fired at his chest . . . and commuting for four years to see his kids, only to have her cut him off from them for the last six . . . and now she was calling to say Hamish was dead. He didn't even know what he felt, for his old friend turned traitor . . . for her . . . or himself . . . he couldn't even think.

"Matt? Are you there?" She was talking nonstop and crying in between, something about the funeral, and their children, and did he think Robert should come home for the services, Hamish had been so good to him . . . and her children from Hamish were so young . . . He felt overwhelmed.

"Yes, I'm here." And then he thought of his son. "Do you want me to call Robert and tell him? If you think it will be too tough on him, I can drive down to Stanford." It was odd how fate served one well in life at times. One father had just reentered his life in time for another to disappear. It was odd how those things happened.

"I already called him," she said bluntly, with little thought for the effect on Robert. That was Sally.

"How did he take it?" Matt sounded concerned.

"I don't know. He was crazy about Hamish."

"I'll call him," Matt said quickly, anxious now to hang up.

"Do you want to come to the funeral?" Sally asked, with no concern whatsoever for the distance, the time involved, or his feelings as usual. If nothing else, Hamish had betrayed him, and damn near destroyed his life, with Sally's help.

"No, I don't," he said bluntly.

"Maybe Vanessa and I will bring the children over for Christmas," she said wistfully. "I don't think you should come to see her this week, unless you want to come to the funeral with us." He had been planning to leave for Auckland to see Vanessa on Thursday, after six long, endless, empty years without his kids. But this obviously wasn't the right time.

"I'll wait. I'll come over as soon as things calm down, unless you send her here." He said "send her," not "bring her." He hadn't liked the implication that Sally would come too. He had no desire to see his ex-wife again. "You have other things to think about right now," a funeral to plan, a husband to bury, decisions to make, fresh lives to destroy. His feelings toward her were anything but friendly since her treachery had been exposed by Robert's return. He knew he would never forgive her for what she'd done.

"I can't even imagine what this is going to do to our business," she said plaintively. She always had work on her mind, always had. Nothing had changed.

"That's tough, I know," he said, sounding bitter, but she didn't hear it. "Just sell it, Sal. I did. No big deal. You'll find something else to do. No point hanging on." They were almost the identical words she had said to him ten years before. But she no longer remembered them. No matter what incredibly insensitive life-altering comment she made, she never remembered it, or took responsibility for it later on. Other people's feelings and well-being never even appeared on her radar screen.

"You really think I should sell?" she said seriously, sounding interested, and all he wanted was to hang up and call his son.

"I have no idea. I have to go now. I'm sorry about Hamish. My condolences to his children. I'll let you know when I'm coming over to see Ness. Tell her I'll call her later myself." And with that, he hung up.

He called Robert and got him in his room at Stanford. He wasn't crying, but he sounded subdued and a little forlorn.

"I'm sorry, son. I know you loved him. I always liked him too," before he blew the bottom out of my life, Matt thought.

"I know he screwed up your marriage to Mom, but he was always really good to us. I feel sorry for Mom. She was a mess on the phone." But not too big a mess to discuss the fate of their business with Matt. Her wheels were always turning to her own advantage. It was just the way she was, and had always been. And at the time, Hamish had been a better deal for her. He had more money, more toys, more houses, he was more fun, so she dumped her husband and moved on. It was still hard to take, and Matt knew it would always be. They had cost him too much, everything he'd ever loved and cared for. His wife, his kids, the business was less important to him, but the rest of it was a loss that could never be replaced. Ten heartbreaking years out of his life.

"Are you going over for the funeral?" Matt asked him, and Robert hesitated.

"I should, for Mom, but I've got finals. I talked to Nessie and she thinks Mom'll be okay if I don't. She's got a lot of people with her." And seven other kids. Four of Hamish's, Vanessa, and two of their own. It was a sizable entourage, although he knew Robert was important to her too. "What do you think, Dad?"

"That has to be your decision. I can't make it for you. Do you want me to come down to Stanford?" Matt sounded and was deeply concerned for him.

"That's okay, Dad. I'll be fine. It's just kind of a shock . . . but not totally. He's had two heart attacks, and two bypass surgeries. And he didn't take great care of himself. Mom always said it would come to this." He smoked and drank, and had been overweight for years. He was fifty-two years old.

"I'll come down anytime you want. Just call me. Maybe we can do something this weekend if you're not studying."

"I've got study groups all weekend. I'll call. Thanks, Dad."

Matt sat quietly for a moment, thinking about it, and called Ophélie. He didn't know why, but he was sad about Hamish, maybe because it affected his children, or maybe because he had once been his friend. He felt less sorry for Sally than he did for him.

He told Ophélie what had happened, and as he was, she was concerned for Robert, and for a strange female moment, she wondered what Sally's widowhood would mean to Matt. He had loved her once, passionately, and mourned her for the last ten years. And now she was free. It was unlikely anything would ever happen between them, but you never knew. Stranger things had happened. She was only forty-five years old, and she would be looking for a new man. And she had once loved him, enough to marry and have children with him.

"She said she might bring Vanessa over for Christmas, and to see Robert," Matt informed her. "I hope she doesn't. I don't want to see her, just my kids." He was disappointed about not going to Auckland to see Vanessa that week too. But this obviously wasn't the time. There was far too much going on, and Vanessa would be tied up with Hamish's family, her mother, and the other kids. She'd have no time to spend with him, and rightly so. Matt understood. After six years, he knew he could wait another week or two. It was better that way.

"Why would she come too?" Ophélie asked, sounding concerned.

"God knows. Maybe just to annoy me," he said, and laughed. But it had been unsettling talking to her on the phone, and listening to her crying. It didn't move him any closer toward her, it just reminded him of how unhappy she had made him over the years. He had absolutely no idea that Ophélie was suddenly worried about her, and saw her as a potential threat to their budding romance.

The rest of the week was hectic for both of them. Things were tough on the streets with the holidays approaching. People drugged and drank more, lost jobs, and the weather was cold. They found four dead people in one night in the cribs they checked. As always, it was rugged, heart-wrenching work.

Matt drove down to Robert to see him. And he talked to Vanessa on the phone. And for no reason he could fathom, in the midst of all she had to do, Sally called him several times just to talk. He did not want to be her best friend, and he complained about it to Ophélie.

The only moment of peace for all of them

was a sunny Sunday afternoon at the beach. She and Pip drove out to see Matt. Robert couldn't make it, he was still studying for exams. And Christmas was in less than two weeks.

The three of them took a long walk on the beach and Matt told Ophélie about the house he'd rented in Tahoe from Christmas till just after New Year's. He was going to go to Tahoe with Robert to ski, and he was hoping Vanessa would fly over too.

"Is Sally still thinking of coming?" she asked, sounding unconcerned, but wasn't. It surprised even her that the reappearance of his ex-wife bothered her so much, but it did. Particularly now that she was widowed too. Although even Ophélie realized it was more paranoia on her part, than anything real. Matt seemed in no way interested in her, but you never knew. Stranger things happened. Much stranger. Like her husband having a baby with her best friend. It had altered all her points of view.

"God knows. I don't care. I'll have someone drive Nessie up to Tahoe, if she comes. I have no intention of seeing Sally, if she's here," which reassured Ophélie at least. "I'd love you and Pip to come up too. What are you doing for Christmas?" It was a sore subject for her this year, even more than it had been the year before.

"I don't know yet. Our family seems to get

smaller and smaller. Last year we spent it with Andrea." She'd been five months pregnant then. The thought of it made Ophélie shudder now, knowing that the baby was Ted's, and the travesty Andrea's friendship had been. "I think Pip and I will just spend it quietly. Maybe it would be nice to come up to Tahoe the day after. I think we should be alone together on Christmas Day." He nodded, not wanting to intrude on her and Pip. He knew how sensitive she was about that, and it was a bittersweet time for them, full of memories that needed to be honored, however painful. "It would be nice to have something to look forward to the day after." She smiled up at him, and Pip was so far up the beach that he bent his face down to hers and they kissed. And as he did, he felt a jolt of electricity run through him, which he instantly suppressed. He wanted more of her, but too much had been happening in the past few weeks, and he didn't want to rush his fences with her, or scare her off. They were proceeding with great caution, and no speed. He knew she still had a lot of trepidation about getting involved with him. She was not at all sure yet if she wanted to forge ahead. He had only kissed her a few times by then, and he was willing to wait, however long it took. Although he was aware that the passion he felt for her distracted him. He was equally well aware of all the trauma she'd been through, especially recently. And in spite of it, he could feel desire mounting in her too. Whatever reservations she had, she seemed to be growing ever closer to him.

They talked to Pip about Tahoe when she walked back to them, and she loved the idea. And by the time they left that day, Ophélie had agreed. And Matt had tried to extract yet another promise from her.

"I only want one thing for Christmas from you," he said seriously, as they sat by the fire in his living room before she and Pip left.

"And what's that?" She was smiling at him. Pip already had his gift, and Ophélie still had to shop for him.

"I want you to resign from the outreach team." He was serious, and she sighed as she looked at him. He had come to mean so much to her, but she still didn't know what to do about it, when, or if. She felt strongly about him, but her feelings were in constant conflict with her fears. But he wasn't asking for answers or promises. He never put pressure on her, except about this, which he did constantly.

"You know I can't do that, Matt, it's important to me. And to them. I know how right it is for me. And it's hard to get people to work on that team."

"You know why?" he said, looking unhappy. "Because most people are smart enough to be scared out of their wits, and won't do it." It had occurred to him more than once that maybe one of her reasons for doing it was some kind of subliminal suicide wish. But whatever her reasons, he was determined to prevail eventually, and get her to quit. He didn't mind her working at the Center, but he didn't want her on the streets. It wasn't a question of not respecting her, but of saving her from herself, and her altruistic ideas. "Ophélie, I'm serious. I want you to give that up, for your sake, and Pip's. If those people are crazy enough to do it, let them, you can help the homeless in other ways. You owe it to yourself to quit."

"Nothing is as effective as what the outreach guys do. They go to them where they are, give them what they need. The really desperate cases are in no shape to come in for us to help them. We have to go to them," she said, always trying to convince him, as he did her. It was an insoluble battle between them, and she'd been unwavering about it. But he kept trying, and intended to continue to do so. "What you don't realize is that they're not bad guys out there or criminals. They're sad, needy, broken people, in desperate need of help. Some of them are just kids, and old people. I can't walk away from them and figure someone else will do it. If I don't, who will? So many of them are really decent and I have a responsibility to them. What else do you want for Christmas?" she asked, as much to change the subject as because she needed ideas, but all he did was shake his head.

"That's all I want from you. And if you don't give it to me, Santa is going to put coal in your stocking, or reindeer poop." Sometimes he wondered if she was right and he was overreacting. She was very persuasive, but he still wasn't convinced. She laughed at what he said then, unaware of the fact that he already had her gift wrapped and put away, and had for quite a while. He hoped she liked it. And with Ophélie's permission, he had bought Pip a beautiful new bicycle that she could use in the park in town, and at the beach when she came to see him. He was pleased, because it was kind of a fatherly gift, something her mother wouldn't have thought to give her. Ophélie had been shopping for clothes and games for her for weeks. She was at a tough age, somewhere between toys, which she had outgrown, and big girl gifts, which she was only now growing into. At twelve, she was exactly in between. He had hidden the bike in his garage at the beach, under a sheet, and Ophélie had assured him she'd be thrilled.

The one gift Matt didn't want was the one he got the week before Christmas. A call from Sally telling him she was arriving the next day, with Vanessa, and her two youngest kids. Hamish's four children were with their mother for the holidays, and she had decided to come to San Francisco, as she put it, "to see him." All he wanted was to see his daughter, which he was wildly excited about, but not his ex-wife. They were planning to stay at the Ritz. And he called to complain to Ophélie about it, the minute he hung up. She was getting ready to go out with the outreach team.

"What am I supposed to do with that?" he said, sounding irritated. "I'm not going to see her. All I want is to see Nessie. The good news is she's coming to Tahoe with me. Nessie, not Sally," he corrected, but Ophélie was concerned anyway, and didn't want to let on to him that she was. She was far too attached to Matt by now, not to be affected by the specter of his ex-wife. What if he fell in love with her again? If he had before, perhaps he could again, in spite of everything she'd done. She had just been relaxing about her, but Sally's impending arrival set her on edge suddenly. She had a sixth sense that he would see her, and doing so would stir up old feelings for him. Men were naïve about such things, and it was obvious from Sally's insistence on seeing him, that she had something up her sleeve. Ophélie tried as delicately as she could to warn him of it.

"Sally? Don't be ridiculous. That's dead and gone. She's just bored and doesn't know what to do with herself. She's trying to decide what to do with her business. Ophélie, you have nothing to worry about. I'm well out of that, and have been for ten years." He sounded remarkably blithe about it, but all of Ophélie's female antennae were on high alert.

"Stranger things have happened," she warned wisely.

"Not to me. It's been over for me for years, and longer than that for her. She left me, remember. For a guy with more money and more toys," he said, still smarting from the blow.

"Now she's got the money, and he's gone. And she's scared and lonely. Trust me. You haven't heard the last of her." But Matt violently disagreed. Until she got to the Ritz, and called him an hour after she did. Her voice was all honey and sweetness, and she asked him if he'd like to come to tea. She said she was exhausted from the flight, and looked a mess, but she was dying to see him. He was so startled, he wasn't sure what to say.

Ophélie's warnings immediately came to mind, but he dismissed them out of hand. She was just trying to be friendly, for old times' sake, but even that didn't appeal to him. Far from it, after she'd stolen his kids from him. His rational mind hated her, but there were other parts of him, which responded instinctively to memory. It was Pavlovian and irritated him at himself as much as her. It was her way of torturing him, to see if she could still pull the old familiar strings.

"Where's Nessie?" he asked bluntly, desperate to see her, and not Sally. All he wanted was to see his daughter, as soon as he could.

"She's here," Sally said coyly. "She's tired too."

"Tell her she can sleep later. I'll be in the lobby in an hour. Tell her to be there." He was so excited he nearly hung up on Sally, and she promised to convey the message to Vanessa, who was thrilled too, when she did.

He showered, shaved, changed, and was wearing a blazer and gray slacks and looking very handsome as he came through the doors into the lobby of the Ritz-Carlton, and he looked around anxiously. What if he didn't recognize her? If she had changed too much . . . if . . . and then he saw her standing there like a young doe, with the same face she had had as a little girl, a woman's body, and long straight blond hair, and they were both crying as they fell into each other's arms. She buried her face in his neck, and kissed him, and touched his face as he held her. The cruelty of their long separation was apparent in the hunger with which they held each other. He never wanted to let her out of his arms again, and he had to force himself to let go of her just so he could see her. And as he looked at her lovingly, they were both laughing through their tears.

"Oh Daddy . . . you look the same . . . you haven't changed at all . . ." She couldn't stop crying and laughing and he had never seen anyone as beautiful as his youngest child. It almost ripped his heart out of his chest just looking at her, and made him realize how agonizing her long absence from his life had been. Everything he had forced himself not to feel for six years came rushing back at him.

"Well, you sure have changed! Wow!" She had a spectacular figure, just as her mother had as a young girl. Vanessa was wearing a short gray dress and high heels, and just enough makeup to look glamorous but not vulgar, and she had tiny diamond studs at her ears, a gift from Hamish probably, he knew. He had always been generous with Matt's kids. "What do you want to do? Have some tea? Or go somewhere?" All he wanted was to be with her.

Vanessa seemed to hesitate for an instant, and then he saw them in the distance behind her. He had been completely unaware of anyone else from the moment he laid eyes on her. But Sally was standing halfway across the lobby, with a woman who looked like a nanny and two little boys. The years had been kind to her, she was still a good-looking woman, although slightly heavier than she had been in the past. And the boys were cute. They were six and eight. But instead of leaving Vanessa alone with him after all this time, she had intruded on them, which was exactly what Matt didn't want, and he was instantly annoyed as she approached, and Vanessa looked daggers at her. Sally was wearing a short black dress, expensive, sexy shoes, and a mink coat, and the diamonds on her ears were a lot bigger than Vanessa's were, another gift from her late husband undoubtedly.

"I'm sorry, Matt, I hope you don't mind . . . I couldn't resist . . . and I wanted you to meet the boys." The last time he had seen them, in Auckland, they had been two and a few months old. And no matter how cute they were, he wanted to be with his own child now, and not Sally and her kids. She had done enough to him. All he wanted now was for her to let go and disappear.

Matt said hello to the boys, with a warm smile, and ruffled their hair, and nodded politely to the nanny. It wasn't the kids' fault that their mother was inappropriate, but he wanted to be clear with her.

"I think Vanessa and I would like to be alone for a little while. We have a lot of catching up to do."

"Of course, I understand," she said breezily, and didn't. She couldn't have cared less what anyone else needed, especially him. And she totally ignored Vanessa's obvious fury at her. She still hadn't forgiven her mother for keeping Matt away for six years, and swore she never would. "I promised the boys we'd run down to Macy's and see Santa Claus, and maybe stop in at Schwarz. I thought maybe we could all have dinner tomorrow night, if you're free," she said with the smile that had dazzled him from the first time they met, but no more. He knew that behind the smile lived a shark, he had been too deeply bitten by her to fall for it. But she played a great game. Anyone else would have thought her charming and poised, and friendly to him. And whatever she wanted from him, he no longer gave a damn.

"I'll let you know," he said vaguely, and firmly led Vanessa away from them to the portion of the lobby set up to serve tea. A moment later, he saw Sally, the nanny, and the boys sweep through the revolving door to a waiting limousine. She was a rich woman now, even richer than she had been. But from his perspective, it didn't add to her charm. Nothing would. She had everything one could want, looks, talent, brains, style, everything, except a heart.

"I'm sorry about everything, Dad," Vanessa said quietly, as they sat down. She understood, and admired her father a lot for the gracious way he handled it. She had talked to her brother at length about what had happened, and she was far less willing to forgive than Robert, who always made excuses for their mother and said she didn't understand her effect on people. But Vanessa hated her with all the energy of a girl of sixteen, and with good cause in this case. "I hate her, Dad," she said bluntly to her father, and he didn't disagree with her, but he didn't want to fuel the fires, or encourage her to hate her own mother. He tried to be somewhat discreet for Vanessa's sake. But there was no dressing it up, or explaining it. She had kept them from their father, for her own purposes, for six years. Almost half a lifetime for them, and it felt like more than that to him. And all they wanted to do was catch up with him now. "You don't have to have dinner with her tomorrow. I just want to be with you." Vanessa understood all of it, and was wise for her sixteen years. She'd been through a lot too.

"I'd rather be with you," he said honestly. "I

don't want a battle with your mother, but I'm not dying to be best friends either." It was remarkable enough that he was willing to be civil to her, and a tribute to him.

"It's okay, Dad."

They sat and talked for three hours in the lobby of the Ritz. He explained to her again what she already knew, how their six years of separation had happened. And then he went on to ask about her, her friends, her school, her life, her dreams. He loved being with her, and was soaking it all in. She and Robert were going to be spending Christmas in Tahoe with him, *without* their mother. Sally was going to New York to see friends with her two youngest children. She seemed to have nowhere to go now, and was searching for something. If he hadn't disliked her so much, he would have felt sorry for her.

Sally called him again the next day, about dinner, and she tried to convince him to join them. But he was patiently resistant, and instead talked about Vanessa, and sang her praises.

"You did a great job with her. She's wonderful," he said generously.

"She's a good girl," Sally agreed. She said she was going to be around for the next four days, and Matt was anxious for her to leave town. He had no desire to see her. "What about you,

Matt? How's your life?" It was a subject he emphatically did not want to discuss with her.

"Fine, thanks. I'm sorry about Hamish. That's going to be a big change for you. Are you going to stay in Auckland?" He wanted to keep their conversations to business, houses, and his children. But she didn't.

"I have no idea. I've decided to sell the business. I'm tired, Matt. It's time to stop and smell the roses." It was a nice thought, but knowing Sally she was far more likely to crush them, and set fire to the petals. He'd been there.

"That sounds sensible." He kept his responses curt and unemotional. He had no intention of lowering the drawbridge, and hoped the alligators in the moat would devour her if she tried to take the castle.

"I gather you're still painting, you have so damn much talent," she said lavishly. And then she seemed to hesitate for a moment, and sounded childish and sad when she spoke again. It was a tactic she used that he had nearly forgotten, to get what she wanted. "Matt . . ." she hesitated, but only for an instant, "would you hate having dinner with me tonight? I don't want anything from you. I just want to bury the hatchet." She had already done that, he knew, in his back, years before, and it had stayed there, festering and rusting. Removing it now would only make matters worse, and cause him to bleed to death in the process.

"It's a nice thought," he said, sounding tired. She exhausted him. She had so many agendas. "But I don't think dinner is a good idea. There's no point. Let sleeping dogs lie. We don't really have anything to say to each other."

"How about I'm sorry? I owe you a lot of those, don't I?" She was speaking softly and she sounded so vulnerable it nearly killed him. He wanted to scream at her not to do that. It was too easy to remember all that she had once been to him, and too hard, all at the same time. He just couldn't. It would kill him.

"You don't have to say anything, Sally," he said, sounding like the husband he had once been to her, the man she had known and loved, and whom she had nearly destroyed. Whatever had happened in between, they were still the same people, and they both remembered, the good times as well as the bad ones. "It's all behind us."

"I just want to see you. Maybe we can be friends again," she said, sounding hopeful.

"Why? We have friends. We don't need each other."

"We have two children. Maybe it's important for them that we establish a bond again." Amazingly, that hadn't occurred to her for the past six

years. Only now. That it suited her current purpose, whatever that was. Whatever it was, Matt
knew it would be good for her, and surely not
for him. Her intrinsic narcissism always controlled her. It was all about her needs, and no
one else's.

"I don't know . . ." He hesitated. "I don't see
the point."

"Forgiveness. Humanity. Compassion. We
were married for fifteen years. Can't we be
friends now?"

"Is it too rude to remind you that you left me
for one of my best friends, moved thousands of
miles away with my children, and haven't allowed me to have contact with them for the
past six years? That's a lot to swallow, even between 'friends,' as you put it. Just how friendly is
that?"

"I know . . . I know . . . I've made a lot of
mistakes," she said sweepingly, and then she put
on the voice of the confessional, which was exactly what he didn't want with her. "If it's any
consolation, Hamish and I were never happy.
There were a lot of problems."

"I'm sorry to hear that," he said, feeling a chill
run through him. "I always had the impression
that you were very happy. He was very generous
with you, and your children." And he was basi-

cally a good guy. Until he ran off with Sally, Matt had always liked him.

"Generous, yes. But he never really 'got it.' Not like you did. He was kind of a good-time guy, and he drank like a fish, which finally killed him," she said unsympathetically. "We had no sex life."

"Sally, please . . . for chrissake. I don't want to know that." Matt sounded horrified and grim.

"Sorry, I forgot what a prude you are." Socially perhaps, but never in the bedroom. And she knew that about him. She had missed him. Hamish told the filthiest jokes on the planet, and loved looking at lots of tits and ass, but he was just as happy going to bed with a porn video and a bottle as with her.

"Why don't we just stop here? There's no point in this. You can't run the film backward. It's all over. It's done. End of story."

"It's not done. It never was. And you know it." She had hit a nerve that was so raw, it still made him jump. It was what he had been hiding from for a decade. No matter what had happened or how bad it had been, he had always loved her. And she knew it. She could sense it still. She was a shark with a radar screen, and unfailing instincts.

"I don't care. It's over," he said gruffly. And the

tone of his voice, almost hoarse, shot the same chemicals through her, it always had. She had never gotten over him either. She had cut it off, sliced their life away like a limb she no longer wanted, but all the nerves around the stump were still raw and throbbing and alive.

"Don't have dinner with me. Have a drink. Just see me, for God's sake. What difference does it make? Why can't you do that?" Because he didn't want to hurt anymore, he reminded himself, but he felt an irresistible pull toward her and hated himself for it.

"I saw you yesterday, in the lobby."

"No, you didn't. You saw Hamish's widow, his two kids, and your daughter."

"That's who you are, isn't it?" he said miserably, not wanting a different answer from her.

"No, it isn't. Not to you, Matt." The silence between them was deafening, and he groaned. She made him feel insane. She always had. Even after she left him. She could always do that to him. She knew where all the chords were, and the raw nerves, and she loved playing with all of them.

"All right, all right. Half an hour. No more. I'll see you. We'll bury the hatchet, declare ourselves friends, and then for God's sake, get the hell out of my life before you drive me crazy." She had done it. She had gotten to him. She always did. It was the nemesis of his life. The purgatory he'd been living in, and that she'd condemned him to when she left him.

"Thank you, Matt," she said softly. "Six o'-clock tomorrow? Come to the suite. It'll be quiet and we can talk."

"I'll see you then," he said coldly, furious that he had given in to her. And all she could do was pray that in the next twenty-four hours, he wouldn't cancel. She knew that if she saw him, even for half an hour, everything might change. And the worst of it was that, as he hung up the phone, Matt knew it too.

24

MATT DROVE INTO TOWN AT FIVE O'CLOCK THE next day, and arrived fifteen minutes early. He walked around the lobby, looking like he was stalking it, and at precisely six o'clock he was standing outside her suite, and rang the bell. He hadn't wanted to be there, but he knew that once and for all, he had to confront this. If he didn't, it would haunt him forever.

She opened the door looking serious and elegant in a black suit, black stockings, high heels, and her long blond hair was as beautiful as her daughter's. She was still a spectacular-looking woman.

"Hi, Matt," she said easily, and offered him a chair and a martini. She remembered that he had always loved them, although he no longer drank them. But this time he accepted.

She made one for herself too, and sat down on the couch across from him, and the first few minutes were inevitably awkward, but the martinis helped them. And predictably, it didn't take long for either of them to feel the chemistry between them. Or she did, what Matt felt was subtly different. He couldn't identify the differences yet, but he knew that somehow, at the core of his feelings for her, there had been subtle mutations, and he was relieved.

"Why didn't you ever remarry?" she asked, playing with her olives.

"You cured me," he said with a smile, admiring her legs. They were as good as they always had been, and the short skirt gave him an impressive view of them. "I've been living like a hermit for the past ten years. I'm a recluse . . . an artist . . ." He made light of it, and had no desire to make her feel guilty. It was his life now, and he was comfortable with it. In fact, he had come to prefer it to the life they'd led.

"Why do you do that to yourself?" she said, looking concerned.

"Actually, it suits me. I've done what I wanted to in the world. I've proven everything I want to prove. I live on a beach and I paint . . . and talk to stray children, and dogs." He smiled to himself, thinking of Pip, and thought of

Ophélie suddenly, who in her own way, was far more beautiful than this woman. They were infinitely different in every possible way.

"You need a life, Matt," Sally said gently. "Do you ever think of going back to New York?" She had been thinking of it. She had never liked Auckland, or New Zealand. And now she was free, to do whatever she wanted.

"Never. Not for a minute," he said honestly. "Been there. Done that." Thinking of Ophélie, even for a minute, had somehow helped him return to his senses and maintain distance from her.

"What about Paris or London?"

"Maybe. When I get tired of being a beach bum. I'm not there yet. When I do, maybe I'll move to Europe. But now that Robert will be here for the next four years, I'm more motivated to stay." And Vanessa had told him she wanted to go to UCLA in two years, or maybe even Berkeley. He wasn't moving anywhere for the moment. He wanted to be near his children. He had been cheated out of them for long enough, now he wanted to soak up every moment he could with them.

"I'm surprised you're not bored with all that, Matt. The life of a recluse. You were pretty jazzy in the old days." And the art director of the biggest ad agency in New York, with a lot of powerful, important clients. He and Sally had chartered planes and houses and yachts to entertain them. But he no longer had a hunger for it, hadn't in a decade.

"I guess I grew up at some point. It happens to some of us."

"You don't look a day older." She tried another tack, since the others weren't working. She couldn't see herself living in a beach shack with him, that really would have killed her.

"Well, I feel it. But thank you, you don't either." In fact, she looked better than ever, and a little more weight suited her and gave her a slightly more voluptuous figure. She had always been too skinny in the old days, although he had liked it. "So what are you going to do now?" he asked with interest.

"I don't know. I'm trying to figure that out. It's all so fresh." She hardly looked like a grieving widow, and wasn't. She looked more like a liberated felon. Unlike Ophélie, who had been ravaged by the death of her husband. The contrasts between the two women were enormous. "I've been thinking about New York," she said, and then looked at him shyly. "I know it's a crazy idea, but I've been wondering if . . ." Her eyes looked deep into his, and she didn't finish. She didn't need to. He knew her. And that was the issue. He knew her.

"If I'd like to go with you, and try it for a while, see where things go . . . if we could put it all back together, turn back the clock and fall in love all over again . . . God, that would be an idea, wouldn't it? . . ." He filled in for her, looking pensive, and she was nodding. He had understood her. He always had. Better than she knew. "The trouble is . . . that's all I wanted for ten years. Not overtly. I didn't torture myself daily, you were married to Hamish, there was no hope for us . . . and now you're not, he's gone . . . and the funny thing is, Sally . . . I realize now that I couldn't do it. You're beautiful, just as beautiful as you always were, and with another couple of martinis, I'd fall into bed with you and figure I'd died and gone to Heaven . . . but then what? You're still you, and I'm me . . . and all the reasons it blew to smithereens before are still there and always would be . . . I probably bore you. And the truth is, much as I love you and maybe always will, I don't want to be with you anymore. The cost is too high to me. I want to be with a woman who loves me. I'm not sure you ever did. Love isn't just an object, a purchase, a sale, it's an exchange, a trade, a gift you give and receive . . . I want the gift next time . . . I want to get it, and give it . . ." He felt remarkably at peace as he said it to her. He had had the chance he wanted for ten years, and found that he didn't really want it. It was an incredible feeling of liberation, and at the same time of loss . . . of disappointment, victory, and freedom.

"You always were such a romantic," she said, sounding slightly irritated. Things weren't going the way she wanted.

"And you weren't," he said, smiling. "Maybe that's the problem. I believe in all that romantic drivel. You want to get on with it. Bury one guy, and exhume another. Not to mention what you did with our kids. The trouble is you damn near killed me, and my spirit is floating out there somewhere, it's free now . . . and I think it likes it that way . . ."

"You always were a little crazy." She laughed. But he had never been as sane in his life, and he knew it. "What about an affair?" She was playing let's make a deal now and he felt sorry for her.

"That would be foolish, and confusing. Don't you think? Then what? I'd like nothing more than to go to bed with you. But that's when all the trouble starts. I care. You don't. Someone else comes along. I get tossed on my head out a window. It's not exactly my favorite form of

transportation. Sleeping with you is a dangerous sport, for me at least. And I have a healthy
respect for my own pain threshold. I don't think
I could do it. In fact, I know I couldn't."

"So now what?" She looked frustrated and
angry as she poured herself another martini.
Her third now. He had left his first one unfin-
ished. He had outgrown those too. It didn't
taste as good as it used to.

"Now we do what you said we would. We declare ourselves friends, wish each other luck, say
good-bye, and go on about our business. You go
to New York, have a good time, find a new husband, move to Paris or London or Palm Beach,
bring up your kids, and I'll see you at Robert
and Vanessa's weddings." It was all he wanted
both for her and from her. And nothing more.

"And what about you, Matt?" she spat at him.
"You rot at the beach forever?"

"Maybe. Or maybe I grow like a strong old
tree, put down roots, and enjoy my life with the
people who sit under it and don't want to shake
the tree every ten minutes, or chop it down.
Sometimes a quiet life is a good thing." The
concept was entirely foreign to her. She loved
excitement. No matter what she had to do to
create it.

"You're not old enough to think that way.

You're only forty-seven, for chrissake. Hamish was fifty-two and he acted half your age."

"And now he's dead. So maybe that wasn't such a hot idea either. Maybe somewhere in the middle works. But whatever the case, your path and mine have gone in different directions forever. I would drive you insane, and you would kill me. Not a pretty picture."

"Is there someone else?"

"Maybe. But that's not the issue. If I were in love with you, I would drop everything and follow you to the ends of the earth forever. You know me. Romantic fool, all that stuff you think is so incredibly stupid. But I'd do it. The trouble is, I'm not in love with you. I thought I was. But I guess I got off the train somewhere along the way, and didn't know it. I love our kids, and our memories, and some crazy, young lost ancient part of me will forever love you. But I don't love you enough to try again, Sally, or to follow you forever." And with that, he stood up, bent down, and kissed the top of her head, and she didn't move as she watched him walk to the door and open it. She didn't try to stop him. She knew better. He meant every word he said. He always did, always had, always would. And as he stood there, he took one last look at her before he left her life forever.

"Bye, Sally," he said, feeling better than he had in years. "Good luck."

"I hate you," she said, feeling drunk, as the door closed.

And for Matt, the spell was broken at last. It was finally over.

25

MATT HAD DINNER WITH PIP AND OPHÉLIE AT their house, to exchange presents with them the night before Christmas Eve. They had decorated the tree, and Ophélie had insisted on cooking a goose for him, because it was a French tradition. Pip hated it and was going to eat a hamburger, but Ophélie had wanted to have a nice Christmas with him, and she had never seen him look better.

They had both been busy and had hardly talked in the past week. He had never mentioned to her that he had seen Sally, and he wasn't sure yet if he would. What had happened between them still seemed private to him, and he wasn't ready yet to share it with her. But there was no question, it had liberated him, and although Ophélie didn't know what had happened, she could sense it. And as always, he was extraordinarily gentle and loving with her.

They were planning to exchange gifts that night, but Pip couldn't wait until after dinner. She insisted on giving hers to him, and wanted him to open it immediately, when he threatened to save it till Christmas.

"No! Now!" She hopped up and down and clapped her hands, watching him excitedly as he tore off the paper, and as soon as he saw what it was, he burst into laughter. They were a man-sized pair of giant yellow, fluffy Big Bird slippers, and they fit him.

"I love them!" he said, hugging her. He put them on and kept them on through dinner. "They're perfect. Now we can all wear them in Tahoe. You and your mom have to bring Grover and Elmo." Pip promised to do that, and then was overwhelmed when he gave her the beautiful bicycle he had gotten for her. She rode through the dining room and living room, nearly knocked over the tree, and then took it outside to ride it down the block while her mother finished cooking dinner.

"What about you?" he asked Ophélie, as they each sipped a glass of white wine. "Are you ready for a present?" He knew his would be a double-edged sword, and there was a chance it might upset her, but in the long run he thought she would be pleased. "Do you have a minute?" She nodded and they sat down, while Pip was still outside trying out her new bike. And Matt was glad to have a moment alone with her mother. He handed her the wrapped gift, and she couldn't imagine what it was. It was in a large flat box and didn't rattle.

"What is it?" she asked, looking touched before she even saw it.

"You'll see." She tore off the paper and opened the box. It was bubble-wrapped and flat, and she made her way cautiously through the wrappings, and then as the last bit of paper came away, she gasped, and her eyes filled with tears instantly. She put a hand to her mouth and closed her eyes. It was Chad, and it looked just like him. He had made a portrait of him to match the one he had done of Pip for her birthday. She opened her eyes and looked at him then, and then sank against his chest, crying.

"Oh my God, Matt . . . thank you . . . thank you . . ." She looked at the portrait again. It was like seeing her son again, as he smiled at her. It made her realize yet again how much she missed him, and at the same time it put balm on the pain. It was perfect. "How did you do it?" It looked exactly like Chad, even the smile was exactly him.

Matt pulled something out of his pocket and handed it to her. It was the framed photograph of Chad he had taken from her living room when he first thought of it. "I apologize. I'm a kleptomaniac." She laughed when she saw it.

"You know, I looked for that. I couldn't figure out where it went. I thought Pip had taken it, and I didn't want to upset her by asking. I thought she was hiding it in her room, or a drawer . . . but I spent weeks looking for it." She set it back on the table in the living room from where he'd taken it to do the portrait. "Matt, how can I ever thank you?"

"You don't have to. I love you. And I want you to be happy." He was about to say more, as Pip flew through the door, with Mousse barking behind her. He had been running along beside her.

"I love my bike!" she shouted, as she crashed past a table in the front hall, and narrowly missed another one, and then came to a screeching halt in front of them as she put the brakes on. It was a very grown-up bike, and it was obvious that she loved it. And then Ophélie showed her the portrait of Chad, and Pip grew silent.

"Wow . . . it looks just like him . . ." She looked at her mother, and the two of them held hands and stared at it for a long time. All three of them had tears in their eyes. It was a tender moment, and then Ophélie smelled disaster brewing in the kitchen. The goose was not only cooked, but nearly burning.

"Yuk!" Pip said as Ophélie served it.

They had a delicious dinner and a wonderful evening, and Ophélie waited to give Matt her gift until Pip went up to bed. It was special, and important to her, and she hoped he'd like it. And his face, when he opened it, was as moved as hers had been when she saw the portrait. It was an old Breguet watch of her father's, from the fifties. It was a handsome piece, and she had no one to give it to now. No husband, no son, no brother. She had been saving it for Chad, and she wanted Matt to have it. He put it on reverently, and was as pleased and touched as she was with Chad's portrait.

"I don't know what to say," he said, as he looked at the beautiful timepiece and then kissed her. "I love you, Ophélie," he said quietly. What they shared was everything he wanted it to be, not like what he had shared with Sally. This was quiet and powerful and real, two good people slowly and solidly bonding to each other. He would have done almost anything for her, and she knew it. And for Pip as well. She was a good woman, a great woman even, and he felt incredibly lucky. He felt totally safe when he was with her, as she did with him. Nothing could touch them within the circle of the powerful force that they shared.

"I love you too, Matt . . . Merry Christmas," she whispered, and then kissed him. And in the kiss was everything she felt for him, and all the passion she'd been resisting.

And when he left that night, he was wearing her father's watch, she lay in bed looking at Chad's portrait with a smile on her face, and the red bike was propped against Pip's bed, where she had left it. It truly was the magic of Christmas.

The "real" Christmas Eve that Pip and Ophélie shared was far more difficult, and inevitably painful. Despite all their efforts to make it otherwise, it wound up being less about who was there than who wasn't. Andrea's absence was felt, and the continuing absence of Ted and Chad was like an ongoing bad joke that never seemed to end. Halfway through the day, Ophélie wanted to throw up her hands and scream "Okay, enough! You can come out now!" But they didn't and never would again.

And along with their absence, she felt overwhelmed by the realization that the memories
she had once cherished of their marriage had
been irretrievably tainted by what had happened with Andrea, and her baby.

It was a difficult day, and they were both glad
to see it end. They climbed into Ophélie's bed
that night, and the only thing that cheered
them was that they were going to Tahoe to see
Matt and his family the next morning. And as
promised, Pip packed their Grover and Elmo
slippers. By ten o'clock, she was sound asleep in
her mother's arms, and Ophélie lay awake for a
long time, holding her little girl close to her.

The holidays had been better than they had
been the year before, mostly because they were
getting used to it, the reality that half their family was gone. But in some ways, it was harder
too, because they were beginning to realize that
it was never going to change. Life as they had
known and cherished it in their family was
gone for good. Things might be happy again
one day, but they would never, ever be the
same. And Ophélie, and even Pip, understood that.

It had helped them both hearing frequently
from Matt. Ophélie had heard nothing from
Andrea, and had no desire to. Andrea was out of

their life forever. Pip had talked about her once, saw her mother's face, and never mentioned her again. The message from Ophélie was loud and clear. Andrea no longer existed in their world.

And as she lay in bed, thinking about it all, Ophélie's thoughts drifted first to Ted and Chad, and then to Matt. She loved the portrait he had done, and the way he was with Pip. His kindness to them had been without measure ever since they'd met. And she could feel herself falling in love with him, and ever more attracted to him, but she didn't know what she wanted to do. She wasn't sure she was ready for another man in her life, and didn't know if she ever would be. Not only because she had been in love with Ted, but also because since Thanksgiving, she had lost all faith in what love could mean between two people. It meant sorrow and disappointment and betrayal to her now, and loss of everything you once believed and trusted. She didn't want to go through that again, with anyone, no matter how lovely and kind Matt seemed. He was human, and human beings did terrible things to each other, most often in the guise and the name of love. Asking anyone to believe in that again, and risk everything seemed almost too much to her. She was no longer sure, and knew she could never trust anyone as she once had, not even Matt. He deserved better than that, particularly after what he'd gone through with Sally.

But she and Pip were both in good spirits when they left the next day. She had brought chains with her in case they ran into snow on the way. But the roads were clear all the way to Truckee, and with his directions, she made her way easily to Squaw Valley. He had rented a spectacular house, with two extra bedrooms for her and Pip. And three more for him and his kids.

Vanessa and Robert were out skiing when they arrived, and Matt was waiting for them in the living room with a roaring fire, hot chocolate, and a plate of sandwiches for both of them. It was an elegant and luxurious house, and he was wearing black ski pants and a heavy gray sweater, and looked as handsome and rugged as ever. He was a good-looking man, and Ophélie felt instantly drawn to him. He appealed to her enormously, but she was still afraid to do anything about it. It still wasn't too late to turn back, although she knew it would disappoint him immensely. But disappointment might be better for both of them than eventual despair and destruction. The risks of allowing herself to abandon herself to him seemed dangerously high to her, yet at the same time doing so appealed to her immensely. She was in constant conflict about him, and all the while, she felt ever closer to him. She could no longer imagine her life without him. And in spite of her fears, she knew she loved him.

"Did you bring the Elmo and Grover slippers?" Matt asked Pip almost immediately, and she nodded her head and grinned.

"Me too. I brought Big Bird with me." Before the others got back, the three of them put them on, and sat laughing by the fire, as he put on some music. And a little while later, Vanessa and Robert came in. They were great-looking kids, and Vanessa enjoyed meeting Ophélie and Pip. She had an instant affinity for the child, and looked with shy admiration at her mother. There was a gentleness about Ophélie that appealed to her, and a kindness that was almost tangible. She saw all the same things in her as Matt, and she said as much to him later, when she was helping him start dinner, and Pip and Ophélie were in their rooms, unpacking.

"I see why you like her, Dad. She's a good person, and really nice. She looks so sad sometimes, even when she smiles. It makes you want to give her a hug." It did the same thing to him. "And I love Pip. She's so cute!"

The two girls were fast friends by that night, and Vanessa invited Pip to sleep in her room, and the younger girl was thrilled. She thought Vanessa was fabulous, really beautiful, and extremely cool, as she told her mother when she put on her pajamas. And after the young people went to bed, Ophélie and Matt sat in front of the fire for hours, until there was nothing left but glowing embers. They talked about music and art, and politics in France, their children and parents, his painting and their dreams. They talked about people they had known, and dogs they had had when they were children. In the process of getting to know each other better and better, they left no stone unturned, and wanted to know everything about each other. And before they each went to their own rooms, he kissed her, and it took them forever to leave each other. What they knew of each other was a powerful force between them.

The next morning all five of them left the house together, and stood on line for the lifts. Robert wanted to ski with some friends from college he'd run into, Vanessa took off with Pip, and Matt offered to stay with Ophélie.

"I don't want to hold you back," she said cautiously, wearing a black ski suit she'd had for years, but it looked simple and elegant on her. She wore it with a big fur hat, and looked very glamorous to him. But she insisted that her skill on the slopes was not equal to the ski suit.

"Believe me, you won't hold me back," he reassured her. "I haven't skied for five years. I came up here for the kids. You'll be doing me a favor, you may have to rescue me." But as it turned out, they were equally matched, and enjoyed a morning of gentle skiing on the intermediate slopes. It was all either of them wanted, and by lunchtime, they were waiting in the restaurant for the kids, who arrived minutes later, looking red-faced and athletic. Pip looked ecstatic as she pulled off her cap and gloves. She was having a ball, and Vanessa looked happy too. She had seen some cute boys, and they had followed her on the slopes. But mostly, she just thought it was in good fun. She didn't appear to be out of control, or wild, unlike her mother at the same age.

The kids skied all afternoon, and Matt and Ophélie enjoyed one long run. And when it started to snow, they went home. Matt lit the fire and put the music on, and Ophélie made them both hot toddies with rum. They settled back on the couch with a stack of magazines and books, and looked up and smiled at each other from time to time. Ophélie was amazed by how easy it was to be with him. Ted had been so much more difficult and demanding, and anxious and argumentative about nearly everything. She commented on the difference to Matt. Their match was a blend of comfort, barely concealed passion, and deep affection. And in addition, they were best friends.

"I like this too," he said easily, and he decided to tell her then about the last time he'd seen Sally.

"You didn't feel anything for her?" Ophélie asked, taking a sip of the hot rum and watching him for clues. She had been worried about Sally for a while, particularly since she'd been widowed.

"A lot less than I expected to, or was afraid I would. I was afraid I would have to fight her off, in my head if nowhere else. And it wasn't like that. It seemed sad and funny, and everything that had always been wrong between us. All she wanted was to manipulate me to get what she wanted, and instead of being in love with her, I felt sorry for her. She's a very sad woman. Not to mention the fact that her husband of nearly ten years had been dead for less than a month. Loyalty isn't one of Sally's strong suits."

"I guess not." Ophélie was a little shocked by the brazenness of what she'd done, after all the pain she had caused him. But she didn't seem to suffer from guilt either. Most of all, Ophélie was relieved. "Why didn't you tell me you'd seen her?" He told her so many things about his life that it seemed odd that he hadn't.

"I think I needed to sort it out after it happened. But I walked out of that room a free man, for the first time in ten years. Going to see her was one of the best things I've ever done." He looked pleased with himself, as he looked at Ophélie, and she smiled at him.

"I'm glad," Ophélie said quietly, wishing that her own feelings about her marriage could be as easily resolved. But there was no one to see, no one to talk to, no one to rail at, or argue with, or cry on, or explain to her why it had happened, or why he had done what he'd done. The only choice she had was to resolve it herself, with time, in solitude and silence.

When the kids came home from skiing, Ophélie cooked dinner that night, and then they all sat around telling stories by the fire. Vanessa talked about her many boyfriends in Auckland, while Pip looked at her admiringly, and Robert teased them both. It was a comfortable family scene that touched both of the adults' hearts. It was what Matt had longed for, for all the years that his children had been gone, and what Ophélie missed so much now that Ted and Chad were gone. There was a wholeness to it, a normalcy that came from being two adults, surrounded by three children, laughing and sitting by a fire. It was what neither of them had ever really had in their previous lives, but always wanted.

"Nice, isn't it?" Matt smiled at her, as they met in the kitchen, while she put some cookies on a plate for the kids, and he poured a glass of wine for Ophélie and himself.

"Very nice," she said, smiling at him. By most of the world's standards, and even theirs, it was a dream come true. And all Matt wanted was for it to last forever. He knew she had issues to wrestle with, and fears to overcome, just as he did, but he wanted them both to come to the same conclusions and find each other at the end. But he was ever cautious with her. He knew how skittish she was. Better than anyone. Because he knew, or at least as much as she did, what Ted had done. It was almost as bad as if he had put a curse on her, or damned her, or condemned her to distrust for the rest of her life. And no one knew better than Matt what a curse that was. But at least they were free of it for the moment, in their safe little world in Tahoe.

They went to a nearby restaurant for dinner on New Year's Eve, and then stopped in at a hotel to see the festivities there. People were wearing ski clothes and big, bright sweaters, and only a few, like Ophélie, were wearing fur. She looked very chic in a black velvet jumpsuit, with a black fox jacket over it, and a matching hat.

"You look like a black mushroom, Mom," Pip said to her mother with a disapproving look. But Vanessa pronounced the outfit "cool." And Ophélie would have worn it anyway. She was impervious to Pip's more conservative fashion advice, and Matt loved the way she looked. No matter what she wore, or how well she spoke English, Ophélie always looked very French. It was either a scarf she wore, or a pair of earrings, or an old Hermès bag on a strap over her shoulder that she had owned since she was nineteen. But somehow the bits and pieces she extracted from her closet, and the way she wore them, always gave her nationality away.

And in light of her origins, and the atmosphere of the surroundings, she let Pip have a glass of champagne on New Year's Eve. Matt did the same with Vanessa, and although he wasn't of legal drinking age, since Robert wasn't driving, Matt offered his son some wine. He seemed to handle it fairly well, and his father was sure that legal or not, he did his share of drinking at Stanford just like everyone else. He was a reasonable young man.

They were in the lodge at the hotel when the clock struck midnight, and all of them kissed each other, French style on both cheeks, and wished each other a Happy New Year. It wasn't until they got home, and the kids had gone to bed an hour later, that Matt kissed her with more passion. They were alone in the living room by then, cuddled together in front of a dying fire, but the room was still warm. It had been a nice night. Especially for the kids, who seemed to be getting along extremely well, but so were they. Matt had never been as happy in his life, and Ophélie felt remarkably at peace. Despite everything she'd been through in recent months, and even the past year, she could feel the burdens that had rested on her for so long slowly fall away from her, one by one.

"Happy?" Matt asked her as he held her close to him. They were whispering in the dark room, lit only by the fire, and they were both sure that all the kids were asleep by then. Pip was once again in Vanessa's room. The two had become fast friends. And Pip looked up to the older girl like the big sister she'd never had and wished she did. And Vanessa's only siblings, both older and younger, were boys, so it was a nice change for her too.

"Very happy," Ophélie answered softly. She was always happy with him. She felt protected and safe and loved in his world. She had a sense that no harm could come to her as long as she was with him. And all he wanted was to protect her, shield her from all the agonies she'd been through, and put balm on her many wounds. The prospect of that didn't daunt him.

He kissed her again then, and they gently and quietly explored each other more than they ever had before. And as she felt his hands roving slowly over her, she realized how hungry for him she was. It was as though everything about her as a woman had died in the past fourteen months, since Ted had died, and she was coming alive again slowly in Matt's hands. And he was overwhelmed with desire for her. They sat there together for a long time, and then lay on the couch, their bodies and limbs intertwined, until he finally whispered to her.

"We're going to get ourselves into trouble if we stay out here for much longer." She giggled in answer, feeling like a young girl again for the first time in years. It took him all the courage he could muster to ask her the next question, but the time seemed to be right, finally, for both of them. "Do you want to come to my room?" he whispered in her ear, and she nodded, as his heart nearly broke with relief. He had wanted this for so long, wanted her, more than he had even dared admit to himself.

They both stood up and he took her by the hand, and led her to his room, as they both tip-toed on silent feet. Ophélie nearly laughed, there was something so funny about hiding from their children, but everyone in the house was asleep. And as soon as they were in Matt's room, he closed the door behind them and locked it, and then swept her up in his arms and walked her to the bed, where he gently set her down. And a moment later, he was lying next to her.

"I love you so much, Ophélie," he whispered, with the moonlight streaming into the room. It was cozy and warm as they kissed and un-dressed each other, and within seconds they were under the sheets. And ever so gently, he reached out to her. He could feel her trembling next to him, and all he wanted to do was make her feel happy and loved.

"I love you, Matt," she whispered back, and he could hear the tremor in her voice. He could sense how frightened she was, and for a long time he just held her close to him, pressing her against him. "It's all right, darling . . . you're safe with me . . . nothing bad is going to happen to you, I promise . . ."

He could feel tears on her cheeks when he kissed her, and she whispered to him, "I'm so scared, Matt . . ."

"Please don't be . . . I love you so much . . . I'll never hurt you. I promise." She believed him, but she no longer believed in life. Life would hurt them, given the opportunity. Terrible things would happen if she let down her guard and allowed him into her world completely. She would lose him, or he would betray her, or he would leave her or die. Nothing was sure anymore, she knew. She couldn't trust anyone or anything, not even him. Not this close. She realized then that she had been foolish to think she could do this.

"Matt, I can't . . ." she said in an anguished voice. "I'm too scared." She couldn't make love to him, couldn't let him that close to her. It was too frightening to care that much, and once she let him into her life and her soul and her body and heart, nothing would be safe anymore. He would own it all, and the demons that ruined people's lives would own them.

"I love you," he said quietly. "We can wait . . . there's no rush . . . I'm not going away. I'm not going to leave you, or hurt you, or scare you . . . it's okay. I love you." He defined the meaning of the word, as no other man had before, not even Ted. Least of all Ted. She felt terrible for disappointing Matt. But she knew she wasn't ready, and she didn't know now if she ever would be. It was impossible to say. All she knew was that she couldn't now. It would have been too terrifying to let him in. And he was willing to wait for her.

He held her in his arms for a long time that night, feeling her graceful body next to his, and he longed for her, but he was grateful for what they had. If that was all it could be for now, it was enough. Light was dawning as she finally got up, and put on her clothes again. She had dozed next to him, and clung to him all night. She wasn't even embarrassed to be naked next to him. She wanted him, but not enough.

He kissed her before she left his room, and she went back to her own bed and slept. She slept fitfully for two hours, and when she woke up, she felt the familiar lead weight on her chest. But it was different this time. It wasn't for Chad or for Ted, it was for what she hadn't been able to do with Matt the night before. She felt as though she had cheated him, and hated herself for disappointing him. She showered and dressed feeling anxious about seeing him, but as soon as she did, she knew it was fine. He smiled at her from across the room, and came to put an arm around her to reassure her. He was an incredible man, and in an odd way, she felt as though she had made love with him. She was even more comfortable with him now than she had been before. And she felt foolish for having panicked. Yet grateful to him for having waited.

They skied together on New Year's Day without ever talking about the night before. They just skied and chatted, and had fun together, and they spent the last night eating dinner with all the kids. Vanessa was going back to Auckland the next day, much to Matt's chagrin, but Matt was flying out to see her the following month. Pip and Ophélie were driving home in the morning, and the day after that, Pip had to go back to school. Robert had two more weeks' vacation, and was going to Heavenly to ski with friends. And Matt was going back to the beach. The vacation was over, but it had been a lovely week. Nothing had been resolved between Ophélie and Matt, but they both knew they were on no one's timetable but their own. And she knew without a doubt that if he had pushed her that night, or forced her, or been angry at her, even the hope of a romance between them would be gone. But Matt was far wiser than that, and he loved her more. They left each other the next morning with no promises, no certainties between them, only love and hope. It was far more than either of them had had when they met, and enough for both of them for now.

26

MATT STOPPED BY TO SEE OPHÉLIE AND PIP after dropping Vanessa off at the airport to go to Auckland. He was sad after leaving her, and grateful for a cup of tea before going back to his solitary life at the beach. He realized more than ever now that the life they had all shared for the past week was what he wanted. He was tired of his solitude. But for the moment, there was no other option. Ophélie was not ready for more than they had, which was friendship with a promise of future passion and romance. She was in no way ready for more than that yet. He had no other choice but to wait and see what happened between them, if anything ever did. And if it didn't, if she was never able to reach out to him, then at least he could be a friend to her and Pip. He knew that was a possibility too.

There were no guarantees in life. They had all had ample proof of that.

He was pleased to see, as he walked into the house, that the portraits he had done of Pip and Chad were hung in the living room in a place of honor.

"They look beautiful, don't they?" She smiled proudly and thanked him again. "How was Vanessa before she left?" Ophélie had become extremely fond of her, and Robert too. Like their father, they were nice people, with good manners, good hearts, and good values. She truly liked them.

"Vanessa was sad to leave," he answered Ophélie's question, and had to fight back the memory of the night he had spent with Ophélie naked in his bed. He wished she had been able to trust him, and could only hope it would come later, if they were lucky. "I'll see her in a few weeks. She loved you and Pip."

"We loved her too," Ophélie said gently. And when Pip went upstairs to do her homework, she looked at Matt sadly. "I'm sorry about what happened in Tahoe." It was the first time either of them had mentioned it. He hadn't wanted to embarrass her by referring to it, nor to press her. He thought it was better left unspoken between them. "I shouldn't have done that. In

French, you call that being an *allumeuse*. I think there's a much more unattractive word for it in English. But it's not a nice thing to be. I wasn't trying to tease you, or fool you. I think if anything, I fooled me. I thought I was ready, and I wasn't."

He didn't like talking to her about it, he was afraid that even doing that would push her to extreme conclusions. And he didn't want to close any doors between them. He wanted to leave them wide open, and give her the chance to come through them when she was ready. Whenever that happened, if it did, he'd be waiting for her. And in the meantime, all he could do was love her as best he could, even if the relationship was limited. "You didn't fool anyone, Ophélie. Time is a funny thing. You can't define it, can't buy it, can't predict its effect on people. Some people need more, some less. Take whatever time you need."

"And if I never get there?" she asked him sadly. She was afraid she might not. The depth of her fears, and their paralyzing effect, had frightened her.

"If you never get there, I love you anyway," he assured her, which was all she needed to hear. As always, he made her feel safe, unpressured, unharried. Being with Matt was always like a long, peaceful walk on the beach. It rested her soul. "Don't torture yourself. You have enough other things to worry about. Don't add me to that list. I'm fine." He smiled at her, and leaned across the table to kiss her on the lips, and she didn't resist. In fact, she welcomed it. In her heart of hearts, she loved him, she just didn't know what to do about it yet. If she loved anyone, and allowed herself to live again, she knew it would be Matt. But she recognized the possibility that Ted might have ended her life as a woman for good. He didn't deserve to have that power over her, but much as she hated to admit it to herself, he still did. He had destroyed some essential part of her she could no longer find or retrieve. Like a sock that had gotten lost. But the sock was filled with love and trust. And she had no idea where it was. Gone, it would seem. Ted had thrown it away. He hadn't even taken it with him. She kept wondering what she had meant to him, and if he had loved her when he died. Or ever. And she would never know the answers. All she had left now were the questions.

"What are you up to tonight?" Matt asked her before he left.

She started to tell him and then hesitated as their eyes met. From the look on her face he knew, and hated it.

"The outreach team?"

"Yes," she said, putting their cups in the sink. She didn't want to argue about it with him.

"God, I wish you'd stop doing that. I don't know what it's going to take to convince you. One of these days, Ophélie, something terrible is going to happen. I just don't want it to happen to you. They've been lucky, but they can't be lucky forever. Your exposure is too great, and so is theirs. You're out there two nights a week. Sooner or later the odds will get you, if nothing else."

"I'll be all right," she tried to reassure him, but as always, he was unconvinced.

He left at five, and a few minutes later, Alice came to baby-sit for Pip. It was routine by now. Ophélie had been doing it since September, and she felt completely confident about it, unlike Matt, who had constant forebodings of disaster. But Ophélie didn't share them. She knew the team well, and how capable they were. They were always sensible and cautious. They were cowboys, as they said themselves, but cowboys who knew their way around the streets, and watched their backs, and hers. And she had grown skilled at what she was doing too. She was no longer an innocent on the streets.

By seven o'clock, she was in the van, with Bob driving, and Jeff and Millie in the other van. They had added more supplies for their route, a number of food items, more medical supplies, warm clothes, condoms, and there was a wholesaler donating down jackets to them regularly. The vans were loaded that night, and the night was bitter cold. Bob told her with a grin that she should have worn long johns.

"So how's by you?" he chatted amiably, as they always did. "How was Christmas?"

"Pretty good. The day was tough." They had both been through it, and he nodded. "But we went to Tahoe the day after. We went skiing with friends. It was fun."

"Yeah, we went up to Alpine last year too. I've got to get the kids up this year. It's expensive though." It made her aware again of how lucky she was not to have those worries. He had three mouths to feed and very little money. But he did everything he could for his children. "How's your romance, by the way?" They shared a lot, driving around all night, and they had their kids and widowhood in common. They exchanged a lot of advice and information, and talked more than they would have in an office. This was no desk job.

"What romance?" She looked innocent, and he shoved her playfully.

"Don't give me that, you phony. Couple a months ago you had a twinkle in your eye. Looked like Cupid got you in the ass . . . so what happened?" He liked her. She was a good woman with a lot of heart, and from what he'd seen on the streets working with her, a lotta balls, as he'd often said to Jeff. She was afraid of almost nothing. She had never held back, never hung back, she was right out there, night after night, every week, helping with the others. And all three of the regulars loved her. "So what's with the romance?" he persisted. They had time to chat as they headed toward the Mission.

"I'm chicken. Sounds stupid, I guess. He's a wonderful man, and I love him, but I just can't, Bob. Or not yet at least. I think too much has happened." There was no point explaining to him about Ted and Andrea's baby, or the horrifying things she had said about Ophélie and Chad in her letter, which implied that Ted agreed with her, that Ophélie was incompetent and had handled their mentally ill son abominably and was the cause of his problems. The sheer cruelty of it still killed her. She had even asked herself if what Andrea had said was true, and she had exacerbated Chad's problems. Even if she'd been manipulating Ted, maybe there was some truth to it. She had tortured herself endlessly over the letter and finally burned it, so Pip would never find it and read it, as she had.

"I know, I know. A lotta shit happened to me too, when my wife died. It's hard to believe now, but you get over it. Enough to put your life back together. And by the way." He tried to look nonchalant as he glanced out the window and not at "Opie," as they all called her. She had come to like it. "I'm getting married." He dropped the bomb on her, and she cheered when she heard it.

"Good for you! That's terrific. What do your kids think?"

"They like her . . . they love her . . . they always did." Ophélie knew his fiancée had been his wife's best friend, which seemed to be a familiar story among widowers. They married their late wives' sisters or best friends. It was familiar to them.

"When?" Ophélie was pleased for him.

"Ah shit, I dunno . . . she's never been married before, so she wants to make it a big deal. I just want to go down to City Hall and get it over with."

"Don't be such a spoilsport. Enjoy it. Hopefully, you'll never get married again."

"Yeah, I hope not. She's a good woman though, and kinda like my best friend."

"That's the best way." Like the way she was with Matt. It was just too bad that she couldn't get over her own terrors enough to have a real relationship with him. She almost envied Bob. But his wife had been gone longer than Ted.

Maybe one day, she hoped, she could throw caution and terror to the winds, and do it.

They skirted the edges of the Mission after that, did their drop-offs in Hunters Point, and had no trouble at all. It reminded her of how unnecessary Matt's fears for her were when she was on the streets. She was completely relaxed, and joking with Millie and Jeff when they stopped for hot coffee and something to eat. It was freezing outside, and the people on the street were miserable, and grateful for everything they gave them.

"Man, it's coooolllldddd tonight," Bob said as they drove off again. They covered the loading docks and the railroad tracks, the underpasses and the back alleys, as they always did. They worked Third, Fourth, Fifth, and Sixth Streets, although Bob said he never liked them. There were too many drug deals going down and people who could feel threatened by them, and thought they might interfere. It was never a good idea to interrupt business on the street. The people they wanted to reach were those who were simply trying to survive, not those who were preying on them. Sometimes the signals could get mixed. But Jeff liked that neighborhood, and he was right at times, there were huge numbers of homeless lying in the doorways and back alleys, under rags and tarps, and in the boxes they called "cribs."

They cut into an alley called Jesse between Fifth and Sixth, because Millie told Jeff she saw a couple of people at the far end of it, and both of them hopped out. Bob and Ophélie waited, and figured with only a few people visible, the others could handle it, but Jeff signaled to them for sleeping bags and coats, which were stored in Bob and Ophélie's van. And she hopped out first.

"I'll get it," she called back over her shoulder, and Bob hesitated, but she moved so fast, she was halfway down the alley with the bags and coats in her arms before Bob could get out.

"Hold on!" he shouted after her, and followed her, but the alley looked deserted, except for a crib at the far end. Jeff and Millie were already down there, and Ophélie had nearly reached them when a tall thin man stepped out of a doorway and grabbed her. Bob saw him reach for her, and started running toward them. The man was holding Ophélie by one arm, but oddly enough, she wasn't frightened. As she had learned to do instinctively, she looked him right in the eye, and smiled at him.

"Do you want a sleeping bag and a jacket?" She could tell he was high on something, speed probably, or crystal meth, but her firm gaze telegraphed to him that she wasn't afraid and meant him no harm.

"No, baby, I don't. What else you got? You got anything I want?" The man had huge wild eyes that darted around him.

"Food, medicine, warm coats, some rain ponchos, sleeping bags, scarves, hats, socks, duffel bags, tarps, whatever you want."

"You selling this shit?" he asked angrily, just as Bob reached them, and took in the scene.

"No, we're giving it to you," she said calmly.

"Why?" He was hostile and speedy, and looked nervous. Bob stood very still. He could sense trouble, and didn't want to upset the delicate balance between them.

"I figured you might need it."

"Who's the dude?" He still had Ophélie by the arm and his grip had tightened. "Is he a cop?"

"No, he isn't. We're from the Wexler Center. What can I give you?"

"A blow job, you bitch. I don't need any shit from you."

"That's enough." Bob stepped in quietly, as Jeff and Millie approached slowly from the other end of the alley. They knew something was happening, but they couldn't see what yet, but they could hear him. "Let her go, man," Bob said quietly but firmly.

"What are you? Her pimp?"

"You don't need trouble, and neither do we. Give it up, man. Let her go," he said clearly, and was sorry he no longer carried a gun. Seeing it drawn would have backed the guy off. By then, Jeff and Millie walked up, and the man holding Ophélie in his grip looked angry and yanked her suddenly toward him.

"What is this? Undercover? You guys look like cops to me."

"We're not cops," Jeff shouted clearly. "I used to be a Navy SEAL, and I'm gonna kick your ass if you don't knock it off and give her up." He had pulled Ophélie halfway across the alley toward a doorway where Bob could see there were two more guys waiting for him impatiently. It was the situation they hated most, they had walked into a drug deal in progress. "We don't give a shit what you're doing. We've got medicine and food and clothes for people here. You don't want them, fine, but we got work to do. Go on about your business. It's no skin off my ass." All they could do was talk tough when things got tough, they had nothing to back it up. And the drug dealer who has hanging on to Ophélie looked like he didn't believe them.

"What's she? She looks like a cop too." He pointed at Millie, and Ophélie kept silent. Millie always looked like a policewoman to her too.

"Used to be. She got kicked off the force for prostitution," Jeff said valiantly, but the guy didn't buy it.

"You're bullshitting. She stinks of cop to me, and so does this one," and with that he let go of Ophélie's arm, and shoved her backward toward them, and sent her reeling. She nearly fell, and hadn't expected it, and as she caught her balance and stood up, they all heard gunshots. They had never even seen him pull the gun. And within a split second, he seemed to do a twirl and a jump in space, leaped like a ballet dancer, and started to run.

Jeff started to run after him, and Bob shouted after him as the two men in the doorway vanished into thin air. They disappeared and a door closed. Everything happened so fast, and the whole focus was on Jeff and the man he was chasing, as Millie ran faster and shouted at Jeff too. They weren't armed, there was no point chasing him down. If they got him, there was nothing they could do except risk being shot while they wrestled him to the ground. They weren't cops, and what Bob wanted to do was get the hell out. He turned to tell Ophélie to run to the van, and as he did, he saw she had dropped where she stood, and there was blood everywhere. The man with the gun had shot her.

"Fuck, Opie . . . what did you do?" he said, as he got down on his knees and tried to pick her up. He wanted to get her out of there, hoping it was a surface wound, but he saw instantly that she was too badly injured to move, and they were sitting ducks with her lying where they were. There were drug deals going down. The alley had been a bad move.

Bob shouted as loud as he could, and Millie heard him first. He signaled to her, and she called out to Jeff. They had seen Ophélie on the ground in Bob's arms by then, and came back at a dead run. Jeff had his cell phone in his hand, and was already calling 911. They were back with Bob and Ophélie within seconds. Bob looked like he was in shock, and she was unconscious, but he had found a pulse, and she was still breathing, but barely.

"Shit," Jeff said, as he got on his knees next to her and Millie ran to the mouth of the alley to wave the paramedics in when they got there. "Is she gonna make it?"

"Doesn't look good," Bob said through clenched teeth. He was pissed at Jeff. The alley had been a bad decision. It was the first dumb one they'd made in a long time. And he was even more pissed at himself for letting her do it,

and not following her more closely. But without guns, there was almost nothing they could
do to protect each other in situations like this.
They had talked about bulletproof vests at one
point, but decided they didn't need them. And
until then they hadn't. "She's a widow with a
kid," Bob said to Jeff as they watched her.

"I know, man . . . I know . . . where the fuck
are they?"

"Coming, I hear them," Bob said, watching
her, and keeping his fingers on the pulse in her
neck. It was getting weaker, and it had only
been minutes, but it felt like lifetimes. But they
could hear the sirens coming, and a second
later, Jeff saw Millie waving, as the paramedics
came running.

They loaded her onto the gurney quickly, as
one of them ran a line into her arm while they
were still moving. "How many shots were
there?" one of them asked Jeff as he ran beside
them. Bob ran to get into his van, so he could
follow the ambulance to General. They had the
best trauma unit in town. And he could hear
himself praying as he started the van and turned
it around.

"Three shots," Jeff told them, as they put the
gurney in the ambulance as fast as possible, and
both paramedics jumped in. They took off as
one of them closed the door. And Jeff ran back

to his van. Millie was already behind the wheel. Both vans followed the ambulance at full speed. It was the first incident like it that had happened to them, but it was no consolation now.

"Think she'll make it?" Millie asked, weaving in and out of traffic, her eyes on the road, and her foot lead on the gas.

Jeff took a breath and shook his head. He hated to say it but he didn't, and neither did she. "No, I don't," he said honestly. "She took three bullets at close range. Unless the guy was firing a peashooter, she's dead. No one can survive that. Not a woman at least."

"I did," she said grimly. It had blown her off the force and put her on disability, and it took a hell of a long time, but she'd lived. Her male partner who was shot at the same time, hadn't. Sometimes it was just the luck of the draw in situations like this.

They were at the hospital in seven minutes, and all three of them got out of the two vans, and followed the gurney inside. They had cut off her clothes by then, and she was lying half naked, exposed, and with so much blood on her you couldn't see what was happening. And within seconds, she disappeared into the trauma unit, unconscious, with an oxygen mask on her face. Her three co-workers sat silently, not knowing who to call, or if they should. It seemed sinful to call a kid, and they figured there was a baby-sitter. At least someone had to know.

"What do you think, guys?" Jeff asked. He was in charge, but it was a tough call.

"My kids would want to know," Bob said quietly. They all looked sick, and Jeff turned to him again before he walked to a pay phone in the hall.

"How old is her kid?"

"Twelve. Her name is Pip."

"Do you want me to call the baby-sitter or talk to her?" Millie offered. It might be less scary if a woman called. But how much more scary could it be than telling her that her mom had been shot twice in the chest and once in the stomach. Jeff shook his head and headed for the phone, as the others waited, leaning against the wall near the trauma unit door. At least no one had come out yet to tell them she had died. But Bob felt sure it wouldn't be long before they did.

The phone rang in the bungalow at Safe Harbour just after two A.M. Matt had been asleep for nearly two hours, but he woke suddenly. Now that he had kids again, he never turned off the phone, and worried if anyone called him at an unusual hour. He wondered if it was

Robert, or Vanessa in Auckland. He hoped it wasn't Sally.

"Hello?" he said sleepily, after he had groped for the phone.

"Matt." It was Pip, and in the single word he could hear that her voice was shaking.

"Is something wrong?" But he knew it before she said it, as a wave of terror filled him.

"It's my mom. She's been shot. She's in the hospital. Can you come?"

"Right now," he said, throwing back the covers, and stepping onto the floor, still holding the phone. "What happened?"

"I don't know. They called Alice, and then I talked to them. The man said she was shot three times."

"Is she alive?" He nearly choked when he asked her.

"Yes." Her voice was very small, and she was crying.

"Did he say how it happened?"

"No. Will you come?"

"I'll be there as fast as I can get there." He didn't know whether to go to the hospital, or to Pip at home. He wanted to be with Ophélie, but it sounded as though Pip needed him.

"Can I go with you?"

He hesitated for only a fraction of an instant, and grabbed a pair of jeans as he listened to her.

"Okay. Get dressed. I'll be there as soon as I can. Where is she?"

"SF General. She just got there. It just happened. That's all I know."

"I love you, Pip. Good-bye." He didn't want to waste time talking to her, or reassuring her. He got dressed, picked up his wallet and car keys, and ran to the car. He didn't even bother to lock his front door. He called the hospital from the car. They had no news, except that she was in critical condition, in surgery, and they had no further idea how she was.

Matt drove as fast as he dared over the mountain, and then hit the gas once he got to the freeway. He nearly flew over the bridge, and threw the money at the woman in the tollbooth, and he was at Pip and Ophélie's house within twenty-four minutes of her call. He didn't waste time going in, only honked the horn, and she ran out wearing blue jeans and her ski parka, which she had found in the hall. She looked deathly pale and terrified.

"Are you okay?" he asked her, and she shook her head. But she was too frightened now even to cry. She looked like she was about to faint, and he prayed she wouldn't. He was praying far harder for her mother. And he didn't comment to Pip about the insanity of her mother being on the streets late at night with the outreach team. This was what he had feared, and predicted, all along. But there was no comfort now in having been right. He couldn't see how she would survive. And Pip couldn't either. Three bullets sounded like more than any one human could survive, although Matt knew some had.

They drove to the hospital in anguished silence, and he parked the car in one of the slots for emergency vehicles, and then he and Pip ran inside. Jeff, Bob, and Millie saw them as soon as they came through the door and knew instantly who they were, or at least the child. She looked just like her mother except for the red hair.

"Pip?" Bob approached her and patted her shoulder. "I'm Bob."

"I know." Pip recognized him from her mother's description, and the others. "Where's my mom?" she asked, looking nervous, but remarkably composed. Matt introduced himself to them with an angry frown. He couldn't blame them for what she'd been doing, she had chosen to do it, but he was angry anyway.

"They're taking the bullets out now," Millie explained.

"How is she?" Matt asked, looking straight at Jeff, sensing that he was in charge.

"We don't know. They haven't told us a word since she came in." They all stood there for what seemed like hours, and finally sat down.

Bob went to get coffee, and Millie held Pip's hand, as she clung to Matt's with her other one. They sat in silence, there was nothing anyone could say, to excuse, or explain, or comfort. None of them had much hope, including Pip, and no one wanted to lie to her. The likelihood of Ophélie surviving was slim to none.

"Did they catch the guy who shot her?" Matt finally asked.

"No, but we got a good make on him. If they've got mug shots on him, we'll get him. I ran after him, but I couldn't catch him, and I didn't want to just leave her," Jeff explained, and Matt nodded. And even if they caught him, what difference would it make if she was dead? None to him, or Pip. Nothing was going to bring her back if she died. But at least she wasn't dead yet.

He went to the desk several times and asked them, but all they could tell him was that she was still in surgery. In the end, she was there for seven hours. But at the end of it, she was still alive.

Jeff had called the Center by then, and reporters had called the desk, but fortunately no one had shown up yet. And at nine-thirty in the morning a surgeon finally came out to talk to them. Matt was terrified of what he would say, and so was Pip. He hadn't let go of her hand since they'd arrived, and whatever he did, he did with the other hand. She had a death grip on him, and he on her.

"She's alive," the surgeon said to reassure them. "We don't know what's going to happen yet. The first bullet went straight through her lung and out her back. The other one came out the back of her neck, and missed her spine. All things considered, she was pretty lucky, but she's not out of the woods yet. The third bullet took out an ovary and her appendix, and did some nasty damage to her stomach and her intestines. We've been working on that for the last four hours. She had four surgeons working on her. That's about as good as it gets around here."

"Can we see her?" Pip piped up in a voice that was barely more than a croak. She hadn't said a word all night, and the surgeon shook his head.

"Not yet. She's in surgical ICU. But in a couple of hours, if her vitals are stable, you can come up. She's still unconscious from the anesthetic, but she should wake up in a few hours. She'll be pretty groggy, and we're going to keep her that way for now."

"Is she going to die?" Pip asked, squeezing

Matt's hand so tight it felt like a vise, and he held his breath as the surgeon answered.

"We hope not," he said, looking straight at Pip. "She still could, she's very, very badly injured. But she survived the surgery and the trauma. She's pretty tough. And we're doing everything we can."

"Damn right," Bob said, praying that she would.

Pip sat down again then, and looked like a little wooden statue. She was not going anywhere, and neither were Matt and the others. They just sat there and waited, and at noon, a nurse said that they could go up to the ICU. It was a scary place, and the glass enclosure where Ophélie was, was filled with machines and monitors and lines running everywhere. Three people were monitoring her, and every inch of her seemed to be covered with needles and bandages and tubes. She looked deathly pale, and her eyes were closed as Matt and Pip walked into the room.

"I love you, Mommy," she said, standing at the foot of the bed, next to Matt, and he did everything he could to fight back tears so Pip wouldn't see it. He knew he needed to be strong for her, but all he wanted to do was reach out and touch Ophélie, as though to will life into her. They seemed to be doing everything they could for her. And the whole time they stood there, she never moved. They were just about to leave, when the nurse told them their time was up. She could have visitors for only five minutes every hour, and there were tears rolling down Pip's cheeks. She was terrified she was going to lose her mother too. And Ophélie was all she had left. Her mother was the only family she had in the world. And as though sensing her distress, Ophélie opened her eyes and looked straight at her, and then at Matt. And as though to encourage them, she smiled, and then closed her eyes again.

"Mommy?" Pip spoke out in the tiny glass cubicle. "Can you hear me?" She nodded yes. The only thing that didn't hurt was her head. And there was an oxygen mask on her nose.

"I love you, Pip," she whispered, and then looked at Matt. The look that passed between them said that she knew what he would have said. It was the last thing she thought of as she went down, that he had been right, and then everything went black. And now he was standing there, and she was afraid he was mad at her. She was glad he was with Pip, and wondered how that had happened. Pip must have called him. "Hi, Matt," Ophélie said, and then closed her eyes and drifted off to sleep again. They were both crying when they left, but they were tears of relief as much as distress. She looked as though she might make it, but they both knew that was not yet sure.

"How is she?" the others asked as soon as they came back. They had been waiting anxiously in the ICU waiting room, and were worried sick when they saw Pip and Matt in tears. They were afraid she had died while they were in the room.

"She talked to us," Pip said, and wiped her eyes.

"She did?" Bob looked shocked and thrilled. "What did she say?"

"That she loves me." Pip looked pleased. But it was clear to all of them, even Pip, what a long, delicate treacherous haul it would be. She was by no means out of the woods.

The others went back to the Center that afternoon, but promised to come back that night, while they were on their route. They had to get home and get a few hours' sleep. And there was a meeting planned at the Center, to discuss the safety issues of the outreach team. This had been a shock for everyone. And Bob and Jeff had already said that from then on they were going to be carrying guns, since they all still had permits to do so, and Millie agreed. There was a major question now as to whether the outreach team was an appropriate placement for volunteers. It was obvious to everyone that it wasn't. But too late for Ophélie.

Matt stayed at the hospital with Pip all afternoon, and they saw Ophélie again twice. The first time she was sleeping, and the second she appeared to be in pain. And as soon as they left, they gave her morphine. He tried to talk Pip into going home for an hour then, to rest and clean up and get something to eat. And after they'd given her mother the shot to make her sleep, she finally agreed, although reluctantly. He went back to the house with her, and Mousse greeted them. And then Matt went to make scrambled eggs and toast for them. There were two messages on the machine from Pip's school, expressing their concern for her. Alice had apparently called them that morning before she left, and she had left a note on the kitchen table, telling Pip to call if she needed anything. And she had left another note saying she had come back to walk Mousse that afternoon.

Matt took him for a walk before they ate, and then he and Pip sat at the kitchen table, looking like shipwreck survivors. Pip was so exhausted she could hardly eat, and Matt couldn't eat either.

"Do you think we should go back yet?" she asked nervously. She didn't want anything to happen, good or bad, while she was gone, and she was like a cat on a hot stove, waiting for him to finish.

"How about a shower before we go back, for both of us?" he asked patiently. They both looked a mess. Not to mention the fact that they both needed sleep. They'd have to get some eventually, and he tried to talk Pip into a nap at least before they went back.

"I'm not tired," she said valiantly, and he didn't push her. They agreed to shower and clean up, and then Pip wanted to go back to the hospital for the night. He didn't argue with her. He wanted to be there too. He drove her back, after he walked Mousse again, and they settled onto the couch together in the ICU waiting room.

The nurse told them that their friends had come by to check on Ophélie, but she'd been asleep, and she was again. When Matt checked she was still in critical condition. And as soon as Pip sat down on the couch in the waiting room, she fell sound asleep, and he was relieved. He sat watching her, wondering what would happen to her if Ophélie died. He couldn't bear to think of it, but it was a possibility. If they let him, he would bring Pip to live with him, or take an apartment in the city. His mind was whirling with ugly possibilities, when the nurse came to get him at two A.M. She looked serious, and Matt panicked the minute he saw her.

"Your wife wants to see you," she said quietly, and he didn't correct her. He just set Pip's hand down gently and followed the nurse into the ICU. Ophélie was awake and she looked anxious to see him. She beckoned him to come close to her, and he was terrified she was having a premonition of worse to come, and as soon as he bent next to her, and touched her cheek gently, she started to talk to Matt in a whisper. It was obviously hard for her to breathe.

"I'm so sorry, Matt . . . you were right . . . I'm so sorry . . . will you take care of Pip?" It was what he had feared. She was afraid she was dying, and wanted him to make some arrangement for Pip. He knew she had very little family, except distant cousins in Paris. There was no one to take her but him.

"You know I will . . . Ophélie, I love you . . . don't go anywhere, sweetheart . . . stay here with us . . . we both need you . . . you have to get well . . ." He was pleading with her.

"I will," she promised, and then drifted off to sleep as the nurse signaled to him to leave.

"How is she?" he asked the nurse at the desk as he left. "Has anything changed?"

"She's holding her own," the nurse reassured him. She was impressed that he and the child had been there all day and night. Things like that made a difference, and it always surprised her how many people didn't bother. But Pip and Matt had hardly moved, except for their brief trip home for less than two hours. And in the morning, when the shifts changed, they were still there. But Ophélie seemed a little better.

He took Pip home again, and told her he either had to buy some clothes or drive home to get his own. They discussed it over breakfast, and decided to stop at Macy's on the way back to pick up some things for him. It was obvious that Pip didn't want him to leave, so he didn't.

He finally got a minute to call Robert and tell him that morning, and made an arrangement with Alice to walk the dog regularly. He called Pip's school, and they assured him that she didn't need to come in. They were very sympathetic and hoped that Mrs. Mackenzie would be better soon. There had been several distressed calls from the Wexler Center, but he had no desire whatsoever to talk to them, and didn't.

And after a brief stop at Macy's, they went back to the hospital, and took up their vigil again at the ICU. And finally, by that night, Ophélie looked a little better. Bob, Jeff, and Millie had come by to see her, and noticed it too. And after they left, he was tucking Pip in with a warm blanket a nurse had given them, when she looked up at him from the couch.

"I love you, Matt."

"I love you too, Pip," he said quietly. He had bought enough clothes and underwear to keep him going for a week. Sooner or later, he'd have to go back to the beach, but he was planning to stay in the city with Pip for as long as he was needed. It didn't look like he'd be going home anytime soon.

"Do you love my mom too?" She'd never been exactly sure of what had gone on between them. They were both extremely discreet about it.

"Yes, I do." He smiled down at her, and she smiled at him.

"Will you marry her when she gets better?" He liked the fact that she had said when and not if. He wanted to think of it that way too. "She needs you, Matt. And I need you too." It almost made him cry listening to her, and he wasn't sure what to say to her. Before she'd been shot, Ophélie had been by no means sure of how she felt about him, or what she wanted to do about it, although he was totally sure of how he felt about her.

"I'd like to, Pip," he said honestly. "I think we'd have to ask her, don't you?"

"I think she loves you too. She's just scared.

My dad wasn't always so nice to her. He shouted a lot, mostly about Chad. Chad was pretty sick, and he did some pretty bad things, like try to kill himself. And my dad didn't think he was sick, so he shouted at my mom, and thought she was weird." It was a fairly accurate account of what had happened, from what Matt knew too, although Pip had expressed it in her own terms. "I think maybe she's scared you might be mean to her too, although you've never been mean to us, but maybe she's afraid you would be if she married you. My dad was really grumpy and really smart, and maybe he wasn't as nice to her as he should have been . . . and she could be worried that you might die, because she really loved him, even though he was grumpy and mean and he never talked to us much. He was always busy, but I think he loved us anyway . . . do you think you could tell her that you'll be nice to us, and then she'll say yes. What do you think?" He didn't know whether to laugh or cry as he listened to her, and he leaned down and kissed her on the forehead instead.

"I think if she doesn't marry me, I should marry you. You make a lot of sense, Pip. That's what I think."

She guffawed as she lay on the couch in the deserted waiting room. They were the only people there again that night, and she grinned at him. "You're too old for me, Matt, but you're pretty cute, for an old guy . . . like a father, I mean."

"You're pretty cute too."

"Will you ask her?" Pip looked anxious again. She had a lot on her mind.

"I'll do my best. I think we should wait till she feels better though, don't you?"

Pip thought about it, and then frowned at him. "I don't think you should wait too long. And it might make her feel better if you ask her to marry you. What do you think? It might help her feel a lot better, and give her something to look forward to."

"It's a thought." Or it might scare her to death. He knew there was that possibility, better than Pip. He remembered only too well the night in Tahoe when she had been too afraid to make love to him. Marriage may not have been the solution Pip hoped it would be. But as she did, he wished it would. She drifted off to sleep then, pleased about having spoken to him, and he sat there for a long time, watching her with a quiet smile.

He went to call Robert again then, he had promised he would, and reported what was happening. He had offered to come in from Stanford that morning. But Matt explained that

Robert couldn't see her anyway, so he said he would call him to let him know how she was. And Robert was immensely relieved to hear from his father that at least she was still alive. He had been shocked when he first heard the news.

Ophélie's shooting was all over the eleven o'-clock news that night. But the hospital had kept reporters away. And they reported with somber faces on the news that the volunteer from the Wexler Center who'd been shot was still in critical condition at San Francisco General, but still alive.

Jeff showed up at midnight then, to tell Matt the shooter had been caught. They spoke in whispers as Pip slept, and Jeff was pleased to be able to report that to him. He and the others had gone to the police station and identified mug shots of him. And he'd been apprehended completing a drug transaction only three blocks from Jesse, the alley where she'd been shot. The suspect still had the gun on him. They were going to try to identify him in a lineup the next day, but there was no question about who he was. And he was going to be sent away for a long time. He had a criminal record an arm long. So far, it was all good news. Except for her. Her life still hung in the balance and it was early days yet.

But when they saw her the next morning, she smiled at both of them, and asked when she could go home. They moved her from critical to serious condition, and the surgeon in charge said she was doing well. No one was more relieved than Pip, except Matt. And Ophélie herself told them both to go home and get some rest. She looked pale, but she was more coherent and seemed to be in less pain. Matt said he was going to take Pip home for a while, but they promised to come back that afternoon. And on their way out of the ICU, Pip looked at him conspiratorially and asked him if he thought he should talk to her mother now, about the matter they had discussed the night before.

"Now?" He looked startled. "Don't you think we should wait until she feels a little better? She might be more receptive if she's not in so much pain."

"Maybe it would be better if you talk to her when she's still a little dopey and on drugs." Pip was willing to resort to any means to get the desired results, and he laughed at her, as they left the hospital and headed for his car.

"Apparently you think she needs to be doped up to agree to marry me," he said, feeling a lot more jovial than he had since Ophélie got shot. Things were starting to look a little less precarious, and the patient looked a lot better than she had. But he was still nervous and worried about her.

"Well, it might help," Pip said, responding to his comment about Ophélie being sedated when he proposed. "You know how stubborn she is, and she's pretty scared of getting married again. She told me so."

"Well, I won't shoot her at least. That ought to count for something," he said with a grim look.

"It might," Pip said, and laughed.

They went home, and Mousse was ecstatic to see them. He couldn't understand why everyone had abandoned him. Matt cooked for all three of them, and lay down for a little while. He'd been up for two nights straight. And Pip seemed in better spirits as she bustled around the house. She loved having Matt there, and he had promised to stay with her until Ophélie came home.

They went back to the hospital later than they'd planned, and Ophélie was having a rough night. The nurse said it was expected, postsurgery, after the trauma she'd had. She was in a lot of pain, and they had sedated her pretty heavily with morphine. But her condition was moved from serious to stable in spite of it. She was making a remarkable recovery, much to everyone's amazement, and that night Matt decided to take Pip home. He told her they could both use a night in a real bed, and reluctantly she agreed. She kissed her mother goodnight before leaving her, but Ophélie was sound asleep. And by nine o'clock that night, they were home, and half an hour later Pip was in a deep sleep in her own bed, and Matt was unconscious in Ophélie's.

Neither of them woke till morning, and they had breakfast before going to the hospital. And when they saw Ophélie, they were both immensely relieved. She had a little color in her face, and the nasogastric tube that had been bothering her had been removed. She was still listed in stable condition, and she was complaining about everything, which the nurse said was a good sign. And she smiled when she saw Matt and Pip walk in.

"What have you two been up to?" she asked as though she had been there for a rest and not three gunshot wounds, and both of her visitors beamed at her.

"He made French toast for breakfast, Mom. And he says he makes great pancakes."

"Good. Bring me some," she said, but they both knew that she was going to be on a liquid diet for a long time, and she was still on IVs. And then she turned to Matt with a serious look. "Thank you for taking care of Pip for me." She had no one else to ask, which they both knew. Time and circumstances, and Ted, had isolated her from a lot of people. And she had no real relatives other than Pip. "I'm sorry all this happened. It was stupid of me, I guess." But she had loved her work with the outreach team.

"I won't say I told you so, but you know how I feel. Jeff tells me they're not going to let volunteers do that work anymore, which seems right to me. It was a wonderful idea, but much too dangerous."

"I know. It sure got out of hand fast that night. I didn't even know what had hit me when I went down." It didn't bear thinking about what could have happened to her, and they talked about it for a while, while Pip gave him meaningful looks and he tried to keep a straight face. He discussed it with her again over lunch.

"I can't just ask her like that with you standing there."

"Well, you'd better do it soon," Pip threatened him, and he laughed.

"Why? She's not going anywhere. What's the rush?"

"Because I want you two to get married." Pip looked like she was going to stamp her foot.

"What if she won't?"

"Okay, then I'll marry you, even if you are too old. Sheeshh . . . I've never seen anyone so slow!" she scolded him. And the next time he went in to see her, Pip sent him in alone with a stern look.

"I'm not promising anything," he reminded her. "I'll see how she feels." He hedged his bets, and didn't want to disappoint Pip any more than himself. He didn't want to push, no matter what Pip thought. He had to trust his own instincts, not those of a child of twelve, although she had the right idea and her heart was in the right place, and he loved her too.

"You're the biggest chicken I know!" she accused him, and he laughed on the way in, and when he got to the cubicle, he found Ophélie looking peaceful and then concerned.

"Where's Pip?"

"Asleep on the couch in the waiting room," he lied, feeling ridiculous, and then suddenly he wondered if Pip was right. Maybe the shooting had changed everything. Life was short, and it was real, and they loved each other. Maybe it was time to put his heart on the line to her again. It was worth the risk.

"I'm sorry I've put everyone through this," she said, looking guilty. "I never thought this would happen," she said, looking tired. She still had a long way to go, and the doctor said it would be a long recovery, which was hardly surprising, given the damage the bullets had done. But it could have been a lot worse, and nearly was.

"I was always afraid it would happen," Matt said honestly.

"I know you were. You were right," she said, as he took her hand. He was standing next to her, and stroking her hair.

"I'm right about a lot of things sometimes, and wrong about others."

"You haven't been wrong about much," she said, looking up at him gratefully, which was comforting to hear.

"I'm glad you think so."

"Thank God Pip picked you up on the beach," she said, and they both laughed.

"As I recall, you weren't too thrilled about that."

"I thought you were a child molester," she said breezily. "Wrong again." She smiled at him and closed her eyes, and then opened them again and looked at him. She seemed surprisingly at peace, given all she'd been through. She was a very brave woman, and he loved her with all his heart.

"And what do you think now?" he asked softly.

"About you? That you're the best friend I ever had . . . and I love you . . ." she added cautiously, looking into his eyes. "Very much, in fact." More than she ever knew. He was almost more than she deserved, or so she thought, particularly after all the trouble she had caused Pip, him, and herself. It had been a hell of a jolt for all of them.

"I love you too, Ophélie . . ." He was afraid to ask her, and then thought of Pip berating him again, and the thought of it made him smile and drove him on. "Do you love me enough to marry me?" he asked her, and she looked up at him, shocked.

"Did you just say what I think you said, or is it the drugs?"

"Could be both. What did it sound like to you?"

Tears filled her eyes as she looked at him, and she was still scared, but not as much as she had been. She had nearly lost everything when she got shot. How much more could she lose? And she had everything to gain with him.

"It sounds good to me," she said in a whisper, and a tear rolled down her cheek. "Just don't die on me. Please, Matt . . . I couldn't go through that again . . ."

"I won't," he said as he bent down to kiss her. "Not for a long time at least. And I'd appreciate it if you'd make an effort not to get shot again. I'm not the one who nearly died here," and then he added seriously, ". . . I would die if I lost you, Ophélie . . . I love you so damn much . . ."

"Me too," she said, and then he kissed her, and as he did, the nurse appeared, and told them he had to leave again, their time was up. ICU patients couldn't have visitors for longer than five minutes, ten at the most, but it had been long enough to find out what they both needed to know.

"Is it official, then?" he asked her, before he left. "Will you marry me?" He wanted to hear it from her lips.

"Yes, I will," she said softly but meant every word of it. She was ready. And it was time.

"Can I tell Pip?" he asked as the nurse waved him toward the door.

"Yes, you can," she said, smiling from ear to ear as he left, and she looked up at the nurse with a grin. "I'm engaged."

"I thought you were married," she said, looking surprised.

"I am . . . but I'm not . . . well, I was . . . I almost am . . . I will be," she explained. She was giddy, she was so excited. All it had taken was getting shot three times to figure it out. A small price to pay.

"Congratulations," the nurse said, and took her temperature, just as Matt walked back into the waiting room, and Pip stared at him to try and figure out what he'd done.

"Did you chicken out?" she accused him with a worried look, and he shook his head, trying to conceal his excitement from her so he wouldn't give it away.

"No, I didn't."

Her eyes opened wide. "Did you ask her?"

"Yes, I did."

Pip could hardly contain herself and neither could he. "What did she say?" She was holding her breath, as he smiled and put his arms around her. She was almost his.

"She said yes," he said, with tears in his eyes again. It had been a very emotional day.

"She did? OhmyGod! Wow!! We're going to marry you! OhmyGod! Matt!" She put her arms around him, and he swung her around the room. "You did it! You did it!"

"We did it! Thank you for the idea, and the courage, and the kick in the pants. If you hadn't pushed me, I probably would have waited another year."

"Maybe it was a good thing she got shot, sort of, well . . . you know . . ." Pip said thoughtfully.

"No, I don't know. And if she ever does something like that again, I'm going to kill her my-self."

"Me too," Pip agreed, as they sat side by side together, partners in crime. Everything had worked out exactly as planned, thanks to Pip. All they had to do now was pick a date.

27

OPHÉLIE WAS IN THE HOSPITAL FOR THREE weeks. And Matt stayed at the house with Pip for the entire time. She went back to school after her mother had been in the hospital for a week, but she went to visit her every afternoon. Matt spent the mornings in the hospital with Ophélie, then picked Pip up at school, and would bring her to see her mother in the hospital after school. They settled into a routine for nearly three weeks. And when she came home, Matt carried Ophélie upstairs to her room. She had to take it easy for another six weeks.

They had saved the lung and repaired her stomach, and they said the intestines wouldn't be a problem. She could manage with one ovary, and even have more babies if she wanted to, and the appendix was gone for good. She had been unbelievably lucky, and Louise An-

derson from the Center had come to apologize
to her for letting her put herself at risk. But
Ophélie reminded her repeatedly that it was
what she had wanted to do. It had been her
choice. But there were going to be no more
volunteers on the outreach team, which was
just as well, although Ophélie had loved working with them. And she promised to come back
to work at the Center itself in a few months, if
Matt agreed. He had a say in it now, and he was
no longer sure. He thought she should stay
home with Pip, and him.

He slept in Ted's old den after Ophélie got
home. He wanted to be there in case she
needed him, and she was happy to have him
there. She still needed help, and it made her feel
secure. And Pip was thrilled.

Their wedding plans were going forward, and
they had agreed to get married in June, when
Vanessa could be there too. Matt had called her
in Auckland to tell her, and she was happy for
him. And they told Robert when he came to
the hospital to see Ophélie.

"We're going to be a family again," Pip told
her mother with a big grin when she got
home. It was obvious that Pip loved the idea,
but so did Ophélie. It had taken a lot to get her
there, too much probably, but she felt comfortable with their decision, and she and Matt were

talking about a honeymoon in France, and maybe even taking the kids. Pip loved that idea.

Ophélie was resting quietly on her bed one afternoon, while Matt went to get Pip in school. It was six weeks after the shooting, and she was feeling stronger, but she couldn't drive yet, and she had only been out of the house a few times. She was excited about being able to go downstairs for dinner.

The outreach team had visited her at home several times too. She was thinking about them, when the phone rang and she answered it. The voice at the other end was familiar, but not welcome, and sounded very weak. It was Andrea, and Ophélie thought about just hanging up. But Andrea sensed that, and begged her not to before she could.

"Please . . . let me just talk to you for a minute . . . it's important." She sounded strange and said she'd heard about the shooting and had been horrified. "I wanted to write to you, but I was in the hospital too." The way she sounded made Ophélie keep listening.

"Did you have an accident?" she asked coolly, but nonetheless concerned. They had been such good friends for so many years.

"No," Andrea hesitated, "I'm sick."

"What do you mean, sick?"

There was an endless pause. Andrea had

wanted to call her for months, but she didn't
dare. And she had to know. "I have cancer," she
said quietly. "They discovered it two months
ago. They think I've had it for a long time. I had
stomach pains for about a year, and I thought it
was just nerves. It started as ovarian, supposedly,
but it's in my lungs, and now my bones. It's
moving pretty fast." She sounded almost re-
signed, but sad. And Ophélie was shocked. No
matter how angry she was at her, she didn't
want this for her, and it brought tears to her
eyes.

"Have you had chemo?"

"Yes, I'm still doing it now. I've had two surgeries, and they'll do radiation after the chemo,
but I don't think . . . I don't think I'll make it
that far," she said honestly. "It looks pretty
bad . . . I know you probably don't want to see
me, but I need to know something . . . will you
take Willie for me?" They were both crying by
the time she asked.

"Now?" Ophélie sounded stunned.

"No," she said sadly, "when I die. I don't think
it's going to be too long. Maybe a few months."
Ophélie was sobbing by then. Life was so un-
predictable, so unfair, so wrong. How did this
happen to people? To Ted, to Chad . . . and
now to her. Thinking about it made her all the

more grateful for Matt. But she was still shaken by all that she had just heard. No matter what Andrea had done to her, she didn't deserve this, but apparently she didn't agree. "Maybe this is God's punishment for what I did to you, Ophélie. I know 'sorry' doesn't begin to cover it, but I am. I've had a lot of time to think about it . . . I'm so sorry . . . will you take Willie?" she asked again, and Ophélie just cried. It was all so cruel.

"Yes, I will," she said through her tears. All she could think of was what Matt had done for her with Pip, and she had only known him for eight months, nearly nine. She knew that Andrea had no one else, and no other choice. She was his godmother, it was right, even if he was Ted's child. It wasn't the baby's fault. "Where is he now? Has someone been helping you take care of him?"

"I hired an au pair," Andrea said, sounding tired again. "I want him here with me, till the end." She spoke of it as a sure thing. It was terrible. So unbelievable. She was forty-five years old, and her son would never know either of his parents.

Matt walked in while Ophélie was still talking to her, and he looked puzzled. He could see that Ophélie had been crying, and he walked out of the room again. He didn't want to intrude. He assumed she would tell him about it later.

"Is there anything I can do for you now?" Ophélie asked sadly. She didn't want to leave any bad blood between them, especially now, although she knew that it would have been hard to bridge the chasm that had formed between them.

"I'd like to see you again," Andrea said, sounding weak. "But I feel sick most of the time. The chemo is pretty awful."

"And I can't go out yet. As soon as I can, I'll come over."

"I'm going to have a new will drawn up, if it's okay with you, leaving Willie to you. Are you sure you can handle it, and you won't hate him for what I did?"

"I don't hate you," she said calmly, "I'm just sad. I was hurt." But just listening to her, she knew she had forgiven her. And she hadn't done it alone. Ted had been part of it too. That had been the hardest part of it for her. But so much had happened since.

"I'll stay in touch and let you know how I'm doing," Andrea said practically. "I'll put your number on my emergency forms." It had been there before, but after what had happened between them, she had taken it off. "And I'll give it to the au pair, in case something happens and I don't get a chance to call."

"You have to hold on, Andrea. You can't give up." She was feeling deeply affected by all she'd heard and the way Andrea sounded, and she was sorry that she couldn't get out yet. She knew that seeing Andrea again would be stressful for her. It was still too soon after all she'd been through herself. "I'll call you. Let me know how you are."

"I will," she said, crying openly. "Thank you. I know you'll take good care of him."

"I promise you I will," and then she decided to tell her about Matt. She had a right to know now. "I'm getting married in June. To Matt."

There was a long silence, and a slow sigh. As though she felt absolved somehow, and she hadn't totally destroyed Ophélie's life, which she hadn't. "I'm so glad. He's a nice guy. I hope you'll both be happy," she said peacefully.

"Me too. I'll call you soon. Take care, Andrea."

"I love you . . . and I'm sorry," she said in a whisper, and hung up. Ophélie set the phone down gently, as Matt came back into the room.

"What was that about?" he asked, looking concerned. Ophélie was obviously upset.

"Andrea," she said, looking straight at him.

"Is this the first time you heard from her?" She nodded.

"Was she begging your forgiveness? She damn well should." He was still outraged over what she and Ted had done, and then Ophélie realized suddenly that she should have asked him about the baby. But how could she refuse? She didn't think she could, nor should. He was, after all, Pip's half brother, and Ted's child.

"She's dying."

"When did that happen?" He looked stunned.

"She found out two months ago. She has ovarian cancer, and it metastasized to her lungs and bones. She doesn't think she has more than a few months. She wants me to take the baby. Us . . ." She decided to make a clean breast of it immediately. "I said yes. How do you feel about that? I told her we were getting married, and I can tell her we can't, if you don't want to. But she doesn't have anyone else. How do you feel about it?" He sat at the foot of her bed for a minute and thought about it. It was certainly a major addition to their life, and not one he had expected, but he could see her point. It would be hard to refuse, and in some ways harder still for her, because the baby was Ted's, and Pip's half brother. It was a very peculiar situation.

"Our family seems to be growing exponentially, doesn't it? I don't see how you can't take him. Do you really think she'll die?"

"Sounds like it. She sounded pretty bad."

"I don't think we have much choice. At least he's cute," he said, leaning over to kiss her. He was an incredibly good sport. And they agreed not to tell Pip about it for the time being. It was too depressing, and she had been through enough trauma with her mother over the past six weeks. She didn't need to know Andrea was dying. It was just too much.

Ophélie got a note from Andrea, thanking her, a few days later, and she didn't call after that. Ophélie was going to call her, but she was so tired and weak herself, she kept putting it off and it still upset her. Matt drove her to the beach two weeks later, with Pip and the dog. They took a short walk, and sat in the sunshine. It already felt like summer, and was only March. They talked about their wedding plans. They had decided to do it quietly at the beach, with just their children present, and a priest Matt knew in Bolinas. It sounded just right to them. Neither of them wanted a fancy social event.

And two days after they'd taken Pip to the beach, they went back out together on a brilliantly sunny day. She said that she thought the sea air had been good for her, and he agreed, but he had something else in mind. They packed a picnic lunch in the city, since he had nothing to eat out there. And as soon as they got to the house in Safe Harbour, he set the basket on the table, and put some music on. She had a fair idea of what he was thinking, and she was ready this time. They had waited a long, long time for this. It was what should have happened in Tahoe, and didn't.

As soon as they walked in, he put his arms around her and kissed her, and she looked up at him. Long before he ever touched her, she was already his, and wanted to be. She followed him into his bedroom, and he took her clothes off gently and laid her down on his bed, and then he joined her, and they cuddled quietly under the sheets, until passion overtook them, and swept them away on a gentle sea. It was the joining of two lives, two people, two hearts, two worlds, and was all they wanted it to be. It was what they had both hoped for and had only dreamed. And together in each other's arms, at Safe Harbour, the dream came true at last.

28

OPHÉLIE HAD BEEN PLANNING TO CALL AN-
drea ever since she'd heard from her two weeks
before. But she'd been overwhelmed, trying to
catch up on things that had piled up when she
was sick. She had to go to a suppression hearing
in the case against her assailant, because the defense wanted to suppress her testimony and
prevent her from testifying at the trial. After an
exhausting morning in court, which Matt at-
tended with her, the defense's motion was de-
nied. And she was still tired. Something always
seemed to stop her when she was going to call
Andrea. She had promised herself finally that
she was going to call that afternoon, before Pip
came home. She was about to dial the number,
when Andrea's au pair called.

"I was just going to call her," Ophélie said
pleasantly. "How is she? I'm glad you called."

The voice at the other end sounded uncomfortable, and hated to tell her the news. "She died this morning, just before noon," she said, and Ophélie felt as though she'd been hit by a brick.

"Oh my God . . . I'm so sorry . . . I didn't know . . . I thought . . . she told me it would be a few months . . . I had no idea it would be so soon." Death didn't always come on schedule, or as planned. In fact, it never did. And all she could think of as she sat there was of having been at the delivery with her, less than a year before. It had been so exciting and so joyful, and so moving, and as she thought of it, she realized that that was how she would remember her. And suddenly she was glad that she hadn't seen her when she was sick. After nearly twenty years of friendship, their lives had become unhooked, but maybe it was meant to be that way. Andrea had a path to follow that no longer included Ophélie. She had made a terrible mistake that had hurt Ophélie terribly, but a child had come of it, and now he was coming home to her. All of life's strange twists and turns never led where you expected them to. It was impossible to even guess at one's destiny.

"Is there a funeral?" Ophélie asked her, wondering if she was supposed to organize it. How odd that was too, they had always talked about weddings and affairs, and Ophélie had given a christening party for Willie because she was his godmother. And now they had to have a funeral for his mother. But the au pair explained that that wasn't what Andrea had wanted. They had already come to get her, she wanted to be cremated and sprinkled at sea. No service, no memorial, no mourners, no tombstone anywhere, just people's memories. It seemed cleaner to her that way, and for once Ophélie agreed. Under the circumstances, it was going to be less painful for everyone that way.

She had made her own arrangements to get rid of her apartment, and her things. All that was left was Willie. The au pair offered to bring him over later that day. Which meant that Ophélie had to tell Pip.

She was waiting for her in the kitchen when she came home from school with Matt. And Pip instantly reacted to the look on her mother's face. Matt already knew. She had called him in the car while he was on the way to school. And he had said he would do everything he could to support her, and Pip.

"Is something wrong?" Pip still remembered the last time she had seen her mother look like that, it had been a lot worse, but it frightened her anyway. She was afraid she was going to tell her that she and Matt had decided not to get married, but Ophélie instantly assured her that everything was all right, but she had sad news.

"Is it Mousse?" He was out in the garden and she hadn't seen him, and Ophélie smiled at her. Other than Matt, they had no one else left.

"No, it's Andrea. She died today." Pip looked shocked at first and then sad. "She was very sick. She called me over two weeks ago, but I didn't want to tell you for a while."

"Were you still mad at her?" Pip asked, watching her mother's face.

"Not really. We kind of made up when she called and told me she was sick."

"What did she do to you?" Ophélie exchanged a look with Matt and he wondered what she would say, and he approved of what she did say to Pip.

"I'll tell you all about it one day, when you're grown up, but not till then."

"It must have been very bad," Pip said solemnly. She knew her mother well enough to know that she would have forgiven Andrea sooner otherwise, and seen her again.

"I thought it was." But Pip also needed to know that Willie was her half brother one day.

"What's going to happen to Willie?" Pip asked sadly. He was an orphan now. It was a terrible thought, even to her.

"He's coming to live with us," she said calmly, and Pip's eyes grew wide.

"He is? Now?"

"Today." Pip looked pleased, and Matt smiled. It was a strange turn of events certainly, but like everything else, meant to be, if it happened that way. It made him realize again how odd life was. If things had turned out differently, Ophélie might have died of her gunshot wounds. Instead, they were getting married, and another woman's baby, who was also Ted's, was coming to live with them. Life and its extraordinary and often complicated and unexpected turn of events.

The au pair brought Willie over with all his belongings late that afternoon, and Ophélie and Pip were waiting for him when he arrived. It was an emotional moment for Ophélie, because the baby was not only Ted's, but Andrea's, and they had been friends for eighteen years. He had grown a lot, they hadn't seen him in four months, and Ophélie asked the woman if she would be willing to stay and work for them, and she agreed. The household was getting busier and more crowded by the minute. But Ophélie wasn't up to taking care of him herself yet. And it would have been a full-time job. For Pip and Matt's sake, she wanted help with him, or she wouldn't have enough time or energy for them.

She did some quick thinking and spoke to Matt for a few minutes, and he was willing, if she thought it would be all right with Pip, which she was sure it would be. She asked him to move into her bedroom, since they were getting married anyway. And she gave Ted's den, where Matt had been sleeping, to the baby and the au pair. It worked for the time being. Chad's room was still considered sacred ground and off-limits. But she had to agree with Matt, they were going to need a new house soon. She wanted to have guest rooms too for Robert and Vanessa. As things were now, Vanessa would have to sleep with Pip when she came to visit, which delighted Pip, and was certainly possible. But they were beginning to burst at the seams. And the house at Safe Harbour, with its single bedroom and cozy living room, was only going to work for Matt and Ophélie as a romantic re-treat, which didn't seem like such a bad idea.

By late that night, once the baby and au pair were settled, and Pip was asleep in bed with Mousse at her feet, Matt was in bed next to Ophélie, and he turned to her with a grin.

"Things are certainly changing around here quickly, aren't they, my love?"

"You can say that again. Imagine if I get pregnant!" She was only teasing him. With Willie's arrival, their family seemed big enough, and she had no intention of adding to it, now or later. Before they fell asleep, she thanked Matt for what a good sport he'd been about everything.

"You never know what's going to happen around here from one day to the next," he said happily. "I'm beginning to enjoy it."

"Me too." She snuggled down next to him as she said it. And a few minutes later, all the residents of the house on Clay Street were sound asleep.

29

THEIR WEDDING DAY IN JUNE DAWNED BRIL-
liantly sunny. It was a perfect day, with bright
sun and a gentle breeze. There were little fishing
boats on the horizon, and the beach looked
swept clean. Safe Harbour had never looked
better.

The priest had arrived at eleven-thirty, and
the wedding was set for noon. Ophélie was
wearing a simple white lace dress, to her ankles,
and carrying a bouquet of tuberoses, and
Vanessa and Pip were wearing white linen
dresses. Matt and Robert were wearing slacks
and blazers. And Willie, in the nanny's arms, was
wearing a little blue and white sailor suit. He
had just started walking and was wearing his
first pair of shoes. And Ophélie couldn't help
noticing he looked just like his mother, which
was something of a relief. The alternative would

have been harder to explain, although he did look a little like Pip. There was a definite family air. And when people commented on it, Pip was pleased. She had no idea, and wouldn't for a long time, her mother hoped, that it was true, that Willie was in fact her family, although not Ophélie's.

They were all in good spirits, and they were leaving for France the next day. They were going to spend a week in Paris, and then two in Cap d'Antibes, at the Eden Roc. It was an extravagant honeymoon that Matt had insisted on treating them all to, but he said he had hardly spent a penny in years. And they were all looking forward to it. And as soon as they got back, Ophélie and Matt had agreed to look for a new house. The house on Clay Street was about to burst at the seams.

Robert was his father's best man, and Vanessa the maid of honor, Pip the official bridesmaid. They had thought of using Willie as a ring bearer, but he was teething again, and they were afraid he'd swallow the rings.

The priest spoke briefly and touchingly about bringing lives and families together, about the resurrection of the spirit, and the sorrows of past lives being healed. He spoke of hope and joy and sharing and family, and the kind of love and blessings that brought and kept families together. And as Ophélie listened to him, her eyes drifted down to the beach, to precisely the place where Matt had been working when Pip must have found him almost exactly a year before. It was impossible not to think of the serendipity and good fortune and blind luck that had brought them together. All because of one little girl walking down the beach with her dog.

Matt saw Ophélie's eyes wander toward the beach, and thought of exactly the same thing, and as he looked at her, she looked back at him and their eyes met and held. It had been remarkable good fortune that had brought them together. But it had taken more than luck and happy accidents or even love. It had taken wisdom and courage to put their lives back together, and to have the sheer grit it took to reach out and hold on tight. It would have been so much easier to never try, to never touch at all, to run away and hide, while protecting old wounds. Instead, they had dared, they had danced, they had trudged on through the dark and the cold, defied the demons, faced the terrors, and refused to run away. It was more than just an act of love they were celebrating that day, it was an act of courage, and of faith, and hope and belief. All the bits and pieces had come together, the tiny threads, loosely bound at first, and now carefully threaded and woven into the fabric of their new life. It was above all a choice they had made, not to give in to death, but to embrace life. A choice not so easily made. It was a tightrope Ophélie and Matt had walked, a delicate balance to reach safety on the other side. They had found what they wanted, and fought for it, until they reached safe harbor, and escaped the storms at last.

And when the priest asked Ophélie if she took this man for the rest of her life, Pip spoke up softly and whispered in unison with her mother, "I do."